Hamid Ismailov

A Poet and Bin-Laden

A reality novel

A Poet and Bin-Laden
By Hamid Ismailov

Supported by English PEN
and
Arts Council England

First published in Russian as "Дорога к смерти больше,
чем смерть" in 2005 by Black Quadrat

Translated from Russian by Andrew Bromfield
Poems translated by Richard MacKane

© Hamid Ismailov 2011

© 2012, Glagoslav Publications, United Kingdom

Glagoslav Publications Ltd
88-90 Hatton Garden
EC1N 8PN London
United Kingdom

www.glagoslav.com

ISBN: 978-1-909156-33-3

Contents

A Second Part

To Christopher MacLehose who inspired me to write this book.

Acknowledgements

I am indebted to all those who helped me with this book and first of all to my wife Razia Sultanova and children Rano and Daniar Ismailov, to Andrew Bromfield who beautifully translated the novel and Richard McKane who translated the poems, as well as to Hugh Barnes who wrote a Preface. Monica Whitlock, John Spurling, Jill Shoolman and David Halpern kindly agreed to be the critical readers, checking the draft and making useful suggestions along the way. Their input is invaluable, and I am very grateful to them for their support. I am also indebted to late Anne-Marie Schimmel, Resat Niyazi and Shousha Guppy along with my friends Robert Chandler, Philippa Vaughan, Gwyneth Williams, Sian Glaessner and Zia Shakib for their encouragement and help with this book. Many thanks are due also to Lena Chibor, who bravely brought out the Russian version of the book, my agent Marc Koralnik, Liepman Ag, English PEN, Arts Council England, the Publisher Maxim Hodak for his passion and determination in making this book happen, to the Editor Camilla Stein, to the Marketing Manager Yana Kovalskaya and my friends mentioned in the novel.

In Place of a Preface

A Poet and Bin-Laden is a novel set in Central Asia at the turn of the 21st century against a swirling backdrop of Islamic fundamentalism in the Ferghana Valley and beyond. It tells the story of the poet Belgi, who may be a grown-up version of "the boy" in Hamid Ismailov's book *The Railway*. The new novel is equally rich in descriptive passages and teems with vivid personalities but, whereas the mood of *The Railway* was nostalgic and its setting a provincial backwater in Uzbekistan during the Soviet years, *A Poet and Bin-Laden* tackles the most urgent and topical subject of today's world – the "war on terror" – and the novel's scope is correspondingly international, with the action straddling the borders of Uzbekistan, Kyrgyzstan, Tajikistan and Afghanistan. However, in *A Poet and Bin-Laden* documentary elements, instead of folklore, are used to propel the narrative. Real events and characters, including Osama bin Laden, who has a walk-on role, bulk large and give the novel its unique quality.

The hero of *A Poet and Bin-Laden* is Belgi, whose presumed death in 2001, while fighting on the side of the Taliban, prompts the narrator to ask, *Citizen Kane*-style: how did a Sufi recluse living in harmony with nature come to die with other Islamic militants on the hilltops of Afghanistan? To answer this question, he retraces the story of Belgi's life in the setting of some of the key events of Central Asia's post-Soviet history: the purging of the democratic opposition, the rise of Hizb-ut-Tahrir ("Party of Freedom") and the emergence of Islamic militancy, the cross-border wars of the 1990s, including the 1999 terror attacks in Tashkent, and the Batken insurgency of the following year. The novel also includes flashforwards to fighting in Vaziristan and the May 2005 massacre of civilians in the Uzbek town of Andijan. But the primary focus of the narrative is the image of this poet who becomes a terrorist in the eyes of the world. This wonderfully original construct allows Ismailov to explore the relationship between the timeless and dreamlike aspects of Uzbek culture – already familiar from *The Railway*, and now personified in Belgi – and the harsh reality of life caught between the dictatorship of President Karimov and jihadism.

11

The story begins on the eve of 9/11, with the narrator's haunting description of the airplane attack on the Twin Towers as seen on TV while he is on holiday in Central Asia. Subsequent chapters shift backwards and forwards in time, but two main themes emerge: the rise of the Islamic Movement of Uzbekistan under the charismatic but reclusive leadership of Tahir Yuldash and Juma Namangani; and Belgi's movement from the outer edge of the circle, from the mountains of Osh, into the inner sanctum of al-Qaeda, and ultimately to a meeting with Sheikh bin Laden himself. His journey begins with a search for a Sufi spiritual master and ends in guerrilla warfare, and it is this tension between a transcendental and a violent response to oppression, between the book and the bomb, that gives the novel its specific poignancy. Along the way, Ismailov provides wonderfully vivid accounts of historical events (as witnessed by Belgi) such as the siege of Kunduz, the breakout from Shebergan prison – a kind of Afghan Guantanamo – and the insurgency in the Ferghana Valley.

In the Tajik village of Hoit, an IMU stronghold, he is recruited by the Islamists and subsequently crosses the border with Afghanistan during the US bombings. He is taken prisoner by the anti-Taliban Northern Alliance, but after escaping from Shebergan is reunited with his defeated comrades – and all this time he is writing poetry!

His poems, along with the stories of eyewitnesses and participants in events leading up to the Andijan massacre, grant the reader insight into the very heart of a secretive world previously concealed from outside view. This, of course, is a very topical book, with reports of the death of the Taliban in 2001 now clearly exaggerated. From a journalistic point of view, it is so rich in first-hand and exclusive material, not least the appearance of bin Laden, that it is certain to attract a great deal of interest. But the real achievement of *A Poet and Bin-Laden* is an imaginative one – this is a very powerful story about the forces of extremism in human nature, good and evil, poetry and terror. It is in every way a grown-up version of *The Railway*.

Hugh Barnes

On your road there are nails, staples,
rusted corks, the dried apricot of time,
a concrete path, the railway, grass here and there,
a living snowdrop or simple, ordinary wire...

In actual fact, in fact all this leads one
to think then, but at the same time your premonition
realises: your life in its complete uselessness
can be tied in with these things.

Do not grieve about this,
death in fact is neither high nor low.
It is not death that is greater
but the thought of the road to death
that overcomes death itself.

-Belgi

Cast of Main Characters and a Simple
Timeline of Events

Belgi, aka Yosir – an Uzbek "new generation" poet, widely translated in the West, who becomes a militant,

Bakh, aka Haroun – his friend, interested in Sufism, who is killed by militants,

Alish, aka Umar – Belgi's friend and his translator, who also joins the militants,

Sher – Belgi's brother, killed by the Uzbek authorities while being held in detention,

Caroline Rowley – an American journalist, Belgi's girlfriend,

President Islam Karimov – the current Uzbek President who came to power in 1989,

Tahir Yuldash – aka Amir Muhammad Farruk – leader of the Islamic Movement of Uzbekistan, killed in 2009,

Juma Namangani – military commander of the IMU, killed in 2001,

Zubair – spokesman for the IMU, killed in 2001,

Zainiddin Askarov – aka Abdurahman Mansur, former spokesman for the IMU, died in an Uzbek prison,

Abdurashid Dostum – an Afghani general who is an ethnic Uzbek.

Numerous journalists and experts, who have contributed materials, memoirs and stories, as well as many militants and members of the Taliban.

1989 – Islam Karimov comes to power as the First Secretary of Uzbekistan's Communist Party. He later becomes President of Uzbekistan;

1992 – a standoff between Islam Karimov and Tahir Yuldash, when the Muslims of Namangan effectively take the President hostage, and he promises an Islamic state. This is when Belgi first names him "Comrade Islam";

1992-1996 – President Karimov crushes the secular opposition and dissenters take refuge in the mosques, he launches his campaign against Islam in the country under the pretext of fighting Wahabbism;

1998 – the mutilated body of Belgi's brother Sher is handed over to him by the police, who claim that he committed suicide. Belgi and his friends end up in a militant camp in Hoit.

1999 – six explosions that occur in Tashkent are blamed on Islamic militants, but later substantial evidence indicates the involvement of the

Uzbek special services; the authorities imprison thousands of believers, thousands flee to Tajikistan and Afghanistan;

1999 -2000 – in summer Islamic militants make incursions into Kyrgyzstan and Uzbekistan: the so-called Batken war;

2001 – "9/11": the Americans start bombing Afghanistan: Belgi is arrested by the Americans, then released and, like many Uzbek militants, he disappears.

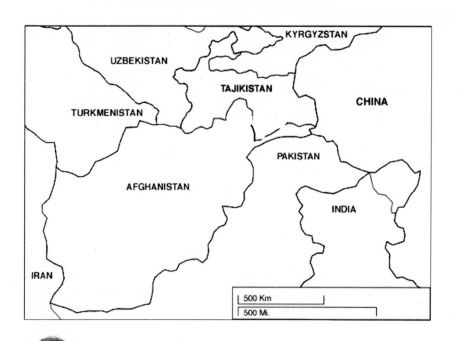

Map of Central Asia

Hamid Ismailov

11/09/2001

The website "Conference of the Refined" at *http://library.ferghana.ru/uz/index.htm* provides the following information about Belgi (real name Asror Abutov, *nom de guerre* Yosir):

> Belgi is a poet of the Uzbek "new wave" and author of the volumes of poetry *Yo'l* (*The Path*), *Ikkinchi kitob* (*The Second Book*), *Bambergiana* and *Moskva Daftari* (*Moscow Notebook*). The recently published English book *Poet for Poet* included a number of poems by Belgi, as well as this brief biographical note: "Born in 1961 in Osh in the Ferghana Valley, applied unsuccessfully to the Literary Institute, took work where he could find it, travelled widely. Now living in seclusion in the mountains of his native province... "

When I asked the author of this note about the final sentence, he exclaimed: "At that time how could I have known that this reclusive Sufi retreat in search of a spiritual master would lead to Afghanistan?" And indeed, at the time when those words were written, the mountains of the Osh province were far from being a theatre of military operations where Islamic militants made annual forays or a political bazaar where some traded in politics and others in narcotics or foreign hostages.

I shall try to recount all this in detail, but I shall start, I think, from the very end.

On September 11, 2001 I was on holiday with my family at Issyk-Kul Lake: how can you expect any Tashkent or Central Asian intellectual to summon up the effort to go any further than that? Before lunch we had been swimming and riding in a catamaran, and after lunch we were relaxing at home. In an attempt to salvage something from those meaningless, monotonous days when, as Pushkin said *"Fare niente* is my law", I was sitting there with a pen and a sheet of paper and a gradually mounting sense of frustration with the members of my household because of the pointlessness of it all. The members of my household were applying their own precautionary defensive measures: in other words, it was normal family life during a holiday. Eventually we decided to

walk to the lake again, I blamed my fruitless depression on my wife's zealous attitude, she got even with me for absenting myself from family activities for two hours, and our two children automatically took mental note of the new cracks between their parents in order later to coerce one into buying ice cream and the other into the interminable construction of skyscrapers of sand.

And now I attempt to recall every little detail, as if there had been some kind of portent, the way a bird will occasionally fly for some distance in front of the windscreen of your car, or the silence is suddenly sucked into both your ears in a contracting sphere of dread, but there was nothing like that, except perhaps for those sandcastles that were washed away by the cold water of the lake.

We got back to our room in the early evening, but there was still some time to go before supper and so on this occasion I felt justified in switching on the television and flicking through the channels. It was strange, though – the foreign satellite channels were all showing a picture of a fire that had started in some tower or other. For some reason I thought about the Tate Gallery in London – I had recently read about it being opened in the magazine *Ogonyok*. Why did I think about London? Most likely because there was someone speaking from London: then I realised it was the BBC channel and I started listening carefully. I wouldn't claim that my English is very advanced – sure, I studied it in school and passed the minimum postgraduate reading requirement, but I'd say I'm probably better at expressing myself in Uzbek at the market than understanding what those analysts are barking about in all those dreary, identical studios. Even so, I did make out the words "New York" a couple of times. And while I was wondering just what it all had to do with New York, the little aeroplane appeared on the screen, exactly like in a second take, and flew slowly and surely into another tower concealed behind the first one. This time I understood without any words – simply from the childish cry emitted by the anchor man – that they weren't showing a Hollywood film, that these unimaginable things were happening even as I watched, and at that moment the entire world was turning into one big Hollywood....

Our whole family sat in front of the television all that evening, missing supper – no great loss – and later, after the whole chilling event had been dubbed and explained by the Russian language channels, in the dead of that cold Issyk-Kul night I had a strange dream that I still remember to this day.

In one of the *kishlaks*, or mountain villages, where I used to be sent for Young Pioneer camp, I walked out of the gate and saw a car hurtling along in my direction. The car's wheels were running along the unbroken line of yellowing clay fences sticking up out of the white

snow, as if these fences marked its only road through the snowfall; it was attached to these fences, and its impetuous motion followed their curves. I would have thought the car was racing along almost vertically, if it had not gone whooshing past me, turned in a steep arc and shot off beyond the dark forms of the bridge and the river that I could see down below. "Lunatic!" I thought, and was about to carry on walking downhill when the car emerged from a dip, swung round and set off back across the bridge. Now it was aiming for me. I went dashing across the snow to get as far away as possible from those fences that held the car the way the electric wires hold a suburban train, but the car made a sharp U-turn and seemed to come lunging after me. I dashed along through snow up to my knees, sometimes slipping into steep holes, but in any case leaving a deep track behind me as I fled. The car could easily pinpoint my location. I put on two rapid spurts of speed and slid down the side of the hollow, all the way to the channel of the glimmering river, and a thought flashed through my mind like lightning: "The car will run straight off into the river here!" True, there was also the thought that it might hook me and pull me with it, but the thought that came after that was even more frightening: "What if the driver comes after me without his car…" How could I defend myself on the white snow?

Woken by a chilly shiver of fear in that black, cold, Issyk-Kul or, rather, Tian-Shan night, I gazed out through the window of our wooden hotel building at the morning twilight advancing from the east, unwilling to admit to myself that this fear under my skin was changing my life forever. And this fear is the point from which I wish to start my story.

Chapter One

"When did it all begin?" Yosir thought in his solitude. On either the sixteenth or the seventeenth day of the month of Sha'ban in the year 1422 of the Hidjra (November 2001), when the time for the after-sunset prayer was approaching, they were ordered to assemble on the southern outskirts of the Zulmat *kishlak*, which fortunately the Americans had not bombed yet. When Yosir asked the messenger if they should turn out with their things – since any other question that was natural in other places and other circles, such as "What for?", "What's going to happen?", "Will it be for long?" could cost you dear – the messenger replied briefly: "As usual!" and Yosir and Hamsa began hastily packing their *hurdjuns*, or traveller's bags, and the AKMS automatic rifles wrapped in Afghan felt cloaks.

Seven minutes later they were sitting in the yard of one of the local mosques after putting their *hurdjuns* down beside the clay fence nearby.

Some men were counting off their prayer beads, some were intently reciting to themselves the most glorious names of God, and a few of those who had only just joined them were bent over in the afternoon prayer that had been missed. But there was something here that went beyond an ordinary gathering, as if the sound of the myna-bird's light, delicate whistle was about to be replaced by the first sound of a plane and a bomb or rocket flying through the air, and the chirring of the first cricket in the corner, its voice cracked from the drought, was about to be drowned out by the rattle of a machine gun replying to the imperturbable plane....

The yard of the mosque filled up quickly, someone ordered the doors to be closed and, glancing from under his brows, Yosir noticed a tall, burly figure appear in the doorway of the mosque itself and move rapidly to the front of the gathering, accompanied by several armed guards. It was Muhammad Tahir Farruk (Tahir Yuldash – the Amir of the Islamic Movement of Uzbekistan). Like everyone else in the mosque, Yosir was sitting with his head bowed low, but since he was in one of the front rows, out of the corner of his eye he saw the Amir halt facing the gathering, while three of his bodyguards walked on further and three stayed beside him on his right, probing the community with their eyes. That had never happened before. Yosir had prayed with the Amir numerous times, and the Amir had very rarely played the part of an Imam, preferring to make himself inconspicuous somewhere in the general body of the community, but everything was different now.

In a low, hoarse voice the Amir read out the obligatory *hamd* and *naat* – the blessing in the name of Allah and his Prophet – and then, with mounting fervour, he moved on to the sermon itself. He spoke of *jihad*, a holy war against the infidels and above all against the empire of Satan – America; he spoke of *shahids*, who had died a righteous death on this path, of children who had been made orphans, but also avengers, and yet again Yosir wondered in amazement where Muhammad Tahir found that blazing passion that spoke prophetically above and beyond his own thoughts, will and lips, so that he never faltered, or hesitated or stumbled over a misplaced breath. He didn't learn it all off by heart, did he, he didn't rehearse it all in front of a mirror – for where would he get a mirror?

Yosir suddenly remembered that when he came back to Mazari-Sharif from Kabul with the film, they have been shooting, in the afternoon of the twenty-third day of the month of Jumad Al-Sani in year 1422 of the Hidjra (September 11, 2001) and entered a house belonging to Uzbek fighters on Puli Havoi Street, the Amir was sitting in the yard, shaving the head of one of his bodyguards by the light of a small flaming torch. The other two bodyguards were sitting nearby with their already shaven heads bleeding.

A certain alarm, not exactly fear, must have shown in Yosir's eyes, and the Amir had laughed and spoken first, before he could say anything: "Look, I am letting the bad blood out of their heads. It's very good for you, would you like to try it?" He made several cuts in his bodyguard's cleanly shaven skin and covered them with a glass jar heated briefly over a flame, the way in which a cold is usually treated. Blood covered the walls of the jar like dark paint. The bodyguard tensed up, but he didn't groan. "He's short of iron! Look how brown the blood is! You're all short of iron!" the Amir had joked and then, leaving his bodyguards in the yard, he had gone into the house to talk to Yosir.

That evening, following communal prayers in the yard of that house, at which people had gathered, as usual, by making their way through openings between one yard and the next, so that no one in the street could possibly guess who they were and what they were doing there, Yosir, who was tired after his long journey, had decided to go to bed early, without telling the curious all the latest news from Kabul and the Turkistan *madrasah* there. But no sooner had the final mountain passes before Mazari Sharif flashed in front of his eyes than he heard sounds from the next room, where the three sentries on duty were listening to the BBC, the Voice of America and Radio Liberty respectively: a loud braying in three voices was followed by rapid repetitions of "Allah-u Akbar!" – "Allah is great!" over and over again. Everybody in the house jumped up and, in defiance of the rules, went dashing towards the room on the upper floor, but one of the sentries was already flying down towards them with a radio pressed against his ear, and all Yosir could hear was "New York" and then something else, followed by "destroyed". The sentry went rushing past – to do as he was supposed to do and report the extraordinary news to the Amir, who was dealing with somebody in the basement. For some strange reason Yosir caught himself thinking of the gigantic wave that was expected when half of a Spanish island slipped into the sea, and felt horrified as he imagined it:

Hovliqar u, talpinar u, shoshar u,
Go'ringizdan na'ra tortib toshar u...

He had once translated these words of Chulpon about a wave of fire into Russian, and now, in the milling throng of that dark house, he tried to recall the ending:

And the wave will seethe and surge and rage
And scorch your coffins with a mighty roar ...

And from there it was but half a step to Brodsky:

Someday it and not, alas, we
Will flood along the railings of the promenade,
Advancing to shouts of: "Don't!.."

"Don't!" the Amir shouted and Yosir, adrift on his sea of memories, shuddered when he suddenly saw the bodyguards, who had pointed their rifles up into the sky, towards the sources of the rumbling that had been expanding for so long, lower their gun barrels, and heard the Amir first shout after them in his wheezing, sleepless voice: "Death to America! Death to the empire of Satan! Allah-u Akbar!" and then order everyone to leave the house one at a time and assemble immediately in the trenches.

Running out of the mosque when the bombing had already begun, Yosir glanced up as if for the last time at the sky, which was scored across by several long, bloody slashes, as if someone had decided to let the sky's bad blood, and high up above, slicing imperviously through the air and glittering like sharp blades in the cuts, he saw the American super-heavy B-1 bombers. Or that same wave of fire....

Chapter Two

To this pool,

to the trees in this pool,
beyond the trees,
the sudden fear of falling
in the bottomless cloud-filled sky,
closing wet eyes.

Within oneself,
in the veins within oneself,
beyond the veins
a groan on which one cannot hang words,
or in non-revelation
that is wider than this, more boundless,
more borderless than this.

I was suddenly afraid of falling.

-Belgi

Hamid Ismailov

After the prolonged and ultimately unsuccessful defence of Kunduz, when each of the commanders blamed another for the failure, and all of them secretly blamed Juma, who had been killed or disappeared; when the soldiers who were still alive – Pakistanis, Afghanis, Chechens and Uzbeks – had all thanked the one God in their various tongues for the slushy road back to possible freedom, Yosir knew for certain what lay ahead for him in the torture chambers of General Dostum. I have a photograph in front of me – the bombed-out building of the Sultan Razia Lyceum in Mazar Sharif, where the Uzbek fighters from the Islamic Movement of Uzbekistan took refuge in October 2001, together with the Taliban and Arabs from Al-Qaeda. A little earlier, in September 2001, the US administration had included the Islamic Movement of Uzbekistan in its list of terrorist organisations. At the same time the leader, or Amirul-Muminin of this movement, Muhammud Tahir Farruk[1] had declared in an interview with the Uzbek service of the BBC that they were prepared to fight on the side of the Taliban.

After the Americans started bombing Afghanistan and NATO – which had previously occupied no more than a tenth of the country – suddenly came to life and went on the offensive, the Taliban in Kabul had sworn publicly to "stand to the death against the aggression of the infidels", and the analysts had argued about a protracted guerrilla war, like the previous war against the Soviets, but there had not been any effective resistance. The local commanders, who had all grown beards under the Taliban, began shaving them off and switching their loyalty once again just as soon as they could tell which way the wind was blowing. And the only ones who were left hostage to the situation were the foreigners: Arabs, Uzbeks, Chechens, Kashmiris and Uigurs, each of whom was here for his own particular reason.

---

1   The factual information here and below has been downloaded from the Internet, and the hand of the special services can be clearly felt in it. I am leaving it just as it is – *Author's note.*

    Tahir Yuldash (Yuldashev) was born on October 2, 1968 in the Namangan region of Uzbekistan. He attended the Muhadillia-Husain regional seminary. In 1991 Yuldashev became the leader of the Namangan Islamist movement "Adolat". He was involved in the establishment of the Islamic organisations "Ishlom lashkorlari" and "Tovba". In 1992, after the persecution of Islamists began, Yuldashev moved from Uzbekistan to Afghanistan, where he became leader of the Uzbek Islamic Opposition in exile. In 1996 he became political head of the Islamic Movement of Uzbekistan (IMU). Yuldashev established extensive ties with many Islamic organisations and also raised funds for the Islamic Opposition of Uzbekistan. For these purposes he visited Pakistan, Saudi Arabia and the United Arab Emirates. In February 1999 he was one of the leading organisers of an attempted coup in Uzbekistan. In late 1999-early 2000 he held meetings with the leaders of opposition movements in order to unite all the forces opposing President Islam Karimov. Yuldashev's primary residence was in Afghanistan, in an area controlled by the Taliban movement. Killed in 2009 in Vaziristan. See http://news.bbc.co.uk/1/hi/world/south_asia/8287714.stm.

The [2] slaughter at Kal'ai Jangi, in the former citadel of General Dostum , was only one page in the story of those troubled late autumn days, when it was discovered who was really fighting in Afghanistan.

The Afghan journalist Daud Qorizade recalls: "After the Americans began bombing the north of Afghanistan, many local commanders changed their allegiance once again and went over to the side of General Dostum, who had appeared in the region. With these forces Dostum first moved against Mazari Sharif and quickly took it; then he moved against Kunduz. That was when two contradictory pieces of news appeared: according to General Dostum himself, when he was speaking to the Uzbek service of the BBC, the military commander of the Islamic Movement of Uzbekistan (IMU), Juma Namangani , had been killed in the fighting at Mazari Sharif.

2 Born in the village of Hojadukuh in the Shebergan district of the province of Juzjan. The son of a peasant. His father was an Uzbek (according to some sources, from a family of Uzbeks who emigrated from the USSR during the struggle against the counterrevolutionary *basmachestvo* movement). Graduated from a three-month officer training course at the Tashkent advanced training school of the KGB of the USSR (early 1980s). Until the April revolution of 1978 was an oilfield worker in Shebergan.

Graduated from a regimental school and soon became a brigade commander. From 1983 commander of a national (Uzbek) battalion and a national brigade at Shebergan.

In 1991 fought with Rabbani, Masud and Hekmatiar on the side of Najibulla. In January 1992 Dostum abandons Najibulla to enter a coalition with A. Sh. Masud, the regime collapses and all factions consolidate the positions they have managed to seize at the time. In April 1992 he airlifts his units (four thousand soldiers) to Kabul, forestalling G. Hekmatyar, who is about to "surrender" Kabul to Najibulla, and soon he is joined by Masud's forces. After the Taliban take Kabul (September 1996), he opposes them.

In May 1997, after switching to the side of General Malik's Taliban forces, he was forced to flee to Uzbekistan, and then to Turkey. In 2001 he returned to Afghanistan and in the early autumn of that year he assembled several detachments and led the attack on Mazari Sharif. In October 2001 Rabbani appointed him "Commander in Chief of North Afghanistan" for the "United Front of the National Liberation of Afghanistan" (the "Northern Alliance"). Since December 2001 – deputy minister of defence in the government of Hamid Karzai. Now has no official posts.

3 Jumaboi Ahmadjonovich Hodjiev (better known as Juma Namangani) was born on June 12, 1969 in the village of Hodja in the Namangan district of the Namangan region. He graduated from Secondary Technical School 28 in the town of Namangan. In November 1987 he was drafted for military service in the airborne forces. In 1988 he fought in Afghanistan. When demobilised in 1989, he returned to his homeland and contacted Islamic activists. In 1991 he established close contacts with the most radically inclined leaders of the Party of Islamic Revival of Uzbekistan (PIRU), and a year later he moved to Afghanistan. In Afghanistan Namangani found his way into a training camp for the Tajiki opposition, located in the northern province of Kunduz, which borders on Tajikistan. When he returned from Afghanistan in the summer of 1993, Juma Namangani founded his own camp in the Karategin Valley in Tajikistan in order to train fighters for the Islamic opposition of Uzbekistan. He later established an entire network of military and training camps in the north of Tajikistan. A detachment under his command was actively involved in the civil war on the side of the United Tajik Opposition (UTO). Juma Namangani's central headquarters were located in the locality of Hoit in the Tajikabad region of northern Tajikistan. The fighting units were armed with almost every possible kind of firearm. Their heavy armaments included several infantry combat vehicles and armoured

According to other accounts, besieged Kunduz was under the control of foreign mercenaries who were commanded by none other than Juma Namangani. In any event, General Dostum did not attack the town; instead he offered the chance of unconditional capitulation, promising freedom to every Afghani who surrendered. "Lay down your arms and go wherever you wish!" That was his appeal to the Afghani commanders in the town. What the fate of the mercenaries would be was not clear. But when the Taliban capitulated and surrendered the town, the foreigners had no choice but to do likewise. However, rumours circulated in the town about a huge military helicopter with no identifying markings that had carried the top leadership of the foreigners away from the besieged town to an unknown destination.

The foreign fighters were loaded into trucks and taken to the citadel of Kal'ai Jangi for further debriefing. They were first locked in the barracks hut and then interrogated. The interrogations were conducted by American instructors, who everyone there knew to be CIA field operatives.

Later the other prisoners said that when one of these operatives was interrogating a group of foreigners, including the American Abdul Hamid, he asked them in very arrogant manner: "Who invited you here? What are you doing here anyway? Why did you suddenly turn up here?" And then one of the Chechens threw himself on him with his bare hands, saying: "Your kind should be killed!"

In the confusion the other foreigners threw themselves on the guards and very quickly not only disarmed them, but killed them all. The guns they now had were used to start the so called uprising at Kal'ai Jangi, which was suppressed in three days with the help of American bombing raids, basements flooded with water and rocket strikes. The number of casualties was huge: more than four hundred foreigners – Arabs, Pakistanis, Chechens and Uzbeks – were killed in this uprising."

And so this was the very time when rumours began circulating that Juma Namangani, an IMU field commander and former paratrooper who had fought in Afghanistan before on the side of the Soviets, had been appointed commander in chief of this entire "foreign legion" in the northern region of Aghanistan. Although, as Daud Qorizade mentions, at the very height of the negotiations at Kunduz, when General Dostum offered the foreigners and the Taliban freedom in

---

personnel carriers, as well as recoil-free cannons, several "Grad" rocket launchers and anti-aircraft defence systems. In 1997 Juma Namangani became "commander in chief of the armed forces of the Islamic Movement of Uzbekistan". In November 1997 his fighters infiltrated the territory of Uzbekistan from Kyrgyzstan and made several attacks on Interior Ministry personnel in the town of Yangiabad in the Tashkent province. In 2000 these incursions were repeated. Juma Namangani is believed to have been killed at the beginning of the American bombing of Afghanistan in autumn 2001, when he had been appointed commander in chief of Taliban forces in the northern region.

exchange for laying down their arms, he also said, in an interview with the Uzbek service of the BBC, that Juma Namangani had been killed in one of the American bombing raids.

How did it happen that Juma Namangani, a former Soviet paratrooper, and Tahir Yuldash, who graduated from a Soviet school with a gold medal, and, most surprisingly of all, Belgi – a poet whose works were being read at that time in French, German and English in the clubs and studios of London, Paris and Berlin – were still fighting in a place where even the Taliban had decided it was better to disguise themselves or run? What kept them there in that war-torn land, why and how did they find themselves in this foreign country beyond mountains and rivers, a neighbour to their own homeland in space but far removed from it in time?

Chapter Three

> *To build new disorder*
> *out of the old chaotic disorder*
> *– perhaps that is to live...*

> -Belgi

What gave rise to the Islamic Movement of Uzbekistan? When and how? Mountains of scholarly sociological material have already been written on this subject, but I am a writer and I am interested in the fate of human beings. For me nothing happens outside of human lives, relationships and bonds. And therefore, while this book is full of documents of the time, the selection of those documents is dictated by my writer's intuition and, as I fumble at the knots of those human relationships, I am also trying to find the answer to that same question. And above all I am interested in the events that were suppressed, those that never became newspaper headlines, but had a significantly greater influence on those ten or fifteen years than the clamorous headlines that explained nothing. One such event took place in Namangan in December 1991, and so....

---

4 On October 5, 2001 the journal *Missives* presented Belgi's poetry to the public at the Raspaille theatre in Paris.

Hamid Ismailov

December 21, 1991,
the town of Namangan

On that day the president of Uzbekistan, Islam Karimov [5], who had held a number of election campaign meetings in Namangan the previous day and then left for Tashkent, was forced to return to Namangan at the demand of thousands of Muslims demonstrating in the central square of the city. The presidential election was due to take place in a few days, and this turn of events was clearly not to the advantage of a president who had still not firmly established himself in his position.

Only a month or two before, he had survived an attempted palace coup when parliament rebelled against him, and now the people were out in the square. An amateur video of the entire meeting has survived, showing President Karimov effectively as a hostage, being forced to appear and make the following speech in Uzbek, which has never been published anywhere before.

President Karimov: "In the first place, yesterday before my arrival in Namangan I sent several men here, they were supposed to meet with the people here and agree who I ought to meet during the two or three days at my disposal. People have different opinions and different problems, so in order to make things easier for myself, I asked them to let me know where I ought to go first. Please now, come on, please… (he is trying to calm the people)… and so according to their instructions in this place, in this region, in our very own Namangan region, concerning whom I ought to meet… if we were wrong, you should know that it was my mistake, but I'd like to say that the first suggestion was – go to a mosque. Meet with the mullahs whom people respect, where they gather, in the first place meet with the Muslims, Comrade President. Listen to what they say, then you can go to other places of work, that's what they asked me to do. And so what did I do

---

5   Born in Samarkand in 1938, Islam Karimov was raised in a Soviet orphanage before studying engineering and economics at university. He initially worked as an aircraft engineer, and then as an economic planner. He became First Secretary of the Communist Party of Uzbekistan in 1989 and was elected president of independent Uzbekistan in December 1991, in what Human Rights Watch described as a "seriously marred" poll. In 1995 he extended his term of office by referendum. He was re-elected in January 2000, and again in 2007, when the international community raised serious concerns about the poll's fairness. Although he has been in power for nearly 20 years, he remains intent on stifling any political opposition. He tolerates no dissent and has banned many opposition groups, in particular Islamic organisations. Mr. Karimov has been keen to track down those he views as Muslim extremists, intent on taking over the country. Whatever the real extent of the Islamic threat, his critics agree that he has used it to crack down on any form of opposition – militant or otherwise. In May 2005, Karimov's administration was heavily criticised by the international community for a bloody crackdown on protesters in the city of Andijan. He blamed the violence on Islamist extremists, describing them as driven by "hatred and aversion to the secular path of development". Human rights groups estimate that thousands of ordinary Muslims are in jail, accused of plotting against the government. The state also maintains tight control of the media and no criticism of the president and his policies is permitted.

when I arrived at the airport? First of all I went to the new mosque. When I got to the new mosque... I performed my ablutions, since I also can... I also cannot enter any mosque without washing first, I went into the mosque (the crowd shouts "Allah-u Akbar") and when I was in the mosque I met with the Ulema, the old men, respected representatives of their religion, I agreed to listen to their demands, to stay in close contact with them, so that was the first place I went to. If I was not right, I ask forgiveness from all of you (the crowd sings "God is great"). I... there are another couple of mosques in Namangan, if I had known I ought to have gone to those mosques first. If I did this out of ignorance, I ask you once again, I am ready to go down on my knees the next time I come, I will meet with you first. (Chanting) But I was at fault... and yet, let me tell you one thing, do not take it amiss, they say that only God is beyond reproach (the crowd cries "Allah-u Akbar"), I was wrong, and so I acknowledge my mistake, looking into your faces, into your eyes, forgive me.

Now about the serious problems, let me tell you frankly all that is in my heart. Friends, brothers and parents say to me that I have been in the post of president for a year and a half. Which of my commands, decisions or decrees have been directed against even a single person? Who can stand up and say that any one of my decisions has been directed against the people? Is there anyone at all who will say this is not so? (Voices in the crowd shout "Yes, there is!")

In the first place, the gates must be open for Afghanistan, Pakistan, Iran, Turkestan (he means Turkey). Becoming their friends, receiving their help, if we become a united Muslim state, what is bad about that? So there are actions directed towards that. From this point of view, I am travelling to Turkey this December, then to Pakistan... recently an important minister came from Pakistan and asked me to visit Pakistan, and then the Iranian minister of foreign affairs, Mr. Velayati came, saying let us and Uzbekistan be friends. So in January, with your permission, if you do not dismiss me from my job, if you do not hack away my roots with an axe, if it is written in my fate, I plan to visit three Islamic states, and I shall try to act together with them to defend Uzbekistan, the Muslims of Uzbekistan and as well as that, the Muslims living right across Central Asia. (The crowd shouts "Allah-u Akbar!" Tahir Yuldash takes the microphone, Karimov says: "And you stay where you are, let me have my say too. When you were speaking, we listened, so let us have our say too".)

Now our younger brother (he points to Tahir) says: Why do you not talk about meat and about cattle? So, just think – there is Russia – there is Belorussia – there is Ukraine, we're all tied together. 60 to 65 per cent of the clothes we and our children wear are brought from there. This is the path of colonialism that lasted for 74 years. So, if it goes on, the Ukraine, for instance, has become independent, it is moving over to its own currency, they are abandoning the old Soviet currency and introducing their own. So what will be the consequences for Uzbekistan? And so tell me, respected elders, if Yeltsin raises prices tomorrow... we get 10 million tonnes of oil, and he wants to increase the price by ten times. Our young Muslim neighbour, my friend Niyazov in Turkmenistan, has raised the

price of oil by a factor of ten. And so should Uzbekistan defend itself in this matter or not? Of course it should. What have we done? I went against my own interests, I said, let my power come to an end, but the people must not suffer, I said: "Tomorrow sacks, briefcases and bags full of money will arrive from Russia and sweep the shelves in our shops clean," and then I said: "Today we have 1,000 roubles, tomorrow they could turn into kopecks," so I turned to our people and I said: "Take all your savings and spend them, otherwise tomorrow that money will be affected by inflation". I said: "Buy up everything in our shops". If they come tomorrow and sweep everything off our shelves, who will be to blame? I shall be to blame.... For everything that is wrong in the republic I am to blame in the first instance.

And therefore... our young brother (he points to Tahir Yuldash) has raised this question. All right, meat is expensive, but you should know that in a year and a half, because of the opportunities we have given our peasants, livestock holdings have doubled. We must defend ourselves, that is my responsibility. All right, even if I am not president tomorrow, I shall still serve you to the end of my life, whether you want it or not!

Prices at the markets are rising, but I have given orders for the neediest to be given 1.5 kg. of meat and a certain amount of wheat and sugar out of our budget, I know it isn't enough, but tomorrow, if necessary, I shall take our gold to Switzerland and take out credits, then exchange them for money, I have to finish this job. Then I shall try to regulate prices. That is why I do not feel guilty about what I told you on the television, I have to talk to people and tell them the truth, that's why I ask you, you must not misunderstand me if tomorrow I should give you the bad news without any warning, that not only in Namangan, but in all Uzbekistan there is nothing left. Do not misunderstand me, this is temporary, for a week, a week and a half, two weeks, I am negotiating now to buy wheat in Kazakhstan, that is my answer to all of you.

The second question. Yesterday, when I met the representatives of religion in the mosque, I said to them: "When I swore my oath, I held the Koran in front of me. I shall never deny my Muslim faith, I shall never regret that I am a Muslim and I shall never be ashamed of this. No man should abandon his religion that is what I always say. If we follow that path, nothing will happen.

You should know that now the three Slavic – they are bringing back the old words – the three Slavic republics – Russia, Belorussia and Ukraine – are meeting in Belorussia. Muslims, the Uzbeks do not know about it, this is my opinion: if it is necessary... I have already spoken with the five Central Asian leaders, we could meet in Tashkent or in Ashkhabad or in some other place, and we will talk with each other in our central Asian, Muslim language, and I shall try to defend (Tahir Yuldash tries to bring him back to the initial subject) these Muslim countries.

What I would like to say is, if the situation gets worse, in the way it is now, you must know that there is no other path for Uzbekistan, it must renounce the USSR. That is why I say, looking straight into your eyes: If there is aggression from the north tomorrow, what must we do? We must

defend ourselves. And from this point of view I have another request: there are no problems that cannot be solved, give me time, and secondly, be patient, we shall do it all together and if necessary I shall put my life into this!

And so, your main demand, to declare our state an Islamic state. I would like to express my views on this matter. I have to speak frankly in front of this large assembly. I promise you that I shall personally raise this question with Parliament (chanting: "Allah-u Akbar!"), if Parliament decides unanimously, with the participation of your representatives from Namangan, to proclaim an Islamic state, then so be it, but the majority of our people must vote for it.

The other problem, listen... now (the crowd is dissatisfied)... there is a demand to postpone the presidential election. I must say... how many republics in the USSR have not yet elected their presidents? Yesterday the last one, Moldova, elected a president. What does that mean? If I want to become President, or Solih, or someone else does, that gives the power to you. I have to go to Turkey, to the other Islamic states, they will ask me: Who are you? Was I elected by the people or by 500 deputies? This is a natural question. We should have held it three months ago. Do not misunderstand me, but we are on the brink of famine, I have to struggle against that, I have to take every possible measure. Just one example. They say the USSR ran up debts of 43 billion roubles. You have to pay back that money, they say. Uzbekistan together with all the rest. There are three places that produce gold, including Uzbekistan (Russia and Kazakhstan). So they say that we have to pay the debts. I am fighting against this. I do not intend to sign this, just like Azerbaijan. But I must have your support behind me! If you have other ideas on this question, so be it, but my request is that whoever becomes president, he must be empowered by the people as soon as possible and act in their name, or else we shall be crushed.

The final problem. (A man from the crowd arrives and says: "The militia has blocked the road to stop people coming to meet their president". He asks for them to be let through.) (Chanting)

Karimov: We shall solve this..... Let them through, tell the militia that is my order, we are speaking frankly here, what should I be afraid of? Dear friends, the final question. Declare Islam the state religion. If the majority is for this and votes for this, if each person votes for it, then why should I be against it? And then the question of dissolving Parliament. In the seventh session of Parliament – you saw it – it was on October 30 (he turns to Tahir Yuldash), you tell me, my young brother, my dear young brother says they are my supporters... absolutely not! If you saw the session, I don't have a majority of supporters in Parliament at all. You saw the kind of attacks I was subjected to, the conspiracy they formed against me, the coup they tried to organise. Historically the struggle for positions has destroyed our country. Important people fight for a position, but who suffers? The poor ordinary man suffers. That is why I ask you, if we wish to win our independence we must unite. For example, in Pakistan, when they were fighting for their independence, all their parties united and then, after independence, they decided to share out the positions and the jobs.

The meeting was broken off here, since someone else from the crowd approached the microphone, and then they were supposed to have questions and answers, but after negotiations it was decided that representatives from the meeting would meet with President Karimov face to face immediately, right there in the building, and then inform the meeting of their decisions.

And so, after this meeting President Islam Karimov (whom Belgi ever after referred to as "Comrade Islam") was obliged to spend several more hours in negotiations with representatives of the Muslim community of Namangan, sitting shoulder to shoulder with Tahir Yuldash, who was then the leader of the informal organisation "Islom lashkarlari" ("Warriors of Islam").

To Karimov's credit as a politician, it should be said that he rather quickly overcame his initial humiliation and fear and little by little seized the initiative, effectively demolishing point after point and totally rejecting the demands of the meeting, but as a man, an ambitious and dictatorial man, a vindictive and vengeful man, he could never forgive either this open humiliation or this public display of fear. It took him only a short time to gather his strength.

Chapter Four

Day after day, night after night, withdrawing into the furthest corner of the Shebergan prison, Yosir recalled his life, grain by grain. If there was one memory that had haunted him for the past two or three years, it was the memory of electric light. Neither at Hoit, nor at Kunduz, nor at Mazari Sharif had there been any electric light during the evenings and the nights. Only when he arrived in Kabul and stayed in a detached house on Vazir Akbarhon Street, had the electricity supply provided dim light for a short period, but even that had frequently failed. All this reminded him of his childhood on the outskirts of Osh, where sometimes his grandmother and sometimes his uncle would clean the kerosene lamp for every evening, and by its flickering light he was allowed to read his grandmother either the tales from *A Hundred and One Nights* or Mashrab's *gazelles*.

But the initial ache of nostalgia had been replaced long ago by either weary habit or a state of permanent irritation as the smoky light of a candle or a kerosene lamp, or even a simple wad of cotton wool or rag doused in oil sucked out his inflamed and bloodshot eyes.

In the Shebergan prison, where they had been taken from Kal'ai Jangi after the bloody massacre, lying with his battered and broken back on

the straw covering the damp clay floor – that way the pain was soothed by the piercing cold – Yosir was quite simply unable to extinguish the naked lamp bulb in his mind, or rather the filament that hung there in a blinding zigzag in front of his eyes, whether he closed them or opened them, and this slim thread prevented him from seeing the bodies around him or the barred windows at the sides, even though the incessant groans drifted into the curves of this filament from all sides.

They were beaten methodically and regularly, in the same way they were given food, But instead of water there were streams of abuse. The Arabs, Pakistanis and Chechens were threatened with being left to rot if they weren't shot. But the Uzbeks were threatened with being sent to Karimov: "Let him fuck you up the ass!" They had been beaten from the very first day, when they were led out of Kunduz after surrendering and the Afghanis were set free, while all the foreigners were loaded into trucks. The Red Cross is going to investigate your cases, they were told, and under that pretext they had been brought to the citadel of Kal'ai, where they were locked in the barracks hut. But it wasn't the Red Cross that investigated, it was several American soldiers, accompanied by General Dostum's toadies, who worked out their own old betrayals on the prisoners.

The darkness of the prison was the only refuge in which there were no thoughts and no feelings – nothing but the oblivion that he had been seeking for so long – but his body clutched with all its pain at his soul and would not let go, and with the pain the nightmares of life returned: the first blow of a rifle-butt against his coccyx when they were being herded into the trucks – that was where Yosir had suddenly seen the dazed face of the journalist who was standing a little distance away and had even shouted something after him, but the blow of the rifle-butt had driven Yosir into the closed truck, where he had collapsed on to the prickly straw for the first time, and then there had been the same kind of straw at Kal'ai Jangi, which had reminded him of the regional Machine and Tractor Station at home, with its dereliction and its smell and its scattered black-fading-into-purple patches of diesel oil....

And again Yosir was called out for interrogation, and again the barking American tried to prove that he understood what he was saying, and the local Uzbek, supposedly translating these words, threatened him every now and again with being handed over to the authorities in Uzbekistan, where they didn't mollycoddle you in the prisons like here, but simply sat you on a bayonet or sluiced boiling water over you. Every now and again Yosir said that he had been working on a film in Kunduz and he didn't know any Juma Namangani or Tahir Yuldash. "Who were you working for?" the American shouted in unison with the Uzbek, and Yosir named a certain Zubair, whose surname and whereabouts he had

never known. "What was this film about? Bomb-making or terrorist activity?" the American persisted, putting his feet up on the table in front of Yosir's face. Yosir waited for the translation, although his impatience was only restrained by the dull ache in all of his body, and then he said yet again: "About people who were forced to flee from Uzbekistan because of the persecution..."

The Afghani Uzbek came out from behind the American and swung the hardest punch he could manage into Yosir's face. The blow landed on his cheek, but it was his lips or teeth that started bleeding, because together with the scorching pain Yosir felt a warm, salty taste in his mouth. His hand instinctively jerked up in a protective reflex, but the infuriated Afghani was already kicking him in the stomach and shrieking: "I've been in Uzbekistan, I lived like a king, and you say it's impossible to live there! I'll show you where it's impossible to live!" The American waited for the beating to end, then lazily got to his feet and dragged the interpreter back behind the desk.

Hunched over from the pain in his belly, Yosir sat there on the straw scattered across the damp clay floor, while the American asked him once again in a conciliatory tone exactly which people his film was about. Yosir felt as if the film were running endlessly in front of his eyes. He was reading some subtitles or other that didn't fit properly: about the family they had brought to him from the Shirbirgan hospital, about the woman from Khoresm in Kabul, about the man from Ferghana in Mazar. The man from Ferghana had fled to Turkmenistan with the remaining members of his family who had not been arrested, and then he, his wife and their one-year-old son had made their way to the Afghan border and begun waiting for the night in order to swim across the Amu-Darya. Of course, he was the only one who could swim, but his strength should have been enough for his wife and his son. Night came, he quietly lowered himself into the cold, murky water, took his wife and son in his arms and at first started wading. The moon rose above the horizon and just when he finally decided to swim, the beam of a searchlight suddenly flashed on above his head and the Turkmen border guards opened fire on them. The young man was under the water, his wife on his back was wounded in the leg and she howled in pain and let go of the child. Speaking to camera, the young man said he would have plunged after his son, but his wife had clung on to him so tightly in her fear of death that he was unable to swim off in pursuit of the little infant, who howled once and then fell silent in the murky torrent. He and his wife had only been saved by the superhuman strength of terror, but on the Afghani riverbank the wife tried to throw herself back into the water to get the child, and now it was the husband who clutched her wounded body and dragged her away from the terrible force drawing her back to the country from which they had just fled....

The pain in his body kept trying to match the pain that lay deeper, to rise to the same level, and everyone around him seemed to be trying to help it: twisting his arms behind his back and tying them there with a cattle noose until they turned blue and numb, punching him as he walked to his darkness in the cell, kicking him on the coccyx in the doorway before slamming the barred door of the damp, welcoming darkness behind him.

And then again those two zigzag filaments sprang to life in his eyes and those uncontrollable, unwanted pictures began slipping along them.

Chapter Five

It seemed to me that Belgi had inherited his elegance of spirit, love of religion and passion for writing from his forebears. I should say that I reached this conclusion a long time ago, although for the most part I had only seen the secular, social side of Belgi's life. In 1996, when seven of us were invited to the small Bavarian town of Bamberg for a conference on "Uzbekness", we all found ourselves accommodated in the picturesque Walkmuhle – a former mill standing on a fork in the river. Our little house was essentially an island surrounded on all sides by the branches of the river, cataracts, waterfalls, streams and bridges. Add to that a dark autumnal avenue of maples and oaks leading off into the forest and in the distance the building of the Constanze rising up over the river and its trembling reflection, and you will understand many of Belgi's poems of that period.

In the mornings we were woken by the chiming of the distant bells of Bamberg cathedral, the town hall and a dozen small churches, and in the midst of the low-key luxury of the house's numerous compartments we gathered together in the kitchen, where everything was within easy reach if you just held out your hand. Hot, thick coffee, cereals, jams and preserves, and especially that fragrant black German bread and those intelligent, so highly intelligent conversations – never in my life had I had known such a cosy and comfortable feeling as I did there and then.

And then there were morning walks along the sluggish river and down those dawn-radiant avenues over the red autumnal sand crumbling under our feet. Belgi loved to hum songs by the Beatles and Demis Roussos while we decided the future of Russo-Uzbek relations or compared Fitrat with Luther and Goethe with Navoi. One morning there Belgi said that he was planning to write a poetic symphony about this town and call it Bambergiana. He had been struck most of all by the robust stone substance of the town, its immutability over the

centuries. He told me that now when he arrived in his native Osh, his home district, he would not recognise it – every year one clay building was replaced by another, the son rebuilt the father's work, the grandson his grandfather's. The only thing that remained untouched was the stonework of the mosque on the Suleiman-mountain in the centre of the town, but even its ground was already a patchwork of graves and paths and pipes. And even Babur's house, which had stood on top of the hill for five centuries – someone had managed to get hold of that and demolish it… But here, in our time, everything was still standing as it had stood in the time of the crusaders, in the time of the first Popes…. It was strange suddenly to feel that *you* were the variable factor, he told me then, and suddenly fell silent.

Our afternoons were wasted on the conference, but Sokrat-aka, the oldest among us, decided to arrange soirées for each of us in the evenings, and when it came to Belgi's evening, instead of reading his poems, which he simply handed out to each of us, he unexpectedly suggested that we should listen to what he called a "documentary story" about his grandfather.

Immediately after the poems he handed out copies of the criminal proceedings against Mirzaraimov Abut and began his story with the very last day of this man's life, the last day before he was shot in February 1939. I won't retell his story here, because that very evening one of us bluntly asked Belgi to let him have the entire story line, saying he would include it in his novel *The Railway,* which he was finishing writing at the time. And the story of the grandfather – Obid-kori – really is there in his book. I recommend you to read that section of it to acquire a better understanding of the life and fate of the poet whom I first met in that far-away Bavarian town with the bell-chime name of Bamberg….

Chapter Six

> *Dark path,*
> *Bandit's tamarisk*
> *Why do you beat so, heart*
> *That which you fear like providence is a mountain,*
> *That which you fear like death is a star*
> *Will your insane guide – whether you stare or not -*
> *Sell you rocks and planets?*

> -Belgi

President Karimov, having won his victory over the poet Muhammad Solih in the presidential elections of December 1991, barely even had time to draw breath in order to set about consolidating his forces, before thousands of students came out on to the streets of Tashkent on February 21, 1992.

The events of that time are recalled by the journalist Hamid Ismailov:

In February 1992 I was approached by a production group from BBC television who were planning to shoot four films at the same time about the four Central Asian republics. They asked me to be their consultant on Uzbekistan. At that time I was living in Moscow and working as the representative of the Union of Writers of Uzbekistan at the Union of Writers of the USSR. Although by then the Soviet Union had effectively already disintegrated, the Union of Writers was still functioning as it had before. I agreed to fly to Uzbekistan, but I made it a condition of my involvement in the making of the film that I would be helped by the poet Belgi, since he was then living in the Ferghana Valley and knew everything that was going on there from the inside. So that was our arrangement.

In addition to general consultation, my assignment included travelling ahead of the film unit and looking for people to interview for the film, deciding how interesting and representative their views were and arranging possible filming sessions with them. Just recently I reviewed all the ten or twelve hours of raw footage for the half-hour film, and I was amazed at how much historical material we gathered back then: there are interviews with the former mufti Muhammad Sadik Yusuf, the dissident writer Mamadali Mahmudov, the religious leader Abdullah Utaev, who disappeared without trace, the poet and politician Muhammad Solih, who emigrated, the leader of the "Birlik" movement, Abdurahim Pulatov, and the patriarch of the religious movement, Hakim-kori Vasiev. In short, apart from president Karimov, who refused to meet with us, we filmed every figure of even the slightest significance in the Uzbekistan of ten years ago.

One of those who were interviewed at length was the leader of the religious movement "Islom Lashkarlari" in Namangan, Tahir Yuldashev. I first heard this name from Belgi when, after visiting the poet Shamshad Abdullaev in Ferghana, I travelled on to Osh and met my young friend there. He it was who told me about the confrontation in which President Karimov was forced to return to Namangan to face that meeting of thousands organised by Tahir Yuldashev in December 1991. And now Belgi told me that after that meeting Yuldashev's organisation had been given the Municipal Communist Party Committee Building, and he had almost completely replaced the local militia with members of his organisation.

We decided to travel to Namangan together. If I exclude my early childhood, I had never been to Namangan before and so, when our taxi was about to cross the boundary of the region and the millionaire traffic-militiamen stopped it in order to question us about where we were going and why, my Moscow arrogance flared up momentarily and I said that I was from the Union of Writers of the USSR: however, that failed to make the slightest impression on the local militiamen. "But the Soviet

Union doesn't exist," one of them said with a yawn and carried on asking questions. Nowhere else have I ever encountered such a meticulously organised network of suspicion as I did there – at the next post we were met by militiamen who asked if we were the poets on our way to a meeting in the local department of propaganda and literature.

Well, all right, they were militiamen, but when our old Andijan Volga drove up to the former Communist Party Committee building and we got out and asked the first security guard we met where we could meet Tahir Yuldashev, the young guard launched into exactly the same round of questions: 'And where would you be from? And what do you want to see him for? And who gave you this address?'

I quickly lost patience, above all with the Namangani manner of asking you questions in the third person: And where would they be from? And why do they want to see them? And who gave them this address? – and I very nearly started teasing the over-inquisitive security guard by asking: And exactly what business is it of theirs? But Belgi tugged on my sleeve and intervened with a gentle explanation that just before Ramadan the BBC was making a programme about Islam in Uzbekistan and the first thing they had decided to do was visit Namangan, as the bastion of Islam in Central Asia, and therefore....

Just at that very moment an entire procession appeared from the other direction and walking along in the middle of it was a tall young man with a sparse beard, wearing a Namangani *chapan*, or simple caftan, with light blue tracksuit trousers showing below it. The crowd around him was moving disjointedly and awkwardly, with some of them trying to explain something to him, but in the middle of a proposal from someone the young man suddenly looked round and shouted to a person on the other side of the street, telling him how he ought to do this and do that.

I don't remember whether Belgi already knew Tahir Yuldashev by sight, but he responded to my intuitive query with a simple nod, and then I took the bull by the horns: walking up to the front of the crowd, I greeted the men loudly and said I would like to have a talk with Tahir Yuldashev. 'Tahir Yuldash?' the young man echoed, cutting off the Russian ending and looking me up and down, before asking: 'And who might they be?'

After that Belgi spoke for me: he was always a lot better than I was with all these Namangani formal courtesies – who serves the tea to whom and how, and the way he has to tap his finger against the bowl as he does it. In short, he built me right up so that the haughty Tahir Yuldash was intrigued and invited us inside, gesturing to the others to go on about their business.

To be quite honest, owing to all the various elements of psychological stress, I have forgotten what our first conversation was about, the only thing I know is that we agreed to bring the BBC crew there to film our interview about Islam in Namangan as soon as possible, because Ramadan was about to begin. I remember that was when Tahir Yuldash said: "It is Namangan now, but you can also call it Islamabad".

We did everything we could to get to Namangan as soon as possible, but the filming of the unfortunate 'national hero' Ahmadjan Adylov (a

legendary Soviet farmer, who suffered arrest for political reasons both under the Soviets and after independence), or perhaps the new capitalist Anvar Tillyahojaev (a banker, who was later arrested and killed while in the prison), in his crimson jacket, or someone else delayed our arrival until the very first day of Ramadan. And on the first day of the Muslim holy month, the month of the fast, our entire assault team disembarked opposite the former Municipal Communist Party Committee building. I won't describe the full membership of the group, but I will make special mention of our interpreter Olga – a young model type from Moscow. Apart from trips to the West, this young woman had never been anywhere outside the central district of Moscow bounded by the Garden Ring Road, and so she had come to Uzbekistan expecting it to be like the Bahamas or Hawaii, a place with lots of sun where she could get a free tan. As consultants to the project, Belgi and I had explained several times to her and the producer of the film – a Pakistani by the name of Farrah – that it was not appropriate to appear looking the way she did in the very heart of Islamic Uzbekistan. Either Farrah was an advocate of the right of Muslim women to absolute equality, or Olga was unable to find anything suitable in the local cooperative shops, but in any event she showed up for all the meetings with the grey-bearded mullahs and the staid imams in her miniskirt, and since – for lack of any chairs and in accordance with local tradition – we often had to sit on the floor, although the righteous men's gazes were directed downwards at the ground (also by tradition) they could not help but stumble across the exposed charms of our supermodel.

Olga was also entrusted with interviewing Tahir Yuldashev on the first day of the holy month of Ramadan. Here is the full transcript of that interview.

Question: Tell us about your Islamic Army.

Firstly I would like to say welcome to you, may God be praised that we are meeting and we already understand that if I give you an interview, I must explain this to you. This Islamic Army was formed here in Namangan eight months ago, it has already been working for eight months. The reason for this is that among the people, in the city, in the region, there were many criminals. If we regard ourselves as Muslims, we must not just look upon any crime, we have been given a command from God and also from the prophet Muhammad, alaihissalam, that if someone does something bad, if we have seen a criminal, we must immediately stop him, restrain him bodily. That is our duty. Therefore, the reason was that the militia, and the Soviet army, you understand, they weren't working, they simply took their pay and that was all. If there was a crime, they took a lot of bribes and let the criminal go. This is why we founded the Islamic Army, to help the poor people or the weak people, and we shall fight against crime. That is our task.

Question: Is it true that you do not recognise the secular authorities, and in that case what kind of government do you want?

You understand, we have laws. The law is the Koran, from God, from Allah. The Koran was given to us by God, it is our path. We wish to see the kind of Islam that will make our army the kind that is shown in the Koran. And the kind that Muhammad, alaihissalam, showed in the Hadith, that is how we wish to arrange things. We submit only to these laws. The Koran and the word of Muhammad, alaihissalam, our Prophet. We want to see some man or other take charge and submit to the Koran and the word of the Prophet Muhammad, alaihissalam.

Question: Will it be easy now to bring back the Islamic traditions when so many years have passed since they were followed?

You understand, Olga... (the producer and interpreter interrupt and tell him not to address Olga directly). Sorry, sorry...

Islam has passed so many examinations. These seventy-four years are also considered an examination. People understand, and I also understand, that if they make an effort it will not be difficult. Our first task is that the way they are now, people have to be shown the true road, because many of them have lost their way. We must show them and we shall try to show them. I think it will not be difficult, it will be easy.

Question: is it true that you use violent methods, and if not, what methods do you use in your activities?

There are many methods. The first method is that we wish to win people over to the true faith, to the true Islam, and we try to explain to the people in this way. But if anyone opposes Islam, if that is what they want, then we are ready to reply to them with force. Islam must never be first to start a war. But if someone opposes it, whoever he is, we can respond.

Question: Does your organisation have a military structure, that is, is it really an Islamic Army?

You understand, I want to explain to you. I think it is not an army. A real army has to have weapons... but our weapon is God. Our most important weapon is the faith that is in the heart. I think it is not an army, they are simply true Muslims who are opposed to injustice. And we think of ourselves as mujahids. "Mujahid" translates like this: with all the strength that a man has, he must help Islam, perhaps someone will teach another man, someone will build a mosque, that is a mujahid. A mujahid must not be understood as someone picking up an automatic rifle or some weapon and firing. No, a mujahid must help Islam with everything he has and he does help. That is what is called a mujahid. That is why I do not want to say "army".

Question: What are your plans if things go on as they are?

I do not think I can feel any changes. Things are still the same as they have been so far. But what will come next, I do not know. When Ramadan

is over here, the Prophet Muhammad, alaihissalam, says: You will see a new moon in the sky and enter into Ramadan, you will see a new moon in the sky and come out of Ramadan. And so what will come next, I do not know. Only God knows. We have lived until this time – this we can know, but what will be next, what we shall do, I cannot say anything about that. If they will change things or not change things, only God knows. We are asked many times the question: What are you going to do? This I do not know. I do not know if in an hour I shall be alive or not. This God knows. And so I cannot answer.

Question: Is it true that Islam will spread across Central Asia from the Ferghana Valley, and why precisely from here?

You understand, I think this is not right. When I read in the newspaper that Mike Tyson accepted Islam, they said that Islam was spreading from America too. The very first Islam came from Mecca, from Arabistan. In order to be genuine Muslims, we must give away everything that we have. Muhammad, alaihissalam, says: You are not Muslims if you love something and will not give it to others. Therefore we love our faith and our prayer, and we love God and try – if we wish to be true Muslims – to give this to others, to explain. Therefore, as many Muslims as there are living on earth, in the world, they must try to explain Islam to others. And so I do not know yet if it will be from the Ferghana Valley, or… and so if someone considers himself a Muslim, he must help explain Islam to others.

Question: What do you think, how will your relations with the authorities develop, especially with the militia, whose functions you have taken over?

You understand, people no longer trust them, those militiamen, policemen. For eight months now we have answered the people, our group has received something like two hundred representations and we have answered the people. We have taken millions from criminals and given them back to people. If someone's money was taken, we gave it back to him. I think the militia is still asleep. If the people go on like this, soon they will have to abolish the police. The local officers don't work here either. If things continue like this, I think we will not have any militia, the Islamic Army, as you called it, will take its place.

Question: Can you foresee what might happen, say, by the end of the year? Will the attitude of the authorities change?

You understand, when we dealt with things, we punished many militiamen too. If they took bribes or committed crimes, we punished many of them. Now in these times they are trying just a little bit to help the people. Perhaps they will carry on doing that, but I think… I cannot answer what will happen in seven months.

Question: Is it true that because of you Russians are fleeing from the Ferghana Valley and do you regard them as kafirs, or rejecters?

That is not right. We in Islam make no difference between nations. If we did, I would not even be talking to you. For example, while I am now their leader, no difference is made between nations with us. We are children of the one procreator. Our first father is Adam. Muhammad, alaihissalam, says: All people who live on earth are children of Adam. Many are afraid now that if Islam is built in Uzbekistan, people who believe in something else, in other religions, they will have to leave. No, that is not true. Whether it is Namangan, Uzbekistan, Turkestan or even Moscow, it is not mine, not yours, because it is ours in common. Because the Koran says: Whatever is on earth and in heaven, it is all for God. Because I do not have the right to say that this land is ours, that only the Uzbek or the Muslim must live in Namangan. With Muslims there is no Uzbek, no Arab, if someone believes, he is a Muslim. And so it is not right if someone says, if there will be many Muslims here, then those who believe in other religions will have to leave, that is not true. Let him live here. They are our friends, they are our brothers. And so Islam must not coerce others, that is also the word of God. And so let him be reassured, we do not drive anyone away.

Question: But do you not think that the rise of Islam here will force them to leave?

No, you understand, there is the word of the Prophet Muhammad, alaihissalam, (the producer intervenes to ask him not to cover his face with his hands). The prophet Muhammad, alaihissalam, says that a believer must not abuse one who believes in another religion, for instance, if he is a Christian or some other. And so if he has abused him, it is as if he has abused me. And so this is no reason, if Islam spreads here, for them to go away from here… It is no reason, perhaps he wishes to live in his native city, for example, if you are from Moscow or some other city, if he wants to go to his native city, that is his… right.

Question: What are your personal plans for the future?

You understand, that is a very interesting question, but I have already said that what will come next, I do not know. I cannot answer. But we will continue marching forward to the end of our life. How much life we have – that is known to God, and so we shall not stop until our life is good. Until the end of our life we shall work for Islam, that is our duty. But what will be, that is a difficult question, I cannot answer.

Question: If the situation in Uzbekistan and the Ferghana Valley deteriorates, what will you do?

If things go on as they are, the poor people, if it still as bad for the people, I think we shall have to carry on working, work more. I believe that a man can take the true path for himself from Islam. And so I think that the people can only find their true path with Islam. And we shall carry on with the struggle more rapidly.

Question: Who does your organisation mostly consist of?

Our members are anyone who regards himself as a Muslim. We will accept him no matter what nation he is from. We even have a lot of women members. There is no difference. In our number we have Georgians, and we have Russians too, and Chechens. Anyone who regards himself as a Muslim, we accept him.

Question: Are there many members in your organisation?

That I cannot tell you. We do not believe in nations, we do not believe in men, we believe in God. That is why we have taken a stand. God helps us. It is not important how many people there are. If I am left alone, I shall fight to the end of my life. How many members there will be, many or few – that does not interest us.

Question: Who finances you?

We take from our own pocket. And also for the poor we have the zakaat. If a man has forty sheep, then he must give one. It is the same with money. With us the rich help the poor. And for this we spend money from our own pocket.

Hamid Ismailov continues:

That was the first international interview with Tahir Yuldashev. Now, when we review these images, we can see how awkward he is in front of the camera, how tightly his hands clench, and even later in the mosque, when he was reading his sermon, or *va'z*, it is still noticeable how young and inexperienced he is, how susceptible to influence. But even so, that was the very occasion when Belgi exclaimed in delight: "If only poets could read their poems like that, they could fill the Marakana stadium in Brazil, not just the Luzhniki stadium!"

Afterwards in the common room in the hotel in Ferghana Belgi and I discussed our impressions, and I remember him saying: "It's the first time I've seen what an inflexible man is like". At the time I didn't actually understand the sense in which these words were spoken, since in the Uzbek language inflexibility is not as unequivocally positive as in Russian, as can be seen from the plasticine-soft posture of almost every Uzbek.

Hamid Ismailov

Chapter Seven

Mir Kaligulaev recounts:

"In 1997, I think the year was – I definitely remember that it was quite a spell after Bamberg – Belgi came to Tashkent from Osh and phoned me at home to suggest that we should meet and have a chat. I was happy to agree, after all Tashkent may be a big city, but there isn't really anyone to talk to: 'the others are not here, and they are far away' – as the great Sufi poet Saadi said. I was renting a room on my Kara-Kamish Street and I invited him to come over, but he said that he was invited to visit two Uzbek writers whose names I didn't know, and so he suggested meeting at their place. To be quite honest, I didn't really want to visit people I didn't know, and I suggested a compromise: Why didn't he bring them to my modest hovel, and I could promise traditional pilaf and wine? And that was what we agreed.

"The next day I really did make pilaf, and after a delay that was only natural – you just try getting to Kara-Kamish on a Sunday evening! – Belgi entered my room in the company of two slightly tipsy Uzbek writers whose faces I didn't recognise. They had brought two string bags of Kibrai beer with them, and they immediately started opening it and handed a bottle to everyone.

"I don't remember their names, they didn't bother to introduce themselves, although Belgi introduced me as his friend, whom he had met in Germany the year before. Then he immediately listed off from memory everything that I had written, and since there was not much on the list that had been published, the others simply shrugged. I was astonished at the retentiveness of his memory, he didn't even miss a story from twenty years earlier that I had sent, in vain, to "Yunost", a Soviet literary magazine for young people published at that time.

"While we ate our pilaf, with breaks for swigging beer, there wasn't any conversation as such. Belgi spoke by turns in Uzbek and in Russian (for me) about his latest translations of Mandelstam and how in Uzbek it was like Chulpon, and how he had almost finished translating *Stone* – I had once given him a first edition of it.

"By this time the pilaf had already been eaten and half of the stack of beer had been drunk and so, to be quite honest, even I had reached the stage where I no longer felt embarrassed that I didn't understand Uzbek perfectly, although I had always got excellent marks for the subject in school. But my guests were not standing on ceremony with me either, and one of them said that *Stone* must be a Masonic work and Belgi should be wary of translating it into Uzbek, which just made Belgi laugh.

"But the belligerent writer wouldn't let it go. As far as I can recall, he was talking about a conspiracy of the Jews and the Armenians against the Uzbeks, scattering names and facts at random. First he mentioned the Turkestan Autonomous Region, which he said had been crushed by the Dashnaktsutyun, the Armenian Nationalist Party. Then he moved on to the Stalinist repressions and said that to judge from the KGB archives, the flower of the Uzbek nation had been arrested by various Vyshinskys and Apresyans, and the latest so-called "Uzbek case" had been led by Gdlyans, Melkunovs and Kalustyans.

"I was astounded by the reply given by Belgi, on whom our belligerent colleague had dumped this rhetorical avalanche. He said: 'On the other hand, in our literature, starting with Navoi, there is a cult, let's say, of the Armenian woman. Shirin is Armenian. Usman Nasyr wrote his poem *Nakshon* about a beautiful Armenian woman whose eyelashes cast a shadow on her breasts. Erkin Vohidov wrote his famous *Azganush*. And while you were speaking, I remembered that even I, sinner that I am, have a poem about an Armenian girl'. And without the slightest preparation he began reciting this poem:

> I know, I know that between us nothing
> Can happen, but every day, as evening approaches,
> Locking myself in my room I pine
> In torment, wracked by one thought,
>
> The single thought that I indulge each evening -
> I know, I know that between us there is
> No space for anything, that space is emptiness.
> If so, how can this thought, this verse, be any defence?

"But even so, after that evening I was left with a bitter feeling in my heart. And not really because of that interminable discussion: I had heard worse things in other countries, in other company. No, that wasn't the reason. It was simply that by that time the conversation had finally shifted into Uzbek, and there I was sitting in my own room, alone with my illusion of understanding and forgiveness, not needed by anyone, and the friend who had come to visit me had been completely absorbed by other arguments and subjects, and even his final words in the doorway: 'I'm sorry, we didn't manage to talk...' had the ring of politeness, rather than regret.

"As it turned out, that was the last time that we met."

Hamid Ismailov

Chapter Eight

One of Belgi's uncles told me how, in the mid-1930's, when their grandfather was arrested, his brothers and their father decided to make their escape through the Alai Passes to Kashgar, and the Kyrgyz people of Alai, who knew all the paths that bypassed the border guards and the frontier posts, helped them make the journey, how they walked through gorges with deadly rivers roaring down below, along ledges only four times the width of a man's foot, where the horses, freed of their bales and even their saddles, chafed their sides until they bled. Belgi could never have imagined that someday he would also have to make treks like that.

In the late summer of 1997 a terrible event occurred that changed Belgi's life irrevocably. At that time he was friendly with two young men, Alisher and Bakhtiyar – Alish and Bakh – with whom he used to visit the Andijan mosque two years earlier in order to listen to the sermons of the independent Imam Abduvali, who later disappeared without trace. Alisher worked as a translator in some foreign organisation, either the Soros Foundation or somewhere else, while Bakhtiyar practiced Sufism and even got Belgi's younger brother, Sher, involved in it. I was told all this by the journalist Caroline Rowley, with whom Belgi had a special relationship. When I asked Caroline what "special" meant, she answered simply: "He was my boyfriend".

Well then, about the terrible thing that happened. On one of the evenings when Belgi was sitting at home with his typewriter, Bakh came bursting in, as pale as a sheet, and said that Sher had been arrested immediately after a *halka* or Sufi ritual session at the home of one of his friends. Belgi and his friends went rushing to the militia station and spent the whole night searching for his brother and it was only with Caroline's help that they discovered, two days later, that Sher had been arrested by the NSS – the National Security Service. A week later the body of Belgi's brother was delivered to him: he had supposedly hanged himself in prison.

I don't know whether one of Belgi's friends was a special services agent or it was someone else, but one of my colleagues came back from a trip with a heap of documents belonging to the Islamic Movement of Uzbekistan and among them there were several disks and cassettes marked "Yosir". I printed them out or transcribed them. This is the first of the transcripts, which shows what happened.

Bakh: Take courage, brother! We are all in the hand of death....

Alish: Be strong! May God, by which I mean Allah, grant you patience and self-control in this hour...

Bakh: Do you remember what the great sheikh Ahmad Yassavi said: Die before your death! In this too there is God's providence and God's mystery... For life is given in order to free us of attachments and the true man is a true Sufi, who has detached his heart from all that is worldly and been left face to face with God....

(a pause)

Alish: We ought to say a prayer.... Go on, Bakh!

Bakh: (reads a prayer in Arabic)

Alish: How did this happen? Everything was all right.... That is, I mean....

Bakh: You mean you think that sitting behind bars in the security service's dungeons is "all right"?

Alish: No, no, what I meant was that Sher was alive and well up until our last meeting....

Belgi: Alive – but was he well? Take a look at the body while the women are washing it. It's covered all over in bruises and burns.... The brutes! They mocked and abused him every way they could! My poor brother! (He sobs)

Bakh: All right, the judgement of Allah will be visited upon them too!

Belgi: When will it? After the end of the world? On Doomsday? They're doing all this today! Here, read this! (a rustle of paper)

Alish: Let me read it, my sight's keener. Notification. Issued to citizen Belgi in confirmation of the fact that his younger brother Sher, eighteen years of age, having been arrested on suspicion of religious extremism and anti-constitutional activity, while detained in a holding cell did, for reasons unknown, end his own life, committing suicide by means of hanging himself. Investigator for especially important cases such-and-such.... Seal!

Bakh: Is this true?

Belgi: (sobbing) But he couldn't have hanged himself, he couldn't have.... Not because Islam forbids suicide... no, I raised him right from the cradle, after our parents were killed and I was left with him, a six-months-old child... I knew him better than I know myself, because I was always more concerned for him than for myself, worried he might have a pain somewhere, or a slight temperature, whether he was hiding a bruise when he came back from school, whether he'd been punched and beaten because of his girl....

Bakh: And he was devoted to you, like a young nestling... he adored you.

Alish: The images you use....

Belgi: Several days after Sher was arrested following the Sufi meeting, they let me see him. And that was only last week. He was sure that it was all just a misunderstanding, he hadn't broken any laws, he hadn't done anything forbidden, all he'd done was go to those meetings and rituals.... So is that religious extremism? Or anti-constitutional activity?

Bakh: But did you notice any marks then, from beatings or...?

Belgi: No, he simply seemed exhausted from lack of sleep, although he was putting on a brave face.... I honestly thought it was natural, no one in his place, who had got into such a bind, would be able to sleep at night.... But now I realise they had been interrogating him all night long....

Alish: All night long? But I expect investigators like to sleep at night too, don't they?

Bakh: Ours follow the Stalinist routine: all the dirty work starts at midnight....

Belgi: He kept using his hand to shield his face from a spot of sunlight in the room and then once, out of the blue, he said: "It's like a kilowatt lamp in my eyes..." I didn't realise then what that might mean.

Bakh: They often do that. Shine a searchlight in your face and interrogate you all night until morning....

Alish: And how do you know? Have you been in prison, then?

Bakh: Thank God, I haven't been in prison yet. But it's the same here as in Russia: you never know when your turn's coming.... People who have been inside told me.... Caroline's written about it....

Alish: Yes, by the way, does Caroline know about this?

Belgi: I don't know...

Bakh: Yes, I called her. She should be on her way.... (a pause) To be quite honest, I blame myself for what's happened.... After all I was the one Sher persuaded to take him to a Sufi *zikr*. I asked him: "What does a medical student like you want with Sufism?" And he answered; "A doctor learns to cure illnesses of the body, but all illnesses start with the soul, don't they? And doesn't Sufism teach the means to heal the soul?" When our Pir saw his zeal for improvement, he walked up to him after the meeting and kissed him on the forehead without saying a word.... (a pause) perhaps I should never have introduced him to our circle in the first place....

Alish: That's nonsense. It reminds me of a joke about a man who was being treated because he thought he was a grain of wheat and he was afraid of cockerels, and he seemed to have been cured. Well now, they asked him, now do you see that you're not a grain of wheat, but a man? I do, he said. He was discharged from hospital, but five minutes later

he came running back in, terrified. There's a cockerel outside, he said…. They repeated the same thing: But you know that you're not a grain of wheat! Yes, I know that I'm not a grain of wheat, but the cockerel doesn't know that…. If they want to arrest someone, they can arrest and… any one of us…. To them we're just little grains to be pecked…. If you ask me, it's time we became cockerels ourselves….

Belgi: They killed him, they killed him, those monsters! When it happened to other people, I couldn't really believe it completely, I thought the state couldn't be lying to us…. Even if some investigator put everything down to suicide, after all there's the forensic autopsy, there's the public prosecutor's office that's supposed to make sure everything's legal, after all there's…. But now that it's happened to Sher, my little boy, the child I nursed since he wore nappies, who can I trust? Where can I go to find the truth?

Bakh: Surely you remember the words of the great Hafiz: My heart was a treasure hoard of mysteries, but the hand of providence locked me shut and handed the key to the tormentress of my heart…. The mystery of death is concealed from us, so take courage, brother.

(the sound of a woman wailing)

Alish: I thought you were going to say that the key was handed to the jailor…. I'll be back in a moment…. I'm just going to check…

Bakh: Is it Caroline? (a vague noise)

Belgi: (in a trembling voice) They've killed our little boy, Caroline…. An innocent boy…. before his life had even begun….

Caroline: Yes, I know everything…. My ambassador told me all about it…. I'm going to write about this appalling case….

Alish: (horrified) But he's scorched all over…. It looks as if he was dipped in acid while he was alive…. There's bloody pulp where his nails should be, the hairs on his body are singed, his face is a mass of cuts and bruises….

Belgi: I couldn't even look at *that*….

Bakh: And the investigator issued an official notification that Sher committed suicide, supposedly he hanged himself in unexplained circumstances….

Caroline: I remember him when he was still a schoolboy, when you brought him to America…. You and I had only just met then…. See how many years have flown by already…. He was such a sweet boy…. The first day, when I started talking to him in English, he tried to answer, but he'd forgotten what to say…. So he blushed and burst into tears…. But a day later he was taking us to Central Park and downtown, and translating everything himself. He knew all your poems off by heart.

Hamid Ismailov

When you went away to Philadelphia to read lectures, we went to where I worked in one of the Twin Towers and in the cafe up on the top he recited this:

> *And this time what*
> *I say makes no sense...*
>
> *the same place again,*
> *the same rain, the same quagmire of mud,*
> *the same roofs, the same landscape,*
>
> *the same sad standing,*
> *the trousers hung on the wire and not drying,*
> *the same choice,*
> *feeling, as though attached to this space,*
>
> *or rather the same thought,*
> *and not the thought – a bitter and sharp*
> *doubt, attached to this space:*
>
> *if space returns, but time does not,*
> *yet what does sadness that has named the draught*
> *still search for in the interval?*

(a pause)

Alish: Caroline, don't forget that's my translation into English.... (more wailing from the house)

Caroline: If you'll allow it, Belgi, I think we ought to photograph... the body... the whole thing.... I can send it for expert examination....

Bakh: Do you think that will help? In general we Muslims aren't allowed to do that.... We're supposed just to suffer in silence....

Alish: All right, drop that. Let the Americans shaft our side up the ass....

Belgi: You think that will help? But how? Nothing will bring back my brother, my little boy, now.... How can I live now without him? What good is some kind of reconstructed truth or triumphant justice to me without him? All I've ever done is put words together to make poems. But I see now that this world is not for words.... Maybe it would be better if I put my own head in a noose, so that these scumbags can balance their books?

Bakh: Do not tempt Allah, brother! What are you saying? We are all in the hand of death....

Caroline and Alish: What about the other people?

50

Alish: And vengeance?

Belgi: Other people.... Vengeance.... Truth.... Justice.... these are all hollow words.... And beyond all that there is nothing but real death... death...death... Everything's jumbled up inside my head. I don't know how to go on living in this cursed world.... What am I to do, maintain total, absolute silence, shout out loud to the whole world, destroy everything I come across? I don't know which of you is right.... My boy, my little boy, won't you at least tell me.... (he sobs).

Chapter Nine

I know from Caroline that Belgi went to the investigator who wrote that letter, but he didn't get the truth out of him; instead the investigator threatened to arrest Belgi himself "for failing to raise his underage brother properly" and also for the poem that was found on his brother, in which Belgi had written:

> Out of the old chaotic disorder
> to create a new disorder –
> this, perhaps, is to live...

claiming that Belgi was inciting public disorder.... The investigator was also going to arrest Bakh and Alish, who had been brought to him to check their stories against Belgi's, and it was only thanks to the intervention of Caroline and the US embassy that Belgi was let out of the investigator's room at all. And then Caroline persuaded Belgi to go away to Tajikistan for a while, since a famous sheikh from the still-functioning Sufi religious order, or *tarikat*, of Nakshbandi had arrived there from India.

Belgi agreed only grudgingly, when Bakh and Alish decided to join him. Although in fact the trip really did mean a great deal to him, for his interest went back to his grandfather who, according to stories his grandmother used to tell, had belonged to this Sufi order, and from whom Belgi had inherited two books, which were buried in the yard – an immense commentary on the Koran and a volume of the epistles of Imam Rabbani – one of the most important books for the *tarikat* of Nakshbandi.

And then, the very fact that it was the school of Nakshbandi, whose motto "the heart for God, the hands for work" had been adopted by Jami and Navoi and Babur, was enough in itself. Everyone who knew Belgi called him a modern-day Sufi for his poems and his way of life, but Belgi did not want this vulgar definition, that was not what he used to argue about for hours on end with all those modern writers and poets

who wanted Sufism without Islam. After all, that was just the same as building a house consisting of nothing but roofs.... And suddenly, here was a real live sheik from out of this uninterrupted past – the latest in the chain of Poles of Faith, as they were known in more noble times.

The next morning they hitched a ride in a huge KAMAZ truck going their way, to Horog, and rode out on to the main highway. It was an Indian summer, and the first half of the day was almost gone, but as the highway ran on along the Kyrgyz Valley, gradually rising higher up the mountain, about half an hour after the strip of rutted, loose stone had divided into two, one road going in the direction of Jirgatala and the other to Pamir, fog suddenly descended on the mountain, or perhaps it was clouds. Higher up, at first a damp, cold rain started falling out of these clouds, and then, after a few more steep bends and spirals, thick snow began pouring down. The road was invisible now, especially from the height of the truck's cabin. The only reference point that the driver – a morose mountain Tajik – had to guide him was the wall of the mountain just an arm's length away and in this total darkness that not even the huge headlights could pierce, it seemed to Belgi that the driver was literally groping his way along, holding one arm out of the window in order not to lose contact with the rock face and go plunging into the formless, impenetrable abyss.

It was only Belgi's acute sense of balance that told him the truck was still climbing higher and higher, even though it seemed as if there was nowhere higher they could go except up above the snow, into the clear sky, where there are never any clouds, but the imminent menace of this thought frightened him, rather than promising any relief. To the eye, the truck was simply droning on the spot, and the three of them were suspended there in the cabin between the earth and the sky, and this went on for hour after hour.

Through the insistent, aching pain for his dead brother, he was occasionally visited by the memory of why they were there, but now even the thought of the sheikh, which had set his heart racing for the last few days, seemed as dull and dreary as the cramped, uncomfortable space around him that had no intelligible form.

Both Alisher and Bakh knew what it was to seek for a Teacher for, strangely enough, in almost every Uzbek family the children of their generation had mostly been raised by women – the men were no longer men, but mere tea-drinkers. According to the sharp-tongued grandmothers, the last generation of men had been shot in the late thirties, and any of them who were left alive had been killed in the war. And that was why, from their very youngest days they had been drawn towards old men, in the hope of somehow managing to touch that which had been denied to their fathers. This wise old man came unbroken from

out of the dark obscurity of history, but were not these five metres of foggy obscurity illuminated by their truck's headlights equally dark?

In any case, they eventually emerged into a night free of mist, with the solitary lights of dwellings that must have been far away peeping through it, and never in their lives had they felt safer than they did then, at a height of four and a half thousand metres. But this false sense of security was the start of an unpredictable series of misadventures. They were stopped at checkpoint after checkpoint, security post after security post, and sometimes simply by armed individuals, and they all took money from them for granting passage along the road. The most frightening occasion of all was late at night in a pass, when they were hauled out, half-asleep, into the icy-cold air, and because they didn't have any cash the men started undressing them and stood them up against the stony cliff face, which apparently had not really disappeared in all the time they had been travelling, and said they were going to shoot them. "And we'll throw the bodies down there..." said one who spoke Russian, pointing back behind himself. And then the driver, who had already paid for himself, shouted something hoarse and guttural from his cabin and paid their ransom, although by now they were already semi-naked. Their windbreakers were left behind, or rather, acquired by the members of this final checkpoint before the next pre-dawn pass, through which the driver refused to take them, for the sake of their own safety. He left them close to some old trailer home that still displayed the features of a former roadside café.

They didn't know whether to thank their driver with the thick moustache, who tossed them two old sheepskin *chapans* from out of the jumble behind his back, or to shout curses after him as they stood there in the middle of the empty road that had long ago ceased to be a road, but now they had to survive somehow at a distance of about a day's journey from the well-fed, peaceful life that they could already no longer remember. They walked towards the little light in that isolated trailer that looked so absurd in those wild surroundings and knocked at the door of this old, Soviet-looking former dwelling of some mountain patrolman, or perhaps former headquarters of some mobile armoured column. When they were already trembling violently from the cold, or perhaps from their mute anticipation, the dirty material of a curtain was cautiously drawn aside from a small top window to reveal a quarter of the fox-like face of a Kyrgyz with a sparse beard. Eventually, when he had made certain that they weren't holding anything in their hands, he opened the door, although he didn't invite them into his home straight away. But they must have looked really destitute, and he finally gestured for them to come in, and the stale air of that unventilated dwelling scalded them with its fetid heat. And so they stayed there, in the prefabricated trailer of that Kyrgyz, who himself

was only living there because the trailer still happened to be standing. As far as I can tell, one of the cassettes that have come into my hands was recorded in that trailer.

Transcript:

Alish: Salaam aleikum, our host, we, er... have lost our way.... We came across your trailer....

Host: Where have you come from?

Alish: Tashkent....

Host: That's a long way....

Alish: Yes it is...

Host: Why? (the sound of him getting up and clanking something, obviously a weapon, then ordering them abruptly) Sit down! (the sound of bodies dropping into seats)

Host: (Speaking in a thunderous voice and laughing for a long time). Sit over here! We're going to drink tea and have a talk.... (chairs are moved; the sound of tea being poured)

Alish: Thank you, our host, if not for you, we would be lying as frozen corpses on the mountain road...

Host: There's still time for that. But maybe there's some reason for you to stay alive.... (he chuckles at his joke)

Alish: You know, the men who took us out of our truck in the pass and stood us against the rock face to take everything that we were wearing and everything we had with us, they said the same thing...

Host: Here in the mountains everyone speaks the naked truth! The law of the mountains is the survival of the strongest!

(a pause)

Alish: You don't even ask how we found your trailer....

Host: Who needs to ask? Everyone who gets lost wanders in here, if they don't die. For a hundred kilometres on every side there's nothing but mountains, mountains, mountains. And there's only one road....

Alish: Pardon me for asking, but how did you yourself come to be here? How, so to speak, did the hand of providence cast you up here?

Host: Well, aren't you the polite and clever one... pardon me for asking... the hand of providence... the hand of providence had nothing to do with it, it was just the Soviet army that sent me to monitor the snowdrifts on this mountain road....

Belgi: And now?

Host: What now? Now I monitor the snowdrifts for good men (a pause) and bad men....

Alish: And have you had the Kalashnikov since Soviet times?

Host: Great knowledge brings great sorrow. The more you know, the sooner you'll be dead, get it?

(everybody falls silent)

Host: Where was it you were headed for? That hand you mentioned, providence, wasn't it, why did it cast you up into our mountain country? Right up into the Pamiro-Alai mountain crest? I don't suppose you're mountaineers, are you?

Alish: (pointing at Bakh) There's our mountaineer, although it's the peaks of the soul that he conquers. This Sufi led us here....

Bakh: Do you know if the leader of the Sufis, the famous Sheikh Gilani, has arrived in Horog from Afghanistan? Have you heard anything? To be honest, we were on our way to see him....

Host: A sheikh, you say? There are plenty of all kinds of sheikhs here.... You could say I'm a sheikh myself....

Belgi: So you were meditating before we came in?

Host: Exactly! That's the very word.... What was it you said?

Belgi: Meditating... transcending... undergoing catharsis... orgasm....

Host: (delighted) Bai-bai-bai! Such fine words! Exactly, exactly.... That's it....

Alish: And do you inhale it or mainline it?

Host: Both ways! And now the hand of – who was it you said? – has sent you to me for company, and now you'll get warm and do a bit of that – what was that you said? Anyway, we'll keep each other company for a while – how was it you put it? – inhaling and mainlining....

Bakh: You know, our host, our friend is still in mourning... As they say in our parts...

Host: (interrupting before Bakh can finish) And in our parts they say that all life is mourning! If those fine fellows hadn't let you go in the pass, I'd be sitting here in mourning now. It's never too late to mourn (a pause)... or too soon!

Alish: Why, our host, you are a true philosopher....

Host: (clattering his automatic rifle) I won't stand for any insults around here!

All: (in fright) Oh no, he didn't mean to insult you... On the contrary, he was praising you....

Host: Right then! I haven't got any vodka, but there's a hookah under the table! Everyone takes three draws, and then I lay the table. If there's a single peep out of you, I'll be mourning for all three of you on my own.

Alish: Ah, here we go then. (he takes one draw) Not bad! Our host, you said only three times, right?

Host: I fancy the look of you, lad!

Alish: No, I was only asking… to make sure….

Bakh: Forgive us all, Allah.

All-merciful and all-forgiving is He,
Wherefore your sinful, rebellious groan?
Today you are dead drunk in the tavern
Die and your skeleton, not you, will be absolved!

(he takes draw after draw)

Alish: (speaking unclearly) Total Apollinairo-Omar-Hayamian psychodelia… (a pause, then suddenly they all start laughing and chuckling cacophonously)

Host: Right, now I'll go and bring some food, and you have a merry time here, but don't break anything!

(the sound of him going outside)

Belgi: Looks like we're in a real mess here, lads! Out of the frying pan into the fire. We thought we'd escaped from the men who stripped us naked in the pass, but we've ended up here with this Cyclops with a Kalashnikov. What are we going to do?

Alish: (still laughing) Have fun, brother, have fun…. He'll get stoned now too

Bakh: Come what may, we have to get to Badakhshan, to Horog. His Holiness Sheikh Gilani is there now. There is no one in the world more holy than him now…. And then, Caroline said she would meet us there….

Alish: Caroline – that's good… But then look where you've landed us now…. We've almost been killed twice. Once by those bandits in the pass, and the second time by this… (he glances warily at the door and lowers his voice)… monster. I hope at least he's not a cannibal, or he'll start boiling us one by one and salting the meat for winter….

Bakh: That's exactly why we have to go to Horog. For us Sheikh Ginali is like Simurgh….

Alish: Like who?

Bakh: Simurgh, the mythical celestial bird. Surely you know the great Attar's parable of how a great flock of birds gathered for a journey to reach this celestial bird, in whose presence they would all achieve perfection....

Alish: And then what happened?

Bakh: They flew through the valleys of Penitence, the fields of Renunciation and the gardens of Love, past the mountain peaks of Pride and the ravines of Fear, just like us, overcoming tremendous difficulties and suffering, losing their comrades along the way, and only thirty birds reached the promised land of Simurgh. And they told the celestial bird's doorkeeper that they had come from far-away lands in search of perfection in the presence of Simurgh, but Simurgh did not appear before them. And then Attar said that these thirty birds were themselves Simurgh, for Simurgh translates from the Persian as "thirty birds" and their journey, full of suffering and losses, was itself the journey to perfection....

(everyone falls silent)

Alish: In our department of scientific communism we used to have a poster on the wall with Marx's words: "In science there is no broad highway, and only he who scrambles up its rocky paths, fearing no weariness, will attain its radiant summits..." exactly like what you said. I hope this Attar of yours wasn't a Marxist?

Belgi: It's probably the other way round, Marx was a secret Sufi....

Bakh: Well, he certainly had the beard for it! (they all laugh uncontrollably again)

Belgi: But we're getting distracted. What are we going to do next?

Bakh: We can't go back to Tashkent. Caroline said they would stick us behind bars straight away. And you first of all, Belgi. If it wasn't for her, you'd already be inside....

Alish: And we'd be right there in the two cells beside you.... A holy trinity....

Bakh: So there's only one place we can go – to Horog, to see His Holiness Sheikh Gilani. We'll serve him for forty days, receive initiation, and Allah will reveal to us our onward paths.... And Caroline promised to come too....

Alish: Caroline – that's good... so it's "over hill and over dale, the division moved on" again, is it?

Belgi: If we get out of here alive.... Our host seems to have got lost.... I just hope everything's all right....

Alish: You leave him to me. I'll find a way of talking to him. I'm a professional interpreter. I'm good at straight talking.

Bakh: I hope you won't straight-talk us into smoking dope with him the whole night long! (suddenly the door swings open and their host comes into the room with a deep, rumbling laugh)

Host: You haven't run off then, my little sheep? I'm going to feed you now, and then put you down to sleep... (he pours soup into bowls) This soup's better than any – what was that you said? – meditism? Say that beautiful word again....

Belgi: Idiotism? Moronity? Schizophrenia? Paranoia?

Host: (quite obviously delighted).... That's good, that's good! They're not much like the first words, but they're still beautiful anyway.... Let's drink to those words (the sound of him draining his bowl of soup)

Alish: Ai-ai-ai! That tastes good! What sort of soup is this?

Host: A soup that brings the dead to life... but doesn't kill the living... (he laughs at his own joke) And now let's have some fun. I'll sing to you first, and you accompany me on the kettle, a bowl and a spoon.... one of you hits the kettle, one hits the bowl, and the other hits the hookah with a spoon....

Alish: How can there be Sufism without dervish dances? Come on Bakh, let us recall the spirit of the Mevlevi....

Bakh: (mumbling something incomprehensible) Mmmmmm....

Alish: Our host, I am afraid of offending you again, but you are a genuine *manaschi*, a folk bard....

Host: That was well said, I think I'll have a dance with you, if someone will strike up a song....

Bakh: Belgi, give us your "Bakhshiyona"....

Belgi:

> *Maskovdami, Toshkanda*
> *yuzma-yuz o'tirganda*
> *kirlangan yuragimni*
> *ishqab-ishqab tozalay.*
> *Ozoda ko'ngil bormi,*
> *oqqan qon yoqqan qormi,*
> *bu dunyo menga tormi, -*
> *qay biridan saralay?*

Host: Ai, kara kush. Ah, dark force, what power! Sing, my fine fellow, sing!

Belgi: (singing)

Otangni siyla desam
 odim otar uchqur ot,
onangni o'yla desam
qush qoqadi qo'sh qanot,
elingni so'yla desam o'z-
o'ziga elim yot,
o'zing ham bo'yla desam
mendan badtar bu hayot,
bu hayotni o'lim ham
eplay olmas harqalay.

Alish: (shouting) Go on, Bakh!

Bakh: Up against the wall! I told you, up against the wall!

Host: What are you doing, lads! This isn't the M-Muslim way!

Bakh: And forcing your guests to smoke themselves into a trance on pain of death, is that the Muslim way?

Host: I only wanted us to have some fun....

Bakh: We've had enough fun already! Get up against the wall, legs together. Alish, you tie his feet, don't worry, I'll be aiming at his head and his body.... And now get down on your stomach, hands behind your back. Belgi, tie his hands!

Belgi: Maybe we shouldn't do this, lads? After all, the man sang with us....

Bakh: Alish, you do it, Belgi's having another poetic fit....

Alish: And he also said: I like the look of you, lad.... How would you like me to grab you know what and say I like the look of you?

Host: Lads, this isn't the man's way, three against one...

Bakh: Don't you worry, we won't touch you. We'll just wait until the morning and go. We'll even leave you your gun. Just as long as you don't bother us again until morning ...

Belgi: This isn't right somehow.... He welcomed us, and we....

Alish: The law here in the mountains is the survival of the strongest!

Belgi: Well, we should at least put him on the bed, or he'll peg out on the floor....

Alish: I've had just about enough of your humanism....

Host: Please don't swear....

Belgi: But how will we give him his rifle?

Bakh: We'll take the bullets and leave him the gun.

Belgi: Do you think he hasn't got any more bullets?

Alish: (yawning) Come on, guys, let's get some sleep! As the French sleepyhead said: "Tomorrow is a new day". We'll work it out then....

The tape breaks off at this point. But I know, from the interrogations of this "Host", that during the night someone knocked on the door of the trailer, and although the knock was cautious and stealthy, it woke up all of them except their drugged and bound Kyrgyz host, who was snoring away. Two men in sheepskin coats and tall fox-fur caps came in, with rifles at the ready. Realising something was wrong, they quickly disarmed Bakh and then stood the travellers against the wall and untied the Kyrgyz.

The host started explaining, and now the fine thread of their lives lay in his hands – these two men with guns could simply snap it with a single shot or a burst of fire. When they heard about the sheikh, one of the dark-faced men said in perfect Uzbek: "The sheikh flew to Dushanbe a long time ago already". Alisher began explaining that he had been told to go to Horog, and he didn't know anything about the sheikh flying from Horog to Dushanbe, otherwise he would have flown there directly himself. "I was wondering what you were doing here," the Uzbek said, but then he added: "We'll have time to get to the bottom of things" and asked their host to feed the horses, which he said were in the usual place. "Take your package out of the back saddle-bag," he shouted after the Kyrgyz, but then asked his partner to go and check on him, while he aimed his automatic rifle at the three of them and sat down to start asking questions.

It's possible to master your initial fear, but it's harder to overcome the constant sense of humiliation when even an amicable response to a curious question from someone who, apart from having a gun, seems like a casual conversation partner ("When did you set out? Do you have many things with you? Where are you going to go now?") becomes part of the script of an interrogation. Among Uzbeks the question "What passport do you have?" is nothing unusual, because an Uzbek could turn out to be from Tajikistan or from Kazakhstan, his citizenship could be Turkmenistani, or Kyrgyz, or Afghani or Chinese or God knows what else. But this very question from his armed compatriot greatly agitated Alish, who suddenly jumped up from under his sheepskin coat and reached into the back pocket of his jeans for his travel document from work. The armed man also jumped to his feet, but just at that moment the door swung open and the host and the other man came in from the frost, and that defused the situation a bit. By this time Belgi had also got up and was rather overeagerly holding out his writer's union membership card to the man asking the questions.

He cautiously tugged on Alisher's sleeve, and Alisher shuddered furiously, but in the darkness the two men didn't notice this moment, and they started whispering to each other, while keeping an eye on the three of them standing against the end wall of the trailer. Several long moments passed like that, but then, in the strange way that things happen in a dream, the tension was suddenly relieved when the leader of the two Uzbeks asked: "Do you pray?" and when Belgi, Alisher and Bakh nodded he said: "It's time for the *bamdad* already."

The *bamdad* is the predawn ritual prayer that the Prophet says should be recited during that period of the fading night when it is impossible to tell a white thread from a black one, and in the dim light before that dawn, this celebrated expression seemed designed to test the very threads of their fate. They couldn't tell whether the armed man really meant: "Pray now for the last time in your life and then get up against the wall!" or he simply wanted to check if they really were God- fearing, but he handed them the jug of water that the other Uzbek had brought in from outside and the three of them went outside to perform their ablutions under the surveillance of the armed man.

No, he hadn't taken them outside to shoot them, in fact they all prayed together in the trailer, although the newcomers didn't take the guns off their shoulders, and every time Belgi genuflected, his head touched the gun butt on the imam's back.

After the prayer they ate the dried meat that the horsemen offered them for breakfast, and over tea the leader asked them if they still wanted to see the sheikh. This question caught Belgi and Alisher and Bakh unawares: this was what they had come here for, but now, after all their misadventures on this treacherous journey, did they really still want to see the sheikh? It was probably their doubts that made them answer with a question: "Where and how?" But could these men possibly be angels that God had sent to meet them, for the same Uzbek said noncommittally: "We're going in that direction anyway".

Belgi looked at Alish and Bakh, they looked at Belgi, and he nodded without speaking. "Then we have to set out before the sun has risen," said the Uzbek, and brusquely grabbing the sheepskin coats that they had used to cover themselves at night, he said: "Put them on!" They put on the sheepskins, went out of the trailer and walked to two horses laden with saddlebags who were hidden close by. There they said goodbye to their disappointed host, the Kyrgyz, and set out into a cold morning of sheer-walled ravines with rivers running on their bottom and rocky paths only four times the width of a man's foot where the horses, freed of their loads, and even their saddles, chafed their sides until they bled.

Chapter Ten

Those two still-hot horses
without saddles, without reins,
without any horsemen,
foaming, insisting, crazy,
thrust, and heaved like death.

Hamid Ismailov

My four eyes became four men on four sides
and rushed and ran. The crowd dispersed and screamed,
anyone left was trampled pitilessly on the road,
the rest flew, like gushing blood. (a fragment)

-Belgi

After a series of convulsions in late 1991 and 1992 the former boxer Islam Karimov, now slightly battered and groggy, managed nonetheless to stay on his feet and, even more than that, he began gradually scoring points or, to use the language of politics, consolidating his power. The first to feel this were those immediately around him – the members of his team and the deputies of the Supreme Soviet but also, ludicrously enough, the criminal world. One of the criminal bosses, or "authorities", who lived in Kara-Kamish and went to the same school as me, told me later that a minister came in person to his house seven times and asked him to go away somewhere, if only temporarily, saying that all the others had already bolted to various places. But this one wouldn't do as he was told, and so, as he put it, they "banged him up". And it was only when, in his words, he "put the entire zone (i.e the prison camps and jails) on hunger strike", and a certain Armenian came from Russia to ransom him with a bag full of money from the thieves' mutual assistance fund, that he was released – on condition that he wouldn't show his face in Uzbekistan.

When Islam Karimov asked for six to eight months while he was addressing the crowd of students, his audience took him to mean that people's general welfare would improve or at least be held at its former level, which was now rapidly being devastated, but it is doubtful if that was really what the president himself meant, since what happened during those six to eight months radically changed the political map of Uzbekistan and the balance of power in the country, bringing about an entirely different outcome. In a certain sense Karimov carried out his promise to change everything, but he did it in a way that no one had anticipated or expected.

In May, out of sheer inertia, Birlik held its congress and the chairman of the Peasants' Party of Uzbekistan distributed a list of members of the "shadow cabinet" to the delegates; the dissident Babur Sharipov, newly returned from America and still unknown to anyone, made the rounds of the reception rooms of the opposition parties, collecting signatures for the establishment of a National Assembly; and a parliamentary group went to the airport to meet the "Uzbek Solzhenitsyn", Dr. Baimirza Hayit. But only a week or two afterwards, everything had already begun sliding down a slippery slope.

A Poet and Bin-Laden

The journalist Hamid Ismailov recalls:

At that time I was working as the Uzbekistan correspondent for *The Literary Gazette*, and the old Soviet times were still in evidence in the 31-model Volga with a state licence-plate that I had for my use and a "hot-line" phone in my office, and I also was registered at the "government polyclinic". But the first call on that phone came when I was suddenly summoned to the Ministry of Justice, to the office of the minister himself, who at that time was Babur-Malik Malikov – later a political émigré. He laid in front of me an article published in the *Gazette*, one that I had absolutely nothing to do with, and told me that the time of Moscow's rule was over, that now the laws were written in Tashkent.

And that, indeed, was the very time when the Ministry of Justice demanded that the opposition parties Birlik and Erk must submit documents for registration, but did not register either of them, although we should not forget that just then there were intensive negotiations taking place in order to bring the whole of the opposition together under the aegis of a unitary Forum, which the disgraced ex-vice president, Shukurulla Mirsaidov, was going to lead, in hopes of following "the Yeltsin model". And after Muhammad Solih demonstratively discarded his Supreme Soviet credentials and walked out in protest against the incipient dictatorship, Erk and Birlik planned a joint mass demonstration.

During those days, Belgi came to my office with a stack of poems, and since he had always been wary of politics and avoided politicians because they disgusted him, when I suggested that he might accompany me round all the various headquarters where they were planning the mass demonstration, he preferred to stay in my office and simply answer all the phone calls, since at that time there weren't any answering machines. In the evenings I used to give him a lift home and, sitting in the Volga, he always identified the car that was following us with the keen eye of someone from out of town – most often it was a dirty-yellow Moskvich with four criminal-type heavies in it – and then the driver assigned to me, Gennady Alexandrovich Rabinovich, would just shrug and say: "They've been following us for a month already..."

But on one of those evenings when we were sitting over the foreword to his first book of poems, there was a ring at the door. I went to open it and there were two militiamen standing in the doorway, with a man in civilian clothes. Without bothering to introduce themselves, they addressed me by name and suggested rather coolly that I should accompany them. I must say, in all honesty, that I had only recently moved to Tashkent from Moscow, and I was still carrying more than my fair share of 'All-Union conceit', so I tried to steamroller them: Why should I have to go, didn't they understand that it could cause an inter-state scandal, and so on and so forth.

One of them, the one in civilian clothes, said that he had known about me for a long time, because he had enjoyed reading my articles and he had even attended my lecture at the Central House of Writers on the occasion of Erkin Vahidov's fiftieth birthday, and his boss was simply asking me to call in to see him because he wanted to ask my advice about something or other....

Then I said that I would call my car and come in an hour, but the man in civilian clothes said in a gentle voice: "Our car's waiting downstairs. Why should you bother your driver? And afterwards, inshallah, we'll bring you home.

Naturally, I couldn't take Belgi with me, so I asked the militiamen to wait for me downstairs and quickly explained the situation to him, although I only succeeding in confusing him totally. But there was one thing I did tell him for certain: not to tell my wife anything if she arrived before I got back and, secondly, if I wasn't back before nine in the evening, to phone certain numbers in Moscow immediately and raise the alarm....

I must admit that although I tried to put a brave face on things, it was terrifying to leave my own home and set out into the unknown future that these "admirers of my talent" had in store for me, and it was only at the very last moment that I had the idea of taking along my broken Sony dictaphone –strictly for swank, as we used to say back in my childhood days.

I rode in the police van, sandwiched between the two men in uniform, and the connoisseur of literature in the front tootled his siren at the crossroads. They brought me to the municipal militia office on Shevchenko Street, and led me down long corridors to the office of the deputy chief, who was sitting there with the deputy municipal public prosecutor. That was how they introduced themselves to me. I pretended that I was going to record everything that happened to me, but the deputy chief said: "Don't make me laugh, do you know where you are? Why don't you tell me what you know about the forthcoming demonstration that Birlik and Erk are organising?' I shrugged and asked: "Why are you asking me? I'm not a member of Birlik or Erk."– "Then why do you attend all of their meetings?" – "Who told you that?" – "We know!" – "I'm a journalist, I'm the correspondent for *The Literary Gazette*!" – "Then stick to your literature!"

That was how the conversation went, wave after wave: they try to swamp me, and I tried to feel out their weak points, declaring that the next day I would report the incident to the Office of the President's Administration, at which they chortled, but their faces turned more serious.

They let me go the same day, without ever explaining what they had wanted to accuse me of, or perhaps I myself was too preoccupied with them to grasp the essential meaning of this summons fully, but the deputy head of militia and the deputy municipal public prosecutor drove away together in the same van that had brought me to the municipal office: they were on their way, as I subsequently discovered, to interrogate Abdurahim Pulatov, the leader of Birlik, in the Chilanzar district station. But that interrogation ended less peacefully than in my case – after the interrogation Pulatov was attacked by unidentified criminal thugs with concrete rods who beat him half to death, and that evening he was taken to the Casualty Centre at the Alai Market.

That was how the violent reprisals against dissent began. The millstones of repression creaked into motion. The next day Dr. Baimirza Hayit was due to return to his homeland from Germany, but instead of driving out to the meeting at the airport, I took Belgi and went straight from home to visit Pulatov at the Casualty Centre. And, as I was told later, Baimirza Hayit

got himself into trouble immediately: as soon as he had kissed the ground, he enquired after Pulatov's health, and that question sealed his fate. The president himself had been planning to receive "our Solzhenitsyn", but after those words specially mobilised "grass roots activists" in the Namangan province wrote a collective letter to the government, saying that there was no place in free Uzbekistan for Nazi underlings, and some time later the national hero was dispatched abroad forever.

Belgi stayed with me for a whole week that time, not for the sake of his poems, but simply to be there beside me: he watched out for the unshaven thugs driving after us, or answered the knock at the door when the next messenger brought the next summons to visit the Public Prosecutor's Office or the militia, or walked my daughter to school and took her by various roundabout routes to make sure that nothing happened along the way....

He advised me to leave when my complaints to the Office of the President were met by friends of mine who had been given posts there with the philosophical comment that "you can't make an omelette without breaking eggs" and a categorical refusal to interfere. This all happened after the latest demonstration had failed to take place when the full might of the militia, backed up by the Interior Ministry's forces, was thrown into the streets of Tashkent and arrests began being made right and left. In fact, Belgi suggested we should go to his place in Osh, but we decided to take refuge as a family in the back of beyond at Maleevka, outside Moscow....

It should be said that the close-grinding millstones of this repression were set in motion against anyone who had "offended" the president in recent times: against the machinery of state and parliament, when one of Karimov's inner circle, his "personnel officer" Mavlan Umurzakov, was removed from his post and then arrested; against the secular opposition, when Pulatov senior was beaten up and Pulatov junior was arrested on the territory of Kyrgyzstan, while Muhammad Solih was forced to emigrate under threat of imprisonment: against the student population, when a metal fence was erected at the Student Campus and the journalism faculty, which had organised the February demonstration, was disbanded; against the Islamists, when the mufti Muhammad Sadyk Muhammad Yusuf was removed from his position and emigrated, the Leader of the Islamic Party of the Rebirth of Uzbekistan was arrested, and Tahir Yuldash and his group fled to Tajikistan.

But the strange thing was that at this time the criminal community, who had been the first to flee, started coming back to Uzbekistan and, what's more, their foothold in the country grew stronger and stronger. All the other "injured parties" repeatedly accused Islam Karimov of fostering this binding together of the machinery of state and the machinery of the mafia, but it is more likely that the key role in encouraging this union was played by the forces of the army, police, state security, etc. on whom the president relied, using them indiscriminately to settle grudges against all his opponents. These "executors of policy" were the only appointees that the President did not change for an entire decade.

Chapter Eleven

In the mountains you lose the sense of time. There is something greater than time that takes its place. It is not that time is reduced to something petty and inessential in the face of this colossal majesty, although there is a suggestion of something of the kind, especially in the violet skies of the dawn and in the early evening, which seem to alternate more frequently than in the ordinary life down on the plains. That was not it, during this period of transition, whether it was a week, or ten days, or perhaps only two, they simply had to survive. There was no fear left, for fear was everything – all they had left were their naked instincts: to grab hold, scramble, to lick their wounds, to prevail.

When they emerged into a valley, as suddenly as if someone had pronounced the magical word "simsim", it was as painful for their snow-blinded eyes as it was for their empty lungs, inflating with the excruciating space, but here time began again. A couple of hours later they were already in a foothills village on the bank of a river, being greeted by armed sentries who embraced the two men in fox fur caps and examined Belgi, Alish and Bakh, who were plodding along behind the heavy-laden horses, with suspicion. "Put them in the infirmary," the two men said, and for some reason this strange phrase immediately allayed the excessive suspicion of the menacing sentries.

They were accommodated in a room in a small clay house that did indeed resemble an infirmary: three bunk beds and a small iron stove with a chimney that ran into the wall. The bearded young man set to look after them made them get undressed, and that was a painful business. Their frozen and swollen fingers would not obey them, and they could not untie the solid-frozen laces on their boots, but even after the boots had been set close to the stove and unfrozen, they seemed to have fused with their socks, which in turn had fused with the skin of their feet, and all their efforts to overcome the boots' absolute refusal to come off inflicted terrible stabs of a pain, a sensation that had been forgotten but was now returning.

The first night they didn't sleep, but howled in a hoarse trio at the unbearable agony in their legs, which were returning to life under a thick layer of mutton fat – that afternoon the bearded man had smeared their aching, exhausted, sleepless bodies with grease and fed them greasy *shurpa*, or spiced lamb soup. He nursed them back to health, and when they finally emerged, pale after a week spent in bed, into the thin blue air, he led them through the communicating yard into the next house and left them in the *dakhliz*, or hallway, in the care of an armed sentry, before going back to his infirmary. After a while a young man with a sparse beard and a face like a Kipchak came out of a room and invited all three of them inside.

In the *tor*, or far corner of the room, which is considered the place of honour, a man in patchy-coloured combat fatigues was sitting at a *khontakhta*, or low and very wide table, looking through some papers. There was a lighted lamp beside him, and when he raised his head, the flame in the lamp fluttered, casting a flickering shadow on his face, and this seemed to distort his features for a moment. He said: "Welcome!" and the three of them greeted him in reply. The soldier invited them to sit down and the young man who looked like a Kipchak sat down first, beside the door. When they tried to sit down, their bones ached painfully with every movement and the soldier laughed at them and said: "City men, no doubt, not used to squatting on your haunches.... I'm sorry, don't take it amiss, but we don't have any chairs here..."

The man had a strange voice: his chanting intonation reminded them of the voice of a mullah, but this soft voice was entirely out of keeping with the military uniform, the two strange shoulder-belts that crossed on his chest, and especially his sharp face with the sparse beard and lank hair, in particular those keen eyes, as sharp as two knives that could slice straight through you and carve you up....

Now they could see that the papers lying in front of him were their identity documents and a couple of rough drafts that Belgi had written in the Kyrgyz's trailer up on the Pamiro-Alai. The commander must have studied the papers very closely, because now, without looking at them or consulting them, he started asking questions, citing numbers, dates and lines from memory. This interrogation lasted until evening. The commander suspected that they were agents of the National Security Service or NSS – the former KGB – sent to spy on them and subvert their cause. They tried to appeal to logic – after all they had not been on their way here, and they hadn't even wanted to come here, but the soldier only asked curtly: "Then why did you tag on to our men?" And then they would launch yet again into the story about the sheikh and their journey to the Pamir, and time and again the keen-eyed commander compared the details of their stories, every time trying to catch them out in something that didn't fit.

Eventually even he seemed to grow tired of these repetitions and simply concluded: "If we find out that you are agents, you'll be strung up in the village instead of streetlamps". And he handed them back to the young man who looked like a Kipchak, and he led them back to the infirmary and the bearded young man. But their documents and papers stayed with the commander who had the voice of a mullah. And that was all they learned during their first days there, since no one introduced themselves or tried to get to know them, and everything was top secret and anonymous.

It took them a few days after their recovery to fit into the local order of things, learning in the process that they were living in the village of

Hoit. They got up early, before dawn, for the morning prayer, after the prayer they drank their morning tea, and then they went up into the mountains to gather firewood, accompanied by the bearded young man, who turned out to be known by the Arab name of Anas, although he was actually an Uzbek from Khiva and must have had a different name – Atageldy or Matyakub. At first they were not even trusted with an axe for cutting *archovnik*, or mountain pine, so that they wouldn't kill their overseer and make their escape. At about midday they returned with a huge bundle of dry branches and stacked everything under an awning in the yard for winter. At this time other men were returning from their military instruction or field training exercises. Then they all went to the midday prayer, after which they had lunch and were allowed to doze for a while, or at least they were allowed to go home and no one followed them, since almost everyone apart from the sentries was asleep. Then came the time for the afternoon prayer, after which everyone went outside, simply to chat, while the three of them were interrogated again until sunset by the same man, until the muezzin called them to the after-sunset prayer. After that, just like during the cotton harvest when they were young, they took their bowls and went to the communal kitchen again for supper, which was also exactly the same as at the cotton harvest – either macaroni or potatoes or occasionally rice, and even more occasionally meat with the macaroni, potatoes or occasional rice. And finally, after the evening prayer, they tumbled into their beds to sleep, only occasionally managing to take a look at the Koran or popular books on the beginnings of Islam, in which the faces of the faithful had been neatly blanked out with black ink.

Strangely enough, they didn't have enough time to discuss the situation during those days, since they were never left alone for a moment and even up in the mountains the young man Anas with his partner, who changed all the time, separated the three of them off to the sides, while they worked away with their axes in the middle.

About two weeks went by in this way until one day, after the midday prayer, they sensed a certain stirring in the camp and the courier who looked like a Kipchak suddenly came for them again and demanded that they follow him immediately to the HQ. They were led through the yard, past the house where the commander had initially interrogated them, and on into another yard, where there was another ordinary-looking little house that seemed to be half-buried in the ground, but when they went down the stone steps, the hallway turned out to be a lot more spacious even than the commander's room. And after the hallway they went through a row of rooms guarded by sentries, and at the end of the row the courier left them under the supervision of two armed men and one who looked like a secretary, sitting beside a huge apparatus that must have been a satellite phone, while he himself knocked timidly on a door and entered.

After a little while he reappeared in the doorway and nodded to the three of them, then let them through into a large room where Tahir Yuldash was sitting, surrounded by several men. Belgi recognised him immediately, and Yuldash also recognised Belgi. He asked in surprise, with a half-laugh: "Hey, poet, what are you doing here?" Of course, the question was phrased, as usual, in the third person plural: What are they doing here? And so yet again Belgi started telling the story of their journey to the Pamir on the way to see the sheikh. Tahir heard him out and then spoke again while everyone else remained silent: "So they are seeking a spiritual mentor, a *Pir*? Well then, it is the will of Allah himself for them to stay here for a while and then, inshallah, they will have a chance to meet our Pir, who is the Pir of all Pirs..." He did not detain them in the room, but merely looked hard at Belgi and asked: "And are these brothers of ours well known to them?" – "Yes, we used to go to hear the sermons of Imam Abduvali together in Andijan." – "Do they not know where they are now?" Tahir asked, this time addressing Alisher, who merely shrugged in reply. And then Tahir gave Belgi a look that he would remember for a long time.

They were released, and after that their lives changed abruptly. Instead of gathering firewood, they were put through the compulsory three-month general military training course, and a very well-mannered man by the name of Yunus was attached to them for the period after lunch, when he gave them intensive classes in Arabic and the Koran.

Later something happened that separated Belgi and Alish, who were now known as Yosir and Umar, from Bakh, who was now known as Haroun, probably forever.... But for a long time Belgi-Yosir still felt that memorable look on him: passionate and suspicious, loving and wary, cruel and repentant, but never betraying itself in a single false word, let alone deed.

Chapter Twelve

The sheep I let roam on the mountainsides have dispersed.
The sea chases its flocks one after another.

I remembered last year in Koktebel,
but my mind could not gather in a single poem.

-Belgi

The journalist Hamid Ismailov recalls:

In 1994 I started working for the BBC in the newly established Uzbek Service. We first heard about Uzbek Islamist fighters in 1995, when our Moscow correspondent, Timur Klychev, came back from a trip to Tajikistan and told us about the "Uzbek" or, more accurately, "Namangan" battalion under the command of a certain field commander by the name of Juma. According to Timur this battalion, which had so far fought in Tavildara, was regarded as one of the bravest and most highly skilled in the ranks of the Tajik Islamic opposition, and it consisted, as its name indicated, of several hundred men from Namangan, who had gone to Tajikistan after the start of the repression started.

The first thing we did after hearing this news, which was also confirmed from Tajikistan, was to contact the Hokim, or Governor, of the Namangan region at the time, Burgutali Rapigaliev. I can still hear his voice saying: "Come now, why would men from Namangan be there? It's just a load of silly stories! Don't go spreading all sorts of rumours!"

In 1996 I went to North Afghanistan and General Dostum himself told me how Tahir Yuldash, who he said was now the deputy leader of the Tajik Islamic Opposition, had once come to him and suggested that they should collaborate, but the general had declined. At that time the Taliban were just beginning their conquests, and almost half of Afghanistan was under the control of forces loyal to General Dostum.

On that same trip, after visiting Dostum's citadel of Kal'ai Jangi, we were given a chance to go to the Tajik refugees' camp at Sahi, not far from Mazar Sharif – the same camp that would be used by the Islamic Movement of Uzbekistan in the late nineties.

Although this camp was on territory that belonged to General Dostum and was under the aegis of the UN, it was quite clear that it was controlled by Said Abdullo Nuri, since his portrait hung everywhere on the clay daub huts, and the room where we decided to interview a few people contained a pile of magazines and brochures published by the Tajik Islamic Opposition. In the same room I also interviewed several Uzbeks, who had initially fled from the Ferghana Valley to Tajikistan and then found themselves here, in the Tajik refugee camp. They were drivers, mechanics and labourers who had fled, as they explained it, from religious persecution, but to be quite honest, at that time this still sounded rather strange to a journalist's ear.

The main item on the agenda back then was repression of the secular opposition. The mosques that had suddenly appeared everywhere during the years immediately after independence, when the criminal bosses and the communists both regarded it as their duty to contribute their mite to the construction of a district or municipal house of God, had only just become places where you could express an opinion opposed to everything that was being preached all around you – on the radio and television and in the press. The mosques had only just become a bastion of anti-government dissidence, the famous Imam Obid-kori Nazarov was still thundering his wrathful denunciations against the powers-that-be from his old town mosque in Tashkent, drawing crowds of thousands to his Friday sermons, most of them young people, for whom the mosque had become the only channel for the expression of social protest after the secular opposition was crushed.

And so, the young Uzbeks we saw who had ended up in the camp of the Tajik Islamic Opposition in Afghanistan were a symptomatic phenomenon, a testimony to obscure, deep-rooted, latent processes taking place in Uzbek society.

In 1996 we made a series of radio programmes devoted to questions of Islam in Uzbekistan. One of these programmes began with these words by President Karimov: "I wish to say concerning the creation of an Islamic state in which, so to speak, the state is ruled by the Koran and not the Constitution, that we are opposed to this model. We support the secular form of state governance. Under our Constitution, religion is separated from the state. It is very dangerous when the religion of Islam is spoken of as an extremist religion, this is absolutely wrong. In my understanding the Islamic religion is the most democratic religion. It is the religion of our fathers, and we respect it. And today in Uzbekistan we are doing everything possible to allow this religion to be practiced freely. Under the Soviet system in Uzbekistan almost all the mosques were closed. Today in Uzbekistan there are fifteen thousand working mosques. But under no circumstances will we allow certain forces to exploit Islam for political ends. We are categorically opposed to the concept of an Islamic state. Within a state people must be allowed to practice the religions that they wish to practice. As well as Islam, people here profess the Christian religion and we even have many synagogues in which the Jews take every opportunity to worship their God. And they are quite contented; in this regard, to use your foreign way of speaking, the situation here is 'no problem'."

But there were problems, although not yet with armed fighters, and not with Hizb ut-Tahrir, whose goal is to combine all Muslim countries into a unitary Islamic state ruled by Islamic law and headed by an elected head of state or caliph.

Chapter Thirteen

Going towards the thirty-three bones
buried in the earth
the thirty-three bones on the earth
are uniting
having rented an alien house
living
drops, leaking from the ceiling,
grasses, pushing out of the earth...

-Belgi

71

In order to give a sense of the problems associated with Islam at that time in Uzbekistan, I have decided to transcribe one of those broadcasts by the BBC Uzbek Service. The broadcast began with those words that were spoken by President Karimov in Paris in May 1996, and then the presenter continued as follows:

These words from the President of Uzbekistan, Islam Karimov, certainly define the policy of the leadership of Uzbekistan towards Islam, but the fact that the President says 'no problem', also certainly does not mean that there are no problems and does not guarantee the absence of these problems. On the one hand, of course, according to the imam of the Andijan mosque, Gishtli Saifiddin Hoji Nasriddin-ogli, the government and Islam simply adore one another:

"Praise be to God, thanks to this independence our government has opened the road to Islam, it has opened a wide road. Thanks to this the call to Islam has appeared among Muslims, and with this the love that has formed between the government and Islam has grown even stronger. Their love for each other now fills them to overflowing..."

However, let us take a look at a case from that self-same Andijan concerning the imam of the collegiate mosque of Avduvali Kori or another scandal, concerning the former imam of the Tokhtabai mosque in Tashkent, Obid-kori Sobithan-ogli. It is February 24, a Saturday. The Tokhtabai Mosque is crowded with people. The deputy chairman of the Office of Religion, Yusufhan Shakirov, walks in, accompanied by members of the militia, for a meeting with the faithful. He addresses the congregation:

"This mosque was opened at the command of God and by decree of the government. And so it should be used for its proper purpose. A mosque should not be used for any other objectives..."

A voice from the crowd: "What other objectives are those?" There is hubbub. Yusufkhan Shakirov continues:

"The fact is that the imam of a mosque is appointed by the Spiritual Administration. The imam is removed from his position, from his job, by the Spiritual Administration..." The crowd becomes noisy: "By what right is that? Show us the reason for it!" Yusufhan tries to keep control of the meeting: "Muslims, please, I beg you, in the name of the Spiritual Administration of Mawarannahr (Transoxiana), in the name of the Hokimiat (local government) of the city of Tashkent, please, we have brought you a new imam..."

Shouts: "We don't want your imam! Give us back our own!"

The gathering of five thousand is opposed to the removal of their imam by the Office of Religion, but His Holiness Yusufhan Shakirov announces that a new imam has been brought. What happened in the days before this? During that period we discussed this question with the mufti and chairman of the Office of Religion, Muhtarhon Abdullaev:

"In the mosques some imams have a strong grounding, and some have a weak one, some of them are on the borderline between recognition and non-recognition by the Spritual Administration. The Office of Religion

of Muslims of the Mawarannahr decided to verify the qualifications of imams, and some of the imams refused to come to the test, including Obid-kori. But it is not only Obid-kori, there is also Shamsiddin from the Shakh Aziz mosque, whom we have summoned four times. He also has not shown up. And so we removed him from his job for disobeying the Spiritual Adminstration."

The suggestion that Obidhon-kori's qualifications had not been verified was confirmed by Yusufhan Shakirov:

"In our Constitution, that is, in our fundamental law, it says that every mosque must obey the Spiritual Administration. If a mosque does not obey, if its imam does not follow our instructions, then the activity of that mosque is halted. That is what it says. We wrote letters to the mosque, saying that because he had not obeyed us and had not followed our instructions, he was relieved of his position."

But in actual fact the reasons lay deeper than this. After he had been removed from his post, Obidhon-kori Sobithon-ogli spoke to us and explained the cause of what had happened:

"The words claiming that the authorities were behind all this, that the state itself orders this, were spoken by representatives of the Spiritual Administration. Until recently I believed that this was not the case, since under the Constitution of Uzbekistan religion is separated from the state and, according to Article 61, the state does not interfere in the activities of religious organisations, but the respected Mufti Muhtaron and the venerable Yusufhan Shakirov apparently said that such things are done by the authorities, that the state interferes in our activity, since we are independent now.... I do not know under which law they made this bold declaration, but it is erroneous. Apart from ourselves, several other imams were removed from their positions on the pretext of verifying their qualifications. If you ask what we are guilty of, then in my opinion, our guilt lies in having been impartial, we have never said a word against the Constitution, against the state. I personally do not feel any enmity for anyone, neither for the state, nor for the Spiritual Administration. But at the same time, I am guilty of not loving blindly, not closing my eyes to everything and praising people. In Sharia law and under Islamic statutes, to grovel to anyone is a sin. It is said you may only flatter your parents, you may only flatter a Teacher when you acquire knowledge. But to flatter for the sake of a position, for greed, for money, for the good things of life, that is a sin. I have not flattered the government or the Spiritual Administration. I have not praised them, but neither have I disparaged anyone publicly, I have not conducted any activity against the government, but neither have I promoted the activities of the authorities through the microphones of the mosque, since it is my conviction that this contradicts the Constitution of Uzbekistan.

Eighty per cent of the community that attends our mosque are young people. This also seems to have irritated people in the administration: they say, he has gathered young people and women around him, he is leading them astray... But I say, why, do young people not need faith, do women not need faith? If young people and women are righteous, that is

to the benefit of this country, this state, this people. They will be pure. We appeal to young people to master not only religious knowledge, but also the secular sciences, to be good specialists. But apparently there are some who do not like this. They are not capable of leading anyone, they are not capable of enthralling anyone with their words, and so they are annoyed. But one more comment – if there are no impartial people, then there will be little advantage to this nation and this state..."

And so, on the one hand, a decree was issued stating that Obidhon-kori had failed to obey the Spiritual Administration but, on the other hand, he claimed that the state authorities had interfered in the matter. But what was the general attitude of the authorities to these problems? In an interview with the BBC, Evgenii Abdullaev, a member of the President of Uzbekistan's Centre for Strategic Research, declared:

"At that time the situation that had arisen posed a threat to the stability of the republic. In effect, a certain alliance, if you wish, had come into being between the opposition and radical religious factions. Their goal was to overthrow the government and, in a certain sense, to build an Islamic state. This situation, however, ran counter to the interests of the bulk of the republic's population. But the policy of the state must protect the interests of this bulk of the population."

The state's interference in this matter at that time was noted later by Obidhon-kori. In particular, he claimed that he had been summoned to the President's secretariat and been interviewed by them several times:

"Up at the top, in the President's secretariat, there is a man by the name of Royikov Bahadyr, he was the man who summoned us on September 25, 1995 and told us: 'You are interfering with state policy in your sermons!', but he was not able to prove this. I said to him then: 'On the contrary, all this is a consequence of the fact that I do not interfere in state policy...' and I said that I had never confused religion with any personality, or any ideology, or any self-interest, or any politics, that I was a supporter of pure and impartial religion. But he said: 'You don't seem to understand, other people will talk to you now, and in a different way...' So for a year now, just as he promised, the other people have been talking, and in a different way..."

What, then, was the basis for the authorities' fear of Obidhon-kori and other religious figures like him? Primarily, of course, it was the extent of the influence these imams had on the public, on the people. Thousands of people gathered for Imam Obidhon's Friday sermons at the Tokhtabai mosque in Tashkent. And these sermons were not only listened to in the mosque itself, but recorded on cassettes and distributed throughout Tashkent and the regions of the republic. The sermons were devoted not only to religious problems, but also to problems of daily life and sometimes to political problems. For instance, in one of his sermons, speaking with undisguised regret about the impossibility of introducing Sharia laws into daily life at the present time, Obidhon-kori remarked:

"Muslims have nothing in their hands. Do Muslims have prisons? Do Muslims have courts and public prosecutors? Muslims do not have

prisons. Muslims do not have a hell in this world, they have nothing. And so they are treated only according to their words. If they repent, then we accept them into the ranks of Muslims. But... but the most humiliating and terrible thing is what will happen tomorrow in the presence of Allah..."

And concerning moral problems, in particular the problem that has become so topical recently of Muslim women wearing or not wearing the veil, the former imam of the Tokhtabai mosque said the following in one of his sermons:

"Truly, the position of women is hard. If the parents have not understood this, then they are pitiless, stonehearted, cruel parents who trespass upon their daughter's holiest values. When the courage of these girls proves lofty in the face of the incapability of their mothers, if no one forces them and they themselves wish to cover themselves with the veil, what happiness this is. For after all, you cannot force anyone to wear the veil if they do not wish to, even by holding a pistol to their head, and you are not supposed to force them! If a girl has herself decided to put on the veil, then a believer should weep at this. How long will this shame of semi-naked maidens continue?"

Of course, it would certainly be hard to find people who could speak face to face with these people who have such passion and such faith in their own words, or who would be capable of battling on equal terms against the ideas that imams like Obidhon-kori have placed on the agenda. And the people, naturally, are quick to notice this. For after all, according to the proverb, it is not the water that makes dough into dough, or even the flour, but the yeast. This is the reason why, as the congregation at the Tokhtabai mosque grew, and the number of imams like Obidhon-kori increased, observers began speaking of the authorities' fear of this phenomenon. However, this is only one side of the scandal surrounding the Tashkent imams and Obidhon-kori Sobithon-ogli in particular. We shall cover the other side in our next broadcast.

At about the same time the following interview with Tahir Yuldash was broadcast. At the time he called himself the deputy leader of the Islamic Opposition of Tajikistan.

TY: First of all it should be said that today the enemies of Islam have found and are using the expression "Wahhabism" to denounce Muslims, especially those who are fighting for their freedom. But the use of this name for those who are fighting for freedom and truth is reminiscent of the way that seventy years ago our fathers and grandfathers who were fighting for freedom were called basmachi. For us this has no meaning. The events that have taken place in Khorezm show resistance to a dictatorial regime. And so, neither in Uzbekistan nor in Chechnya nor in other countries bordering on this region do I know of any movement that would call itself "Wahhabite" and I have not come across any.

Question: President Karimov said recently during a visit to Bulgaria that Wahhabism is spreading nowadays and the philosophy of this

movement is: "If you are not with us, you are against us". If we take your movement, is it committed to the same philosophy?

TY: First of all, what Karimov said is nothing new to us. But this philosophy is a false philosophy. Showing your enemy as more than what he is will encourage your political allies. It is not surprising that Karimov is asking for help from political allies. Karimov and Russia, Kazakhstan, Kyrgyzstan have started uniting against Muslims, against Allah. A Muslim can never act against another Muslim, and this is proved by history. Today in Uzbekistan, if anything happens with some Christian mission or Judaism, then… it shows the true nature of Karimov's government, and the Muslim people knows that very well. And as for our movement, the Islamic Movement of Uzbekistan has never called itself "Wahhabite" and it belongs to the hanafit mazkhab, or school. We are adherents of ahli sunnah wal jama'ah, the perfect balance. Therefore we do not accept this name.

Question: Do the Arab countries provide any help to your movement?

TY: To the present day no Arab countries have helped our movement, since the Arab states themselves are colonies. Some of them are under Israel, some in the hands of America. And so, since they cannot solve their own problems, they cannot provide help to others. We have not so far heard of any help from Arab countries and we do not acknowledge it.

Chapter Fourteen

In autumn of that year refugees from Uzbekistan flooded into Hoit. As a rule they arrived in families, although the families were not complete, since either a father or a brother or a husband had been arrested by the militia and the remaining family members had fled to Tajikistan in fear of further arrests. Many took the train to Dushanbe, where they got into a taxi, taking their scant belongings with them, and the taxi, hung all over with bundles of various kinds, usually arrived in Hoit in the evening. It was met by people who first of all put it through a kind of quarantine, spending a long time asking where the fugitives had come from, and why they had come here, and only when they were finally convinced for one reason or other that the newcomers were telling the truth did they find them places in the houses that were becoming increasingly overcrowded.

The men and youths immediately started gathering firewood or taking military training and the women looked after their little children at home, baked bread cakes foreveryone and dried dung with straw for the winter.

That was when Yosir (Belgi), Umar (Alish) and Haroun (Bakh) were instructed to collect all the terrifying stories that the refugees had to tell

and think about what could be done with them: make a film, record them and make multiple copies of the cassettes, or send them off to foreign radio stations. And that was also the time when Yosir, Umar and Haroun, while engaged in this work, had their first chance in all this time to discuss the situation and think hastily about what they ought to do next.

The largest group there were followers of two imams, Abduvali from Andijan and Obidhon from Tashkent, and Yosir found the story of one of the latter's assistants both strange and intriguing.

Obidhon-kori had a twenty-five-year old assistant by the name of Tahir Ibrahimov. This young man was from Dunshanbe, but after studying in Bukhara and then in Tashkent, he had stayed in the Uzbek capital, at the Tokhtabai mosque. After the persecution of his teacher began and the Office of Religion finally removed Obidhon-kori from his post as imam of the mosque, Tahir Ibrahimov temporarily took his place, and the congregation of several thousand people united round him in a spontaneous campaign to have their imam restored to his position. But the Spiritual Administration was not drowsing either: on the one hand, its agents went round the surrounding old city districts, or *mahallas*, collecting signatures for a letter accusing Obidhon of "Wahhabism" – by this time Wahhabism had become the official bogeyman – and on the other hand, the leaders of the Spiritual Administration, in particular the Mufti's deputy, Yusufhan Shakirov, arrived in the mosque on February 24, 1996 to propose a new imam for the insubordinate mosque.

And then the people, led by Tahir Ibrahimov, rebelled. People shouted: "We don't want your new imam!", "Bring back Obidhon-kori", "The people chooses it leaders, but only your KGB knows how you got on to the board of the Spiritual Administration!" In short, things started getting out of hand and went so far that Yusufhan Shakirov exclaimed furiously: "Do what you like with your mosque, you're not part of our Spiritual Administration any longer!" and left the mosque.

But the very evening after this happened, many activists from that meeting in the mosque were arrested, including Tahir Ibrahimov, and he happened to be arrested by another man who was also called Tahir Ibrahimov, a lieutenant-colonel in the National Security Service or NSS, the successor to the KGB. This Tahir Ibrahimov was infamous among the faithful as one of the most ruthless infidels, the dread of all the old city mosques, madrasahs and religious circles. His fervour in the struggle against Wahhabism was legendary among his colleagues and a source of terror to the pious.

He was the first to interrogate his own namesake, in whose pockets, naturally, two small packets of marijuana had been discovered. The first of these two men swore and cursed in a blue fury, saying that he would fuck the other up the ass there and then, while the second, undaunted,

appealed to God. The religious Tahir Ibrahimov was put in a cellar with criminals whose natural response was to taunt and jeer at a lover of God, he was tortured and interrogated for several days, then tied up and taken to Hojent, from where he was sent to his native town of Dushanbe, where they started interrogating him again, although this time there was no torture.

And the other Tahir Ibrahimov said they would let this little imam rot in prison, where he had been sent initially for eight years.

Yosir confided to Umar and Haroun that he sensed in this story a strange similarity that went beyond just the names: there was a certain common relentless fanaticism, although under different banners, but he immediately added in embarrassment that it might just be his own poetic side's eternal search for rhymes.

Chapter Fifteen

That year the holy month of Ramadan came when the war was at its height. In the mountain regions of Afghanistan darkness comes early, and so it was not really difficult to observe the external aspect of the fast and not eat during the hours of daylight. And even with the prayers, including the evening *tarawih* – when the thirty parts of the Divine Word of the Koran are read, evening after evening – all went well, he was always in a group where at least one man knew the Koran off by heart, whether they were in a village mosque, in a cave or in the roadside house of a good-hearted fellow believer.

But that year Yosir found it harder than at any time before in his life to part with Ramadan and this closeness to God. He had never felt such regret at this parting, such sorrow at this ending. Quite the opposite in fact – in his previous years in Afghanistan he had counted off the days of the fast one by one, nostalgically anticipating the return to normal life, when he could eat his fill of the pilaf in Kabul halfway through the market day, when he could glance surreptitiously at the jaunty step of some mysterious girl in a blue *chadrah*, clattering along the battered asphalt with her fashionable high, narrow heels, when in some car giving him a lift out of town to the first Taliban checkpoint he could hear Pakistani music that had been smuggled in, or maybe even the British band "Oasis".

But this time, this year, in the middle of the war, he didn't want any of these things, he wanted to remain with God, listening to His ponderous word, as if when Yosir stopped doing this, the link would be broken, as if when he returned to ordinary life, God would forget about him, in the

same way that Yosir forgot about Him. Yosir felt that He too probably had a need for human love and faithfulness, otherwise what was the point of this ordeal?

Apart from, that, his thoughts were occupied with petty matters: his memory would suddenly throw up "Purity" tooth powder, with that kid with the gleaming white teeth on the lid, and then his memory would slowly open that lid in order to see the layer of parchment paper that you had to slit open with the sharp end of your toothbrush, and the sudden impulse sent the powder scattering across the surface of the parchment paper, and then the moistened toothbrush was lowered into the soft powder and picked up a dry, fragrant crust. And the first thing your mouth felt was the dryness of the outer particles as they scattered across your teeth, diffusing the scent of mint, and something else sharp and bitter, and then the taste dispersed with every stroke of the brush, and it would never be the same again…. That powder didn't exist anymore, that life didn't exist anymore…. Nothing but that sharp taste in his mouth where half the teeth were missing, and the fresh pure sense of a beginning.

Or else he would see buses, one after another, at first little GAZ buses with those hinged windows, and then he recalled the stained-glass windows he had seen in the cathedrals in the West, and the same buses appeared in front of his eyes with hinged stained-glass windows at the back, and with doors that the driver opened with a long nickel-plated bar that ran from him to the door, and then they were followed by massive ZIS buses with steep, blunt foreheads and two doors that opened automatically, only the most memorable thing wasn't the doors, but the loophole-shaped recesses, those steep brow-bones with the brightly lit glass forms underneath them that were the just same as they were later in the first trolleybuses: it was only later that everything had become flat – flat windows, flat houses, flat people – but all of these things that came out of nowhere and went back to nowhere were still toy-like, handmade, the art of craftsmen.

Is there anything in which man cannot take solace? After all, the last books that Yosir had re- read in his former life were his children's books: *Tarantul*, with the pictures, in which the chapter "The Arrest of the Spy" was intimately associated with a one-armed man with round eyes in a peaked cap, shooting with his only hand, and although this disagreeable figure shooting straight at *you* made the word "spy" clear, for a long time he didn't understand the word "arrest", and he was afraid to ask the grown-ups, because the book was his mother's. So he either imagined this word was the crumpled little peaked cap – although in the word itself here was something forthright and harsh that refused to accept that battered condition – or he thought that the slope running down from under the

one-armed cripple's feet must be the "Arrest", especially since he and his mother had once ridden past a metro station that was called "Arys".

Every picture in this book spoke for itself, telling its own story that wasn't written in the book. How afraid he had been of the picture of the prickly burr in the book *Periwinkle*: and deep inside him there was still a fear of something that was shaggy rather than prickly, formless rather than bright-coloured. And then again, just as one bus had followed another, the books paraded by: *Battle En Route, Knockout, The Cutlass, The Pleiades, The Blue Parcel.*

There was a time when Yosir had wanted to write a book about these books, about how it was not great volumes, but these trashy publications that had shaped his imagination and framed his mind, and how the keys to his heart were hidden in them, but was it really only the books....

There were the records, and the "Komsomol Lake", with its painted, steep little bridges and heavenly islands, with the young-pioneer train that was like a toy but real, as if it had been invented for childhood and then deliberately destroyed afterwards, and the films: *Sky of the Baltic, The Secret of the Two Oceans, The Seventh Journey of Sinbad...* And the big square biscuits and the pastries, the New Year shows or the "Rot Front" chocolate that his mother used to buy on the way home from the kindergarten....

And....

The things out of which a man grows....

Chapter Sixteen

One can't lose what doesn't exist.

I hammered in the stake and tied up the cow.
Perhaps I equated the rope to life
with the written words.

There is a hole at the bottom of my heart.
However many words I compressed and hurled out
this mouth of the hole never closes.

One can't lose what doesn't exist.

Before my eyes are the clouds of grass.
This too will one day disperse.
That's all, enough now, I say.

A Poet and Bin-Laden

We sucked the unboiled milk of a pure dream.
Clamping the heart we smeared blood.
Flying up into the blue we fell to earth.

The tongue grinds and the ears don't hear.

One can't lose what doesn't exist.
One can't lose what doesn't exist.

-Belgi

It somehow happens that I skip all the important historical events: I find myself in completely the wrong place at completely the right time. For instance, until January 1966 and again from September of that year, I lived in Tashkent, but I missed the famous earthquake. At thetime, my mother took me to see my grandmother up in the mountains, to breathe the fresh air and build up my strength before I started school. I also missed the terrible avalanche of mud and stone that descended on Kizil-kiya in the late nineteen-seventies. I went away to take part in a handball competition, and when I got back to the little town where I was doing my summer practical work, the mud that covered the ruined walls right up to the roof was already drying out. Eyewitnesses of both events told me about the horrors of all the forces of nature uniting together to spark an intense fear in people who would later feel honoured to have been involved in something bigger than everyday life.

In the same way I missed the explosions in Tashkent on February 16, 1999. I was in a train on my way back from Orienburg after visiting a friend.

It's strange, but when I do happen to be present at something that is later called "historical", I honestly don't want to remember it, either because of the blatant discrepancy between what I saw and what has been inscribed in the annals, or because of the grotesque absurdity of what I actually did see.

On August 19, 1991 I took the morning flight from Tashkent to Moscow. When I was already on my way to the airport, I heard a voice on the radio that sounded like the Soviet war-time announcer Levitan, relating terrible events. On that day, when power shifted from Gorbachev to the State Emergency Committee, no more than 15 passengers out of 250 flew to Moscow, and I was one of them. The people sitting near me leafed intently through their telephone books, crossing out beforehand the numbers they didn't want any more, while I was wondering who it would be safe for me to go to, which of my outspoken friends would already have

been arrested, and who they might come for the next time around.

I was pondering these dark thoughts when we arrived in wretched Moscow and landed, not at Domodedovo, as we should have done, but at Sheremetievo, where the terminal building was half-empty, if you didn't count the soldiers and armed militiamen who made up a good half of the people there. And instead of pestering you in their usual manner, the taxi drivers waited politely for their hurrying customers in a long, orderly queue. I decided to go to Mir Kaligulaev in Bibirevo although, with his democratic fervour, he could easily have been picked up on the very first day. But on mature reflection I decided that it would be several days at least before the Uzbek authorities would inform the State Emergency Committee about him, and then I would be able to take a look around and move, say, to stay with the artist Shavkat Avdusalamov. Artists are a more easygoing bunch than writers and poets.

I got into a taxi, and from the very beginning of the journey I saw tanks on the shoulder of the road, in fact there were lines of tanks all the way, especially along the Leningrad Chaussée as far as Khimki and then along the ring road, and the bewildered young soldiers, who had never been called on to encircle Moscow before, were passing the time by clustering in a queue for the field kitchen, clutching bowls in their hands, or lining up with a jerry can to get diesel fuel for a tank smoking in a ditch. I had a strange feeling, as if it was all put on, a show, for after all, these young soldiers, whose presence ought to have been frightening, were more frightened themselves, and even the huge tanks had a decorative look about them, as compared to the junk-heap Zhigulis and Volgas that went flashing by.

Half an hour later I was on Leskov Street in Bibirevo. I rang the doorbell and no one answered. The door gave no signs of life at all. I stood in front of it, pondering my contingency plans, but then decided to knock at the neighbours' doors. Fortunately the neighbour opposite turned out to be an old Tatar woman, and when she learned that I had just arrived from Tashkent, she started pattering away in Tatar and dragging me over to her table for *belyashi*, which are like fried meat ravioli. I pulled one of our inevitable Uzbek melons out of my bag. She started keening even more loudly, saying that her neighbour was here, she had seen him that morning, when he was throwing out the rubbish.

I calmed down, and over tea I asked her what was going on in the city. She shook her head and said, with an ineradicable Tatar accent: "Eeee, it's bad, they'll arrest Gorbachev, Yanaev has come. The Emergency, putsch Emergency.... Just like Stalin it'll be now.... Son, have more tea, drink your tea..." she told me, and I suddenly realised that despite everything, life still goes on. In the evening my friend, the Uzbek writer Erkin Agzam, came to see me.

That night, after all the talking and watching the famous press conference on television with our hands shaking, we couldn't get to sleep, each of us tormented by our own thoughts. But in the morning for some reason I woke up in a quite excellent mood, feeling as if I had read through the entire script for some dark, heavy drama in advance, before watching it on the stage. And first thing that morning I suggested to Erkin that we should go into the city.

We went first to the Union of Writers, or rather, the Central House of the Writer (CHW), as it now was, where we had a coffee and a cheese sandwich before moving on in the direction of the White House. And then – I can see this as if it were happening now – some drunks who had not been allowed into the CHW, or perhaps the House of Cinema opposite, were shouting to each other: "Mityok, bring over a girder..." – and some scruffy, drunk Mityok strained and heaved against a pillar, tearing his shirt on it, but failed to push it down and walked on a bit further to a rubbish bin, which he tipped over and rolled towards the White House for the barricade.

I don't wish to say anything bad, but to my Tashkent outsider's eye, it looked if all the riff- raff of the old Russian capital had ganged up there to revel in doing what they would never be allowed to do again. You could batter and crush a telephone kiosk, then drag the wires out of it, piss on the steps of the parliament building, light a fire in the middle of the square and put the cover of a streetlamp on it instead of a kettle. Beat people, drink, make merry, guys! When will life give you another chance for a romp like this?

That is the unhistorical memory I have of the putsch by the State Emergency Committee and the people's unanimous rejection of it, but that is not what I was talking about. I was talking about how I missed the explosions in Tashkent on February 16, 1999.

Chapter Seventeen

Even if you know that a lie is a lie –
The lie doesn't cease to be a lie...

- Belgi

Here is the official announcement of those explosions by the Uzbek press:

On February 16 a series of explosions took place in Tashkent in the buildings of the Cabinet of Ministers and the National Bank of Uzbekistan, and also close to the airport and the embassies of Belorussia, Turkmenistan, Tajikistan and Georgia. Initial reports indicate that at least six cars filled with explosives were used. According to the Uzbek Ministry of the Interior, about 1,250 people were hurt and fifteen were killed. The municipal authorities have allocated forty million Sums for the medical treatment and rehabilitation of the victims. One of the explosions occurred on Pedagogicheskaya Street.

Although the Uzbek press, and also the Uzbek authorities, claimed quite definitely from the very beginning that Islamists were behind the explosions, the majority of observers who did not belong to either of these two circles were not so sure, even after the show trial of the individuals who were accused of organising and carrying out these bombings. This trial, of course, took place in the summer of 1999, and this time I was there, as an accredited representative of the Russian press. I will tell you about the trial a little bit later, especially since after all this time I have just started re-reading the two-volume text of the Official Charges, which came into my hands by a strange, roundabout route, and I must confess that now I see many things differently from the way I did during those hot summer days of the actual trial, when the whole of Tashkent was shrouded in smog and encircled by armed guards.

Let me turn first of all to the analysts, who discussed not just one, but a dozen different versions of events. Here are the versions proposed and analysed by one of the leading specialists on Central Asia, Dr. Rustem Zhangozha.

AN ANALYSIS OF THE POSSIBLE ORIGINS OF INCREASED POLITICAL TENSION IN UZBEKISTAN

1. The "official" version

On the basis of the evidence that we have as of today, it is possible to assert that the main goal of the terrorist attack was an attempt on the life of the President of Uzbekistan, Islam Karimov, who was due to speak in the building of the Cabinet of Ministers at the very moment when the explosions were set off. Immediately after the events in Tashkent, Islam Karimov announced that he would "cut off the hands of the Islamists" whom he believed to be the organisers of this act of terrorism. In his address to a session of the Cabinet of Ministers which, despite a terrorist attack on a scale that had shaken the entire world, took place on the same day and was later broadcast on local television, the president appeared dazed and bewildered, and the address itself was emotional and extremely confused, which, according to the experts, is quite untypical of him.

The declarations made at this same meeting by the heads of the police and security structures of Uzbekistan are highly revealing. For instance,

the Minister of Internal Affairs, Zakir Almatov, stated: "On behalf of the ministry I can say that if we are not able to solve this crime expeditiously, the authority of the militia will be damaged in the eyes of the people. We shall find them and set them face to face with the people, and they will be punished". The head of the National Security Service of Uzbekistan, Rustam Inoyatov, was even more specific in his declaration: "Today we already know who organised and who took part in these events. We have the necessary information about this… We give our word that we shall pull them up by the roots and report the results within a month".

Moscow's *Independent Newspaper* cites the substantial doubts about this version expressed by a western diplomat in an interview with the paper's correspondent: "For me personally, everything that is happening arouses associations with the attempt on the life of President Nasser in 1954. On that occasion Nasser, who for some reason had not put on his bullet-proof vest that day, was shot at seventeen times, but not hit. However, the attempted assassination gave the Egyptian president an opportunity to give short shrift to the fundamentalist opposition. Does it not seem strange to you that the head of the National Security Service promises to catch the criminals within a month – after all, bearing in mind the realities of the local situation, we can be certain that if he doesn't keep his word, he will lose his job. Perhaps, in reality, the minister already has his candidates for the crime 'lined up'? It is curious that immediately following the first explosions, militiamen told the crowd of curious people who gathered to take a look at what had happened that it was the work of 'Islamists'. We know that in Uzbekistan a militiaman would only dare to say something like that with the blessing of the authorities. In this connection it is interesting to note that on the day of the terrorist attacks there was no real security in place in the centre of the city and you could easily drive through the police cordons for a small bribe. Of course, this situation can be explained in part by the lack of discipline and corruption of the militia and security forces, but to a certain extent doubts still remain."

And so, as of today, this account of a failed assassination attempt proposed by the head of state, who also happened to be the intended target, together with the officially announced addresses of the immediate culprits, remain the main "guidelines" for the investigative agencies. However, until such time as the guilty parties are identified by judicial procedure, it will remain permissible to propound other explanations which view these ambiguous events in a wider political context. For after all, what happened in Tashkent can be unambiguously interpreted as a political act. Let us also put forward alternative scenarios for the events that have been enacted in Tashkent.

2. The "Burning of the Reichstag" version.

It is no secret to anyone that the "party of power" in Uzbekistan cherishes no illusions concerning its popularity with the broad strata of the population. In the absence of any economic levers of influence (even of a populist nature), it can only rely on repressive methods to intimidate the electorate. This means, primarily, the creation of powerful police and security structures which are willing to act repressively against a

discontented population. It means the political persecution of all dissenters. But it also means shaping a negative image of the ideological enemy in the eyes of the public – the image of an Islamist prepared to commit any atrocities. This last measure has been targeted at the international human rights organisations, who are frightened by the worldwide emergence in recent years of the stereotype Islamist, a terrorist who must be neutralised using any and all means available.

The above considerations offer cause for serious doubts concerning Islam Karimov's claim that members of the Islamic Movement of Uzbekistan were involved in the terrorist attack. In the first place, the Islamists lack the significant financial resources required to carry out an attack that is so well organised (from the technical point of view), and secondly, there are no really serious groupings among them capable of organising a terrorist attack.

It must be acknowledged that on the eve of the parliamentary elections, and with the presidential election to follow, it is simply very convenient for the president and his entourage to be able to accuse the opposition of committing criminal acts and to take this as grounds for strengthening the regime "in order to support a civilised society". In this context, Islam Karimov's claim concerning the organisers of the terrorist act seems to have been a genuinely "lucky find", providing him with a political trump card that he is quite certain to exploit in the run-up to the election campaign and to increase his influence over his potential electorate.

3. The "Older Brother" version.

Tashkent has recently effectively withdrawn from the "Tashkent Accord". Islam Karimov's political announcement that Uzbekistan does not intend to continue with its involvement in this agreement on the collective security of the countries of the Community of Independent States (CIS), since "the present accord does not correspond to the national interests of the country" provoked a disgruntled response from the Kremlin.

The final scene (or continuation?) of the drama that has unfolded in Tashkent can be written "with closed eyes": even if Islam Karimov does have in his possession irrefutable evidence that the attempt on his life was organised by the Russian "cloak and dagger" agencies, he will keep silent. The investigative agencies of Uzbekistan will dig up Islamist plotters and hold a show trial, at the same time declaring the entire internal opposition outside the law. The official mouthpiece of the president's regime, the newspaper *Truth of the East* has already placed Boris Yeltsin first in a list of leaders from around the world who have expressed their sympathy to the leader of Uzbekistan, and actually singled Yeltsin out by printing an entire paragraph about him. The national mouthpiece of Russia, *The Independent Newspaper*, has already noted this and stated that "Tashkent does not intend even to consider the 'Russian version' of events".

4. The "Step-Brother" version.

Two years ago the Russian sociologist, Andrei Zdravomyslov – a specialist in international conflicts – wrote that "since 1990 the situation in Tajikistan has been developing in the form of a conflict over the nationwide

dominance of one of the ethnic groups in the country... This conflict has a tendency to spill over into a general Central Asian conflict (involving Uzbekistan and other countries in the region)." It is well known that the President of Tajikistan, Rahmonov, who is a Kulyabi, actively opposes the influential pro-Uzbek clan in Leninabad, while Karimov would like to see a member of the clan in Rahmonov's place. The Leninabad region of Tajikistan is populated primarily by ethnic Uzbeks, and this is the region which Colonel Hudaiberdyev recently raided from the territory of Uzbekistan, provoking a strident response from President Rahmonov and accusations that Uzbekistan's President Karimov had aided and abetted the rebellious colonel. Could the terrorist attack in Tashkent perhaps be a response from one president to the other, this time no longer in word, but in deed?

The actions of the security forces of Uzbekistan suggest that the answer to this question could well be positive: as part of the efforts to arrest the criminals, members of the Uzbek militia have been provided with photographs of two citizens of Tajikistan, one of whom is a member of the country's special forces. The cooling of relations between the two central Asian countries is also indicated by the fact that Rahmonov's expression of sympathy, unlike Yeltsin's, was only printed in the Uzbek newspapers after two days had passed.

In this connection one can also consider the possibility of a combined version of the last two scenarios that we have adduced for the events in Tashkent. After all, the "step-brother" now also bears the same relationship to the "older brother", and in the process of verifying this new "brotherhood", could Russia and Tajikistan not perhaps have colluded to give their other "brother" a little fright? In this context special attention should be paid to a comparison of the political situation between Azerbaijan and Georgia, two of Ukraine's partners in GUAM (Georgia, Ukraine, Azerbaijan, Moldova). Like Uzbekistan, these two states have refrained from signing the protocol for the prolongation of the "Tashkent Accord", which expires this year. The comparison is particularly interesting, since as yet there is still no real clarity concerning the planners of last year's attempt on the life of Shevardnadze or, more importantly, who was actually behind it.

In a case where the authorities were all so unanimous, why were the analysts, who cannot possibly be accused of having any connection with militant Islam, by no means so categorical?

Chapter Eighteen

On February 16 Haroun went on duty in the evening, and his shift began with listening to and recording the foreign "voices" speaking in Uzbek. Following the evening reading of the Koran by the dim light of a lamp, Yosir and Umar had gone straight to bed. Yosir must have fallen asleep easily and slept soundly, for when Haroun shook him awake, he thought the night was already over and it was time for the pre-dawn

prayer. But usually everyone was woken for that, and this time for some reason Haroun put his hand over Yosir's mouth and gesticulated strangely. Yosir awoke as easily as he had fallen asleep, with a clear head. Haroun pointed outside and Yosir immediately realised that something had happened. He wrapped himself in his *chapan*, which he always spread on top of the standard-issue hospital blanket, slipped his feet into the rubber galoshes that served him for carpet slippers and crept furtively after Haroun – out under the crystal-clear winter sky.

He started trembling even before anything was said, as if the icy twinkling of those immense stars had been instantly transmitted to his body, and when Haroun started whispering to him about what had happened the day before in Tashkent, this trembling mingled with the trembling of his soul, and his heart was suddenly embraced by the same vague cloud that was scudding across the dumbfounded moon, which seemed ready to explode and scatter across the entire width of the black night sky.

"Who? Who?" he whispered, trying to hurry his friend, who in his agitated state was retelling the entire broadcast word for word, and Haroun became bewildered and jumped straight to a quotation from the Chairman of the National Security Service, Rustam Inogamov, who had apparently promised the President that he knew who had done it and in a month all the guilty parties would be brought to account....

"Was it our people?" Yosir asked in a trembling whisper, which made Haroun lose the thread again, and he shrugged in bewilderment and fell silent, like a radio that has been switched off.

In the morning the commander, Abdurahman, woke them all from their beds with an immediate alert and they skipped the morning prayer and went running up the mountain to the trenches that had been prepared in advance. Yosir, who was short of sleep, was running side by side with Umar and Haroun, who had not slept at all, and when he suddenly blurted out: "So it was our people, then..." Haroun simply nodded his soaking-wet head, as if he were shaking the sweat off his face on to the hard frozen ground. There, in the those foothill trenches overlooking the mouth of the valley, they were issued with guns, and the cold was so fierce that their hands stuck to the barrels, but then the morning suddenly turned overcast and gloomy, bringing first a sharp, fine snow, and then billows of white flakes that covered the rare thawed patches like a thick blanket, and this layer of white made even the trenches a little warmer.

They returned to the village in time for the midday prayer.

It was not the first alert they had had in recent months. Fear made the men in the camp cagey about talking, but they simply could not help talking about the "jihad" that was apparently expected in spring – a holy

war in which the entire Ferghana Valley was supposed to rise up in revolt. And the militants who were especially taciturn would sometimes go off into the mountains in the direction of Jirgatal and Batken and spend a long time there, returning black in the face from the cold and raw from the wind. But neither the invisible commander-in-chief, Jumaboi, nor the omnipresent imam, Abdulaziz (about whom the men said – some in fear and some with pride – that he had killed a dozen infidels by slitting their throats or shooting them, and that when a Namangan militiaman was decapitated, it was his men who did it), nor his follower, the commander Abdurahim, said anything about the jihad and it was only these alerts, coming one after another, that gave them the sense of something inevitable.

And suddenly there were these explosions.... A little before noon Haroun developed a fever. At first no one took it seriously, but when, during the midday prayer, he prostrated himself in a bow and did not rise back up out of it, the entire row of men began complaining, so that the prayer had to be concluded in haste, and then they grabbed the four sides of the brightly coloured *shalcha*, or rug, that served as a prayer carpet and carried Haroun to the "infirmary".

Their young "doctor", who had once worked as a vet, began taking Haroun's pulse, then said that he had to let his blood, but Yosir couldn't bear to see that: when Haroun started groaning dully, he turned away, his eyes suddenly filled with tears. But even so, when the doctor shouted for someone to bring him some burning cotton wool to cauterise the bleeding wound, Yosir automatically went dashing to the stove in the corner, grabbed a coarse wad that was hanging on the wall, thrust it into the flames with his bare hands and, feeling no pain as it burned, dashed back to the "doctor" in two quick strides and handed it to him. His friend howled briefly and the smell of singed cotton fibres and hair spread through the room, but there were three men holding Haroun tight. He began groaning quietly, and as he groaned life returned to him....

Yosir was always astounded at how easily the human body could be cut. There were many there in Hoit who had first-hand experience of this. Until November of the previous year a tall young man by the name of Jura had lived there among them. That infamous cut-throat, the imam Abdulaziz, had introduced him to them. It should be said that Abdulaziz had no great liking for Haroun and Yosir, and if it were not for the initial task that Tahir Yuldash had set them of creating a kind of "chronicle" of the *Hijrat*, or exodus, he would long ago have found some way to put them under the ground. When he introduced Jura to them, the imam had smiled crookedly into his sparse moustache and thin beard and said: "Write down in your history everything that this warrior of the true faith tells you!"

It took Jura three straight days to tell them his story of repeated stalking, house-breaking, robbery and murder, which in his telling became "reconnaissance", "taking up position", "capture", "attack" and "liquidation". It had all begin in 1994, when on the night of March 5 Jura and the notorious criminals Tolib Mamajanov and Sohib Holmatov, led by Abduvali Yuldashev and armed with an automatic rifle, a pistol, a sawn-off shotgun and knives, attacked a customs post in Uchkurgan and slit the throat of the sleeping customs officer in order to steal his uniform and weapon, together with all the money in the pocket of his jacket.

After that, it's true, they lay low, afraid of exposure, until that autumn the imam suggested that they should all "go and join the Hijrat" in Tajikistan. By October – at the very height of the war – they had managed to reach their fellows from Namangan, who at that time were fighting on the side of the Islamic Opposition, and through their mediation they were sent – as "true believers" who already had the blood of "infidels" on their hands – through Horog to Kunduz in Afghanistan, and from there to the Arab military training camps at Gardez. There were seven Uzbeks in that group, and the men who taught them to shoot from small arms, mortars and anti- aircraft guns carried on training them right until the spring of the next year, but somehow or other Abduvali Yuldashev managed to persuade Tahir Yuldash to let them go back to their homeland, and in 1995 the entire gang of them returned to Namangan.

There they started raiding the homes of people who they thought had grown rich unjustly, and their raids became ever more audacious and savage. And so, after several robberies, the proceeds of which they divided up among themselves, while paying a fifth into their "jihad fund", which was called "Baitulmol", they decided to attack the house of the deputy *hokim* of the province, Erkin Mamatkulov. Jura and his accomplices went on three "reconnaissance missions", studied the approaches to the house, the time Mamatkulov came home from work and the habits of his household. And then, early one autumn night, five of them climbed over the fence of his house and made their way into the cellar, where the foodstuffs were stored.

Late that night the deputy *hokim* came home from work, undressed right there in the yard and, after taking a hasty wash, asked his old mother to bring him a melon from the cellar. But then he stopped her when she was halfway there and went to the cellar himself as usual.

That was where they "jumped" him. However, the deputy *hokim* was a big man, too much for even five of them to handle. A wild brawl began, and then the imam Abduvali, who was standing in the corner without a mask, shouted: "Scatter!" and fired a burst from an automatic rifle. Mamatkulov slumped to the ground and the others threw themselves on him with their knives and started slashing at him with vindictive savagery....

Leaving the bloody mess on top of a heap of smashed melons, they dashed out into the yard, firing indiscriminately, then starting tying up the women of the house with wire and rope: the old mother, trembling and begging; the howling wife; the dumbfounded daughters, and after them, the nephew who had slept through it all....

For that raid Jura received from the imam 5,000 roubles, a mink cap and the leather jacket that the murdered deputy *hokim* had worn.

After that, in the spring of 1997, the imam shot dead two militiamen when they became suspicious of him at a railway station and went away to Hoit again. His place was taken by Tolib Mamajanov, and the gang became even more merciless: dressed in militia uniforms, they choked their victims with wire nooses, pressed hot irons against their naked bodies and, in the case of the traffic militiaman Boki Ubaidullaev, whom they had tracked carefully for a long time, they cut off his head and wrapped it, still warm, in a tablecloth, then put it in a plastic bag and hung it on the top corner of the gates of the deputy head of the provincial militia.

Jura became passionately excited as he told them how this *dushman*, or enemy, came home from work late at night and didn't notice anything on his gate, how they kept watch from a flat that they had rented in advance opposite his house, waiting for the morning to come, when the militia boss, having been informed of what had happened to his subordinate, would come out of the gate, still sleepy, and while he was waiting there for his official car he would notice the white plastic bag and feel something soft in it, and then the driver would carry a ladder out of his boss's house in order to climb up on to the crossbar of the gates and take down the bag with the still-warm head inside it....

At this point Yosir was sick, and Jura laughed, turning towards Haroun and Umar and saying that this little poet was still raw, he needed to be boiled and seasoned....

That was the time that Yosir fell ill. He didn't want to live. The world had lost all meaning. Until that day he had heard and recorded only the stories of victims who had suffered almost exactly the same treatment in the concrete cellars of the militia. Then suddenly here were these werewolves putting on militia uniforms, these true-believing imams who slit the throats of sheep for the festival of Kurban-hait, just as they slit the throats of men on ordinary days. If not for Haroun, Yosir would not have survived the last autumn. Haroun pulled him through with herbs that simply emptied the brain of anything except the most basic instincts – eating, sleeping and answering the call of nature.

Chapter Nineteen

Has summer come?
In your life you'll still write another
Twenty-five books in the little square
among the mass of stone, ugly memorials.
Some concrete piece, the existence of a memorial
left by the builders,
turns into the absurd
as though, yes, say as though, in as far as
even if the thought ends
the yearning to continue it
does not end.
Shall I go into the dining room
and soak my hardened
brains in tea
so as to pour into my thought?

Here no one needs you,
but this is just the width and the length
of the fact that you need no one.

-Belgi

The Uzbek authorities' account of the explosions of February 16, 1999 appeared on the same day when, literally only two hours after the event, President Karimov gathered together his team of state functionaries and declared in no uncertain terms that the Islamists were to blame for what had happened. But in the light of the rather fearful statement made at that meeting by the head of the National Security Service, General Rustam Inogamov, this version of events must actually have taken shape even earlier, before the explosions occurred, since the security chief declared that his service already knew who had carried out the attack and started begging the president for a month, in which time he promised to detain and deliver everyone responsible for planning and committing this crime.

There are now many articles on the internet claiming that the photographs of the suspects were distributed to the militia on February 14, and the authors of these claims actually cite their sources.

The explosions in Tashkent: questions without answers....

Sergei Ivakov
April 2000
Extracts from the book *Democracy Uzbek-style:*

Unlike you, I do not conceal my sources of information – Marcel Abdulin, a member of Islam Karimov's security services, told me many interesting things when he was in that state of intense euphoria popularly known as "smashed". The details of the entire conversation are hardly of any interest, but certain points cast light on many dark spots and expose other people as well as you.

And so, the explosions in Tashkent on February 16, 1999 were carefully planned by the Uzbek special services on the initiative of Islam Karimov and under his control, with the goal of neutralising his political opponents and subsequently eliminating them. The operation was planned in conditions of the strictest secrecy.

All the operational services of Uzbekistan, in particular in Tashkent, were put on high alert, with instructions to focus their vigilance at the exact spots where the explosions later took place.

(Is this not too many coincidences?) Just imagine, Mr. Oleg Yakubov, even documentary evidence like the following has surfaced! The special services of Uzbekistan drew up a list of "suspects" in advance (any officer from any local militia district will confirm that).

On February 14 all the local militia districts had already received typeset printed flyers with descriptions and photographs of the "suspects", and also clear instructions not to post the sheets in public before February 17.

It was claimed that the trial of the "perpetrators" of the February events was open. This is a lie – in actual fact the trial was top-secret, the judges did not take evidence from the accused and any alibis they offered were beaten down with truncheons; the court was only interested in "appropriate" confessions, and if one of the accused tried to be awkward, that didn't matter, it was still good enough, the outcome of the trial had in any case been decided long before the court sessions.

> Vitalii Ponomaryov
> Centre for Information on Human Rights in Central Asia

Or here is another document from the same time, concerning the same events:

THE THREAT OF "ISLAMIC EXTREMISM" IN UZBEKISTAN: MYTHS AND REALITY
(POLYGON Independent Information Agency)
October 5, 1999

About 80 people have already been convicted of involvement in the explosions in Tashkent, but many questions still remain unanswered. Karimov announced that "Islamic extremists" were behind the explosions almost immediately after the terrorist attacks, before the special services were in possession of any reliable information about who had organised the explosions. However, many people in Uzbekistan are convinced that the explosions in Tashkent were organised by clan-based factions or staged by the local special services.

A study of the documents of the trial and the investigation can only lead to bewilderment. The explosives and detonators were apparently obtained "from a place not yet identified by the investigation" and the individual who actually obtained them has also not been found. The documents for the rented cars in which the explosives were placed were drawn up in the names of members of a criminal gang in notary's offices in Tashkent three days before the terrorist attack, using the terrorists' genuine passports! The charge sheet speaks of four cars being blown up, although Karimov himself previously mentioned five. It does not say a word about the explosion in the building of the Cabinet of Ministers that was reported by the leading information agencies. The investigation did not therefore have to find an answer to the question of how "Islamic fundamentalists" could have carried explosives into this heavily guarded building.

The official account of who commissioned the criminal acts also appears entirely unconvincing: supposedly it was the leader of the Islamic Movement of Uzbekistan, Tahir Yuldashev, and the chairman of the Erk party, the well known poet Muhammad Solih (they both live abroad). It is difficult to believe that Solih and other activists of the secular democratic party Erk can have agreed to the creation of an Islamic state in Uzbekistan, or that the Islamists, in turn, would be prepared to appoint the leader of a non-religious party as president of such a state.

The substance of the two meetings (two in all these years!) between Yuldashev and Solih is related by some of the accused at third hand and cannot be regarded as convincing evidence. In a western court at least, evidence of this kind would simply not be taken into account.

Clear proof of how the democratic governments of the West (who are anything but sympathetic to "Islamic extremism") regard the Uzbek security services' version of events is provided by the recent decision to offer Solih political asylum in Norway, a decision that was taken with the involvement of the appropriate agencies of the UN. And this despite the numerous statements in the press that Solih is being sought by Interpol as the organiser of the explosions!

An entire treatise could be written about the various kinds of discrepancies in the criminal case built around the explosions that occurred in Tashkent on February 16, but we will make do with a single example. In his verdict, the judge asserts that Solih's money was supposedly used to buy 1.5 tonnes of extremist religious literature calling for a *jihad* and the literature was delivered to Alma-Ata and distributed in Uzbekistan and Kyrgystan, partly through the efforts of the Bishkek Committee for the Defence of Muslim Rights. The author happens to know that religious literature in the Uzbek language definitely was delivered to Alma-Ata late last year, but neither Solih nor, indeed, the "Wahhabites", nor the "supporters of a jihad" had anything to do with this. The works concerned were written by a brilliant adept of Islam living in emigration, the former Uzbek mufti Muhammad-Sodik Muhammad-Yusuf, and they included his research into the attitude of Islam to problems of the family, human rights, etc. The illiteracy of the investigators transformed Sodik (who has never been called a "Wahhabite", even by his enemies) into Solih. But then, the militant opponents of "the fundamentalists" are not really interested in the clarification of such "petty details".

The doubts most often expressed include surprise at the fact that the President arrived late for his meeting with the Cabinet of Ministers and the ease with which a GAZ21automobile packed with 400 kilograms of explosives drove right into the very heart of Tashkent, to the government building, when no one was even allowed access on foot shortly before the arrival of the president.

But to be honest, I must say that, as a writer, I was slightly nonplussed by President Karimov's behaviour just at that moment, behaviour that was disingenuously filmed, but quite ingenuously shown by Uzbekistan TV several weeks later. The car has only just exploded in front of Government House, which is still smoking, and there is the President, surrounded by his retinue, with the bareheaded, frightened Minister of the Interior beside him, calmly looking into the camera, talking and asking questions of the subordinates. Just then there is another explosion, no doubt the one at the National Bank, and the minister involuntarily pulls his head down into his shoulders, while the President carries on talking without a break, as if nothing had happened....

Imagine any president in that situation, with bombs going off one after another in his capital city: the natural response is to declare an emergency, to seek the maximum security for oneself, to try to discover where this threat is coming from. But after only a couple of hours, here he is addressing his assembled party functionaries with a speech prepared in advance....

However, let us not speculate about this, but simply say that despite the immense efforts made by the Uzbek authorities to prove their version of events, there are a number of facts that simply do not fit with that version. I have already said that I am in possession of the two volumes of the official charges brought by the Public Prosecutor's Office of Uzbekistan in this criminal case, which bears the number 8378, so let us go through them.

It is hard to raise any objections to the immense number of facts gathered together in the case materials, demonstrating that in 1994 Tahir Yuldash and his associates fled to Tajikistan, where they joined the ranks of the Islamic opposition, and that by 1996 he had become a significant figure in that movement – to be precise, Said Abdullo Nuri's deputy for foreign affairs. At the same time Juma Namangani's authority as a field commander was on the rise. But after the united opposition of Tajikistan signed a peace agreement with the government of Tajikistan in 1997, and the opposition leaders became members of a coalition government, the Uzbek component of the opposition had to consider its own position, and that was when the Islamic Movement of Uzbekistan was proclaimed, under the leadership of Tahir Yuldash.

Here is one of the interviews from that time, in which Tahir Yuldash, who had relocated his forces to Afghanistan, spoke about the relations between his movement and the Taliban:

In the name of God the Gracious, the Merciful

Today the Taliban are subjected to various kinds of slander, they are accused of things that are not typical of them, and we cannot look on this with indifference, since Allah says in the Koran: "O believers, fear Allah and be on the side of the faithful". Our attitude to them is that they are implanting in the life of Afghanistan and the region the Islam that has been driven out of here over the course of centuries. But the propaganda claims that they are harmful or dangerous for the region are, of course, new falsehoods. They are trying to restore Islam in Afghanistan and their goals are the true goals, and we are proud of them and we are on their side. It is more dangerous for the region that the Russians are introducing new forces into Termez. They are restoring their domination of Central Asia. We have already lived as a Russian colony, but as for the Taliban, they do not wish to colonise anyone.

Question: The Uzbek government is afraid that if the Taliban approach their southern border, they will provide assistance to Islamists in Tajikistan and Uzbekistan. Do you have any contacts with the Taliban?

TY: The threats of the Uzbek and Russian governments concerning the Taliban remind me of the Uzbek saying that the coward is the first to start waving his fists. Seventy years ago, when the Bolsheviks seized our region, those who tried to defend it were accused of working for the English. They called them *basmachi*, meaning "brigands". Or when the Soviet Union attacked Afghanistan and the Muslims of this country, it claimed once again that there were Americans here, that there were Chinese here, in short, it tried to conceal its own crimes by blaming others. Today, the claims by the rulers of Uzbekistan that they will suffer harm if the Taliban reach the border – these claims merely testify to the fear of traitors. And this propaganda by the Uzbek government, claiming that the Taliban might provide support to the Islamic forces of Tajikistan and Uzbekistan – this is testimony to the cowardice of the Uzbek government. As for our contacts with the Taliban, we have good contacts, and we are proud of them, but we are capable of pursuing our own goal without their support, even if they do not make way for us. We do not rely on external forces.

The prosecution materials trace a kind of history of the development of this movement in the words of its leaders – men like Bahrom Abdullaev, Zainnidin Askarov and Olovuddin Boltaev. In May 1997, in the Hotel Elajak in Istanbul, the first "summit meeting" of this movement takes place, attended by Tahir Yuldash, Jumabai Namangani, Bahram Abdullaev (one of the followers of Imam Abduvali Mirzaev, who disappeared without trace), Kazimbek Zakirov (the imam's former driver and bodyguard), Zainnidin Askarov from Namangan (who later became the movement's press secretary), Ruhiddin Fahrutdinov

(the son of a former minister of forestry in Uzbekistan) and Abdullah Ahmedov from the Ferghana Valley. These men decide to unite all the various Islamic movements in Uzbekistan under the aegis of a single Islamic Movement of Uzbekistan, and Tahir declares himself the leader of this movement. He it is who sets the goal of declaring a *jihad* against Karimov's government, carrying out propaganda work among young people, increasing the number of their supporters and sending them to Hattab's military training camp in Chechnya and Juma Namangani's camp in Tavildara.

Work on realising these goals goes ahead at full speed. Bahram Abdullaev travels directly from Istanbul to Chechnya, where he meets with Hattab, who promises to put 20 men through his camps every two months. In all, as many as 5,000 young Uzbeks undergo military training during these years.

The leaders of the movement hold a second meeting in Istanbul in July of the same year, at the home of an eminent religious figure, Haji Abdulla Hodi, who is an ethnic Uzbek. Those who are responsible for various areas of work report on what they have achieved during the preceding months. In addition, a new task is set of selecting capable individuals from among the young people, especially those studying abroad, so that they can be used in the future to help construct an Islamic state.

In November of that same year the leaders of the movement meet to "synchronise their watches" in Baku, at the office of a Turk called Hussein, where they decide to set up a headquarters in Alma-Ata....

Here we shall briefly interrupt our exposition of the criminal charges and accompanying investigation of the discrepancies between the official account of the explosions and what, quite obviously, actually happened, since during this very period one of my friends happens, completely by chance, to meet Tahir Yuldash in Teheran.

Chapter Twenty

in the gap
between myself and the word
everything ends
my yearning to the West is glossed by the East
but no one is answered

- Belgi

97

Hamid Ismailov

One of my friends, who took a serious interest in the Islamic Movement of Uzbekistan, met Tahir Yuldash in 1997. This is what he told me:

In December 1997 I flew to Teheran on an assignment from one of the Moscow newspapers to cover the assembly of the Islamic Conference Organisation. I flew via Istanbul, and after I had boarded the plane and the fantastically polite Turkish air hostesses had already begun demonstrating the safety regulations for the flight, there was a commotion as a number of men entered the cabin, speaking loudly in guttural Arabic. I thought to myself: "It must be some oil sheikhs or other ..." although, as a rule, people like that are not usually so noisy. At that moment a rather ugly-looking young man with a mongoloid face walked past me, followed by Tahir Yuldashev, whom I had interviewed in Soviet times, and then two Arabs. I recognised Tahir immediately, even though he was dressed in white Arab robes and a white Arab skull-cap. He must have recognised me too as he passed by.

Naturally, by that time I had heard that Tahir was part of the Tajik armed opposition, that he had been the deputy of Saeed Abdullo Nuri himself, and after that he had organised the Movement for the Islamic Revival of Uzbekistan, and so you can imagine my excitement at the prospect of even a brief word with him. I imagined what a fine little bomb I could publish in Moscow after all the formalities of the conference. As the flight went on I was pondering how I ought to approach him, how I could reel him in to get an interview with him, and so on and so forth.

Anyway, by the middle of that night flight I couldn't repress the urge any longer and I set out in the direction of the rear toilet, in order to reconnoitre. I walked between the seats, shamelessly scouring the rows with my eyes, and the infrequent bearded men in black who couldn't sleep darted sharp glances at me with hate in their red eyes, as they guarded the faithful wives snoring gently on both their shoulders.

Eventually I spotted those white robes in the last row, but when I approached them sycophantically, I saw that all the men were sleeping peacefully, and especially Tahir, whose face was turned away towards the black window.

We arrived in Teheran between one and two in the morning. Even in Teheran a plane is still a plane, and so everyone flocked to the doors as soon as we landed, and I was swept out into the thick Teheran night. Everything seemed a bit strange and I was a bit wary, since it was the first time I had been in Islamic Iran. It was also strange that the journalists were met by a shrill-voiced woman – not until later did I realise that in Iran everything is essentially run by the women, but at first I found this odd too, so much so that for a while I even forgot about Tahir Yuldash.

But then, a little later, when we journalists were huddled together at the passport control desk under the watchful eye of that same woman in black, wide awake in the middle of the night, Tahir came across and greeted me himself, and asked if I had come for the conference. With my mind fogged by the throng of questions I had prepared to ask, I said that it would be good if we could get together, if only at the conference. A frequent visitor

who knew the city well, he interrupted me to ask where I was staying, and when I named the Lola Hotel, he told me that, if it was Allah's will, he would find me himself. Then he turned away and walked over to the young man with mongoloid features, who was holding his sports bag, and through the glass partition I saw the customs men rummage in the bag and pull out a track suit that was probably used instead of pyjamas, and a few other items of standard luggage for a business trip. Tahir stood there calmly, towering over the busy customs men.

And then later, when I was already sitting in the journalists' bus and looking out of the window, I saw that same tall, snow-white figure being met by several men in a car, but my faint feeling of regret that I might lose the chance for such a fine interview was soon replaced by a gentle curiosity as I surveyed the night-time approaches to the legendary city of Teheran.

The Islamic conference followed its course and in our insolent journalistic fashion we pursued Saeed Abdullo Nuri, who smelled of rose water, or Saparmurat Turkmenbashi with his hennaed hair, or someone else, in the intervals describing the heavy snow that fell on Teheran that December. And then one morning a conference session was postponed precisely because of that snow, and I was sitting in my hotel room, watching the outlandish Iranian television, which in those days was anticipating the birth of the "hidden imam", when the telephone rang and the hotel receptionist said that someone had come to see me.

Without asking who it might be, I went downstairs and saw Tahir Yuldash standing at the counter, accompanied by a tall young man with a short moustache. We said hello, and I suggested going through into the café to drink tea, but Tahir said politely: "Would it not be better if we talked in your room?" I agreed, and then he nodded to the man with him and said: "You wait there for the time being...", and although I invited him too, the young man immediately walked over to the corner of the tea room, while Tahir and I went upstairs.

Let me say straight away that from the very beginning Tahir refused to give a formal interview, saying that there would be an opportunity to give not just one, but many interviews, and now we could simply have a talk. Naturally, he was the one who spoke and I listened almost without interrupting, only occasionally nodding my head or trying briefly to clarify some point. He told me the story of his life since I had interviewed him in Namangan in the early 1990's and even from the time a little earlier than that, when he graduated from secondary school with a gold medal and went to study at the Samarkand Cooperative Financial College.

That was where this well-provided-for son of a goods-depot director had become enthralled with Islam and argued fiercely with his female teacher of scientific communism. He was almost expelled from the college for one of those arguments. He showed me how that teacher used to gasp and splutter and said that she had "raised up a stork's nest on the head of a free woman of the East, but gave no thought at all to the contents of her head". I imagined this woman and her righteous anger with this youth who still had no beard or moustache (actually, his beard and moustache were still sparse, even then) and was unable to suppress my laughter.

Then he skipped to Namangan in the early 1990s, or rather, straight to the events of 1992, when President Karimov began reinforcing his hold on power and they started arresting Islamists one after another in Namangan. That was when the militiamen themselves warned Tahir that his arrest was imminent, and the night before it was due to happen he and his supporters fled to Andijan and then to Tajikistan.

"Tajikistan is a special story, one that would be very long in the telling. I crossed the Afghan border five times, I was wounded in the leg once (he tugged at his trouser leg, indicating his thigh), of course, I had it treated very secretly. Then I took my family over there, the children are in Afghanistan now. I was Saeed Abdullo Nuri's deputy for foreign affairs, and it was mostly our fellows who did the fighting, not the Tajiks," he said.

I asked what he wanted to see happen in Uzbekistan. He laughed and said: "My lads are asking me to be president of Uzbekistan, but I don't want to. I want to win a place in heaven!" Then he started reflecting on what sort of Uzbekistan he would like to see. "I've been in all the Islamic countries, and nowhere have I seen the kind of Islam that we would like to build in Uzbekistan. Iran? Absurd. Take a look at their newspapers, they still believe that their lost imam will come back to them and solve all their problems. My spiritual leader says that they are like children, that they listen to their grandmothers and believe their fairytales. Pakistan? Ninety per cent of the population is illiterate. Afghanistan? Even more ignorant. The Arabs? They can't even unite among themselves, let alone unite the whole of Islam. No, the Islam that we wish to see does not yet exist on earth. It did exist once, but not now. We need intellect..." – he stumbled over the word for a moment, and then repeated – "We need intellectuals..." And then he added: "Like you".

I don't know if I was taken aback or flattered. Probably both. But then I suddenly remembered that a year earlier I had interviewed the renowned Imam Obid-kori in Tashkent, and during the interview he had pronounced the word "homosexuals" with exactly the same diffident intonation. It had always seemed strange to me that these "pillars of the faith" and experts in "extramundane and metaphysical" matters always yielded to this temptation of "worldliness", as if to demonstrate that they could also flaunt their knowledge of the ordinary everyday world, and I had always found this depressing. That was the moment when I admitted to myself that for all his male handsomeness, Tahir's forehead was too low, and his beard was shamefully sparse, and because of that he probably had a whole heap of complexes for which he tried to compensate with his belligerent militancy. Of course, in saying this, no doubt I myself am working out some of my own complexes, the nature of which is not very hard to guess. But then, I am talking about him, not myself...

"At that very moment for some reason Tahir began telling me a parable about the Emir of the Faithful, Umar ibn-Farruk (could that perhaps be where he got his title of "amir" and the name he took, Muhammad Farruk?). The essential meaning of the parable was expressed by the phrase: "My sword is my truth!" and I should say that, owing to all these intellectual thoughts, I failed to remember the parable itself. I have also forgotten the

rest of that "intellectual" conversation on which we spent about two hours in my room.

"We shall speak again about many things," he promised me as he got up, and we walked downstairs together to the foyer of the hotel, where the tall, distinguished-looking young man was still sitting squeezed into the corner of the tea room. I started apologising to the young man for the inconvenience, but Tahir stopped me and said it was his work and there are no inconveniences in work. But even so, I persuaded them to take a bowl of tea and the young man, who brought the tea, suddenly started asking me about myself. I told him that so far, by the will of God, I was still living in Moscow. "But are you going to return to your Homeland?" he asked again. "Inshallah," I joked. Then the young man exchanged glances with Tahir and said to me: "In ancient times the Chinese conquered Central Asia, and some of their troops were left in garrisons on that land for a time. When the main part of the army decided to return to China, they asked those who stayed behind: 'Are you going to come back to the homeland?' and they replied 'We shall return!' The words for that in Chinese are 'dun gan'. The centuries passed, and those soldiers accepted Islam and they still live in Central Asia to this day. They call themselves 'dungans', but they have forgotten that 'dun gan' means 'we shall return'! So take care that you don't become a dungan..."

And we all laughed at this parable from Tahir Yuldash's faithful companion.

Chapter Twenty-One

The lamp wavers in the night, wavers.
A trembling track remains in the black, pitch black sea.

The mountain spreads, a ship that has taken its course in the night,
don't name it, all this is me.

Is it pain or emptiness that ties the swing?
How can I know what measure of the heart is chosen?

What sort of a rustling is this sound, is this suffering?
Is a wave beating or a bird flying, or is it a mirage,

or the pebble telling the stars of its heavy soul?
It is not crying but just a gathering of sounds.

The lamp wavers in the long night, wavers.
A trembling track remains in the black, pitch black sea...

- Belgi

My journalist friend who told me this story added at the time that by pure coincidence they also travelled back from Teheran to Istanbul in the same plane, although this time Tahir was accompanied by a completely different man and he was dressed in some kind of semi-sporting outfit, not Arab robes. And at Istanbul airport he was met by several men who quickly drove him off into the city.

But let us get back to the criminal charges, according to which this was the very time when the so-called "Kabul meeting" between the leadership of the Islamic Movement of Uzbekistan and Muhammad Solih took place, and the latter supposedly committed himself to donating 1.6 million dollars to a jihad, and they supposedly agreed that after the armed coup Muhammad Solih would become the president of Uzbekistan and Tahir Yuldash would be the minister of defence. When I showed these pages of the case materials to my Moscow journalist friend, he laughed and said: "Tahir isn't used to taking second place! And then, he's a lot richer than poor Solih. And thirdly, why make Tahir minister for defence, when they have the famous old war dog Juma?"

But the point I wanted to fish out of the statement of charges was something that happened before this "Kabul meeting" that supposedly finalised the preparations for a jihad. This event was the arrest in Turkmenistan on October 10, 1998 of the Islamic Movement of Uzbekistan's amir for Uzbekistan, Bahrom Abdullaev, and his bodyguard Zahidjan Dehkanov. Bahrom Abdullaev was at the very centre of the movement. As a disciple of the imam Abduvali, he had immediately become one of the movement's most influential authorities, attending all the "summits" and carrying out the most risky assignments, such as negotiations with Hattab, the famous militant Chechen field-commander, about training young Uzbeks in his military operations camps.

In short, if there had been any plan for a jihad, Bahrom Abdullaev would have had to know about it. The Turkmen special forces quickly handed him over to their Uzbek colleagues, and in that same hapless documentary film in which president Karimov gives his fearless interview while Tashkent is still exploding in the background, Bahrom Abdullaev looks straight into the camera and tells the judicial investigator shooting the video: "I told you then that you ought to get rid of Murad Kaziev".

But Murad Kaziev figures in the charges as the most important organiser of the explosions, who was also involved in carrying them out. He it was who arrived at Tashkent's own "Red Square" in an old blue Volga, driving straight up to Goverment House just ten minutes before President Karimov's arrival, he it was who pushed aside the militiaman who came up to him and ran off with his partner in the direction of Anhor, he it was who cried "Allah is great!" as he fired aimlessly from his automatic rifle while the militiamen either lay down on the ground or peeped out of the window and then hid in the safest place they could find

until the two armed men had run almost a kilometre towards Urda, where they hijacked one car, then another and carried on like that unhindered, swapping one car for another, all the way to Chernyaevka on the border with Kazakhstan, then crossed the border and disappeared, first in Alma-Ata and then in Chechnya – and so no one had tried to arrest this Murad Kaziev and get rid of him, although Bahrom Abdullaev, the Islamic Movement of Uzbekistan's amir for Uzbekistan, had advised the special services to do just that.

Here are a few more items extracted from criminal case file No. 8378. On page 121 it says that Bahrom Abdullaev's nephew, who replaced him as the Islamic Movement of Uzbekistan's amir for Uzbekistan, returned from meeting with Tahir Yuldash on February 14 and informed the others that Tahir Yuldash had told him: "There are certain problems in organising a jihad, Juma Namangani has still not returned to Tajikistan from Afghanistan, Muhammad Solih has not yet received the money that he promised, the vehicles for transporting Juma Namangani's troops have not yet been bought, but all actions must go ahead according to plan, and the melting of the snow in the mountains in spring should simplify matters". The claim that Tahir Yuldsh was planning a jihad during the melting of the snows is mentioned in testimony on pages 96, 97 and elsewhere in the case materials.

On April 14, 1999, having learned in a telephone conversation with Kazim Zakirov that something was being planned in Tashkent, supposedly "Olovuddin told him that they would ruin the plan, that Juma Namangani had still not come back to Tajikistan and assembled his forces, the KAMAZ trucks had still not been bought with the funds that had been allocated, Tahir Yuldashev was not back from his trip yet ..." (page 101)

And, in addition, Tahir Yuldash, who was supposedly responsible for the explosions, was in Teheran at the time, and when Rustam Mamajanov brought him videotapes of reports of the explosions from various TV channels, "Tahir Yuldashev spoke with him, but since he had no time that day, because a swarthy military man had come to see him in his hotel, it was only the following day that he (Rustam Mamajanov) spoke with Tahir Yuldashev and gave him the videotapes..." (page 149). This certainly seems like rather strange behaviour for a man who had actually organised the attempt on the president's life, when it would only be logical for him to be waiting expectantly in some place closer to Uzbekistan.

In short, the official charge materials are full of facts that don't quite fit with the official account of the explosions. And on page 511 there is a really strange passage, which I shall try to translate word for word: "Questioned as a witness, Vladimir Viktorovich Ivanov stated that since 1992 he had worked as the deputy head of the operations

information department (OID) of the National Security Service (NSS) of the Republic of Uzbekistan, that on approximately February 17-18, 1999 NSS operations officers had approached him with a request to examine documents concerning the issue of a visa to U. Babajanov and his wife and that, having examined these documents, he reported that the relevant documents for these individuals to leave the country had been formalized by the OID of the NSS within 45 days, in accordance with the law".

And yet according to the case materials, U. Babajanov was the principle individual involved in the purchase of a house on Abdulla Kahara Street, where the tanks of explosive were loaded into the cars and, according to the official version of events, he was also the immediate organiser of the explosions in Tashkent.

---

6 On November 26, 2003 journalists from foreign agencies were invited to Tashtyurma for a meeting with the well-known ex-press secretary of the Islamic Movement of Uzbekistan, Zainiddin Askarov. He began his address by talking about how much conditions had improved in the prisons in Uzbekistan, but halfway through the talk, the NSS officer left the room, and Zainiddin Askarov suddenly came out with a statement in which, citing Bahrom Abdullaev, he said that the special services of Uzbekistan had known about the explosions on February 16, 1999 and had controlled them. Here is a part of what Zainiddin Askarov said: "When Bahrom Abdullaev was sitting in the NSS cellar, they tried to pin crimes on him, saying, you are a mujahid, you train terrorists, you are a cutthroat.... Bahrom Abdullaev had strict orders from Tahirbai – do what you like, kill Izzat if you want, but stop the explosions organised by the supporters of Abduvali-kori. Bahrom told them: 'There are explosions being planned in Tashkent, I came to stop them, I'll give you the addresses, I'll tell you who Izzat is, where he was trained, how much explosive and how many bombs they have. I don't mind even if you shoot them. As for me, reward me or put me in prison – that's up to you. Only stop this, stop it urgently! At first they won't believe it, but then they'll look and see that it's all serious'.

"After Bahrom Abdullaev told them this, they arranged a feast for him and asked him about the details, who wanted to do this and what their goal was. He said they wanted to release Abduvali-kori from jail. After he told them all this, the investigation of Bahrom Abdullaev's case was halted until the time of the explosions, and he was kept in a separate cell. He prayed and feasted.

Doctors examined him, asked how he felt, how his health was.... In short, the state knew what was going to happen. And after that the bombs were welcomed like guests in Tashkent.... Five minutes after the explosions Islam Karimov, Rustam Inoyatov (Head of NSS) and Zokir Almatov (Minister of Interior Affairs at the time) arrived in the square and, as if following a scenario planned in advance, out of the blue they blamed it on 'religious fanatics', saying that they knew who had done this and they would catch them. Why? Because Bahrom Abdullaev had informed them."

Chapter Twenty-Two

The sky is the sky not so it can be reflected in water,
the trees too are not only created to drop leaves on the earth,
but if you say that so much beauty is drunk on itself alone
you would be mistaken. Look at that old mill
while it's turning the power of the torrent into white flour —
your heart also is heavy as a millstone,
and to dispel a handful of sadness in the eyes of this girl
the wind blows, the water flows, time grrrrinds and squeaks like a mill....

-Belgi

If there was a single day in the year that Yosir always remembered, that day was November 22. When he was a child he and his stepfather had read a book about how President John Kennedy was shot on that day, and his step-father had explained to him who Lee Harvey Oswald was and what connection he had with Jack Ruby. But it wasn't the mystery of this story that made Yosir remember this day; he remembered it because it was the day when a classmate of his called Georgii was run over by a car.

And for some reason that day had been notched into Yosir's consciousness forever: every year seemed to revolve around it, as if it were some kind of fixed axis, and every year on that very day his awareness quivered and shook off its patina of humdrum ordinariness. And so when the American told him, in the presence of that Uzbek of his, that in a few days, on precisely November 22, western journalists and the Red Cross would come to see them, those two bright electric filaments that had been glowing in front of Yosir's eyes by day and night suddenly went out, as if the bulbs had burst, and their place was taken by a thick darkness that ticked like a clock.

They stopped beating them and actually arranged washing facilities in one of the cells, they even added all sorts of American muesli and biscuits to the rations. The tongue clings to remembrance more tightly than ephemeral memory, and his tongue suddenly blossomed impetuously with the taste of Bavaria in Germany, and sad poems reflecting the turgid flow of the German river under the massive aspen trees started drifting through the darkness of his brain, and the long-forgotten feeling that he did not belong to himself usurped the place of his reviving body....

There is a certain feeling when feelings are unnecessary, superfluous, when you want to die, not out of despair, but out of fullness, because

all the best things that could happen have already happened, because God has been so kind to you that He didn't even let you notice it – take out any day from behind you and bathe in it as if it were an entire lifetime. And today, after it has turned into yesterday, will become just as inaccessibly sweet, and how long can you go on suffering over this in your bewilderment at life, with its day-before-yesterday melancholy that is still to come?

But on November 22, 2001, when the present coincided with reality for its one day in the year, the representatives of the Red Cross entered their prison at eleven o'clock in the morning, together with the western journalists. They came into the cells in cautious groups of three or four and asked their leisurely questions in the presence of the guards. It was November 22, but the three who came into the cage occupied by Yosir and his motley cellmates were living in the tomorrow of their newspapers, inventing florid banner headlines scraped together out of their trite questions: "How do you feel about 9/11?", "Are you from Al-Qaeda or the Taliban?", "Where is Osama bin-Laden now?"

The doors into the yard were open and for the first time the cold light of the sun glanced into the cell, tinting the straw at his feet an even more sickly shade of yellow. The day of November 22 drained away into the haggard wrinkles of these strange faces. Another two groups came in, checking the information they had obtained, and Yosir sat there in a pose that was now customary, pretending that he was listening to the interpreter and reciting the midday prayer to himself: "Allah does not burden any soul beyond its strength. It will receive that which it has deserved. Our Master, do not chastise us for forgetfulness or delusion: and, our Master, do not lay upon us a responsibility like unto the responsibility that You laid on those who came before us: our Master, do not burden us with that which we do not have the strength to bear; and absolve us of our transgressions, grant us forgiveness, be merciful to us; You are our Lord; and assist us against the unbelievers".

Those people left as well. The prisoners would probably be fed now, because the inspection party was still there. But instead of the clattering of plates, he heard the jangling of the prison cell locks, some being opened and more being closed. How much was still left of November 22? The darkness ticked in front of his eyes.

And suddenly the door creaked open again, a beam of light came slicing diagonally into the cell and a solitary female correspondent, who must have arrived late, came in awkwardly, and it wasn't the face, but the entire awkward approach that suddenly illuminated Yosir's consciousness as the solution to the riddle of this day, and even before she came close enough to be recognised he involuntarily broke off his prayer and exclaimed: "Caroline!"

She moved closer to his cry and flung up her arms. "Belgi? Oh, my God, what are you doing here?" she wailed in Russian as she examined his bearded, battered face. Yes, it was his Caroline....

The last time Belgi had seen Caroline was in the camp in Hoit, but when I showed Caroline one of my transcripts, it turned out that she had never even suspected that her Belgi was concealed behind one of the masks in that mountain village in Tajikistan. Anas had come running to Yosir and Umar and told them that journalists from the UN were on their way to the camp. The camp commander, Yunus, had apparently ordered all weapons to be handed in and the women and children to be brought out into the streets. Anas waved his arms about and shouted: "We are a refugee camp and there are no mujahadin here, so give me your rifle and then get your recordings ready... Have I explained clearly enough? You'll answer to Yunus with your head! If anything goes wrong, you know what he'll do to you..."

And here is that transcript:

Yunus: Well, by the will of Allah, all of us in this camp are refugees... You probably didn't know that before you arrived here?

Caroline: No, I didn't. Everybody believes that here in Hoit there is a guerrilla camp, from which military forays are made into Kyrgyzstan and Uzbekistan. Can I ask you a question about that?

Yunus: You know, I'm the one who asks the questions around here. We don't have any fighting men, only women and children.... All refugees.... You've met them, what did they tell you?

Caroline: That the male population is in Nai-Yailak, undergoing military training.... (the sound of Belgi coughing)

Yunus: Exactly who was it who said that? I'll... look that person hard in the eye.... How can they deceive international public opinion like that.... In the sight of God.... No, I don't understand these people.... Well never mind, I'll sort them out....

Caroline: Please, don't punish them on my account....

Yunus: No, what do you mean, if I wanted to punish them, I'd do it in front of you! And then, when a woman... such a beautiful girl... asks, how can I refuse.... So let the witnesses confirm what I say....

(voices, evidently Belgi and Alish: "Masha Allah!")

Yunus: Are you an American? (a lingering pause)

Alish: (disguising his voice) I can tell from your accent that you're not American!

Caroline: I'm Irish originally...

Yunus: Aha, the IRA, the Irish Republican Army! Then you must help us get in touch with them! They're genuine warriors – mujahadin!

Caroline: (laughing) Well, not exactly... but if you really need to get in touch with them.... By the way the way I have a request for you in return: the boyfriend of a friend of mine set out for Horog with two friends to see Sheikh Gilani, and he disappeared on the way....

Yunus: An American woman's boyfriend, was it?

Caroline: Yes, she's American. But how did you know?

Yunus: I told you. I'm the one who asks the questions here! You say there were three of them?

Caroline: Yes, three.

Yunus: There are three of us too! (laughs at his own joke) Wouldn't you like to take us as boyfriends for you and this friend of yours?

Caroline: There were three of them already without you.... He's a well-known poet. Perhaps you've heard this poem of his, it was set to music as a song....

> *My sadness is the measure of your beauty,*
> *but there is none of this beauty in my sadness..*
>
> *Having written this*
> *I was sitting in a chair,*
> *and when she herself came in I wanted to stand up quickly,*
> *but somehow I had grown a bit old,*
> *somehow I had become lazy, thinking of the finale,*
> *and I stayed put, a novel in my lap*
> *and a kitchen knife on top of it.*
> *The corn on the cob was boiling in the basement kitchen.*
> *All this, without stirring, not refusing*
> *this old game entirely, nor praising to the skies,*
> *but hurting a little inside:*
> *this had vanished, as though I shall return to reality*
> *without all this, or in exchange I must strike this out.*
>
> *My sadness is the measure of your beauty,*
> *but there is none of this beauty in my sadness...*

Alish: (disguising his voice) But who translated it?

Yunus: (interrupting them) I don't read poems, I'm a warrior... phoo, I mean a refugee! And I don't know any poets! Everyone is equal here with me! They're all refugees! So you tell your girlfriend that I

haven't got any poets! Maybe he's somewhere in Afghanistan! And what are you men staring at! You've finished showing the materials, so get back to your stations! I'll have you sent to Afghanistan tomorrow! And as for you, dear lady, the reception is over! Get in your car and go to Dushanbe! Otherwise I'll keep you here, and you won't be reading any poems, you'll be doing what all our women do – washing our tunics and digging trenches! Would you like that? All this nonsense about poems....

Chapter Twenty-Three

Caroline left a strange atmosphere behind her in the cell: most of the men sitting around Yosir understood Russian, and now he felt as if November 22 had closed in tight around him. Not that any of them would have dared suspect him of anything forbidden, but this non-Muslim girl's final words had left Yosir isolated in a separate kind of space, and if anyone there had said: "Beat him!", the entire cell would have thrown themselves on him and torn him to pieces. The really strange thing, though, was that there was no correlation between him the rest of the cell: he didn't glance at them, didn't say a word to them, there was no pride or guilt, he remained just the same as he had been all that morning, locked into a kind of stupor, a state of non-belonging to which no one had found the key....

That was how the day of November 22 passed. At night, when the Americans went away to their barracks huts, the prisoners were allowed to pray as a group. When all the cells lined up for this communal prayer, and he was the last in line in the last cell, the gates of the prison suddenly creaked and cracked. The bark of that American voice caught them as they were genuflecting, the light of a torch, as sharp and sudden as a shot, picked out their line and that Uzbek with the nasal voice who was always dancing round his boss by day and night, shouted : "Yosir, get out here quick!"

And now Yosir could sense the circle of his cellmates' and fellow-believers' sympathy closing in around him: they took people away to America at night, but in groups. "Allahu Akbar!" exclaimed the Chechen imam, and everyone took it up: "Allahu Akbar!" He walked past behind his cellmates, and they all tried to shake his hand, for the last time, for when they came for you at night their intentions were not good. So that's what November 22 is about, he thought and tried to remember when, what time of year it was when his grandmother learned of his grandfather's death... Had it really been in November?

They led him out into the cold yard of the prison. The latches grated shut behind them. The night was clear and piercingly cold. His legs were unused to walking and his knees trembled. And the trembling kept rising higher up his body. Lorca had cried and clutched at the side of the truck. What should he do? Ah, Caroline, Caroline...

The Uzbek shoved him into the back of the jeep, where two of Dostum's armed men were already sitting. The barrels of their automatic rifles glinted coldly in the black night. The doors of the cab slammed shut and they drove out of the yard. Behind them he could still hear the shouts of "Allahu Akbar!" They drove through Shebergan, past the clay buildings, pale in the night, and Yosir caught himself thinking how banal death could be: an unreal night trip that might have surfaced out of a childhood dream: it made no difference if you were still asleep or you had woken up.... And was it really November 22? But what year? The body of one of the soldiers involuntarily swayed against him as they drove over the potholes that were softened by the moonlight, and the contact warmed them both, although the body of the man sitting opposite them was sullen, with a rifle gripped between the knees.

They drove out of the town. I ought to look at the stars, Yosir thought and then stopped himself short: what for? A girl had once told him in a bus at night: I wish I could ride like this with you forever.... Where was she now.... Caroline, Caroline....

Uncertain little lights appeared along the highway in the distance. The jeep stopped and the American turned off the engine. Silence like that is only possible in the steppe at night, when every blade of grass can speak its heart to the wind.

> The grass-blades have grown up to the sky
> and become stars,
> they have not surmounted
> the boundaries of sadness...

The American got out of the cab and started urinating noisily on the road. The Uzbek imitated him, running a little further on and squatting down. The American barked something. The Uzbek, washing his hands in the night-dark dust, translated: "Get out!" the warmth of the adjacent body was torn away, and as soon as Yosir lowered his uncertain feet outside the back of the jeep, a blow to his back from a rifle-butt sent him sprawling face-down on the ground. Something warm started clogging up his beard. The American shouted something. Now there would be a burst of automatic fire....

Or had it already happened?... How did a man die? Was curiosity really stronger than death? He shuddered at the sudden sound of the engine, or was that the gun firing? Or had they decided to crush him in

the middle of this road to nowhere? The jeep really did swing round, it picked up speed and went rushing past him.... But where was that burst of fire from the man who had just been sitting beside him?

Once, a long, long time ago, one of his friends had told him how he had lain under a moving train. Even after the train had gone past him, he still couldn't get up, as if it would come back again the moment he raised his head. Or was it him that had happened to?

The roaring retreated into the distance and a blade of glass began talking to a star....

Chapter Twenty-Four

...seeing other peoples' deaths, we learn about our own

-Belgi

After the explosions on February 16, 1999 a strange situation developed in Hoit. On the one hand, a new stream of refugees began arriving from Uzbekistan, and the people told terrifying stories of how the militia and the NSS were running riot, hunting down all the believers indiscriminately, how at all the guard posts posters had been put up with photographs of hundreds of young men who were wanted.... And yet, despite all this, an inclination to return began to build among those who had already lived here for months, as if there were something more terrible than a rampaging militia in store for them here.

This is what one of the young men who fled from Hoit in the late spring of 1999 recorded on the dictaphone of the journalist Adiba Ataeva:

A guy called Ismail came to us in Khorezm and said that we could study religious learning in Tajikistan and then work in the Office of Religion at home after we came back to Uzbekistan. And so we went. We got to Sarychinar, and saw that they weren't offering any religious learning there, all they taught was how to use weapons, and then it turned out that they were gathering young men there and sending them to the mountain village of Hoit. And when you got there, there was no way back, you couldn't run away, so anyway, it was all a trick. There were seven or eight of us young guys in Sarychinar, from all over – Tashkent, Namangan, Andijan – they were all the same as us, some had come a week earlier, some two or three days ago. We tried to run away from Sarychinar, but they took your passport away there and wouldn't give it back. And after we arrived in Hoit we asked, but they wouldn't give them to us. They've arrested your mother and father there, they said, and if you show up, they'll put you behind bars too – that was the sort of thing they said to us.

Anyway, they trick you and keep you there. They say, if you run off, if you leave the boundary of the camp, we're not responsible for you. And there were twenty-five or thirty men in the camp. They were from all over the place too. And so the lads agreed and tried to escape and go home. We decided to leave in the night and early morning, in groups. Seven or eight in a group. So on the night of May 15 the lads set out from Hoit and Garez and Chigal. You can't walk there at night, so they hid in a field to carry on in the morning. Two groups joined into one there. So then we set off down the road first thing in the morning.

There were seven of us. Altogether there were four or five groups. Something like thirty men altogether. I don't remember exactly.

When we got some distance out of Hoit in the morning, after we'd gone about ten or fifteen kilometres, Abdulaziz and Yunus drove past us in a blue "Niva", and then Saifullo and Bilyal – they're from Namangan. They drove past in a Niva. They had guns. We didn't have any weapons. We were frightened, we thought they'd come to stop us, but no, they drove straight past us. And up in front of us there were those seventeen guys from the two or three groups that had joined together in one place. They were walking about twenty or twenty-five kilometres ahead of us. They were walking towards Dushanbe, and from Dushanbe they wanted to go back to Uzbekistan.

Well, they reached those other guys and said; "Where are you running off to? Without asking permission…" And they said: "We want to go to Uzbekistan." – "No, you're not going anywhere without permission!" And they said: "It's none of your business!" – "Ah, so that's it!" And they shot those seventeen young guys. Eleven from Khorezm, three from Tashkent, two from Bukhara, three from Navoi; one Abdulbatyr from Khorezm, then Umar, Rahmatulla, Abu Jihad, then Abdullah Yosin, Ahmad, Abdulmajid, Umid, Hairulla, Khamza, two Abdulhakims, Abuzar, and there was Muslimaka, Yusuf, Abdulkuddus and Nasrulla.

When you get there, it turns out they don't call you by your own name; when you get there, they change the names. Their names, the ones I remember were: Abdubatyr – Nazarov Fahridin; Yunusov Rihsi – he was Umar; Rahmatulla was Rajapov Husnuddin; Karimov Daniyar was Abu Jihad – he was from Khorezm too; Vafaev Bunyad – he was Abdula Yosin – he was from Khorezm too; Ibodulayev Mumijan was Ahmad; Hudaiberganov Ergash, another one from Khorezm – he was Abdulhakim; Abdulmajid was Islombek Ibodulaev; Atajanov Umid was Muhammad; Muminov Normurod was Hamza – he was from Bukhara; and there was another one called Himmatula…. He was from Navoi… .Muslimaka… he was from Khiva, I don't remember his name…. And there was Haroun too…. Anyway, they shot these young guys and took their good clothes off them, especially their shoes, the trainers, and they took the money out of their pockets… (he repeats this)… then they loaded these bodies into a KAMAZ truck and drove them to the village of Tajikabad and dumped them in a common pit and didn't even cover them with earth.

Then they stopped us, loaded us into the KAMAZ and sent us back to Hoit. About nine days later we said: "Let's go and take a look at the lads…

let's take a look at the lads..." We told the commander we wanted to find out who had been killed. They said "Okay" and took us there. By that time they'd been buried in the Tajikabad cemetery. We went and opened up the graves. We saw the lads lying there in a row.

In bloody clothes. The shoes had been pulled off lots of them. Their pockets were pulled inside out. We came back and we asked the commander by what authority the lads had been killed. We asked Abdulhakim, from Namangan. "That's none of your business, or ours!" he said.

Then a few days after that I ran off early in the morning with two others – Abdurahim and Abdurasul – we walked to Kyrgyzstan and reached Osh, and then used public transport. Lots of men want to go back to Uzbekistan. But now the commanders are all there. Abdulhakim is there, Jumabai came, Jumabai's there now, he arrived about a couple of weeks before we ran off. Tahir Yuldash isn't there. But what they're saying there is, we're going to build an Islamic state, although there aren't very many weapons there....

The recording broke off at that point, but Adiba finished the story. The young man went back to Uzbekistan and went to the militia with a confession, because by then the president had announced in one of his speeches that he would pardon anyone who came back and confessed. He was handed over to the NSS, who interrogated him for a long time and then sent him to Khorezm. But there things became absolutely intolerable. Every now and then the local militia brought him in for questioning and roughed him up, trying to beat more and more evidence out of him against his relatives, his acquaintances and the people who lived in the same village. Eventually, the young man could not stand anymore and he decided to run away. He got in touch with his people again through the old channels, and just when everything was ready for him to set out for the Turkmen border, the militia stormed the house he was in early in the morning.

Knowing what was in store for him, the young man blew himself up with a grenade, taking two militiamen with him....

It was from this recording that I learned that Haroun, i.e. Belgi's friend Bakh, had been killed by the guerrillas as he was trying to get back home....

Chapter Twenty-Five

Let him who gives me a shadow not hold me.
You know the breadth of a star
is not equal to the embrace of the ray.

Hamid Ismailov

> *Let me go, blue holy light,*
> *my shadow is in torment on the black earth.*
> *Am I drunk, or is my road drunk?*
>
> *The snow flows, the earth is white and black.*
> *The word 'I' is a wanderer like I,*
> *you are eternal as an icy, cracked puddle.*
>
> *Did we trip over our shadow*
> *or did the mirage melt in the icy pupil —*
> *a roof, holding up a lamp, when the house moved.*

-Belgi

After Haroun ran away in the late spring with two other young men from Khorezm, the imam Abdulaziz assigned his own overseer to Yosir and Umar. This young man, who was known as Saeed, had recently arrived from Chechnya, and by local standards he was extravagantly talkative.

Every story that Yosir was told by the refugees from Uzbekistan provoked a flood of memories from Saeed, and he could match every event in their lives with one from his own. While Yosir was at work in the house or the courtyard, processing the refugees' stories, with all their terrible details, Saeed never stopped telling the story of what had happened to him, how he also used to go to Imam Abduvali's mosque on Fridays and then, when the imam was picked up at the airport by the KGB, and everybody started going into hiding, he had gone away to Tashkent, where he used to trundle barrow-loads of goods around the race course market.

In Tashkent he had started visiting the Tokhtabai Mosque and listening to Obidhon-kori, but after Obidhon was dismissed, Saeed decided to go back to Andijan. Naturally, there was no work to be had at home and he quickly ran out of money. One day in the mosque he complained about this to a friend of his by the name of Abdukadyr, who took him to a house near the puppet theatre, where several men from various different places were living: Oibek from Khorezm, Bahadyr from Balykcha and a few other lads. Oibek was giving them lessons in the Koran.

The lads got him a job in a bakery that made *samsas*, or small meat pies, and he worked away there quietly, but one day when they were all praying together, they were raided by the militia, who took them all in to the central municipal station. They were separated into different cells, beaten and accused of disseminating *Wahhabism* and being

114

cutthroats and murderers. But then his father came for him and paid a lot of money to get him out.

He worked in the fields at his native village for a couple of months and then ran away back to Andijan, where the lads found him a job in an automobile spare parts shop. So he hung around there until October 1997, and then his friend Shuhrat told him about a chance to go to Alma-Ata and introduced him to a young man by the name of Izzat.

This Izzat said that there was a *hujra,* or hostel, at a madrasah where they taught the Koran and he was going there soon with a few other young men. In late October 1997, Saeed went back home and told his father that he was going away to study in Alma-Ata, and at seven o'clock the next morning he was at the place where Izzat was waiting for him. But that morning Izzat said he had only been testing him.

Three days later he came to the bus terminal again, as he had been told to, and there Izzat gave him and three other young men tickets for a flight from Tashkent to Minvody, then put them in a small Daewoo TIKO, gave them some money for the journey and sent them off to Tashkent. From Tashkent they flew to Minvody, where they were supposed to meet a man called Usman on the second floor of the airport building, but there was no Usman there. They phoned Shuhrat in Andijan and he told them: "Take the suburban train and go as far as Novotur Station, then get a taxi to Serzhantyurt and ask for Hattab, and they'll show you where to go".

So they went to Serzhantyurt and walked to the army base, which was guarded by several men. They did as Izzat had told them and asked for Ozodbek from Uzbekistan. After a while Ozodbek came out of the base and led them back inside, instead of taking them to the *hujra.* They were put in a room for five men. The Arabs did start teaching them the Koran, it's true, but as well as that they had military training, firing automatic weapons and flame-throwers, and they studied military map-making....

There were about a hundred and thirty Uzbeks there: Hotash, Hamza, Zubayir, Abbos, Umar the computer specialist, Bulbul, Ibrohim... they all had aliases. And they all swore on the Koran to be faithful to the Amir Tahir Yuldash, although he himself wasn't there.

Saeed spent three months there and returned to Andijan with a few other young men by the same route. In Andijan Izzat, who was really called Murad Kaziev, told him that he worked for Hattab and didn't take orders from anyone else, and he asked Saeed to draw up maps of the Hanabda military base and another base on Red Army Street. He did all this in a week. And then, through the second wife of one of the young men, they agreed with a Russian major called either Subutov or Subukov to buy armaments from the base – three crates of AKM bullets, six mines, thirty smoke bombs, ten ground flares and two sacks of camouflage

uniforms – all for four thousand dollars. The major also offered them some kind of poisonous substance, but Izzat noticed that its shelf-life had expired and refused to pay for it.

And then Izzat discussed various plans with them at Shuhrat's house: the idea was for him to go to Tashkent and he and the local "Chechen" lads would take Karimov's daughter hostage, or else he would load up a KAMAZ truck with explosives and drive it at full speed into the president's dacha at Durmen or, even better, attack the American embassy. Basically, that he would do something that Hattab himself would be proud of.

Soon Izzat went away and his place in Andijan was taken by a young lad called Ikromiddin, and they started making an explosive substance in a huge cooking-pot at Azizbek's house, out of nine sacks of nitrate fertilizer that they bought and ground down in an electric coffee mill, two sacks of sulphur and a barrel of aluminium powder. Then they tested the substance at the stream outside the town, and stunned fish that drifted away with the current. Ikromiddin told them that a jihad was planned for spring, when the snow melted in the mountains of Tajikistan, that the Taliban would get as far as Termez, and Juma Namangani and his troops would drive into the valley on twenty-five KAMAZ trucks, and that was when they would have to explode all this substance, when the command came down from above ....

But the explosions came a lot sooner than that, on February 16, and neither the Taliban, nor Jumaboi invaded Uzbekistan. Then Saeed and the other lads in Andijan realised there was something wrong, so they phoned Ikromiddin, who was in Bishkek at the time, and then went for an urgent meeting with him, and from there they went back to Chechnya, to see Hattab.

And it was there, in one of one-armed Hattab's camps in Shali, that Saeed saw Izzat, who boasted that he was the one who had arranged the explosions in Tashkent, but when Saeed asked him if there had been orders from Tahir, Izat said: "I don't take orders from any Tahir-Pahir, I have only one commander – Hattab!"

Chapter Twenty-Six

Days, when it rains
or
the wait for the child at music school
or
bitter thoughts in astrology
sudden tripping over

A Poet and Bin-Laden

or
crossing the threshold, receiving a letter in a dream
the style of Shamshad
absent-mindedness in the country
the thudding steps
the crying wires
link after link

if even linking the empty words one to the other
you consider their collection to be the justification of your life
why support a person or give a ring
or
the days of musical instruments, when the stars rain?

-Belgi

Tahir Yuldash never accepted responsibility for the bombings in Tashkent. He admitted to the jihad and subsequent armed forays at Batken and Saryasy, but as for the explosions, he several times denied categorically having anything at all to do with them.

Here is an interview given to the BBC while the trial was actually taking place in Tashkent by the head of the Supreme Council of the Islamic Movement of Uzbekistan and the press-secretary of the movement, Zubair ibn Abdurahim.

Zubair: In the name of God the Gracious and Merciful. We have given statements on this event previously, our policy is a clear policy: when we do something, we say that we have done it, but if we have not done something, then we say that we did not do it. In our policy there is no duplicity. And therefore we say that we had no involvement with the events of February 16.

Question: According to a statement from the Kyrgyzstan Information Agency, Tahir Yuldash has begun uniting all the opposition forces: Hizbut-Tahrir, Birlik, Erk. How reliable is this report?

Zubair: This report is far from the truth since, first of all, these movements, who call themselves the opposition to the regime in Uzbekistan, would have to work things out and come to an agreement among themselves. Until this has happened, any aspiration to unite them is – in our opinion – an illusion. But let it be said that we have no personal conflict with the regime, our disagreements are ideological. Until our principles are accepted, the disagreements will not be resolved.

Question: By that, do you mean that you will continue your so-called jihad? It was reported recently that Juma Namangani and Tahir Yuldash still have about 700 fighting men in Tajikistan. How accurate is this report?

Zubair: Yes, we did declare a jihad, and that jihad is still going on. But as far as the fighting men are concerned, there is no truth in this, and the significance of this report – as we understand it – is that the coward is the first to put up his fists. But our jihad continues.

Question: When you speak of a jihad, do you mean military action, that is, do you wish to introduce to Uzbekistan what has been happening for more than ten years already in Afghanistan, or does your jihad imply something different?

Zubair: Allah be praised, when mention is made of jihad, there are several meanings to this, including the meaning of military action, but what we have declared is a struggle against an oppressive regime and the replacement of the constitutional order by the Sharia law of Allah. But not to such an extent as you say. We have our own blueprints, our own plans, but, of course, this will all be achieved by military means.

Chapter Twenty-Seven

Let this evening go, let it go,
throw it away, don't cling onto it, close your eyes, close the window.
The cloud will fade, the birds will fall silent, the silver dust
will lower itself quietly onto the roof, taking pity on you.

Is what you preserved this girl in the photograph?
Before summer had started the leaves had torn themselves from the trees.
Let this evening go, it means nothing to you,
throw it away, don't cling onto it,
one of these days you...
one of these days you...

-Belgi

The trial of the individuals accused of organising the bombings on February 16 took place in June 1999. Hamid Ismailov, one of the members of the press accredited to cover the proceedings from inside the courtroom, recalls:

The trial took place in the building of the Supreme Court of Uzbekistan, and all the approaches to this building were cut off by cordons of militiamen and soldiers from the interior forces. Snipers in military uniform could be seen on the roofs of the surrounding buildings, in short, extreme security measures had been put in place. Journalists accredited to cover the proceedings had to pass through several control points and only then, after a body search, were they allowed into the courtroom.

The courtroom resembled the hall of an ordinary Soviet cultural institution or club, with about twenty rows of bare chairs with metal legs set close together. Most of them were occupied by the families of the victims, members of the militia and NSS and a few journalists. In the far right-hand corner there was a huge iron cage with the seventeen accused inside it and several armed soldiers standing around it – the cage itself was the first thing to catch my eye, since the people on the other side of the bars looked no different from those sitting all around. They were young men, dressed in their own clothes, their heads hadn't been cropped, they hadn't been shaved – some of them had moustaches, as if they had only just been picked up and brought here. This contrast between their ordinary appearance and what they were supposed to have done was probably the most difficult thing to take in immediately.

From inside the cage it was possible to look around to the sides and forward at the podium where judge and the people's assessors would sit. The courtroom looked at the accused, and they in turn tried to spot at least one familiar or well-disposed face in the courtroom.

After the classic call of "All rise for the judge" (to which a member of the journalistic brotherhood beside me responded with a habitual comical whisper: "All hail to our Soviet court, the most humane court in the world") and the clatter of chairs that followed, the trial itself began and went on for several days, if not two weeks.

I can't remember now all the details that we journalists discussed until we were hoarse, but that is probably for the best, although I must say that at the time I recorded the entire trial from start to finish on tape, and I listened through the tapes after every session. But the reason I say it is all for the best is because with the passage of time, the most important points that I took from that trial have remained stuck in my mind.

I should say that the first thing that really struck me was the sheer motley variety of the group of accused. Their supposed crime was being presented as the work of a tightly organised criminal gang capable of the kind of planning that had almost cost the President his life, but the people in the dock could hardly have been a more mixed bag; from killers to army officers, from businessmen to jobless hobos, from fervent readers of the Koran to Uzbeks who didn't understand the Uzbek language.

It was this very variety that lent the trial an atmosphere of the everyday, in the sense that anyone, including me, could have found himself behind those bars. For instance, when the press secretary of the Islamic Movement of Uzbekistan, Zainiddin Askarov, whom I knew under the name of Abdurahman Mansur, and whom I had interviewed several times on the phone, turned in my direction and declared: "I was instructed by Tahir Yuldash to read out statements that he sent me by fax, and I immediately recited them to various foreign radio stations: Ozodlik, the BBC – Hamid Ismailov ..."

Of course, Zainiddin was being cunning, since he had given those interviews in his own name, but this cunning, which emerged in his sudden exclamation: "Well then, oh cursed of God, who did explode these bombs?" and the highly colourful stories in which he stigmatised Solih for having his head in the clouds and called him *Hayolbek* or "Mr. Dreamer",

and the way he tried to convince everyone that he was a European karate champion and had met the presidents of fifteen countries, ultimately won him a reduction of almost a third of the sentence demanded by the Public Prosecutor, while the others of his calibre, such as Bahrom Abdullaev, were rewarded with the death penalty for their dignified brevity.

"So, when Zainiddin said that, there was absolutely no guarantee that the militia officers sitting close by would not come across to me and slap a pair of handcuffs on my wrists, after all, the men there in the dock had just about as much to do with the explosions as I did, if you discounted the one or two who had actually carried them out. But those few men were the ones who were most "zombified" and controlled by somebody else's will.

Chapter Twenty-Eight

*Like someone who climbs a ladder
I stretch my arms into the future.*

*Like a man on skis
so as not to fall I slide,
slide into the distance.*

*My future is the air,
my past — the ice.*

I've missed my brother, my brother....

-Belgi

That Zainiddin was attempting to be cunning is also made clear by the following interview that he gave to one of the foreign radio channels at the time when he was press secretary of the Islamic Movement of Uzbekistan and known by the name of Abdurahman Mansur. In it he comments on the killings in Namangan and subsequent events.

Question: The men who have been convicted in Namangan and Tashkent, are they from your movement, or have they no connection with you?

AM: The men who have been arrested and convicted now, and the ones before them – they have no connections with our organisation, but they are Muslims, and therefore we sympathise with them. They have not undergone any training with us and they have nothing to do with us.

Question: they are accused of Wahhabism. Do you regard your movement as Wahhabite?

AM: In Central Asia all Muslims belong to the mazhab, or school, of Imam Agzam and are called ahli sunnah da jamaa (people of Tradition and Community). No one there calls himself a Wahhabite. In particular our movement, that of Tahir Yuldash, is not Wahhabite, since Wahhabism is a movement founded on Arab nationalism, for that we would have to be Arabs, but since we are Turks, we are ahli sunnah da jamaa, and not Wahhabites. This is a propaganda term, invented by the KGB in the 1970s in order to divide the Muslims of Central Asia. Even if there were any truth in this Wahhhabism, the mufti Muhammad Sadyk is not a Wahhabite, but he has been attacked, Muhammad Solih, Abdurahim Pulat, all the men who have been arrested now, they have been attacked. Now they say that they are waging a struggle against Wahhabism, but in fact a front is being opened against Islam. There is nothing else in this.

Question: Let us accept that the men who have now been convicted of Wahhabism have nothing to do with you, but why are they accused of having been trained in the guerrilla camps? What is behind this?

AM: What is behind this is the following reality. The men who are called guerrillas in Uzbekistan are armed by Karimov. In what sense? Karimov oppresses the people so badly that they are forced to take up arms. Whether they acknowledge us or not, they are obliged to take up arms, and having caught two or three such people, on this pretext they arrest the others, calling them guerrillas, but Karimov's oppression is arousing the people and forcing them to take up arms. That is what is behind this.

Question: The president of Tajikistan, Imomali Rahmonov, has announced that he has appealed to the opposition to hand over to Uzbekistan forty-five Uzbek guerrillas who are presently on the territory of Tajikistan. Are these forty-five your men?

AM: We have five or six thousand armed mujahedin in Tajikistan under the leadership of Tahir Yuldash and the military commander Jumaboi Namangani. Their leaders are Uzbeks from Namangani, Tashkent and everywhere. But when they say that there are forty-five guerrillas there, and say, if we tell the opposition, then they'll catch them for us, then that is Rahmonov, Yeltsin and Karimov uniting, and the local "commandos" here have been fighting for five or six years against the Tajik government, against the Russian communists, and they have excellent battle experience. Therefore, all we can say is that the union of Yeltsin, Karimov and Rahmonov will only unite the Muslims of Tajikistan, Uzbekistan, Kyrgyzstan, Kazakhstan and all Central Asia. But even if they try to detain them, these experienced mujahedin are capable of defending themselves. Yes, this really is our group. And not just in Tajikistan, but in Afghanistan too, and not forty-five, as Karimov says, but many more.

Question: The interior ministers of several countries are presently meeting in Tashkent, and intend to establish a Committee for the Struggle

Against Wahhabism, against extremists. What is your assessment of this decision?

AM: They call it Wahhabism, but in actual fact these actions are intended, together with Israel, America and Russia, to destroy Islam in Central Asia. In fact, this "Wahhabism" has never existed from the beginning. But whether a committee is being set up or not is of little interest to us. In any case, we shall continue our struggle. But you should know that Wahhabism is only a pretext. Now we shall see that in Uzbekistan they will start to arrest anyone who is a believer, who even goes to the mosque. And from this it follows that their goal is to destroy Islam in Central Asia. Here I wish to say that if defending our people, defending women behind the veil, men with beards, defending our homeland, defending our religion – if this is Wahhabism, if this is terrorism, if this is treason to our homeland, then we are prepared to call ourselves by such a name. But if attempts to eliminate Muslims are made against this, to arrest them and plant marijuana in their pockets, frightening people by saying there are armed forces in Tajikistan and Afghanistan, and all this is called independence, love for the homeland, then we are against this kind of independence and we do not consider that Uzbekistan has become independent. Uzbekistan needs another forty years to become independent.

Question: You say on the one hand that you have armed forces in Tajikistan and Afghanistan, but then you immediately say that the government frightens people with the presence of armed forces. Do you not see any contradiction in this? So are there any armed forces there, and if there are, against whom are they being prepared to fight?

AM: These armed forces exist. But we wish to say..... I was in error, when I said they frighten the people. They frighten the Tajik opposition, saying if you do not give up the Uzbeks, you will not be given a place in the government and so forth. But I wish to say that our forces are even greater than the forces of the Tajik oppositionists. That is, I wish to say, let them not frighten the Tajikis with this, since we have very experienced forces in Tajikistan.

Question: The Uzbek government recently claimed that Pakistan is involved with the camps where your people are trained. How closely does this claim correspond to reality? What are your ties with Pakistan and other countries in the matter of military camps?

AM: Our camps, like the places where we acquire weapons, where our training takes place – all of this is in Afghanistan. None of this is in Pakistan. But this does not mean that we do not have any ties with Pakistan. For instance, we maintain relations with Afghanistan, Pakistan and other countries where there is a jihad movement, and there are more than fifty of them. When necessary, we assist these organisations, and when it is necessary, they will assist us. Now you see that Karimov, Rahmonov, Yeltsin, Israel, America and Russia are uniting, and we too are uniting, although unofficially, with all the mujahedin throughout the world, and since presidents Karimov and Rahmonov seek to live in this world, in order to restore Islam in Central Asia, we are equally prepared

to face death. Therefore, if tomorrow we take to the battlefield, Pakistan and Afghanistan and other Islamic states will rise up after us. We have connections, but not to the extent that the KGB reports to Karimov. In Pakistan now the conditions for camps do not exist. We state quite frankly that our camps are in Afghanistan, our mujahedin are in Tajikistan and we are in both these countries.

Question: Since you have mentioned Afghanistan, does the seventeen-year history of fratricidal war in Afghanistan have anything to teach you, or do you want the same thing for Uzbekistan?

AM: There is one thing you should understand: whether what you speak of will happen or not depends on Karimov and Rahmonov, who carry out orders received from Israel, America and Russia. If they stop oppressing the people, release those who have been arrested illegally, if they stop closing mosques and madrasahs, if they allow freedom of religious practice, then we do not wish for any bloodshed, since Islam is a superior system, founded on kindness. But if Karimov and his henchman continue the oppression, Allah has ordered us in the Koran to carry out a jihad, to kill the infidels, to free the Muslims. And we shall continue to follow this path. But what is happening in Afghanistan, where one group is supported by Russia and another by America, and yet another by Israel – eight factions have taken shape there. From these seventeen years of war in Afghanistan, in Chechnya, in Bosnia, we have acquired immense experience, and so, if we start something in Afghanistan, Tajikistan, Kyrgyzstan, Kazakhstan, in short, throughout all of Turkestan, Allah grant that we shall not fall into this delusion and before long shall liberate Turkestan from the oppression of Karimov and others.

Question: How far do you think that you reflect the thoughts and hopes of the people of Uzbekistan? Perhaps the majority of the people of Uzbekistan are against you?

AM: Concerning people being against us, yes, at first many were against us. But Karimov has managed to make them sympathise with us. At first many people's heads were full of Karimov's propaganda, which said "they are armed terrorists", but the people can see that this is not just an attack against Tahir Yuldash or Muhammad Solih, this is an attack against any Muslim in Uzbekistan, against any person who has money. And that is why almost seventy per cent of the population of Uzbekistan is on our side. Whether it is a man who prays to God or does not pray, a democrat or a nationalist – they all, together, wish to do something about the oppression that has come about in Uzbekistan. And therefore, even those who did not sympathise with us are now seeking contacts with us and wish to unite with us. And so we believe that the time has come to give an answer to the regime that oppresses the people.

Question: Let's continue on this line. Tell me, do you have connections with the democratic forces of opposition?

AM: The democratic, nationalist and other movements know us from a distance and we are familiar with them. We are connected with

some of them by phone, or through published journals, and they are also familiar with us. Our movement is not planning to join with the democratic movements, with the Abdurahims, with Muhammad Solih, with Shukrulla Mirsaidov, but when we take to the field of battle, and they come to us saying "You have been proved right", then we can let them join us. However, we shall not join them, our unity consists only in the fact that, since they are opposed to Karimov, we can exchange opinions on the reasons for this confrontation. But just as Karimov is against us, against men with beards, against armed Islamists, they too have so far been against us. They do not want us. But we say to them: "Whether you want it or not, we have already taken our decision and we will respond to oppression by means of arms, if the regime will not agree to accept our demands peacefully". If they phone, we answer, but so far we have not had any joint council about to what to do, or any joint assembly.

Question: You say that you will take to the battlefield. What does that mean? Starting military operations against Uzbekistan?

AM: The programme of our military actions, when they begin, will be announced by the amir of our movement, Muhammad Tahir Farruk, but if you look more widely at what is happening in Central Asia, it is that Israel, America and Russia are trying to destroy Islam and implant Judaism, Baha'ism, Christianity and Krishnaism, and trying to restore the idolatry that existed three or four thousand years ago. And therefore, even if we succeed in establishing out Sharia rule, we shall take to the battlefield against all this Judaism and Christianity and Krishnaism that is being implanted. And if we take to the battlefield, it will not be against Karimov personally, but against Russia, the Jews, the Baha'is, the Christians, we shall fight against them all. After that our goal is the unification of Turkestan – these five republics – and the construction of a state based on genuine justice. Within this there are many secrets that will be proclaimed to the world as the battle begins. In due time this will be announced to you by our military commander, Jumaboi Namangani, or by the Amir Tahir.

Question: How certain are you that the peoples of Central Asia will follow you?

AM: We cannot help but know, whether we have consulted with the people or not, that the people are ready to explode, because they are hungry, they have no money left, they have been completely cut off from religion: look, they shave off men's beards wherever they see them, they tear away women's chadras, the oppression is universal. Wherever the call is from, the people will not wait, but rise up. And there are millions like that in Central Asia. So we shall continue to struggle for their liberation, although we do not claim that so-and-so many thousands in Uzbekistan support us, or so-and-so many in some other place. But we trust in our strength and intend to start a holy war. If this oppression does not end, then we shall fight, not against the people of Uzbekistan, but against the oppression of dictators who are today introducing Zionism and Freemasonry into their countries. We wish to restore to Turkestan the system from its historical past.

Chapter Twenty-Nine

During the summer of that year, every night Yosir continued the "log book" that he had inherited from Haroun after his friend decided to run off, and he wrote down everything said about the trial by "Ozodlik" and the BBC, and especially the details from the court room itself, and then, as well as that, during the day he wrote down the constantly multiplying stories from members of households of the arrested men on trial, from their relatives and the relatives of those relatives. He no longer understood who he was writing all this down for, after all, no one was interested in these terrible stories, which were all alike, each one differing only in its own specific pain.

No, if there was anything that interested the commanders, then it was the words spoken at the trial by one or another of the accused, and after those words of confession, they either swore at the "snivelling traitors" or boasted that they had always known these men couldn't be trusted, even when they were close to them.... In fact, the number of men who had been close to them before this could be counted on the fingers of one hand, but they were the ones who came in for the worst abuse.

The killer Jura, who had been introduced to Yosir by the sparse-bearded Imam Abdulaziz, was among them, and he was berated most of all by his old accomplice, for he told the court all about their raids on people's houses, and then how they had planned all sorts of scenarios for kidnapping the president's daughter and raiding his mansion and seizing the US ambassador, and even how he himself had tested the explosive quality of a mixture of ground nitrate fertilizer, aluminium powder and sulphur – he even told them that. "Police informer!" the imam said once, but no one paid any attention to these words.

The point was that, after that bloody mess with those seventeen men from Khorezm, Juma Namangani and Tahir Yuldash had immediately come to Hoit. Nobody knew what had happened in the "commander's bunker", but everyone who knew Imam Abdulaziz even slightly had noticed that recently he had become even more nervous and hysterical. The word was that he had fallen out of favour because this whole business had come into the open – the radio "voices" talked about him, and the refugees said there were articles about him in the Uzbek press. But after the mass arrests, Tahir had probably been infected by the same nervousness, and that was why the imperturbable Juma, who had not lost any of his men, apart from those seventeen, suddenly acquired such a prominent role. The word was that he was the one who had told the imam what he thought about everything and threatened him that he could only wash away this blood with more blood...

Yosir certainly knew about this fall from grace, for the "summaries" that he prepared regularly went to the so-called "leadership" of the movement, the *Shuro*, or Supreme Council. After almost half of the previous Council had been arrested, a new one was appointed, and Imam Abdulaziz's name was not on it.... In addition to Tahir and Juma, it included Zubair ibn Abdurahim as chairman of the council and a new press secretary, to whom Yosir supposedly reported directly; the head of counterintelligence was Ali from Tashkent, whom everyone addressed politely, either because he knew so many languages, or out of fear of the position he held; "Ustoz" was the Jordanian Uzbek Abu Anas, who supposedly handled not only intelligence operations, but also communications with the Arab world; and there was also Bilol, who worked as a kind of policeman for the Council, and Sobithon-kori, the head of the Sharia law section – Yosir used to meet him too, since he was also in charge of publishing matters. Apart from them, there were also less important commanders, from the general council of the movement, but Yosir didn't send his "summaries" to them, the "top" commanders must have sent copies on to them afterwards.

Haroun was killed trying to go back home, after Yosir and Umar had left for Afghanistan on the orders of their commander Zubair: they had to discuss when and how to release the video and the book about this exodus of refugees. That was when he saw most of those "top leaders" of the Islamic Movement of Uzbekistan to whom he sent his summaries of the "voices". That was when the Amir came into the room on Vazir Akbarhon Street, where Yosir and Zubair were watching the shots for the video, as they had permission to do in the Taliban's Afghanistan, and said that they needed to think about their own radio, broadcasting from Mazari Sharif, that they needed people like Yosir, and the Sheikh would give them money for this business straight away. Yosir didn't dare to ask who this Sheikh was and, in any case, it was not the done thing here to ask questions.

They often prayed together with this "supreme leadership" and several Taliban members who were always hanging around, although Yosir didn't know their names or their positions. But after the initial curiosity: "Man haza?" ("Who's this?") no one bothered him. And then, during the prayers, when for a while this interminable hierarchy (who was subordinate to whom?) stood in straight lines and bent double, Yosir would be visited by a sense of community, not with these sparse-bearded young men, but with some "golden period" of Samarkand, Bukhara and Delhi, he seemed to be praying with Ibn-Sina and Beruni, Navoi and Babur, Ulugbek and Mashrab... And when he came round again in the company of these "commanders" after his prayers, he suddenly felt like the only keeper in the entire world of this culture that had been abandoned, left with no one to tend it, that had been torn down like

Herat, where he had been a few days earlier. And at those moments he felt so lonely that he wanted to wail, wail so loudly that he would be heard by the whole of Afghanistan, which was called "the country of wails".

Later he would think over this fleeting experience of one-and-a-half-months of Afghanistan, but now, when he had returned to Hoit and was sitting in his clay hut after hearing from the garrulous Saeed that his friend Haroun – no, now he was simply Alisher – had run off and left him and Umar here, that feeling of the "land of wails" seemed to be spreading right around the entire huge world, like the radio waves that he was waiting for here, that filled up this little room, and the whole dark, cold village, all the way to the mountain camp behind the ancient Soviet fence, where in the barracks hundreds more of those "commanders" were getting ready for bed.

And this was the time when his work began.

Chapter Thirty

After his night shifts, Yosir was allowed time to sleep in the morning, but to a certain extent he could manage this time as he thought best: for instance, if he rose early and sat reading the Koran, or joined someone going into the mountains for firewood, no one would criticize him for that. After these spells of "court duty", following the trial, he was unable to sleep, and instead of wasting time tossing from side to side on his bed, he would set off into the mountains with his head on fire.

There is beauty in nature, and even greater beauty in the recollection of nature, but in his present life and his present company, such concepts had no reality, and even within Yosir himself they had gradually been eroded away. The mountains that he had admired in pictures in another life were there to provide cover, to be surmounted, to provide firewood for the winter, and even the knowledge that beyond them lay that same old life with the beauty of nature and the beauty of its recollection no longer touched his hard-baked soul.

How can the sense of beauty remain alive in a body that is barely surviving, or is in pain because it lies beyond the bounds of beauty? How pointless, how idle this sense seems amid the mess of war, where only your instincts and the strength of your grip are of any importance. Only occasionally would age-old landscapes from the most incredible times and places come to him as the recollection of a recollection: a rust-coloured lake in the middle of a shadowy spring forest, a fat fish splashing out and back into the water, circles spreading all the way to the distant

banks, the circles making startled ducks glance back over their shoulders towards the centre of the explosion and quack in a half-whisper to their offspring.... Or the endless shingle of the sea in the motion of its eternal laundering... Or the red and blue glow of stained glass, illuminated by the darkness of a cathedral....

What meaning did these beauties of light have in this place, or in the prison in which his friend Alisher, known here by the alias of Haroun, must have been shut away after he ran off? What meaning did they have in his present life, which he could not remember ever having wanted, which had taken him by surprise, like a sudden snowfall in the mountains in May....

The meaning of his life became less and less clear, the more emphatically it was pointed out to him by those "commanders": for him, the vengeful and bellicose God with whom they constantly frightened him here, had always been light.... the gentle light of the heavens and the earth.... a light like the light from the niche in his grandmother's little clay house, the niche with the old lamp standing in it... the lamp enclosed in glass on which his grandmother would breathe with her warm, pure breath as she cleaned it long and lovingly.... and the soft cotton fibres made the glass gleam as purely as a brilliant star.... Lit from a blessed Tree, an Olive, neither of the East nor of the West, whose oil is well-nigh luminous, though fire scarce touched it... mysterious words... the oil on the murmuring wick burned almost without being touched by the flame.... Light upon Light... and his grandmother would whisper: Allah doth guide whom He will to His Light....

And so, drowned in this blinding light, he wept amid those snowy-white mountains, and with frozen fingers he wrote a single word in the hard-set snow: Allah....

Chapter Thirty-One

And this time what I say
makes no sense...

the same place again,
the same rain, the same quagmire of mud,
the same roofs, the same landscape,

the same sad standing,
the trousers hung on the wire and not drying,

A Poet and Bin-Laden

the same choice,
feeling, as though attached to this space,

or rather the same thought,
and not the thought — a bitter and sharp
doubt, attached to this space:

if space returns, but time does not,
yet what does sadness that has named the draught
still search for in the interval?

-Belgi

In August 1999 the guerrillas broke through into the Batken region of Kyrgyzstan, taking hostage not only several Japanese geologists, but also a general of the Kyrgyz army. This was the beginning of the so-called "Batken war". During one of those autumn days of high tension, the Amir walked into Zubair's room and threw three newspaper clippings down on to his desk. "Learn how to write!" he said, then turned round and walked out. The articles were in Russian, and since Zubair did not have a very good command of this language of the infidels, that same day he asked Yosir to translate the articles into Uzbek as well as he could, and Yosir sat down to the translation.

The Hostage's life

The bearded cutthroats have been holding thirteen men hostage for more than two weeks. This is their trump card, their guarantee that the Kyrgyz forces will not take any drastic measures. For more than two weeks, all the international information agencies have been waiting with bated breath to see what ransom the mujahedin will demand for four foreign citizens, one of our generals and several militiamen.

And in the remote Kyrgyz village of Samarkandyk one woman has not slept a wink for more than two weeks. She is the wife of militia sergeant Kasym Shadybekov, one of the hostages. His four little children do not understand the full meaning of what is happening, but the older daughters, who already go to school, try to help their mother and do everything she tells them to. This is a very hard time for her.

Almost every day for the first two weeks Zamira left her children and her household in the charge of her elderly mother and travelled to the regional centre of Betken, about sixty kilometres from her village. There she laid siege to the doors of high officials and officers of the armed forces, demanding: "Bring back my husband!" The hearts of these statesmen and colonels were wrung by the sight of this woman with her tear-stained face. They did their best to reassure her, explained the situation in the region of the village of Zardaly, to which Sergeant Shadybekov was posted from

the Tayan district militia office during those days of high tension. But the woman kept repeating: "Why could you find the money to pay for the governor, but you can't find any for a simple militiaman?"

This woman's grief rejects the strategy and the tactics of this senseless military conflict. She wants her husband, the father of her children, their breadwinner.

When men from the governor's office and the rural authorities appeared in the doorway of her house, the poor woman's heart almost burst. "Could something really have happened to Kasym?" she thought. A sack of flour, five hundred Soms, rucksacks for school, clothes, a few medicines. "This is humanitarian aid for you, while you have no breadwinner," said the governor of the Batken Region, A.M. Mamataliev, who knows from personal experience what it is like to be a hostage. But the woman started to cry, she was afraid that all this was only because her husband was no longer alive.

"But he's alive, he's alive," they all reassured her. "The shepherds have seen him!"

"I don't want anything. All I want is him!" the woman cried and carried on wailing. Behind her, her mother and Kasym's sister began crying too. Only two sturdy toddlers, Kasym's little sons, just sat there, blinking in confusion. At that moment a lump rose in everyone's throat.

I don't know if those bandits have wives and children in the mountains, if there is anyone waiting for them, anyone who loves them. But I do know that nowhere in the Koran does it say that this is the Muslim way – making children orphans.

Leila SARALAEVA

The second article was clearly from the same newspaper. The face of the young man in the photograph had been blanked out by the Amir's own pen, leaving nothing but a sturdy wounded body bearing a face that was completely black.

The confession of a "warrior of Allah"

Looking at him, you would never guess that this youth with eyelashes as long and soft as a girl's and a clear, innocent look in his eyes believes that he is a warrior of Allah and has deliberately come to our country in order to kill. Indeed, it would be hard to believe this, if not for the bloody trail that he has left behind him and his firm conviction that he and other blind young adventurers like him can "turn the whole of deluded humanity to the one true faith".

Ulugbek Mahmudov, a 22-year-old Uzbek from Tashkent, was detained at a blockhouse manned by a consolidated Interior Forces unit at the village of Kara-Bak in the Batken district between nine and ten in the evening of September 19. When he was detained the following items were confiscated: a Kalashnikov automatic rifle with two magazines (24 and 26 bullets), a home-made knife, a compass, prayer beads, a soldier's belt, maps of Uzbekistan and the Osh region.

During a body search a tattoo was discovered on his right forearm: the banner of Islam with an inscription in Arabic: "Allah Akbar".

My conversation with the "true warrior of Allah" took place immediately after the Kyrgyz operational officers had contacted their Uzbek colleagues and learned that U. Mahmudov was wanted by the interior ministry of Uzekistan for a very grave crime.

"Ulugbek, when did you first meet people who preach the ideas of Islam?"

"I used to live and study in Chimkent. In 1992 my mother, father, brother and I moved to near Tashkent. There I finished twelve classes of school by correspondence. Then I worked as a graphic designer in a provincial department. About three years ago I started going to the mosque in our neighbourhood. Usually it was after the evening *namaz*. About twenty young men like me would gather. First we studied Arabic and memorised the Koran. And then the politics started."

"Did you sense straight away what your mentors were leading up to, or was it all disguised?"

"No, not really. They expounded the ideas of Islam quite openly. And I studied voluntarily. The threats only began after I started dragging my feet in carrying out an order from my mullah to find my cousin Hasan, who had run off to the Jeretal district of Tajikistan straight after the terrorist attacks in Tashkent. They even called me on the phone: 'You're the only one left. When are you going to follow your brother students?' By that time all the young guys I'd been going to the mosque with in the evening really had disappeared in some mysterious way. I was very afraid for my relatives. The men who phoned made open threats: 'If you don't go in September, your whole family will suffer'. So I got a move on ..."

"...And you found yourself in the Batken District. How did you come to be in Kara-Bak?"

"I made several attempts to join the guerrillas and failed, but eventually I succeeded. A friend of mine got me a job as a driver at a company making maps. I often used to drive out to the Uzbek-Kyrgyz border. With maps of the locality, you understand, there was no real problem. I just had to get myself a gun. My teachers told me that a warrior who took his weapon from the enemy was especially respected. One night I attacked a sentry, took his AKM, with two magazines, and set out along the Darin Gorge..."

"Now you know that private Rahimov, who happens to be the same age as you, is still in a coma since you hit him over the head several times with a hammer, do you regret what you did?"

"Believe me, I feel very bad about it. But I had no other way out. Even if I hadn't done it, there was no way I could have gone back home: my brother is fighting against Karimov, and I've been through the training too. I'm afraid for my relatives ..."

"As far as I'm aware, all religions, including Islam, are opposed to any violence, not to mention the killing of innocent people. You must have heard about the outrageous atrocities committed by the guerrillas here in Kyrgyzstan. You knew about that, but you still came to help them. Doesn't that make you an apostate?"

"Yes, our faith rejects all manifestations of cruelty, but in the Koran it also says that a long time ago the prophet Muhammad led holy wars against the infidels. And today there is a struggle going on for the establishment of a unified Islamic state."

"If you had the chance now to send a letter to your brother Hasan, what would it say?"

"I would tell him not to believe in the ideas of fundamentalism. Because while I was on my way to find him, I heard too many stories from the Kyrgyz people about all the 'heroic deeds' of the warriors of Islam. Let him come down from the mountains, and see for himself the old man in Zardaly whose last cow was taken away by his brothers-in-arms. And about myself I would write: I'll serve my time and then definitely get married – in their sleep our mother and father see grandchildren in the yard of our house…"

P.S. *An hour after my conversation with Ulugbek, there was a call from the Interior Ministry of Uzbekistan: Private Rahimov had died without regaining consciousness, and Ulugbek Mahmudov's mother and father had committed suicide*

S. SIDOROV

Concerning the third article, the Amir said: "When you've had it translated, show it to me, and then it has to be faxed to Jumaboi!" – and he gave a crooked smile.

Namangani's Kingdom

We have come into possession of some extremely interesting travel notes by a foreign doctor who travelled to the Jirgatal district last year. The first time he was stopped on Tajik territory was by a patrol of Juma's guerrillas in a UAZ jeep. After checking the doctor's documents and rucksack, the guerrillas warned him…. that he must register with the village council. In a gesture of farewell, one member of the patrol aimed his automatic rifle at the foreigner and laughed. A joke.

The second thing that astounded the doctor was the desperate way the children of the household where he was staying threw themselves on the food he had brought. "There are supplies of food in the village," he writes, sharing his discoveries, "but they are almost all concentrated in the storehouses of the field commander Namangani. As the local inhabitants later told me, in order to survive in the districts controlled by Namangani, they have to carry out various kinds of instructions from his armed men, participating in the smuggling of narcotics out of Afghanistan and the transportation of guns from there. The locals who work for Namangani receive at least some money or food for their labour. The others have to struggle to survive: either they are helped out by relatives from other districts, or they are forced to keep cattle and grow vegetables and fruit. However, constant requisitioning by the guerrillas seriously reduces the rations of local inhabitants like these. Naturally, I

wondered if the situation could really be the same in other districts. My question was answered by an old man who has lived in this village all his life. He told me that by no means all the field commanders had such a bad reputation. The old man believed that Namangani's guerrillas were so hard on the local inhabitants because they had no roots here: 'They're only here temporarily,' he said, 'practically all of them are ethnic Uzbeks, not many can speak Tajik'.

"After that conversation I had more questions than answers. What were Uzbek guerrilla fighters doing on Tajik territory? Why did the other field commanders allow Namangani to treat their own fellow- countrymen so badly? My local translator immediately asked me not to ask any more questions. To get to the bottom of everything, I needed to talk directly with people who knew about Namangani not just from hearsay, but had met him in person."

Soon the doctor was given just such an opportunity. He was taken to treat a wounded guerrilla, a junior commander from one of Namangani's units. The hard-baked warrior, whose name was Rashid, gradually grew to trust the doctor, who managed to get him to open up.

"Rashid used to live in the Namangan region. After he came home from the army he was unable to find work for a long time. Cruel fate turned him into a thief, and he used to travel to Tashkent to steal. He gathered a group of several other men around himself, but their career in stealing didn't last long – they were arrested. One member of the gang had an uncle who worked in the local militia, and he helped his nephew and Rashid and the other accomplices whose families could find the money for a bribe to get out of jail before the trial.

"That was when they met a recruiting agent who offered to take them all as fighting men for the so- called Namangan battalion" that was commanded by Namangani. The recruiting agent promised a good life not just for them, but for their families too. Emphasising that otherwise they would end up behind bars anyway, he promised to make real men of them by sending them for training in Afghanistan or Pakistan. He said that the training given to the "seals" in the USA or the "black berets" in Russia was nothing, compared with the training they would get.

"The result was that Rashid and his friends found themselves in the Afghani province of Faizabad on a three-month training course in sabotage, where they were taught the basics of fighting a partisan war – in particular, how to organise raids behind enemy lines, how to blow up public utilities and communication facilities, how to plan and carry out the physical elimination of state officials. When I said that these are all terrorist acts, Rashid nodded and said his instructors had not tried to hide that, but they had justified these acts as necessary for the victory of Islam in Tajikistan and the other countries of Central Asia. According to Rashid, every military training centre has a mullah who preaches what they think is the true Islam – 'Wahhabism'. For instance, their mullah had said that any means could be used in achieving the goal of the triumph of Wahhabism, and that even a mullah who deviated from the ideas of this movement in Islam should be physically eliminated!"

Once he had started speaking frankly, the guerrilla also told the travelling doctor about Juma Namangani's training centre in the Garm district, not far from the location of his main body of men at the mountain village of Sufien.

"According to Rashid, general training is given by instructors from Afghanistan and Pakistan, while the more delicate means of waging a partisan war, including methods of torture, are taught by instructors from the Muslim terrorist centres in India…. I realised that it was only a short step from the theory that the guerrillas are taught to putting it into practice. And I was proved right. Soon afterwards I heard about the methods and forms of organisation in the terrorist groups of the 'Namangan battalion'. For interest, every guerrilla in Namangani's forces has his own number, and all the guerrillas have to call each other by these numbers. There is harsh punishment in store for those who transgress this law – execution. According to Rashid, four or five men had already been tortured and executed for not complying with this monstrous rule. "Another stringent rule is a prohibition on any contact with the civilian population or the guerrillas of other field commanders that has not been sanctioned by Namangani. In fact, Rashid himself has fallen victim to this rule. He and his friends got into an argument on the boundary between the territories of Namangani and another commander. Rashid was unlucky, and he was winged in an exchange of fire – the kind of wound that cannot be concealed from a superior officer. In order not to attract any attention, he asked to be moved, together with the men under his command, to an outlying observation post. He tried to treat the wound with his own resources, but it turned septic. He heard that a doctor, i.e. me, had appeared in the next village, and that was how we came to meet.

"Rashid told me that he hadn't yet taken part in any raids into Uzbekistan by Namangani's guerrillas, but he has heard about a number of successful raids into the Namangan region. He said that the guerrillas have five or six lines of deployment, mostly through the territory of Kyrgyzstan, and especially through Osh…. Rashid said that with the money Namangani gets from abroad, he could not only saturate the whole of Central Asia with narcotics and weapons, he could afford to tell the authority figures in the Tajik opposition to go to hell. Rashid said that Namangani himself sometimes says as much to his own inner circle. In fact, the belief among the rank and file is that Namangani is rather like the Chechen guerrilla commander Salman Raduev – just as independent in his actions, just as committed to terrorism, only not a fanatic, he does everything for money and propagates the idea of Wahhabism on the instructions of the special forces. One of Rashid's acquaintances from Namangani's inner circle believes that Namangani is an agent of the Saudi Arabian special forces, since he has supposedly witnessed several meetings between Namangani and functionaries from that country. According to Rashid, this acquaintance has heard Namangani claim that he is simply exploiting the goodwill of the top men in the United Tajik Opposition (UTO) and if anyone gets in his way, he will kill them – that's a lesson he has learned very well.

"When his course of treatment was nearing its end, I asked Rashid why he had told me all this. He said that he himself was for peace, but what kind of peace can there be, he asked, if there is nothing but prison waiting for him at home, but here, so to speak, he is a 'master of life'.... Rashid said that probably only Namangani and a few of his comrades-in-arms are willing to wage an armed struggle against their own homeland on someone else's instructions, the others don't want that, they would prefer to stay here, in a foreign country, even though they understand the hopelessness of such a position. Many cherish dreams of growing rich while they are in Namangani's forces, so that they won't go back home empty-handed and will be able to pay for forgiveness from their families or buy pardon for their offences from the authorities. Rashid's conscience has eventually begun tormenting him, and sometimes he wants to let the whole world know about the injustice that people are suffering here. Only he doesn't have the strength to do it, and he is afraid for his family, whom he left behind in Uzbekistan. Namangani constantly hints to his armed men that the price of betraying him and his movement is death, not only for the traitor, but also for his family and loved ones, wherever they might be."

Did the doctor understand everything about "Namangani's kingdom" correctly? Information of a different kind also reaches us. Namangani is supposedly solidly entrenched on Tajik territory. He has the support of the local population since, unlike the other commanders, he does not confiscate food, but buys it. He is on excellent terms with the leadership of the United Tajik Opposition, and one of them, the former field commander Jaga (Mirza Ziyaev, who has taken the post of Minister for Emergencies in the Tajik coalition government!) is not only a close friend, but supposedly also a relative. By the way, Jumabai Namangani really is married to a Tajik woman from the village of Yaz-gulem, who has borne him a son.

The Kyrgyz secret police have received an interesting videotape. A large feast in one of the Tajik villages. About fifty field commanders have gathered together. Everybody addresses Mirza Ziyaev respecfully. There are Europeans at the table. They are introduced. One is German, and the next best thing to the ambassador. Another is some kind of specialist (like the Japanese geologists who ended up as hostages at Batken). The "ambassador" reads a speech written out in advance: on behalf of, and on the instructions of.... I express our deep gratitude for the release of our citizen. The "big commander" is pleased. And, as it happens, sitting there in one of the places of honour is Juma Namangani!

Will Jumabai Namangani be squeezed out of Tajikistan like the pus of a furuncle that has grown too bothersome? Will our borders be closed against his armed bands – as the Tajik authorities have assured us they will? In view of all of the above, it seems unlikely. Namangani apparently feels as much at home as ever on the land of Tajikistan.

Chapter Thirty-Two

I think the time has arrived for me to interrupt my story and put in at least a brief word of clarification. Everything that I have written so far is documentary, and not only in those sections where I cite documents or eyewitness accounts, but also – even more importantly – in the parts where I tell the story of Belgi-Yosir, or rather, where I reproduce reality as seen through his eyes.

This is the point at which I must say that I have not made anything up, and while I am open to the reproach that I have not seen it all with my own eyes, nonetheless I have made it a rule in every case to rely on the words of those who did see things for themselves. Many of these people will never admit what happened to them: for instance Alisher, or Umar, who told me himself how he and Belgi came to be in Hoit, now works in a foreign cultural delegation No one ever found out where he had been and what he had seen, and at work they simply announced– after all, it is a foreign delegation – that he had spent some time at the organisation's head office in Moscow for advanced training: and that dealt with that.

I also have a number of documents sent to me from "over there" by journalist friends, for instance this letter from Zubair, in which he mentions his work with Yosir.

Zubair's Letter:

Hello, Kasymkhan and Abdulkuddus.

"Verily, Allah has bought the souls and the fortunes of the faithful, for which they have heaven! They are fighting on the path of Allah, killing and being killed, according to His true promise in the Torah, the Gospel and the Koran. Who is more faithful in his covenant than Allah? Rejoice in the bargain that you have made with Him! This is great good fortune!" 9:111

Yes, it is so. Glory to our Lord, who has bestowed these words upon us in the Koran.

My brothers, how is your health? I received the cassettes that you sent and was greatly delighted. There is much news at the Centre. Yosir and I are now working on a video film entitled The Groan. One hour and twenty minutes is already complete. There will probably be about two hours. As soon as it is ready, I shall send it to you.

We have set up economic and publishing departments, our political department has been disbanded and a Management Department has been established in its place.

We have also set up a department for religious propaganda, the appeal for education and the struggle against sin; Abu-Abdullakh has been put in charge.

In the days ahead we wish to establish a Sharia court.

I am sending you six videocassettes in the briefcase. Fear Allah. Pray on my behalf. Peace upon you and blessings

Zubair.

Sometimes, of course, I have to reconstitute the reality "over there" grain by grain, when one person's story contains the story of another eyewitness whom I myself have not met: but this is no new practice in the East. By which I mean the history of the hadiths or the utterances of the Prophet Muhammad when, for instance, the Imam Al-Bukhari cites them from the words of such- and-such or so-and-so, the latter of whom heard all this from an eyewitness, Of course, I carefully check such stories against the accounts of other eyewitnesses. These are often accounts given by guerrilla fighters who have returned during the last year or two, or that have been given to the authorities in Uzbekistan by the authorities of Afghanistan, Pakistan and Kyrgyzstan. Materials from court cases, stories by journalists who have interviewed them – I check all of this thoroughly in order to reconstruct that reality "over there" as precisely as possible.

Here, for instance is a list of personal assessments that were clearly carried out by the Islamic
Movement of Uzbekistan:

Assessments:

Abdurashid, born 1980, made the hijrat (i.e. migration) to Tajikistan in the year 2000. Profession: confectioner, miller.
Military profession: heavy and light firearms, mining, reconnaissance, sniper, tactician, mapping.
Character: bad-tempered and serious, but works hard on himself. In good health, robust. Clothing size: 52; hat 56; shoes 42 . (unmarried)

Muhammad, born 1975.
Made the hijrat to Tajikistan in 1998.
Religious education: can read the Koran, good aptitude for the Arabic language. Profession: manual labour trainer, driver, motorcyclist.
Military profession: heavy and light firearms, tactics, mapping, mines, reconnaissance. Character: rather bad-tempered, weak-willed. Begrudges nothing for his brothers, sometimes has headaches (unmarried)
Clothing: size 52; shoes 43; head 56

1 Asadulla 2 Salim, born 1978 (unmarried) Made the hijrat to Takjikistan in 2000.
Profession: fourth class of financial college (economist).

Military profession: heavy and light firearms, reconnaissance, mapping, pistol, tactics, mining.

Character: mild, gentle-tempered, docile. Religious education: Koran reading skills Clothes: size 54; shoes 44; head 58

In good health, sturdy.

Anas, born 1968 (married with two children in the home country). Profession: driver, painter, glazier.

Military profession: heavy and light firearms, mapping, tactics, mining. Religious education: Koran reading skills

Character: polite, talkative, weak-willed, trusting, easily deceived, easily angered, but also easily appeased. Unsuited for responsible work. Suffers from rheumatism in the legs.

Clothes: size 54; shoes 45; head 56.

In addition, since I am writing the biography of a poet, and a poet who is far from simple and already well-known, in the process of correlating this reality with his spiritual world, naturally I cannot manage without his poems, not to mention my own reminiscences and those of the friends we had in common. I can assure you that nothing has found, or will find, its way into this book that has not been checked with at least two or three of the writers in our circle, who must certainly have known Belgi better than I did.

But there are things that only I know about him.

Chapter Thirty-Three

I fell down and crawled at a run,
the poplar was pitiless, the lake a wasteland, the shadow a palm's width,
should I hide in the grave, my soul like a lump in the throat?
The earth quaked behind my back, the sky fell.

What races are these ulak, kupkari, payvak?
There is no chink for you, no hollow, no hole,
the reinforced concrete walls are rotten, the curtains dishevelled,
the neighing of the horses, the rolling thunder guffawed.

Was this voice a loudspeaker?
If you soar into the sky one of the horses is a falcon,
if you drown in the water the other horse is a diver!
Ah, water and blue sky, they say it's a tornado.

A Poet and Bin-Laden

I was tired of being afraid, I turned back
and said to one of the horses as to a human:
'Do what you want, trample, fuck me!'
At that moment both horses fell silent. (a fragment)

- Belgi

During that period, some time around August 25, 1999, Zubair Abdurahim-ogly phoned the BBC. After introducing himself as the press secretary of the Islamic Movement of Uzbekistan and simultaneously the Chairman of its Political Department, he said that he wished to clarify matters concerning the events in Batken and at the same time to read a statement from the Amir of the IMU, Muhammad Tahir Farrouk. The basic content of the statement was that the Islamists had no arguments with Kyrgyzstan. And as for the Kyrgyz citizens and the Japanese who had been seized, they were not hostages (he said they did not take hostages), but prisoners in a "holy war".

The goal of the jihad that had been declared, Zubair stated, was the establishment in Uzbekistan of an Islamic state. Moreover, their arms were directed "only against the dictator Karimov and his entourage". The military action on the territory of Kyrgyzstan, he declared "is only taking place because of the stubbornness and political shortsightedness of the authorities in Bishkek". He claimed that the Uzbek mujahadin wanted only one thing – not to be prevented from returning to their own homeland. But the Kyrgyz authorities had "blocked their way with troops, which had led to armed clashes".

Bishkek, he claimed, had behaved incorrectly towards the mujahadin even earlier by "transgressing all the norms of human rights and blithely flouting the laws of human hospitality" when it handed over "refugees" to the Uzbek authorities. And Bishkek had once again "treacherously broken its oaths" only very recently – that was when they had given the guerrillas fifty thousand dollars for the first hostages and then tried to wipe them out. The present "prisoners", Zubair ibn-Abdurrahim declared, would only be released "when about fifty thousand Muslims thrown behind bars in Uzbekistan are set free".

The statement also set out the guerrillas' demands for the Bishkek regime: "Leave the mujahadin alone, so that the warriors fighting for the faith can make their way to Uzbekistan unhindered", and also they must not provide help to Tashkent in its struggle against the Islamists. If Bishkek did not meet these demands, then "the jihad could be directed entirely against the Akaev regime".

Here is one of his declarations from that time:

Zubair: In the name of God the Gracious and the Merciful.

A statement from the Management Department of the Islamic Movement of Uzbekistan:

The Amir of the Islamic Movement of Uzbekistan and commander in chief of the mujahadin, Muhammad Tahir Farruk, on the advice of the ulema and with the guidance of God, hereby declares a jihad against the dictatorial regime of Karimov. For the pursuance of this jihad there exist the arguments of Sharia law and mujahadin who have undergone the necessary military training. We wish to remind you that the defence of the religion of Islam, which is being trampled underfoot in our region, and of the Muslims who believe in this religion, the liberation from the hands of the oppressors of the wise ulema who disappear without trace and young Muslims who are arrested without cause and condemned to be shot, and the return to the control of Muslims of hundreds of mosques and madrasahs that have been closed, is the very highest idea and goal, and for the establishment of the rule of the Koran and Sharia law, the only path is the path of jihad.

The only cause of the measures of jihad begun in Kyrgyzstan lies in the Bishkek regime, insofar as this regime has handed over to the dictatorial regime in Tashkent thousands of Muslim fugitives who had taken refuge in Kyrgyzstan. In addition, this regime is blocking our mujahadin's route. As for those who have been arrested, until about fifty thousand prisoners in the jails of Uzbekistan are released, this activity will continue. We wish to warn foreigners arriving in the region. The Islamic Movement of Uzbekistan also warns the countries in the region not to provide any assistance to the dictatorial regime of Tashkent. Our jihad will continue until an Islamic state has been built in our country. We declare that there are no foreign mujahadin in our ranks, and we regret this. We demand the immediate resignation of the Tashkent regime, so that Uzbekistan will not be ruined and innocent blood will not be spilled. But if similar events occur in the future, the responsibility for them will lie with the Tashkent regime.

Head of the Management Department of the IMU, Zubair ibn Abdurahim

Question: You say that the individuals who have infiltrated Kyrgyzstan are not foreigners. Who are they, Uzbeks?

ZA: They are our brothers from the Islamic Movement of Uzbekistan, our mujahadin. When we speak of the Islamic Movement of Uzbekistan, there are members of various nationalities living in Uzbekistan, in particular Tajiks. Therefore, these languages might be there, but in certain reports, beyond that, there is mention of foreign languages. There are no such languages in our ranks.

Question: Do these men have anything to do with the Tajik Opposition?

ZA: No, they have nothing to do with the Tajik Opposition. These men are opposed to the regime in Uzbekistan.

I recall that, after the interview with the guerrillas switched into the Uzbek, Kyrgyz and Persian languages, everybody, especially the Japanese agencies and authorities, began jamming our phone lines with calls. They called from Moscow, from Tokyo, from Bishkek, from within London itself. We were the primary link to the guerrillas and through them to the hostages.

I should say that Zubair was a lot less sophisticated and artful in his role of press-secretary of the IMU than his predecessor, the tub-thumping Abdurahman Mansur, aka Zainiddin Askarov, who used simply to pour out a torrent of speech. The new man was rather tongue-tied and not entirely resolute. You could sense him checking every word with Tahir Yuldash, who was probably standing beside him.

As for the Japanese and General Shamkeev being taken hostage, the details of this incident were subsequently clarified by the Japanese geologists' interpreter. The general and two soldiers had come to spend the night with the geologists. During the night the guerrillas had attacked, and when one of the soldiers started shooting back, they had mown him down where he stood. The others had been taken without a struggle.

On August 25 a group of militiamen led by Lieutenant-Colonel of Militia Zholchubek Zheenabaev was also taken hostage. After his release, the lieutenant-colonel recalled that day: "We were captured at half past ten in the evening of August 25. Our shift of nine men had been on duty at the post in the village of Bok-Bashi in the Chon-Alai district. It was raining, and it was dark all around. Four sergeants and I were keeping watch, the others were resting. Apparently the guerrillas were watching us then and they burst in suddenly. We didn't try to resist, because there were shepherds with families in the settlement, a lot of children... If we had opened fire, they would have killed everyone in the village. The guerrillas took us to their base in a mountain village. It was seven hours away from our post on foot. Then they let four of the militiamen from our group go, saying that they knew the *shahada* (i.e., the declaration in the belief of the oneness of God and acceptance of Muhammad as His prophet). But they set a guard to watch the other five of us and warned us immediately that we'd be shot if we made any attempt to escape. The guerrillas are Uzbeks and Tajiks, a lot of young guys about 20 to 25, but there are some old men too. All with beards, dressed in camouflage suits and armed to the teeth.

"At first they thought we were Uzbek militia, but when they realised that we were Kyrgiz, they seemed to soften a bit. They even reduced the guard. After about a week they started taking us out to work – at least that was a bit of amusement for us. Later we began saying the *namaz* together, of our own free will, no one forced us. Our day began at half past four in the morning, we performed our ablutions, at five there was the *namaz* and then breakfast. As soon as it started to get light, they took

us off to work – we cut down trees and undergrowth, laid in firewood, scythed wheat. They ground it into flour. After work they fed us dinner. The dishes were mostly made out of yak meat – *shurpa* (soup), pilaf, roast meat. After dinner there was more work or reading the Koran. They gave each of us a Koran: the letters are ours, but the words are Arabic. That was how we read prayers.

"While we were prisoners they never beat us once, but we didn't even think about trying to escape. They kept us separately from the other hostages – the general and the Japanese – but I saw the Japanese from a distance."

Chapter Thirty-Four

The train runs like time, life, like thought:
this is an old thought, but its pain is new every time.
We drowned, covered in sins like one
of the purest of the undefiled, like one of the biggest bastards.
No I am not saying that we were all united in sin in hell,
however, to wait for hell is a bigger hell than living in hell.
I simply mutter, as one sentenced to death: this cell
is so damp compared with any other possible cells....

-Belgi

Omurbek Zhanakeev, the interpreter for the Japanese geologists taken hostage by the IMU guerrillas, tells his story:

It all happened on the night of August 22 to August 23, 1999 at about one in the morning. That evening General Shamkeev came to us with his bodyguards and stayed for the night in one of the trailers. He had set up a covering force of 15 or 20 soldiers on the high road about two or three kilometres away from, and then they had been joined by several busloads of reinforcements, and they were supposed to sweep the main road leading from the mountains to us and then to Kan. But at one in the morning, when everybody was asleep, the night was suddenly torn asunder by bursts of automatic fire from all sides. Our camp consisted of several trailers, and the open space between the trailers was lit up all night long by floodlights. But the automatic fire came from all around. Shouts of "Allah-u Akbar" mingled with the gunfire, and we ran out into the light, wearing just the underpants and vests that we had been sleeping in, but then went dashing back to the trailers in fright, throwing off on the way everything we had on, to make it clear that we were unarmed....

I threw myself on to the floor of the trailer. My body was shuddering in terror. Bullets were flying straight through the trailer and whizzing around everywhere, leaving tracer trails and bright sparks. After a while the shooting began dying down, but I could already hear shouting in Tajik and Uzbek close beside me. I didn't know what to do: the fear was pounding in my naked body. And then suddenly the barrel of an automatic rifle was thrust in through the window that had been opened beforehand and there was a guttural shout of "Harakat!" I didn't know what that meant, but I got up cautiously, raising my empty hands first and making it clear that I wasn't armed and I wasn't a soldier. Just then somebody's bulky body came tumbling in through the window and a sudden blow to the back with the butt of a rifle knocked me over facedown....

No, because of the shock there wasn't any pain just at that moment, it was only later, after a day or two that my whole body started to ache, but at the time I didn't feel anything except the fear of death. Kicking us and goading us with their rifles, they drove us out of the trailers on to the dark road, threw sacks over our heads and tossed us down down, naked, on our backs on the soaking-wet ground. And I didn't feel the cold at all: there was nothing but the fear that I was about to be killed.

I heard single shots not far away, and they were even more frightening now than the random bursts of tracer fire earlier. The guerrillas were shouting something, and there was one voice that clearly stood out, that the others addressed obediently, calling its owner Tahir. That must have been their commander.

All this time I was shaking. But I don't think it was from the cold. It was more likely the fear. I couldn't stop my teeth chattering. I calmed down a little when, after they gathered us all together on the dark earth road, they first of all started looking for the driver of one of our jeeps. They started asking us who we were. I answered that I was a geologist. But the driver wasn't there. He must have managed to hide in the darkness and run off in the direction of the mountains. I should say, to do justice to our group, that no one gave any one else away. But the guerrillas must have known about us from someone who had access to our camp, because they led the Japanese out of their trailer and the first thing they asked was who their interpreter was.

I was one of two interpreters; the other was a young student on work practice. I felt sorry for him, so I said I'd go and he should stay lying down. 'I am!' I responded, and immediately got another blow from the butt of a gun in my back. 'You said you were a geologist!' They didn't forgive anything. I'm sure they have would cut me down with a burst of gunfire if they could have managed without an interpreter. But they needed me.

Then, when they couldn't find the second driver, they started asking how to drive this Japanese car, and when they found out that, although the driving wheel was on the right hand side, the gear changes were exactly the same, one of them said: 'I'll drive it myself!'

They got us up off the ground and ordered us to get our clothes from the trailers one at a time. With a rifle barrel trained in me, I managed to put on a light jacket over my bare body, a pair of light canvas summer trousers and a pair of trainers on my bare feet.

Meanwhile the guerrillas themselves were dashing through the trailers, grabbing everything in them that was valuable. They were looking for a satellite phone, only they were so stupid they didn't notice that the phone was behind the open door of a trailer, but no one put them right. It was only later that I earned another blow from a rifle butt, by telling them the phone had been left behind the door, but by then we were far away in the mountains.

But at our camp one of the guerrillas carried one of the geological instruments out of a trailer and asked us: 'Is this a satellite phone?' And when we shook out heads, he flung it down on the ground in his fury.

Of course, the one who suffered worst of all there was the poor general. They beat him to a bloody pulp.

Probably only about twenty minutes went by, but it seemed like an entire eternity. Six of us – four Japanese, me and the general – were put in the back of the jeep, while the guerrillas got in the front, and they left all the others in the camp to make sure the trailers were burned and set off in the direction of Kan.

When we drove out on to the high road, even though it was the middle of the night, there were crowds of refugees with their belonging walking along it. The guerrillas started honking their horns and firing in the air and the people began moving aside in fright and making way. After about fifteen minutes we reached the bridge at the entrance to Kan and the guerrillas stopped the car and told us to get out. They stood us facing the cliff beside the water, and at first I thought that now they would start to shoot us because they had no use for us. Logic doesn't apply in that situation. You don't think that if they've driven you this far, then they need you, and they'll take you on further. Every stop seems like the last one.... But no, they loaded us up with everything that they could – ammunition belts and rucksacks – and on top of that, after we went down to the river and started moving up the gorge, when we forded the river, the guerrillas got up on our backs and we had to carry them across the raging river. Just before the far bank I slipped under all the weight and fell. My rider managed to jump up on to the bank, but I got absolutely soaked through. He started drubbing me with his rifle butt, saying I'd done it deliberately.

We groped our way along the ravine on that icy cold summer night. In places the guerrillas shone their torches, looking for marks that only they knew. A little higher up the ravine, when what lay ahead was more frightening than what already lay behind, they hung rifles without any magazines on us and put us up in front – in case we ran into an ambush.

It was on the road there that my body started to ache as the life came back into it, together with the pain, after the initial shock. I had to take off my trainers and give them to an old Japanese man, who was gasping for breath, either because we were so high up in the mountains or simply because he was old, or perhaps both at once. We walked along goat tracks and several times we crossed the river, from one bank to the other. When morning came it was raining, and in those mountains rain quickly turns to snow. I started shaking all over again, but the impossibly heavy load that

the guerrillas had piled on us now kept us warm, and even the metal of a gun rubbing against us seemed to provide some protection against the vicious cold.

There were times when I didn't want to keep walking, I just wanted to throw myself into the ravine and put an end to it all forever. Or even take two or three of these mujahedin with me out of sheer spite, but somehow I kept remembering the poor Japanese, for whom I was now responsible. Their lives depended on me. And it wasn't really a sense of responsibility, but some kind of hospitality that must have been in my blood, that made me keep thinking about them again and again and keep on walking further into the mountains.

There were several halts, when the guerrillas covered their guns with cloths so that they wouldn't glint and given them away to a sniper with binoculars or the pilot of a helicopter. Yes, and sometime about midday a government helicopter did come rumbling across the mountains. We all lay down behind rocks. My heart was pounding, and I wanted to shout out: 'Here we are, why are you turning away?' But the helicopter circled for a while in the distance and strafed the bare mountainsides just in case, then swung round and flew away again.

You should have seen the way the mujahedin's eyes lit up and they gloated after that: look, those are your armed forces, they said, that's all they can do – bombard the mountains aimlessly and send rocks flying down into the ravine, we're the real masters here, they said.... And they really did know everything there: before some turns they sprayed the mountains with automatic fire to start a rock fall and clear the slope before we moved on and went slithering over those rocks, cutting our feet on the splinters, down to the river, where some of them prayed and others stood guard over us....

There were moments when the men who were up in front moved too far ahead, and the ones behind dropped back because they were praying, or because they were taking a bite of their dry rations of raisins or nuts where we hungry helpless prisoners couldn't see them, and then the same thought ran through my head again: Should I hide somewhere in these cold mountains? But then the sobering thought: Will you survive, and what will happen to the Japanese? – would set me moving again after the group up ahead that was hidden from sight. The general must have had the same thoughts, because it was harder for him than anybody else, but his soldier's dignity never deserted him for a moment. I tried to show my respect for him in every way I could, by giving him my hand, or giving him a push uphill, so that this attitude would also affect the guerrillas, who did everything they could to humiliate him, as their immediate enemy.

Apart from that, I tried to get the guerrillas who happened to be beside me to talk. But they were all afraid of each other, and under the wary glances of their brothers-in-arms they immediately started prodding me with the butts of their rifles, or simply gave me a kick up the backside. But when no one could see us, something human came awake in them. I started talking about them and their families, and about literature: about

Aini, Fitrat ...their answer to that was that they had the one Allah, and they didn't want to know anything else ... Although one of them, a Tajik from Pamir, who had come on this sortie to earn a bit of money, did say that his wife had been categorically against it, and she had threatened to take the children and go to her father's house. This poor bearded fellow sang patriotic Soviet songs under his voice while the advance group loosed their thunderous bursts of fire and set the rock falls rumbling, and the men behind prayed one at a time behind a bend in the steep ravine....

In the evening of that day we reached their camp, where the mujahedin exchanged passwords with their comrades-in-arms and were welcomed, and we were all taken down to a meadow sheltered on three sides by mountains, where the mujahedin lit a campfire and crowded close around it to get dry. They didn't let us get close to the fire and the six of us, just as we were, soaked through, lay down back to back, warming each other with our shivering.... But we didn't fall ill.... To this day I'm still amazed at the strength a man can draw on to survive....

Early in the morning, after prayers, we were led further into the mountains. And that was when something happened that still makes me shudder when I remember it. Our single file had stretched out over several hundred metres, and I saw that the old Japanese man was falling further and further behind. Then he completely disappeared from view. At about midday we came out at another halt, where the commander who had been leading the old man joined us after a while and in response to my glance of inquiry, he suddenly said: "He was killed!" Although I knew it would mean another blow from a rifle butt, I exclaimed: "How?" I was indeed knocked off my feet, but I remained conscious enough to hear the commander say: "He couldn't walk any longer, I gave him a horse so he could clear off. But the horse turned stubborn: it stopped in the river and wouldn't budge a step further. Then, to frighten it into moving I fired a shot in that direction, but I hit the old man..." That was the trivial way he told the story.

How my heart ached, how it ached.... Worse than any pain from a rifle butt or a kick to the kidneys.... I walked on as if I was crawling: everything was black in front of my eyes, and I wondered why I hadn't tried to drag that commander down into the steep ravine with me.... Then the old man would still have been alive.... I don't remember how the time came for the pre-sunset prayer, but when for the first time we stood facing Mecca and made our four bows, simply repeating the movements of our imam, as we had been ordered to do, the tears involuntarily sprang to my eyes, and through them I saw the old man staggering towards us, with my huge trainers on his diminutive Japanese feet.... It was a miracle.... It was such a miracle that it never even occurred to me that the commander had simply been joking with me, that he had been joking, not just with me, but with life and death.... It was a miracle, and I only thought about everything else later, high up in the mountains, where they held us as hostages for two months.

Chapter Thirty-Five

Pebble.
A crowding stone.
No language, no heart... stone... stone
stone.
Stone piling one on the other.
Soundless, blind, cold, scentless, closed stone.
As though
this was not
enough, a
stone
on which
my black
shadow
fell.

-Belgi

Here is one of the rare interviews given by the press-secretary of the IMU, Zubair Ibn Abdurahman on military operations during the first Batken war.

Question: What connection do the Islamic fighters who have reportedly seized five villages in the south of Kyrgyzstan have with you?

ZA: These mujahedin who have captured these villages, they are groups acting under the leadership of the Islamic Movement of Uzbekistan, and they are carrying out these actions in accordance with our plans and our goals

Question: According to certain reports, these groups do not take orders from you. Can you tell us how you maintain communication with them? Can you prove that they obey your instructions?

ZA: The events themselves, and the fact that we inform the press about them, prove that these groups are with us and under our leadership. They are under the authority of our leader, Muhammad Tahir Farruk and act in accordance with his orders.

Question: But how do you maintain communication, by telephone or in some other way? How do you control them?

ZA: The events which are taking place now were planned many days, months and even years ago. We have constant communication with them and we maintain this communication.

Question: Then how is this communication carried out: by telephone or by messenger?

ZA: You yourself mention that there are various means of communication. Since this is a military secret, we shall, inshallah, inform you of this in greater detail in the future.

Question: If they are in communication with you, then why have they taken four Japanese geologists hostage and yet do not state their terms to the Kyrgyz government and are not conducting any negotiations?

ZA: In recent times communication has been inconsistent, but as far as these four prisoners are concerned – we call them prisoners, the press says they have been taken hostage, but no, they are prisoners. That is, our Islamic Movement of Uzbekistan is not a commercial organisation, we do not take hostages and trade in them. No, the battles that are taking place now are ideological battles, this is a holy jihad.

Question: If you are not demanding any ransom, then why are you holding them?

ZA: We are holding them because – and we have stated this frankly – our goal is the release by the Tashkent regime of many thousands of people who have been arrested illegally and are being subjected to torture. We can exchange them. That is where our goal lies. They will be kept in our ranks, and there can be no other possible arrangement. We guarantee that they will be kept safe. But they could come under fire or aerial bombardment from the air force of Uzbekistan.

Question: How do you know about the state of health of these hostages? How many hostages are there in the mountains there?

ZA: I repeat, they are not hostages, but prisoners of war, since they were captured in the course of military action.

Question: But they are Japanese geologists, they are not soldiers, how can these civilians be called prisoners of war?

ZA: They were captured in the course of military action. There are four of them. In addition, there are several individuals from the agencies of law enforcement. In all, there are only thirty men in our hands. Of these, six are from the intelligentsia, four of them have accepted the Koran, and so we have released them. They now know us better than before. That is, they know how Muslims regard them, the people.

Question: What are the numbers of mujahedin there in the mountains of Kyrgyzstan?

ZA: The number of mujahedin is a military secret. It lies outside my area of competence.

Question: According to the latest reports, in recent days about ten guerrillas have appeared in Sokh, and the local population has supposedly

risen up against them. What comment would you like to make on these reports? And in general, what kind of relations do you have with the local population in Kyrgyzstan?

ZA: Our relations with the local population are very good. Since our enemy is only the Tashkent regime, and that is the only place on which we have designs. If someone stands in our way and offers armed resistance, then we shall be obliged to break through these barriers

Question: Is it true that your initial goal was to infiltrate Uzbekistan before September 1?

ZA: We do not possess such information, but I would like to talk about the people. Although the people of Uzbekistan have borders with the peoples of Kyrgyzstan and Tajikistan, our ancestors were the same, just as the springs from which we drink were the same, and the rivers and the mountains. There were no boundaries between us. Only the communists introduced these boundaries and then when the time came for them to be destroyed, they started to strengthen them. These, of course, are the plans of America and Israel.

Question: Let us get back to immediate events. Your guerrillas are now in the mountains. In a while the cold season will begin. You are supposedly preparing to infiltrate Uzbekistan, but the borders of Uzbekistan are well guarded. The armed forces of Uzbekistan are on the alert. So what are your plans? Are you really planning to oppose such a force?

ZA: Our goal is Uzbekistan. We have not yet engaged our enemy. That will happen with the help of Allah. But the army officers of Uzbekistan, the agencies of law enforcement, let those criminals know that they are not only opposing Muslims, but Allah himself. Allah is with us....

Question: But let us get back to what you are saying on behalf of all the people. The people of Uzbekistan need peace and they most certainly want peace. But do you think anyone will support you in the Ferghana Valley?

ZA: Let that be the last question. Since at present several tens of thousands of the Muslim people of Uzbekistan are in the prisons, their groans against these criminal law enforcement gangs reach up to the sky, we think that the people understand all this very well. If you ask the people, are they criminals, they will all reply, yes, they are criminals.....

Question: According to the latest reports, the guerrillas in the mountains of Kyrgyzstan are commanded by Juma Namangani. Is this true?

ZA: Juma Namangani is one of the most senior commanders of the Islamic Movement of Uzbekistan.

Question: So he is in command of these guerrillas?

ZA: Juma Namangani is one of our commanders and he is a military commander.

Question: Where is he now: in Kyrgyzstan, in Tajikistan or in Afghanistan?

ZA: We shall reply to that question in the future.

Question: A final question: according to reports, the refugees in Tajikistan, particularly the women and children, have left Tajikistan. Where have they gone to? What has happened to them?

ZA: It is our goal for these people – our people, our women and children, to be with us. They will return to their homeland with us. And that is the only means for them to return to their homeland. But if they start to return according to the promises of the government, then look how many of our brothers have been condemned to death and to long prison sentences. And if they go back, the same fate awaits them. There is only one path left, to return to Uzbekistan by means of jihad, by means of victory. If Allah grants us this path, that is good, if not – Allah himself knows we accept that also.

Question: But where are these women now? In the mountains of Kyrgyzstan? Where are the children?

ZA: They are with the mujahedin. But not in the front ranks. The men who fight are in the front ranks. That is the task of the mujahedin.

Chapter Thirty-Six

I know a great deal of the life of Belgi Abutov (i.e. the poet Belgi, i.e. the guerrilla fighter Yosir), certainly more than I am telling here. Naturally, the greater part of what I know, I learned in the process of working on this book, when I was not only inundated with the materials collected by my journalist friends, but also had my own meetings with writers, which for some reason resembled classic rendezvous between spies: mostly in secret, reached by devious routes, arranged by third parties who constantly glanced around and spoke in whispers, even in their own homes.

I never used to think that I would become a journalist – a profession I had always rather looked down on, rather as a psychoanalyst, say, might look down on a proctologist. But life has changed so much now that the whole of literature is shifting in precisely that direction, into journalism, and once you overcome your fundamental arrogance, you start to understand that there is no way of escaping this: if you want to be read by people, you have to try to grasp events even as they happen.

But that's not what I wanted to say. What I wanted to say is that, although I have reconstructed Yosir's life "over there" grain by grain, there is one period of about a couple of months concerning which,

for all my documentary strivings, I can only guess. I know in detail, from the lips of eyewitnesses, what came later, and it is clear to me what came before this period – indeed, I have already told you about that, and yet these couple of months just before and at the very beginning of "the first Batken war" remain a blank spot for me. But this is precisely the decisive time when Belgi finally became Yosir completely.

Let me try to explain in a little more detail. From long conversations with Umar-Alisher, who was Belgi's close friend for almost a year and a half, I know for certain that Yosir was prepared to go back home – to avoid using the humiliating term "to flee from Afghanistan". Alisher tried fervently to convince me that if Yosir had not been summoned to Afghanistan when he was, after the explosions in Tashkent his inclination was quite definite: he had to leave... "If he had stayed with me, then he would definitely have left with us," Alisher asserted ardently. But there was something about his ardour that somehow made me, a complete stranger, balk at the very feeling, the taste of flight. No, I didn't condemn Alisher – who am I, a mere city bookworm, to condemn his "flight" from his own likely death and the deaths of others? – and yet some little grub of an unspoken question such as: "But why didn't you wait for your friend?" kept gnawing away somewhere inside me. And, in addition, I knew that men had come back from Afghanistan and Iran after Alisher, some on assignments and some of their own free will, but why had Yosir not been among them?

This question still torments me even now, because I cannot answer it unequivocally. And anything that I write about this time and this subject can be no more than my own guesswork.

I immerse myself in Yosir's final poems, written "over there" and try to understand what happened between the time when he was supposedly preparing to come back home, immediately after the February bombings, and the Batken war, following which he and five or six hundred other mujahedin were sent to Afghanistan forever in November.

These four poems that came into my hands thanks to another poet, Khairullo, after he visited Afghanistan, stand completely apart from everything else that I know about Belgi.

With the help of several young Uzbek poets, I have tried to render this poem literally. Why literally? Because for me it is not so much poetry as a document. This is how it turned out:

> *The vision that came to me –*
> *was it in the heart or in the body?*
> *I emerged from the banks (the channel),*
> *but my shadow flowed on, like the Amu (Darya)*

I directed the people/the pupil of my eye
to a burial mound like a cliff,
That elevation was an accumulation/heap of thoughts,
and also an obstacle on the path

Going down and observing a rock/cliff
steeper than the other rock/cliff,
I said: Rumi said:
The true path is as fine as a hair.

It turns out that we have travelled a path
with no return; up on high another wanderer
At this moment has defiled/urinated on the mountain
that we knew as sacred.

In response to my crying out,
a certain Hebrew appeared:
Thought, he said, is by no means a home;
if not a graveyard, does it really count?

At that time the azan/call to prayer sounded
and after making two genuflections.
I hurried into the circle (Sufi ritual);
he and the people wrapped themselves in a blanket.

The sheikh who was on the podium
raised up his hands like a snake
And bit/cut into the earth and the heavens;
was he a magician or a servant of God?

But I, fearful of the steward
and the pit of Canaan,
When I emerged from the circle,
an accomplice and brother-in-arms of the people,

When my shoes, like the lamp/light,
were not where they should be,
From Belgi there sprang forth an uvais/self-enlightener:
My galosh has been lost, do you have it?

Naturally, as my friends have told me, this clumsy translation does not convey even a tenth part of the elegantly powerful poetry contained in the actual gazelle, but I feel that this is still enough for me to reflect on what was going on in Yosir's mind. Let me say straightaway that I

am not certain of the time at which this poem and the others from "over there" were written, but after all there is in poetry a certain precipitate that is enduring, not to say "eternal", something which in the context of other details gives us a certain key to the human heart.

I have never analysed poetry in my life. I know that people like Hamid Ismailov or Shamshad Abdullaev are genuine hermeneutic scholars in this area but, even so, I would not trust them or anybody else to construe this poem, or the other three poems by Belgi that I have in my possession. I do not intend to indulge in literary disquisition here. The *meaning* is what is important to me. And from this point of view a sense of duality, which is initially set with the classic separation of body and soul, can be traced quite clearly throughout the entire poem. The main point here is that, while the poet has had a "vision", it is not clear where he had it, in the soul or in the body, in other words, for instance, the initial intention which took him into the ranks of the IMU could have been an ideological bias, but also, at the same time, a portion of his body, a matter of chance. The one thing that *is* clear is that the man has taken an untested path, like a river that has left its channel.

I can just see how horrified the aforementioned Shamshad Abdullaev or Hamid Ismailov would be if they saw the poem "carved up" in this fashion, since even the very youngest poets who helped me make this literal translation explained to me at very great length that Lyutfi, the great fourteenth-century Uzbek poet, has these lines:

> If thou/Thou hast not made thy/Thy home in the eyes
> of Lyutfi – that is no wonder,
> It is hard to build a house on (the waters of) the Amu.....

and they linked these lines with Belgi's words. But, as I have said, my "vulgar sociological" reading of the adduced text is entirely premeditated.

And so, he leaves his primordial channel, but his shadow still flows like a river. In Central Asia, if a river leaves its old channel, it is the first sign that the river is drying up. And there is nothing more frightening than a man walking along a dried up riverbed with his shadow trailing along in front of him. If we accept that by the river, the writer means Tradition, then the picture of its present condition assumes a black-and-white, photographic clarity. I can read the second *beit*, or couplet of this gazelle literally, or, in other words, as landscape. If you have ever happened to be in the mountain gorges between Hoit and Batken, you will understand immediately what I mean. But even if we take this stanza symbolically, the important thing is that this duality remains with the poet – the elevation or "magic mountain" to which the "pupil of the eye" or "the people" is directed (the Uzbek word "mardum", which is of

Arabic origin, has both these meanings) turns out, to put it crudely, to be a heap of garbage, an obstacle to a clear flow.

The following two stanzas confirm my reading. IMU may claim that it is returning the people to its origins, to its channel, but the poet is saying that the channel has dried up and what is left in the channel of this once mighty river is a mere shadow. And even heaps of books or agglomerations of buildings can only be an obstacle to the pure aspiration of the people. For according to Rumi, the Muslim exegeticist, the path is as fine as a hair, and not like the bed of a river. On this fine hair running between good and evil, between piety and sinfulness, between love and hate – you can continue the list for yourself – there is space for only one person, and on the Day of Judgement no soul will be responsible for any another, this is not a flowing current of water or a crowd, and every individual soul will carry its own burden along this hairline....

Yet even so, the poet identifies himself with "we", conceding that there is no return from the path he has followed within this "we", but up there on the "magic mountain" another wanderer defiles the mountain by urinating on it, no doubt in the belief that his urine is of the same nature as the water of that great river. In other words, to make a halt on my path of commentary, we can assume that, while Belgi accepted that he had become irretrievably a part of the IMU, he regarded what was taught by those on the summit of the pyramid as blasphemy masquerading as pseudo-tradition.

Unfortunately my knowledge of culture is not adequate to decoding the following stanza in which the response to the poet's cry is the appearance of a certain Hebrew (Who is he? Ibn Ezra? Maimonid? Spinoza? Derrida?), and the poet cites his idea that thought is no refuge or domicile unless it is like death. At this particular point I could not possibly be less inclined to the vulgar interpretation that Belgi had somehow become involved in an intellectual circle of militant antisemitism. The spiritual dignity of the tradition of thought to which this gazelle appeals would not permit him to sink as low as such a concept – try to discover even a grain of it in Ibn-Sina, Al-Gazali or Ibn-Arabi.

I deliberately mention these names because (even though I have not understood what I have just read) the following lines tell me that Belgi valued the Islamic nature of Sufism, he not only uses a lot of symbols in the poem, but speaks quite unequivocally about Sufi ritual, the mystical circle.

But now I return to my own vulgar sociological approach: the sheikh – a leader who can be seen as any of the leaders of the IMU: Tahir Yuldash, Juma Namangani or Zubair Abdurahim – may be menacing, with the snake-like gestures of his arms, but this very fact undermines

his faith. For after all, one of the most highly venerated *hadiths*, which is regarded as sacred because it was imparted to the Prophet Muhammad by Allah Himself, says that of those who regard themselves as believers, three groups will be sent to Hell. One of these is the *shahids*, or terrorists. Allah will ask them: What did you do on earth? They will reply: We perished in Your name, on Your path. Allah will exclaim: No, it was not in My name that you perished, but so that men would glorify your courage. Hell is your punishment! Allah will deal in the same way with the mullahs and chanters of the Koran who have revelled in their own voices when they thought they were preaching the word of Allah.

But while the poet is wary of these "administrators" and of the pit of Canaan – the well into which Joseph was thrown by his brothers - he still emerges from the circle accepting the crowd, that is, those unfortunate refugees and mujahedin driven away from their land and their homes by the threat of arrest and torture – but in the final stanza he suddenly brings the entire situation back down to earth with a joke: he has left the Sufi circle only to find that his shoes – the items that render the rocky path painless – have been filched.

Bringing this poem down to earth in my own manner, it is perfectly possible that the poet Belgi, having abandoned poetry for the IMU, lost that which protected him, which served not only for travelling the path, but also illuminated it for, after all, he juxtaposes these lost shoes with a bright lamp that has also been lost, and then in his new desolation and nakedness, he discovers a sign – that is how the word "Belgi" translates – that revelation never manifests itself to the masses, it is unuteachable, untransmittable, it is manifested from above, and each one to whom it is manifested is an *uvais*, a self-enlightener....

This is enough for me to trace in outline what went on in Yosir's mind between the bombings and the start of the war. I have deliberately not confused you even more with something that my translation assistants told me: that in the final line Belgi cites a famous line by a poetess called Uvaisi: "kavshim yo'qoldi, sandamu?" – "My shoe has been lost, do you have it?" – which is addressed to God Himself. These are already subtle poetic matters. For me, it is enough to say that although I do not know the precise date when this poem was written, in this particular case I am inclined to trust Alisher, who fled from Afghanistan, when he says that after the bombings in Tashkent Yosir sat out in the moonlight all night long, writing something in a small notebook that he hid even from his friend....

Hamid Ismailov

Chapter Thirty-Seven

Every evening there's a tree fading,
every evening the leaves of the windows,
every evening falling into the night...

Every evening, when it disappears,
my breathing, empty and restless,
every evening a cigarette smokes...

Every evening, every evening, every evening,
spending the night on the street of a strange town
when the rust unexpectedly covers the stove-bench.

Like the candle of the last leaf, when it has not faded yet,
every evening twinkling till morning,
what is the moon, your window, waiting for?

-Belgi

Tursunbai Bakir-ulu – a member of the Kyrgyz Parliament and a former Kyrgyz Ombudsman – tells his story:

I should preface the story of my negotiations concerning the Batken hostages with the following. In 1996 in Germany, I met Muhammad Solih, the leader of the Erk party, who at that time was living in exile in Frankfurt. Either that year or a year later, when I was in Turkey, I was sought out by some young men from the Islamic Movement of Uzbekistan, which was unknown to me at the time, and they gave me several video films, saying: "We know you are a member of parliament, pass these videos on to your president. We are preparing a jihad against Uzbekistan, let him not stand in our way, let him open a corridor for us. And in that case we shall not touch him. We have nothing against Kyrgyzstan, our hostility is directed only against the regime in Uzbekistan. But if your president stands in our way, then he will not prosper either!" Then when I went back to Kyrgyzstan, I handed on all these video cassettes to our president's administration with the appropriate explanations.

And then in the early autumn of 1999, when I travelled to the Osh region as part of my parliamentary duties, I suddenly got a call from the president's administration, saying: Fly back to Bishkek urgently, military action has begun and the president asks you to return to the capital immediately, you know them, we need your help. I flew back to Bishkek straight away. They told me what had happened: that one of our generals, some Japanese geologists and several of our citizens and soldiers had been taken hostage, and they said: Get in touch with them, start negotiations.

I was installed in the Kabar news agency, which the guerrillas supposedly phoned occasionally to propose their terms, and one day Zubair ibn Abdurahman, their press secretary, called. I took the phone, introduced myself to him and explained that I would like to meet him to discuss the hostages. Zubair said: "We know you well, you have already tried to negotiate with our mujahedin. We have nothing to discuss with you!" I said to him: "You are confusing me with Tursunbai Akhunov, who tried to reach an agreement with the mujahedin. I am a different Tursunbai, Tursunbai Bakir-ulu. I am known to Muhammad Solih, Muhammad Sadyk Muhammad Yusuf and his brother, your Abdurahman Mansur.... Ask them!" Then he thought for a moment and said: "We must first check who you are, and then we will give you our answer".

The phone was silent for two days. We sat there, hardly ever going out, and waited for a reply. Finally, on the third day, the phone rang. It was Zubair ibn Abdurahman. He said that I been checked, and now I could fly to see him in Kabul via Dubai. To be quite honest, I was not very eager to accept this invitation at first. Who knew what might happen to me in the Taliban's Kabul? And so I asked whether it was not possible to meet somewhere else, say, in Dushanbe.... "No!" said Zubair. "Come to Kabul and there's an end to it."

And so, Kabul it was. I had to prepare myself for a flight to the Taliban. A ticket to Dubai was quickly booked for me. I flew there and moved into a hotel and suddenly in the evening a fax was pushed under my door. It said: "'You are being followed by the American and Israeli intelligence services, so move to such- and-such a hotel and then go to the Afghan consulate, your documents will be ready". Well I thought, this is spy mania, if one side doesn't kill me, the other one will. But, on the other hand, I began to feel a certain sense of security – I was being followed, so if anything happened to me, everyone would know about it straightaway.... In the new hotel another fax was pushed under my door, again from them, telling me come at such-and-such a time to the Afghan consulate, which is at such-and-such a place....

I found the Afghan consulate and arrived there with Nuri, an employee of the Tajik embassy who was supposed to interpret for me. We arrived, they met us, we talked about this and that. After the Taliban consul, a man with a great huge beard, learned who I was and what I was there for, he suddenly said: "If all Kyrgyz are like you, then I am your friend!" And I answered: "If all Taliban are like you, then I am your friend too!" We had a laugh and were given our visas, they put us on our Ariane plane themselves and we flew off. There were two important Taliban sitting in front of us. They asked us: "Who are you, where have you come from and what for?" We told them about ourselves. They turned out to be two ministers who were on their way back from Davos. They became friendly with us and they said: "We take good care of our guests, so we'll make sure you're all right!"

As we were approaching Kabul after these friendly conversations, the aeroplane suddenly lost height and flew so low that I thought we would crash into the mountain-tops at any moment. We were very frightened, because we were really hedge-hopping, and they explained that below us the fighting against Ahmad Shah Masud's forces was still going on, and

God forbid that they might launch a rocket and that would be the end of the plane. They said it was flying so low as a precaution. So, frightened out of our wits by the idea of a rocket and the snowy mountains, we finally landed at Kabul airport. The ministers took us to the Intercontinental Hotel in their jeeps and said they would tell the Uzbeks that we had arrived.

The next day guerrilla fighters dressed in black arrived at the hotel in jeeps with black terrorist flags, all carrying automatic rifles and grenade throwers. A terrifying sight! They said: We'll take the men who have arrived with us. But the Taliban said: No, we've been instructed to look after them! Anyway, they agreed that the Uzbek guerrillas would take us and guarantee to bring us back there. They took us in their jeeps and drove us to a two-storey mansion in the centre of the city. There we were met by Zubair ibn Abdurahman himself. He turned out to be a rather small man from Namangan. We said hello, chatted about this and that and started our negotiations. He and I spoke for two days. I kept trying to convince them that they were only harming Muslims both in Kyrgyzstan and in Uzbekistan by their actions. They were showing Muslims as barbarians, extremists, killers. That gave the authorities a free hand in their fight against the faithful. Zubair stood his ground, saying the reason that they had taken a stand to defend the downtrodden rights of Muslims was precisely that Karimov's regime didn't understand anything but force. However, my main efforts were directed towards the negotiations concerning the release of the hostages, and above all of the Japanese geologists, since their seizure cast a shadow on Kyrgyzstan, and beyond that on the Muslims of Central Asia. But Zubair said that on that matter I would have to talk with the amir himself – Muhammad Tahir Faruk.

Two days later a jeep carrying Tahir Yuldash and his bodyguards drove into the courtyard with the same pomp and pageantry. Again men with automatic rifles dressed in black, again the same black militant banners. He spoke with me in far more categorical terms, telling me this is not Europe, welcome to the Taliban's Afghanistan, where you and I will speak in our own language! Before the negotiations we prayed together, and then I tried to say the following: Where in the Koran, I asked, does it say that if you want to have a fight in the family, you should climb over your neighbour's fence? I continued with my thought that all these actions only added to the sufferings of Muslims in Central Asia, and in addition, this situation led to the Russians returning under the pretext of the struggle against terrorism. I spoke, and all the time our negotiations were recorded on video by his men. And then he interrupted me and said: "You know that we can simply execute you here, thank Allah that the time for prayer has come, or you would not have kept your head…"

We prayed together again and sat down to continue our interrupted conversation. I was more careful now, but I still expressed the same idea, saying: "You should release the hostages, so that you and the Muslims throughout Central Asia do not earn a bad reputation"… Anyway, we talked with him face to face for two days.…

All this time my life hung by a thread. They were going to kill me three times, and I was almost ready to bid life farewell. The first time was while

we were negotiating and Tahir Yuldash suddenly arrived in the morning with a transcript of a radio message and showed it to me. It said that the positions of the Islamic guerrillas in Hoit had been bombarded from the air. In fact only cattle and three of the local population had been killed, but Tahir Yuldash was beside himself with fury: "We negotiate with you here, and your people bomb us! What's to stop us from simply executing you here as an example!" I said: "That would be like killing a man called Godfrey who is pronouncing his name and has already said 'God', but has not yet said "'rey'. Let's clarify this, because I know for certain that Kyrgyzstan does not have any aircraft that could have bombarded you.... Let me phone and investigate this...." I barely managed to persuade him.

I called the president on the satellite phone – he didn't answer. It wasn't a working day. I phoned the head of the national security service – he wasn't there either. Whoever I phoned, there was nobody there....

Eventually I contacted one of the top brass in the military. I told him the way things were and that I was being threatened with death. "Order them to stop the bombing," I said. But the general said: "We're not bombing them, it's the Uzbeks who are doing it". I said to him: "Then what am I supposed to do?" And he said: "Try to get out of it the best way you can...."

All right, so I convinced them it wasn't Kyrgyzstan that was bombing them, but Uzbekistan. No sooner had I calmed them down than there was another disaster. This time the Taliban came bursting in: "We have to execute him, because he has betrayed us to the international community. We stated repeatedly that the Islamic Movement of Uzbekistan has nothing to do with us, but he has announced that the negotiations are taking place in Kabul". I picked up the phone again. Apparently at a meeting with delegates of the OSCE, the president had assured them that everything would be all right with the Japanese hostages, saying:

"We've sent our man to Kabul for negotiations...".

So anyway, now I had to convince them that an ambassador cannot be killed. I just barely managed to persuade them by bringing in the Taliban ministers I knew and their promise that I would be safe. No sooner had I dealt with this, than some other Taliban arrived, saying: "They're playing a double game here: some other Tursunbai has turned up at our embassy in Pakistan, saying that he's authorised to conduct negotiations on behalf of the Kyrgyz government...".

Eventually manoeuvring between these different deaths made me fall ill. Then I asked the men to bring me a lot of onions and I ate as much as I could of the bitter stuff. I ate those onions for two days, and during that time Tahir Yuldash arrived. He couldn't stand the smell and asked me what was the matter. The men told him that all this time I had been treating my illness with onions. Then he recited a *hadith* that said a man who has eaten a lot of onions should not appear in the company of people and people should not visit such a man, and he started rebuking his men. They were frightened and they scowled darkly at me. If he'd given the command, they would have torn me to pieces.... I said to them: "I'm sorry, it's my fault, that's the way the old men in our village taught me to cure myself".... They forgave me very grudgingly....

But as they say, if Allah has not ordained a death, it won't happen. Eventually, after all those negotiations, all that fear of death and the illness, I was taken to their camp in the Logar province, where I was shown their firearms training. I fired some of their guns myself. In short, we finally agreed that they would give me a letter from Tahir Yuldash to Juma Namangani, telling him to release three hostages. I said, since I've been through so many deaths, give me at least five... Then Tahir Yuldash told me that Juma had the authority to add another two hostages for me, if I was able to persuade him. That was when I realised that Juma was not entirely under Tahir Yuldash's authority. They gave me the letter and Nuri and I flew to Dushanbe.

In Dushanbe we were met at the plane by armed opposition guerrillas from the twenty-fourth guards unit. There we had meetings with Davlat Usmon and Hodjiakbar Turazhon-zada, and then also with Saeed Abdullo Nuri, who was amazed at our great abilities - it turned out that not even he had been able to convince Tahir Yuldash to make any concessions. "He's my pupil, but it's almost impossible to persuade him to back down," he said. I asked him to give us some help, to get us through the territory of Mulla Abdulla, who took orders from no one – neither the government nor the opposition – to see Juma Namangani at Hoit. He gave us a car and armed guards, but he ordered us very strictly not to stop for a second anywhere, and to drive straight to Hoit without any delays.

And so we set off. We drove past a place called Komsomolobad without stopping, and some other places. The time was approaching for the midday prayer. I said to the driver: "Let's say our prayers and we can have lunch at the same time". "No," he said, "we were ordered not to. This isn't our territory, he said, they could shoot us all...". Not for anything would he agree. But Allah is great! Suddenly he got a puncture. One way or another he had to stop. While he was changing the tyre, we managed to say our prayers and, thank God, no one shot at us. We had a bite to eat and set off again.

When it was almost evening we drove into Hoit, where we were met by the men of a commander called Shakh Iskander. They took us to him. We explained the business that had brought us there, saying, we have to see Juma Namangani, we have a letter for him from Tahir Yuldash. "I don't know any Juma-Puma! There isn't any Juma here," Shakh Iskander told us.

But then, when it was almost midnight, he told us that they had found someone out among the rocks and after a while Uzbek guerrillas arrived on American jeeps. Armed to the teeth again, with those same black militant flags.... They took us. I think Yunus was their commander.... They drove us up into the mountains at night. We didn't know where we were going. Eventually they brought us to a house with a huge courtyard – it was Jumaboi Namangani's house. As soon as we drove into the yard, dozens of guards shouted out to greet us: "Allahu Akbar! Allahu Akbar!" They led us to him and there in the inner part of the houise, or *ichkari*, we saw his children and his wife.... He looked daggers at us: it was a very dark, pitiless look. As if he could see straight through us! I give him the letter from Tahir Yuldash, explained who I was and why I had come....

A very stern man. Quick to anger. He shouted: "Why are your people boasting on the radio that they're enlisting *mergen* snipers as volunteers?

Let them come up here into the mountains, if they're so brave. I'll tear their heads off! They're only brave down there in their offices! I've got that general of yours eating out of my hand, he's so delighted I haven't taken his head off!"

He read the letter and I said to him: "There, Mullah Tahir said you have the authority to add another two hostages..." it would have been better if I hadn't said that then... He jumped to his feet and shouted: "How would you like me to blow your head off" – and aimed his pistol at me.... I told him that all things are in the hands of Allah, and if my head was destined to be blown off here, then that was His will, only I had not come about my head, but in order to help innocent people.... He said: "We let the innocent Muslims go immediately, as soon as they recited the *shahada* for us! There are only prisoners of war left here!"

Anyway, he said one thing, I said another. I brought all my diplomacy into play. Eventually he said to his bodyguards: "Leave us alone!" – and they left the room. "You have found the key to my heart," he said.

In short, the next morning we went to the mujahedin camp in the mountains. There I saw our general and the others. The general was performing his ritual ablutions. They gave me five hostages, and I started again: "Throw in at least one of the Japanese for me as well". Jumaboi raised his pistol again and said: "Shall I shoot you, or put you with those ones over there?" and he pointed to his hostages. In short, he was quick to anger....

They gave me five then, and another nine later. But I won't say anything about the Japanese money that the Kyrgyz and Tajik high state officials made out of this....

Chapter Thirty-Eight

Do you know what it's like crossing the border between two states? Not borders like those between European countries, when you drive along in a car and suddenly find yourself in a different country, but the Tajik-Afghan border, which is guarded by Russian border guards. Where they shoot without warning, and not into the air, but to bring you down.

I have been told of so many ways to cross, from bribing the border guards, especially those of Tajik nationality – the method that the "commanders" mostly used when they didn't cross by air in a state helicopter – to an armed skirmish, when a group of marksmen draws the border guards' fire and the spies take advantage of the shooting to crawl or swim across while the darkness is split by the bright tracerywork of flying bullets.

But Yosir and his experienced partner Jafar made their way to Afghanistan entirely at their own risk. First they were taken as far as Tavildara, then they travelled on donkeys through gorges as far as the

border zone, and early in the night they dressed warmly and set off into the mountains, which Jafar knew like the back of his own hand, a hand that had only four fingers, since the index finger had been shot off in one of the fire fights there. And although he always regarded the novices whom he had to get across to the other side as a burden, the process of crossing the border and exercising his professional skill gave him a measure of enjoyment and satisfaction that actually meant more to him than the hundred or two hundred dollars that he was paid for this operation. He usually trained his wards briefly, and after that relied on unquestioning obedience and blind imitation of what he did himself.

And indeed, what else could they do? They might be strong and healthy, but they were soft, and they pressed their clumsy bodies down hard into every tussock of grass, constantly expecting to be riddled with bullets, or to be swept away by the clear, icy water of a stream.

And yet, despite everything, that was not the way Yosir felt. After the bombings in Tashkent, which had first delighted the men at Hoit and set them boasting, in the belief that the explosions had been carried out by their own people, until they were given strict orders from the commander, Juma, to denounce them, and even more so after the killing of the seventeen young men from Khorezm, including his friend Bakh, Yosir had fallen into such a deep depression that if a bullet had broken off his life here, that would have been easier for him than to carry on living. In reality, he had found himself at the border seeking his own death, in response to its first call. That was why he had initially responded to Zubair, who had long been wanting to have him by his side in the newly established ideological department. After the movement's organisation had been destroyed and its previous press secretary, the tub-thumping Abdurahman Mansur arrested, undistinguished, grey men like Rustam Mahumdov, aka Zubair, had started moving into positions of prominence, and they were in desperate need of bright minds. In fact, Yosir could easily have been advanced long ago by the amir Muhammad Tahir Farruk himself, but until recently he had hidden behind his assignment of assembling a "chronicle" of the Uzbek exodus – the flight of thousands of people, whose woeful stories he recorded one by one in a notebook.

Now here he was, supposedly on his way to Afghanistan, but actually in search of his own death. And so, in the cold, thickening darkness of the night, while they waited for the most difficult time for the border guards, which is not around midnight, but in the small hours just before dawn, the motionless outline of his body jutted far out from the recess in the cliff, annoying Jafar and yet at the same time reassuring him. He had seen all kinds of "mujahedin": some quite shamelessly messed their pants, or broke out in such a sweat in the cold mountain night that the

snow around them started to melt, threatening a landslip, while others tried to drag him back, promising twice as much money as he had been paid for the crossing. But this one just sat there as if he was frozen to the rock and didn't say a word....

In the mountains time flows across the sky: the candle-end of moon is suddenly exposed and slips through the wet cotton wool of a dirty cloud, and then the clouds themselves start to stir, and engulf the moon so that it is barely visible: the sky is the only thing here that is occasionally restless and fidgety, if you don't count ordinary people, that is. People only rarely appear here at night, but those who do can notice how, at such rare moments, time leaps down to the earth – into the water that is suddenly lit up, into the ice that reflects the moon in a harsh glint, into the eyes gaping around in fright....

There is every sort of animal in a man: a snake, creeping noiselessly towards a rustling river; a cat, gently stealing along after it; a muskrat, swimming with only its head exposed, but above all inside a man there is the man himself – fearful of every murmur of the earth and, above all, of another man who has sharpened a knife for him, or aimed a sniper's rifle at him. And yet there is a state in which you call this danger down on yourself: you stop and you wait. And at that moment you realise that the feeling of every danger is connected with a movement: the movement of a snake, a cat, a muskrat....

And that was the way Yosir stood upright there on the bank of the Pyanja, like a ground squirrel readying himself to give a sudden whistle, but instead of getting a knife in the back or a bullet from behind, he was felled bodily by Jafar. Jafar hissed something as he did it, but no louder than the water streaming off his clothes, and he dragged the senseless Yosir across the rough, sharp earth....

Later, much later, Yosir would recall that river in the same way that he recalled a river in his childhood, one that he would have to swim across someday soon, even though he had only just learned how to stay afloat: day after day he had looked at that opposite bank, so close and yet so far out of reach, he had studied all the snags and reeds that he could clutch at for support, and eventually he had made up his mind, and gone floundering in as hard as he could, getting tired out before he had even reached halfway; in very the middle of the current all his strength had deserted him, and he was already imagining the river clutching his water-logged body and bearing it away ever so gently downstream, to the dams in the distance, but then some sudden fear that came from his very heart had set his arms and legs moving convulsively, and when he came to, he was already lying in the thick dust, beneath the laughing faces of the grown-ups, whom he had now joined....

But now the strength that allowed him to overcome his own fragility had been transformed into a burden like that of the wandering Jew: neither fire nor water could harm him now.

Chapter Thirty-Nine

The snow
is falling on my sight.

Not daring
to lift my eyes
I look
at the earth.

- Belgi

Here are another two documents from that time. They are a kind of ultimatum from the IMU, which was never actually made public, but indicates the way in which Juma Namangani and those around him were thinking:

Demand:

1. Leave Tajikistan.
2. All demands to be accepted only in written form.
3. Listen carefully to all their demands or advice.
4. We only carry out orders or any instructions from top officials.
5. There can be no mention of withdrawing to Afghanistan.

Demand:

1. Anyone who wishes to negotiate can negotiate with the Amir.

2. Let us go to Uzbekisan – when we wish and by the route we wish.

3. Give us time until summer. Let them open the passes, and in the meantime we must remain quietly in this region

4. We have no business interfering in the internal affairs of Tajikistan and we do not wish to interfere. For this reason we have several times met your demands and withdrawn to Afghanistan. This time we will not withdraw anywhere except to Uzbekistan.

5. We are not concerned by any threats. If our demands are not accepted and the states start a war, we are prepared for this and we wish for martyrdom (i.e. we are prepared to become shahids).

6. If a national war starts here, the same kind of war can break out in Uzbekistan, because there are about ten million or more ethnic Tajiks in this country. If there is a war, the various problems can only increase.

This attitude was confirmed in a radio interview by the Amir of the IMU, Muhammad Tahir Yuldash:

TY: This meeting with the Russian government took place at the request of the government of Takjikistan. They demanded that we withdraw into Afghanistan. We are not willing to withdraw into Afghanistan. We are willing, inshallah, to return to our homeland. We have not yet taken any decision. They have announced this decision prematurely. As yet negotiations are still continuing.

Question: You say you are not willing to withdraw to Afghanistan, but you do have supporters in Afghanistan, don't you?

TY: Yes, there are supporters of ours there, there are refugees, they are not only in Afghanistan, but in many countries of the world, and they regard themselves as members of our movement

Question: Let's get back to your armed men in Tajikistan. Bearing in mind that they are armed, neither the UN nor any other international organisation can serve as an intermediary for you. In what way, then, do you wish to return to Uzbekistan?

TY: We have only one answer. The Tashkent regime does not understand any language but the language of the gun. We have been warning about this for a long time, through the UN and through international human rights associations, for seven years we have been warning them: do not simply stand and watch the oppression that is taking place in Uzbekistan, we have told you that the consequences of this will be serious.

Question: There is a rather widely held opinion that most of the Muslims in Uzbekistan do not support you, that you are a group of only a few dozen men.

TY: If we were a group of only a few dozen men, then why would the US Secretary of State need to come, in that case Russia and the four countries could destroy a dozen men. But, Allah be praised, our power is the power of a typhoon that Karimov's regime will not be able to stand against.

Chapter Forty

In Kabul – in the two-storey detached house on Vazir Akbarkhon Street that was the IMU's headquarters – Yosir was informed that the Tashkent bombings had been carried out by the Uzbek authorities

themselves. They told him: We were preparing our jihad, but planning it for a later time, the time when the snow will melt in the mountains and all the other conditions will be right for an invasion will be ready. Yosir, who had just arrived from Hoit, knew that although May was almost over, the snow was still lying, not only on the summits but on the slopes of all the surrounding mountains.

Well then, Yosir accepted in his heart that they had not carried out the explosions, but what about the seventeen men from Khorezm who had just been killed, news of whom had even reached this place, Kabul... Zubair was writing all sorts of statements on this matter and preparing for all sorts of interviews, claiming that this was yet another act of provocation by the Uzbek National Security Council, which had sent its spies to join the ranks of the IMU ... But Yosir did not believe this.

And although he worked day and night with Zubair on the film that was provisionally entitled *Nido (The Groan)*, his thoughts constantly went back either to Hoit, or even further – to his homeland. They travelled from one part of Afghanistan to another, since the Uzbeks had now spread everywhere, carrying a document like this:

> The Islamic Emirate of Afghanistan
> Vilayat Balkh
>
> Greetings. The bearers of this letter, a group of four Taliban, are permitted to bear arms, and they are on their way to Herat. Please do not hinder them in their business.
>
> Niyazi, administrator of the Province of Balkh
> 14.7.1419

Part of this film was shot among the Uzbek refugees in Kabul, in particular at two of the local *madrasahs* that had been opened by the IMU: the "Maverannahr" for adult students, and the "Imam Bukhari" for children. What surprised Yosir most of all were not the terrible stories he heard, he had more or less got used to those, but the immense administrative machine of the IMU, which had not merely recovered from the substantial losses of February but seemed to be building up even greater might. Where had they all come from, and how – all these men who were mostly dull and undistinguished, the kind he had known since he was a child, could this all really be Tahir Yuldash's work? Or were there forces behind him that Yosir could not even guess at?

I often wonder why Yosir did not make a career in the Islamic Movement: why did he not become at least its press secretary? After all, that would have given the organisation's authority a tremendous boost. Was it the simple envy of the men around him? Those dull,

undistinguished men? Or a failure to understand his genuine worth, as happened to Joseph in Egypt? Was that the reason why Belgi mentioned the pit of Canaan in his previous poem? But in any case, how would they know that by this time Belgi was being translated into numerous European languages, after all, no one mentioned that on the radio.

But even so, it seems to me that these were not the reasons, that the reason lay in Belgi-Yosir himself. Of course, the individual will of any member of this movement would not be his own property, it would be completely subordinated to higher authority, but I do not think that was so in Yosir's case. I think that a poet's life differs from the life of an ordinary man because his will is always in his own hands. Even when it seems to belong to another.

Here are a couple of gazelles from that time that I was given to study:

> Woe is me when I am unable not only to find
> my beloved/God, but even my own amorousness
> My heart is hard, my spirit is bereft,
> my mind is inured in vengeance.
>
> Lacking courage for the journey,
> not showing the darkness my shadow,
> Since I am scattered like my shadow
> by the light across the face of blackness?
>
> Others are separated in the midst of love,
> a meeting is their hope.
> Ah! This chain of hopelessness
> keeps me away even from hope.
>
> My friend hears not, my enemy is blind,
> the morning wind has overturned the cup
> In myself I am like Hasan,
> having lost his twin Husain
>
> On the stage/in the courtyard of this performance
> like some unwelcome and impersonal sign/Belgi:
> Saying "What was the one promise
> to all about?" if I howl.

And here is the second gazelle:

> The Day of Judgement is like a river channel
> that is empty of water,
> When I broke away from the people/crowd,
> the people and the noise and the cries began to flow.

When I distanced myself from the people/crowd,
with my eyes still on the people,
I saw there was a different sound/voice coming separately
from the fragmented people/crowd.

This sound/voice is the sound/voice of a typhoon,
the mudflow at the start of the riverbed,
Bearing away everything in its path,
not knowing/acknowledging the bridge or the diver.

No avalanche, but the ocean like a typhoon
that rises up to meet it,
An instant will pass and it will reach me –
thinking when I turned away unwittingly,

Washing away the people/crowd
from this channel and this end,
The ocean's twin/double hurls
fear in my direction.

After an instant two terrifying
typhoons from both sides
Transform me into a balance/scales
in a world of shattering blows

From the spirit of Mevlevi and Shamsi Tebrizi
becoming/dying a sign/Belgi,
I beg for a least a splash of foam
in this blueness....

I will not try to analyse these two poems here, but they allow me to understand the state of Yosir's spirit following the explosions in February 1999, and they answer many of those tricky questions that I have been asking myself, from why Yosir did not attain any positions of prominence in the hierarchy of the IMU up to and including why he went to war as a guerrilla, as a *mujahed*.

Chapter Forty-One

I learned from the Japanese geologists' interpreter, Omurbek, who spent almost two months as a prisoner of the mujahedin, that among the guerrillas in the first Batken war there was a certain taciturn young man whom everyone addressed by the name of Yosir. I haven't mentioned yet

that Yosir, or rather, Belgi, or even more accurately, Belgi Abutov, had been a professional soldier – an officer in the tank forces. At the age of seventeen, having grown up in a rural district, during his work experience training and the time he spent hanging about at the local Machine and Tractor Station, behind which he lived, he had learned to drive all kinds of tractors, from the three-wheeled Belarus to the Vladimirets, with its caterpillar treads. At the army recruitment office they recommended that he join the Chirchik tank academy, and his mother, who was already in the final years of her life, was glad that her son would not serve his time in the army somewhere on Chukotka or in Germany, but closer by, and in addition he would acquire a profession that would start to feed him straightaway. So she was all in favour of this recommendation, and as soon as Belgi finished school, he went to Tashkent to take the exams.

When he was in his third year of study, his mother died, orphaning not only Belgi, but his seven-year-old brother, who was taken in by their grandmother, and so, to be quite honest, when Belgi graduated from the military academy, he was torn. On the one hand, events in Afghanistan were already in full flood and, as a young officer, he was desperately keen to go there, but on the other hand, he simply could not imagine abandoning his sick grandmother, or his juvenile brother, who might be left without anyone at all to care for him, and going off to do battle with the "spirits" as they were called by experienced officers who had brought new Afghani conscripts for the short-term training courses that had been set up right there at the academy.

In actual fact, he had been eager to go to Afghanistan immediately after the troops moved in – that was when he was in his second year of study, but although they had been put on alert and moved out, they weren't actually taken any further than Chirchik. And then the zinc coffins started arriving, but the worst thing, as I have already said, was that his mother died, desperately worried that now her son would definitely be sent to Afghanistan. But then, as I have already mentioned, they brought a group of those new Afghani conscripts to the academy, and they were definitely not interested in going back to their own country in tanks, and somehow his initial spontaneous impulse to go to war began fading away, although there was still an itch remaining somewhere deep inside him.

He graduated from the academy with a first-class diploma, and so within certain limits he could make a choice, but then the battalion commander had summoned him before he was posted anywhere and said he wanted to assign him to work on the new courses, teaching the art of driving a tank to those new recruits who had arrived wearing turbans and baggy trousers. And so Belgi had stayed in Chirchik.

During the year after he graduated, he turned grey: almost half of the men he trained were killed, some by a mine, some by a "stinger", some

by a knife, and the other half went over to the side of the mujahedin – but that didn't happen just with his students, it was going on everywhere, so all of this could hardly cast any doubt on his personal qualifications. But the spirit within him broke. He went to the regimental doctor, who prescribed a "Sherba's collar" for a whole month, but the nightmares and hallucinations carried on tormenting Belgi and eventually, a year and a half after graduating from the academy, a medical review board invalided him out of the army.

Immediately after his retirement he moved closer to Tashkent and started earning a bit of money as an assistant instructor at the local branch of DOSAAF, the voluntary society for supporting the armed forces. That was when he decided to take in his nine-year-old brother. Thanks to Altaer Magdi, I am in possession of several short stories he wrote then, which give some insight into how the poet Belgi began. I should mention that at this time Belgi wrote in Russian.

Chapter Forty-Two

Although the guerrillas did eventually retreat in the first Batken war, they still felt as if they had won their jihad. Something that had been postponed for years had finally happened. They had gone to war for their own land. Yosir remembered that during that spring in Kabul the Afghanis and the Arabs and, especially, the Chechens had accused the Uzbeks of indecision, he himself had been present at several such discussions, when even the demoniacal Tahir Yuldash had tried to make them see reason, pointing out that the Chechens were fighting for their freedom against the Russians, just as the Afghanis were, whereas he would have to go against his own people. But they kept insisting that *kafirs* were all the same, no matter whether they were Russians, Jews or Uzbeks, and so, they said, it was high time to take up arms. Then Tahir remarked that his people had borne their arms well in Tajikistan and in Chechnya too, that he himself had received wounds on the Afghan border, and they had nothing to reproach him with, but they kept pressing the point that it was time to open the jihad, that Jumaboi already had enough forces and he was eager for battle, hinting that if Tahir himself did not get the job started, then there was someone who could take his place.... Look, they said, even in Tashkent the mujahedin have acted on their own, without waiting from orders from the Amir... Tahir repeated yet again that that was the very reason why the jihad had now been postponed indefinitely, since that piece of folly had cost him his key men....

In short, it would be wrong to say that they argued until they were hoarse, since all these conversations were held in low voices and hushed tones, as it behoves Muslims to speak. But their content was the precise opposite. Then Yosir had gone back to Hoit, only this time he didn't cross the border on foot, but flew across it in a helicopter with four important Arabs, who were met by Jumaboi Namangani in person. That was when he had the presentiment that something ineluctable and irrevocable had already happened. And it had happened both in Kabul and here in Hoit. The killing of the seventeen men on their way home had cut back everybody's alternatives.

Go back to those two gazelles that I left unanalysed, and you will see that while in the first the poet is still floundering between the idea of going back and his own state of abandonment (compare Belgi's Hasan, left without his twin brother Husein, with himself, having lost his friend Haroun), in the second he has already been caught up by the mudslide, the typhoon, the great waves of water that have come rushing down on him from both sides, and here there is no longer any rational choice, only a single bright glimmer reaching up to the sky, a sign, a burst of foam – an attempt to atone foreverything through an equilibrium at the point where two oceans collide.

If we try nonetheless to rationalise this Koranic reference from the poem, then Yosir's heart, or rather, Belgi's, was still torn between the guerrillas and those they were fighting against. The terrible torrent of state oppression that he had chronicled in Hoit and which, as he writes in the poem, could even reach him, has clashed head-on with an equally terrible torrent which is waterless (remember the motif of the river as Tradition in the original gazelle) and is therefore nothing less than the Day of Judgement, and the poet, caught between these two raging torrents, attempts desperately to balance them within himself, to encompass them like two worlds, in neither of which, as Nasimi expressed it, can he himself be encompassed, and the empty hope that is woven out of foam seeks in one final impulse to liken this movement to the blue sky....

I saw an island in the sky.

Water beating on its shores
turned into clouds.

I saw an island in the sky.

My tears fell
as though the sea itself had toppled over.

Hamid Ismailov

I saw an island in the sky,

now is my road leading to heaven
and has my burial in the earth come to an end?

Chapter Forty-Three

when a lamp goes out and falls from the shelf, at that moment
if you rush after it, what is dearer — a burnt hand or the lamp itself?
At the basis of these words there are 1,000 fine poems,
there is the bird of life, death flying in, the shudder of warm blood,
so many eternities spent in loneliness and peoplessness,
so many signs and echoes of future indifference.
All this without doubt I can interpret,
but in remembering the lamp again, I think that what burned me
was not the glass but the fire;
O God, rich in secrets and as miserly in answers,
or is such an undefined life our payment instead of answers?

The day died. On the 14660th night.
There is no bottle or lamp. You can become drunk
because there is no wine in the bottle, although you understand this,
but the smoke from the burnt hand
is no more than sense, no less than nonsense....

-Belgi

The journalist Hamid Ismailov recalls:

In December 1999 I set out for the Taliban's Afghanistan. I had been invited by the minister for *shahids* and refugees, Mullah Abdul Rakib, an ethnic Uzbek whom I had previously interviewed by phone a couple of times. In the way that things are usually done in the East, he had said to me: "Your opinion of Islamic Afghanistan is mistaken. Come and see it with your own eyes!" and I had accepted this as a genuine invitation. I flew to Islamabad, where I had to find a man called Kuraishi in the Taliban embassy, and he was supposed to arrange all the remaining visa formalities. I flew in on Wednesday, and early on Thursday morning I went to the Afghan embassy, where there was a group of long-bearded guards or petitioners sitting outside, lighting a bonfire as they shuddered in the chilly morning air. Their appearance was strongly reminiscent of civil-war Russia in the works of Andrei Platonov, and subsequently this initial impression of a similarity between the Taliban and the Bolsheviks only grew stronger and stronger.

By nine o'clock luxurious white Toyotas started arriving in the courtyard of the embassy, and men in turbans and white robes, with the beards of prophets, got out. Once out of their vehicles, they embraced each other unhurriedly, and then drifted into the embassy building like outlandish fish on display in some huge aquarium.

The bonfire was now disconsolately burning out, abandoned by the man with a gun and his entourage of bearded cripples, and I reminded the guard once again about the man called Kuraishi. I spent that entire day at the embassy, to which, naturally, I was not admitted, but Kuraishi failed to put in an appearance, having apparently gone away on business to Peshawar, from where he was only expected to get back in the evening.

The next day was Friday, and so the Islamic embassy was not working, and it was not working on Saturday or Sunday either, in accordance with the secular laws of its country of residence. Monday arrived and once again I discovered in front of the embassy that same scene out of Platonov or Babel. But this time the man with the gun told me that today was the first day of the holy month of Ramadan (in fact, I already knew this) and the embassy was closed.

Anticipating some new hitch the next day, I found out the embassy employees' home numbers and set about besieging them by phone, and eventually I found, not the man who was called Kuraishi, but his boss, who promised to pass on my message and asked me to come to the embassy not the next day, but perhaps the day after that....

That was what I did, and the next Wednesday I found the man called Kuraishi, who proved to be a roguish-looking individual with a big beard and a turban on his head, and he began questioning me captiously and at great length aout how I came to know Mullah Abdul Rakib, who had supposedly invited me to visit the Islamic Emirate of Afghanistan. When I explained the story of our telephone conversations, he asked me in a half-whisper: "Then perhaps you know Kori too?" "Which Kori?" I asked in surprise, for some reason immediately thinking about Obid-kori Nazarov, who had disappeared without trace. So he was there, in Afghanistan... I asked Kuraishi: "Do you mean Obid-kori?" Now it was his turn to be surprised, so surprised, indeed, that he blurted out: "Why no, Tahirjan-kori!" and then immediately clammed up. "Ah, the Amir Muhammad Tahir Faruk?" I replied, pronouncing the name like a password, and then he calmed down and nodded in agreement. I nodded back at him. "Kori is very rich now..." the man called Kuraishi said, clicking his tongue and glancing around. "He has bought three hundred houses in Kunduz". And then, after a pause, he added: "By the way, that is where Abdul Rakib happens to be right now.... There has been a battle...."

It turned out that the minister who had invited me was incommunicado and, formally speaking, the man by the name of Kuraishi could not send me to Afghanistan without agreeing it with him. "But can't he be contacted at all?" I asked simplemindedly. "No, there's a war on..." the other man replied forlornly and started clicking his tongue and shaking his head again.

I spent the next two days in the embassy of the Islamic Emirate of Afghanistan, studying the Taliban and their relations with each other while I waited for the eventual return of Mullah Abdul Rakib from war-torn Kunduz to peaceful Kabul. Ever since that time I have often dreamed that I am on a foreign work assignment which simply never ends, despite my boss's urgent insistence that I must "return to base": either I can't buy a plane ticket, or I can't get through on the phone, or I simply can't reach the place I'm trying to get to....

And so my Ramadan continued to be spent among the embassy employees, to whom I had become as familiar as the small iron coffer that contained their one and only cherished official seal. Every day, in response to our enquiries, the Ministry of Foreign Affairs informed us that Mullah Abdul Rakib was still on his mission, which, just like mine, was taking longer than expected, and every evening I explained to my boss that we were already in the final straight and any moment now I would find myself arriving in the Taliban's Aghanistan, where none of our people had ever gone before.

On Friday, when I arrived at the embassy again, to make sure that the man with the gun was lighting his perpetual morning bonfire, instead of telling me: "The embassy's closed today for Juma (Friday)", he didn't say anything, and by nine o'clock, just like the first time the week before, the white Toyotas began arriving at the embassy, and the imposing individuals with long beards who looked like Old Testament prophets started climbing out of them for their long, slow embraces. In response to my expression of surprise, the man with the gun told me that in honour of Ramadan, today there would be a midday prayer here, led by the ambassador, Mullah Hakkani.

In short, I crashed the general prayer meeting and the roguish individual by the name of Kuraishi pointed out Mullah Hakkani, who was sitting in the corner, meditating after the prayer, and when he had finished meditating I launched a full frontal attack. I knew myself what an explosive mixture could be produced by the post-Soviet mishmash of Marxism and Mohammedanism: I ranted that no form of Islam allowed a guest to be humiliated by mistrust, that I had not just been invited by some man in the street, but the minister for *shahids* and refugees, and yet I had been obliged to cool my heels here for more than a week already... in other words, I ranted on and on.

To give Mullah Hakkani his due, he took me to his office without a word and stamped his seal into my passport, and that very day I set off via Peshawar and Turham for the Taliban's Afghanistan.

I won't tell you all the details of the almost two weeks that I spent in the Islamic Emirate of Afghanistan, especially since I have already written about that elsewhere in Uzbek, let me simply tell you what concerns the Islamic Movement of Uzbekistan in one way or another. Strangely enough, I didn't actually seek them out deliberately, assuming that they were only in the north, in Mazari Sharif and Kunduz, although I did suspect that I would be able to find them with the assistance of the minister who had invited me. At the time I did not know that their

headquarters were located right there on Vazir Akbarhan Street, where I spent almost all of my time in Kabul, or that the BBC correspondent Kate Clark had actually been arrested by them, although I saw her almost every day. It was only much later that she told me she had been picked up by men from the IMU and interrogated by someone in a black mask whom everyone had addressed respectfully as "Ustad", and that this Ustad had spoken all sorts of languages, including English. Afterwards she had suspected it was Tahir Yuldash himself, and when I told her that he didn't speak English, she was rather upset. Eventually we agreed that it could have been the IMU's head of counterintelligence, known as Abdullah, who could indeed speak any number of languages, since he was a graduate of one of Tashkent's elite third-level educational establishments.

While I was waiting for my minister, Mullah Abdul Rakib, I struck up an acquaintance with some Uzbeks I happened to meet in the vicinity of his ministry, and they took me home for the evening meal after the day of fasting and once again they asked me suspiciously, but without offending my feelings as a guest, where I had come from and why I had come. They had Pakistani and Indian music playing in their houses, and they removed their turbans in my presence, exposing rather ruffled but fashionable hairstyles. One way or another the conversation turned to Tahir Yuldash and, just like the man who was called Kuraishi, they began clicking their tongues and shaking their heads respectfully. From this I concluded that the Amir Muhammad Tahir Faruk really was well connected in the highest spheres here, and not only here, but in other countries that were no more than legends for these simple men... Certainly, no one gave away anything else about him, and I didn't put any pressure on them, leaving all that for the meeting with the minister, who was bound to be on close terms with Tahir Yuldash.

But the minister still didn't arrive, even though I felt the natural term of my assignment had expired long ago, so then I decided to travel to Kandahar and Herat. At Kandahar I met with one of the leaders of the movement, Mullah Abdulhair Muttaki, a young man with whom I argued about the nature of Persian and Pashtu versification, and he tried to prove to me that contemporary Pashtu poetry was stronger than contemporary Persian poetry, since, in addition to the school of Persian versification, Pashtu poetry had also passed through the school of Russian versification, and I found it strange to hear this in the Taliban's very own lair. That was when I realised just how open to argument these notorious Taliban were, that their entire regime really was just like the infantile disorder of leftism in communism, only in relation to Islam, that all their religious aggression was only the result of a juvenile lack of self-confidence. And at every point I felt that if this regime continued for a while, all the distortions would naturally start to disappear, that life would reassert itself, that they needed to be drawn into the general eddy and flow of international life, that after all they were not to blame for being the thin cream of the defatted milk of Afghan society, when all the rest of the elite had scattered and run.

They were simple men, those Taliban leaders whom I saw on that trip of mine: Mullah Hakkani, Mullah Muttaki, Mullah Abdul Rakib and

several other mullahs. A single example: Mullah Muttaki (Mullah Umar's spokesman) and I were driving in his Jeep, on our way to a meeting with Mullah Mutavakil, when suddenly a truck came darting out from round a bend, travelling at furious speed, and almost rammed into us, and it was only thanks to Mullah Muttaki's dexterity that our car managed to dodge out of the way. I imagined any of our Bolsheviks in his place – they would have shot the road hog on the spot, for disrespect to the authorities, if nothing else. But Mullah Muttaki merely settled his jeep in behind the truck and shrugged his shoulders: "He could break his neck like that, the poor fellow…"

And yet… and yet… I have never in my life seen anything more frightening than an ordinary soldier in a Taliban uniform. There was a time in Kandahar, before the meeting with Mullah Muttaki, when my observer and guide from the ministry of foreign affairs was incautious enough to ask a black-turbaned guard the wrong question, and the time in Herat, when I tried to use my journalist's credentials to get through to see a local official. The Taliban private with the black turban and red eyes tore the permit that gave me access to the heads of states and governments into tiny shreds and aimed his automatic rifle at me. I have never been so close to death as I was then, at the gates of that local official's office, and the soldier would have fired too, if the lazy and pompous official had not called to him from the window, and then my experienced guide had simply tossed me into our car, and we went shooting off, leaving death behind us.

When I nonetheless arrived back safe and well in Kabul, the minister had already arrived from Kunduz, and he came straight to the hotel to get me. He was young and handsome, and even his massive Taliban beard only made his milk-white face with its sunken eyes look slightly paler. He also removed his turban in my presence, and again I saw that fashionable haircut which in our schooldays used to be called the "youthful" style, and had recently been adopted by Leonardo di Caprio in the film "Titanic". I knew from hearsay just how fashionable that blockbuster had been in Afghanistan, and now every one of the many people I spoke to offered me real proof of the fact.

He and I sat together for a long time, again not arguing, because there is no such thing as argument in Muslim etiquette, rather we discussed one subject or another, the minister told me how he had come to be a Taliban leader, about how humane Mullah Umar was. The Uzbek language has the word "sinuk", which is usually translated by the non-equivalent terms "snapped" or "broken". It signifies a man who has broken down his own arrogance, and Mullah Abdul Rakib used this word several times in rapid sequence to characterise the top leader of the Taliban, advising me insistently that I really had to meet him. Unfortunately, I had already been to Kandahar, and instead of the exalted audience that Mullah Muttaki would have arranged, I chose to make an urgent short visit to Herat, to honour the remains of Alisher Navoi. No doubt it was an expression of my resentment at having been made to wait for my visa in Islamabad…. "Well, never mind, next time…" Mullah Abdul Rakib consoled me.

At the end of the conversation I raised the subject of Tahir Yuldash, but the minister politely declined to continue with that topic and

began telling me about the propaganda and organisational work he conducted among the Uzbeks in Kunduz, saying that in general Mullah Umar had instructed him to bring the north over to his side, and that now many things were changing in the north. I didn't insist on talking about Tahir Yuldash, which would have been discourteous to a man who had invited me to Afghanistan to discuss the Taliban, not the IMU.

A little later, however, one of his assistants gave me a kind of pamphlet in Pashtu, saying it was an address to the Taliban by Tahir Yuldash. Here is a brief summary:

A declaration to the people of the Islamic Emirate of Afghanistan

As you know, during the last seven years Islam has not been forgotten in the lands of ancient Bukhara. The peoples of Maverannahr still wish to restore Sharia law. For seventy years the Bolsheviks and their henchmen killed eminent Ulema, the genuine bright stars of Islam. This darkage seemed to have passed away with the collapse of the Soviet Empire, but what had seemed a new beginning for the people of ancient Bukhara proved to be the beginning of new misfortune. Even Amnesty International speaks of fifty thousand Muslims thrown into prisons and four thousand mosques closed, many of them turned into stables for cattle. And even this is not enough for Karimov's dictatorial regime, this regime has launched a campaign against women and their right to wear the hijab.

But now warriors of the faith have appeared on the scene, and they are presently undergoing military training in order to defend their religion and their country. They are prepared to become shahids and take a stand to protect Islam. When all the Muslims of the world pronounce the takbir in a single voice, the kafirs will be set trembling in fear. Many young sons of Bukhara are today willing to sacrifice their lives in order to serve as a beacon to future generations.

Dear brothers in Islam! You know the sacred hadith which says that all Muslims are a single ummah, a community, and if one part of the ummah is injured, it is as if one of a man's organs is injured. Then the healthy parts must come to the help of that part. The way in which you have welcomed us with wide-open arms shows the love that exists in the Muslim world. We are only too well aware that you have welcomed us when your own people are hungry and suffering from the embargo imposed by the USA. That is the very reason why we value this help so much. We promise that we shall not forget this hospitality. We know that the situation of seventy years ago, when the emir of Afghanistan handed fugitives from Bukhara back to the Soviets, will never be repeated in our time. Historically, Afghanis have never acted in that fashion.

We are facing a time of tests. And at this very time I appeal to all Muslims and wish success to all of us. Your brother in the faith, Muhammad Tahir Farruk, Amir of the Islamic Movement of Uzbekistan.

The following day I visited my minister at his Ministry for the Affairs of Shahids and Refugees. There were dozens of people milling about in front of the ministry – mostly cripples, women and children. They were distributing something from a truck, but the huge crowd for this hand-out made it quite impossible to see what it was – blankets, bread cakes or documents. We were led along corridors to the minister's office, which really was ministerial, the kind of office you can walk into in Tashkent, Bishkek or Dushanbe, but they are all empty, while this one was crowded

with people. The minister was sitting with his feet pulled up on to his chair, surrounded by these people. Those around him were sitting in the same pose, if they were not petitioners. He didn't notice us for a while because of the crowd, out of which people walked through to him, accompanied by one secretary or another. I stood by the door, observing how this ministry functioned.

A petitioner would approach the minister, accompanied by an embassy member of staff or secretary, who would bow to Mulla Abdul Rakib and explain the essence of the matter in a whisper. The minister would occasional interrupt him to ask questions, or simply listen and then, taking the sheet of paper held out to him, he would write something on it, following which, as a rule, the people went away, thanking him and bowing, but once or twice they tried to explain something else, but the minister held his open palm up towards them and they backed off, making way for those who followed....

Why am I telling you all this? Because these were typical scenes of life in the official Kabul of 1999 and from them it is possible to guess how the organisation of the IMU functioned and lived in the Taliban's Afghanistan.

Chapter Forty-Four

It is really strange that no one in the IMU ever found out that Yosir had been a professional soldier. They continued to regard him as one of those people who did something or other that was incomprehensible, but took his assignments directly from the top, and so, although the rank-and- file guerrillas were rather suspicious of him, at the same time they were wary, and they didn't talk too freely about him. Who can say how his life would gone if at the first firearms training sessions he had said that flailing away at isolated targets with a grenade thrower is too expensive a luxury, but the class was being led by someone called Ilkhom, who had not only been trained in Chechnya, but had even fought there, and in the process had picked up his own ideas of how one type or another of weapon should be used.In general, as he went through all these courses on tactics, topography and reconnaissance, Yosir silently noted to himself how "incorrect" they were from the viewpoint of the classical art of war, but on the other hand, how well they were grounded in and based on the experience of the revolutionary Che Guevara, the Afghan mujahedin, the Bosnian partisans and God only knew whom else as well. The synopses that had been hastily translated from some other language into Russian, and then into Uzbek, still contained curious little points about reconnoitring Serbian villages or the line of retreat into the Pankisi Gorge....

Here is one of those texts about reconnaissance work and recruiting people from the local population:

Instructions

You must have at your disposal an individual from the nomads or the local population, someone you can trust and whose advice you can follow. Otherwise, even though he speaks part of the truth, generally information from a liar will bring you no benefit. A liar is not a scout to your benefit, on the contrary, he is a scout to your detriment. As you approach hostile territory, you must increase the number of scouts (agents) and, working together with them, distribute sarias (groups of armed men) into the enemy's environment, so that the armed groups cut off the enemy's support forces and vital facilities. The scouts must determine their weak and defenceless points. Choose brave, intelligent, strong comrades-in-arms as scouts. Choose swift horses for them.

Those who are under your protection and care must be tested for loyalty and especially for the ability to tolerate their curators patiently. If they tolerate to your benefit, then we also treat them well and take care of them. Do not oppress those who enter into peace with us and at the same time do not ask them for help against our enemies.

But there was, nonetheless, a fundamental difference between his training in the Chirchik tank academy back in the eighties and his training here in the mountains of Hoit: here the talk of war and death was absolutely serious, it wasn't a matter of some tactic that might possibly be used by a some potential adversary, here every last detail mattered: from lighting a fire without smoke to smoking the metal elements of your automatic rifle, so that they wouldn't give you away to observers from the air.

And then the discipline here was much harsher, especially after the men from Khorezm had been shot, the slightest insubordination was punished by immediate arrest and imprisonment in a damp basement without any wooden flooring. Of course, Yosir was in a special position, since from the very beginning everyone had known about his personal contact with Tahir Yuldash, and the letters that were delivered to him by every courier from the political section – from Zubair – made him in a certain sense "untouchable". But the more often groups went off into the mountains and did not come back again, the more suspicion Yosir could feel from the members of Juma Namangani's immediate circle. There was a certain sense in which he was regarded as "Tahir's man" among them. And although at the beginning, when everybody who arrived in Hoit "from outside" swore their loyalty to the movement's Amir, Tahir Yuldash, on the Koran, and association with the Amir was a guarantee of safety, now as war approached, everything made it quite clear that Juma was gathering power into his own hands: sometimes he

even refused to speak with Kabul on the satellite phone, saying that he was dealing with more urgent matters, and left the report on the current situation to the commander Yunus or the Imam Abdulaziz.

In one of his letters Zubair informed Yosir that it had been decided at the very highest level and on the advice of the Sheikh (that was how he referred to Sheikh Bin-Laden), to launch a jihad against Karimov's faithless regime, and so for this period he asked Yosir to act as the point of contact between the mujahedin and the political department. Zubair explained that he would have to give a lot of interviews, and for that reason he needed to keep up to date with all the latest events. In the same letter Zubair also assured Yosir that the Amir would have a word about this matter with commander Juma.

One summer evening, immediately after the evening prayer, Juma's men took him into the headquarters building to see the commander and left him there alone in the room where Yosir had once met Tahir Yuldash in the company of several Arabs. The room was empty, but Yosir could sense with every pore of his skin that he was bring watched. He was even wary of looking around, he just sat there staring at the floor. After a while Jumaboi himself entered the room, but not from the side where Yosir had been expecting him. Juma didn't bother to greet him, but simply said: "Tahirbai called me. You're going in the radio room studio. The commanders will give you a bulletin and you'll broadcast it to Kabul. But none of your metaphors and petaphors! If anything goes wrong, I'll have everyone's heads…"

The delicate subtlety of Juma's voice had always grated on Yosir's nerves, especially in view of the harsh belligerence of the things he said and the peasant strength of his arms. This shrill voice seemed to belong to a completely different man. Once he had even had the shameful thought that if Tahir's beard was not so sparse and Juma's squeaky voice was a bit more substantial, then perhaps their irrepressible ambitions would be diminished somewhat.

Yosir had not quite understood the final threat – he couldn't tell if it was intended for him or foreveryone who would be giving him these bulletins, or foreverybody who was involved in this exceptionally unmilitary undertaking, all the way up to Tahir at the far end, but somehow he didn't feel it was meant for him, and so he wasn't frightened.

"Any questions?" Juma asked, glancing round at him. "When do I go on air and who with?" Yosir asked. "Wait, you'll be informed!" Juma snapped. As he left the courtyard with a dozen pairs of eyes gazing at his back, Yosir was suddenly struck by the thought that he was actually a few years older than Juma.

Chapter Forty-Five

Heh little bird,
heh real live little bird, sitting
proudly on a post, nonetheless
you will not achieve that living
tree in my memory. It's strange,
when I look at you, although I
see this tree,
I myself,
like a man who has fallen on an unfamiliar road
and then goes through the back gate into his yard,
I cannot return to anything in my life...

Here is the poplar, there the narrow lane...
Heh little bird, why are you trembling so?

- Belgi

I was intending to write about the second Batken war in the same way as I did about the first, but the documents brought back from Afghanistan by my journalist friends included a set of wrinkled white sheets of paper that had been neatly arranged in a file with the title "Autumn 2000", and I decided to offer you the contents of this file instead. I believe that Zubair's department, in which Yosir worked for a certain amount of time, collated these summaries of press coverage of the events of August and September that year. They provide an impression in some depth, not only of what took place on the battlefields, or rather "battle mountains", but also of surrounding events.

The clashes between Islamic insurgents and units of the Tajik state army are continuing in the Zagar region and Kyrgyzstan. The government forces of Kyrgyzstan have so far lost 27 men. This week Uzbekistan has also suffered losses. The Ministry of Defence has announced that twelve soldiers have been killed. There are no independent reports of the insurgents' losses. This is the second occasion on which Islamic insurgents from Tajikistan have invaded neighbouring countries. Last autumn insurgents raided the border region between Tajikistan and Kyrgyzstan, seizing three hostages. Who are these men and what are their demands? Shahid Yakub reports:

Last year when a group of Islamic extremists from Tajikistan invaded the Batken region in southern Kyrgyzstan, the local population and government were taken by surprise. Through the efforts of the

181

government forces of Uzbekistan and Kyrgyzstan, the insurgents were driven back out of the region and forced to withdraw to the mountains. A year later the same scenario is being repeated, but this time the insurgents are fighting not only in southern Kyrgyzstan, but also in the south of Uzbekistan, inflicting large losses on government forces. The insurgents claim that they are members of the Islamic Movement of Uzbekistan, an illegal organisation headed by Tahir Yuldash, the former commander of the Uzbek battalion in the United Tajik Opposition. So what is this movement and who are these insurgents? John Shoeberlein, director of the Central Asia International Crisis Group project, believes that this movement is extremely heterogeneous and the different groups that make it up are pursuing different goals:

"I think that they consist of various groups, although it is true that the information we have about them is very meagre. One of the constituent elements is something relatively well organised that we can call the Islamic Movement of Uzbekistan. But there are undoubtedly other supporters of the movement, including men from Tajikistan, former guerrillas from the civil war. However, the largest element consists of men who have fled from Uzbekistan owing to suppression of the opposition from underground Islamic movements."

The Islamic Movement of Uzbekistan claims that its main goal is to invade Uzbekistan and fight against its political regime, which they regard as a regime of infidels, or *kafirs*. However, since this region is so close to Afghanistan, one of the largest producers of narcotics in the world, some people believe that the Islamic insurgents are simply a covering force that seeks to keep the trails open for drug trafficking. John Shoeberlein believes that in view of the known diversity of the insurgents, this possibility cannot be excluded:

"Some people are interested in the financial gain that is involved, it is possible that there is a certain element of collaboration with the narcotics dealers. But some people, undoubtedly, are sincere Islamists who would like to see a return to more fundamentalist forms of Islam in the region. And some of the insurgents are hostile to the government of Uzbekistan and would in any case like to see the end of the present regime there."

The Kyrgyz authorities have accused their Tajik colleagues of collusion in the incursion of Islamic insurgents into their country, although reports continue to claim that they are not in Tajikistan. The Tajik government has denied these allegations, claiming that all the insurgents were expelled to neighbouring Afghanistan. However, the insurgents themselves claim that they have been living in certain villages in Tajikistan for many years. Experts on Central Asia say that this is the Tajik government's fault for failing to take any action over the insurgents, because it simply does

not have control of the entire territory of the country. Some regions of Tajikistan are effectively under the autonomous control of the field commanders, who are fighting a civil war there. Furthermore, analysts believe that some of the key individuals in the Tajik government have had direct contacts with the insurgents' commanders and might even support them. John Shoeberlein again:

"It is possible that certain elements in Tajikistan, perhaps even in the state circles of Tajikistan, are interested in supporting these men for various reasons. These could include putting pressure on Uzbekistan, since Tajikistan is a relatively weak country and it often comes under pressure from Uzbekistan. Providing the insurgents with shelter could be a way of offering some resistance to the Uzbek pressure."

One of the problems facing the Central Asian states invaded by Islamic insurgents is the mountainous landscape and badly trained armies, which lack experience and the appropriate training for a mountain war. Here is the opinion of Roy Allison, head of the Russia and Eurasia programme at the Royal Institute of International Affairs:

"It is rather difficult for them to deploy the kind of military units that would work well in this mountain terrain. Unfortunately, these are not the forces that the Soviet Army possessed in the past. Not even Russia has many units of mountain warfare ordnance. So, bearing in mind the nature of the terrain, they really do struggle to cope with this kind of military incursion."

Uzbekistan has the largest and most powerful army of all the Central Asian states. Kazakhstan and Kyrgyzstan have only recently begun building up their armies. However, the experts say that no matter how powerful and well-trained the military might be, it would be almost impossible to put an end to the Islamic extremists' activities. One important question is just how much support these insurgents might have from the local population. In a region hit by economic crises, unemployment and the ineffective rule of law, public discontent with the authorities is on the increase. And so any possible support for the Islamic insurgents might not be a sign of a desire to return to Islamic roots, but merely a protest against the authorities.

Chapter Forty-Six

From the pupil of my eye
trickling inside me
this autumn world —
as though a bluish balloon

Hamid Ismailov

not able to find a wall
pokes out
in the emptiness
unable to be caught by the eyes.

-Belgi

Yakubjan Alimjanov, who was in the same class as Belgi, tells us:

When we were children we loved to walk up into the mountains. Our village is in a hollow and it's surrounded by mountains on every side. The Chon-Alai mountain range begins to the south of us and runs off into Tajikistan, then further on into China. That was where our grandfathers went to get away from Soviet power. These peaks are always covered with snow, but in order to reach them you have to walk through hills that gradually get higher and higher. As children we didn't have enough time for that. And so we eagerly looked northwards, to where the entire horizon was covered by red mountains with freakish outcrops that looked like palaces or castles. To us children it seemed strange that we saw these castles in front of our eyes every day, and yet neither the geography teacher nor the older lads ever said anything about them, as if they didn't even exist. We felt there was some kind of mystery in it all.

And although those red mountains began at a distance of five to nine kilometres from the village, while the hills to the south were only a stone's throw away, the mountains were more fascinating for us, and one day we decided to walk in that direction and solve that mystery. And we soon found an excuse: our mothers were terribly fond of sour wild rhubarb, and the Kyrgyz who sold it at the market said that it grew over there beyond the red mountains. And so one Sunday we decided to go to collect wild rhubarb, supposedly in order to please our mothers.

There were three of us, all nine years old: me, Asror and Ilyusha Pentakidi – a Greek classmate of ours who, despite being so young, always knew all the secrets of grown-up life, from dating to kissing. He was our leader – on New Year's Eve the previous winter three of us had dressed up in costumes as the Three Musketeers, and Ilyusha had been out Porthos, in canvas army boots with cardboard tops and a starched gauze cloak.

Naturally, we didn't tell anyone about our expedition. Perhaps our childhood was very free, but nowadays I simply can't imagine my children setting out for distant mountains early in the morning, without telling me anything about it. But that's the way things were then. We set out first thing, after filling our rucksacks with provisions. As I have already said, the mountains began right on the horizon, and in order to get to them we had to cross our entire village, until we reached our river, the Kakyr-Sai, and then follow it as far as the distant village of Yotan, taking our course all the time from its Lombardy poplars. After Yotan there were swamps, and Ilyusha suggested that we should take off our canvas boots and tramp along barefoot, squeezing the mud between our toes. There were prickly

thorns tangled up in the grass on this swamp, and we scratched our feet really badly, so when we reached the other river, which, just to make sure that we would lose our way, flowed in a strange direction, not running down from the mountains, but towards them, leading us on a tortuous, twisting path along the mountain range, it felt really good walking over the huge, smooth boulders after that muddy, tedious swamp. But even so, Ilyusha ordered us to turn perpendicularly towards the mountains. Even the way that Ilyusha applied that word "perpendicularly" to real life showed his grown-up experience. We obeyed and turned on to a road with occasional clumps of sheep or goats....

Half an hour later we were already standing at the foot of one of those red mountains. But I must say that the closer we got to the mountains, the less magnificent those mountain castles became. At first we thought the castles were simply being hidden from view, after all we knew that mountains are always piled up on each other, and behind one there is always another, and we thought that we must be seeing the closest mountain, and the castle was on the next one... But on the first sandy mountain there were only chalky or rocky outcrops, and we failed to recognise them as our castles in the air.

I said "sandy mountain". We felt that from the very first step we took on it. What from our village had always looked like red granite rock, turned out to be sand, the loose dust that they used to cover our basketball and volleyball pitches. We crept upwards with our small load, having already lightened our rucksacks and loaded up our stomachs, although the mountain slope tried to send us sliding back down together with its sand. And then Ilyusha's grown-up savvy came to our rescue again: he said we needed to grab hold of the little bushes growing in that loose scree and use them to support our feet too. Fortunately, there were lots of these prickly little bushes, they were almost everywhere, and we slowly but surely crept upwards again, barking our hands on the way.

And so we conquered the first hill, behind which there was a small dip and then another one – this time higher. On this slope there were fewer little bushes, and so our dashes from one to another became more dangerous as we got higher. And although it seemed as if there was nowhere to fall – the same hollow was still there below us - our slanting path nonetheless brought us closer and closer to the line of a rock fall that ran across these red mountains like a white ribbon, widening towards its bottom. To go slipping down on to that rock fall would have been fatal, even Asror and I understood that, let alone quick-witted Ilyusha.

And then, when we had almost reached the peak of this foothill that was almost a mountain, Ilyusha, who was leading our group, showing us what to cling on to and how, suddenly went sliding down on his belly, still clutching a withered bush in his hands – he slipped down as quickly as if the mountain had turned into a conveyor belt. I was three metres away from him to one side, so all I could do was watch him, and I almost let go of my own bush as I watvhed ... And it was only after I recovered my wits, or rather, the other way round, it was only after I saw Ilyusha hanging on Asror's outstretched leg and Asror clinging on for all he was worth to the

nearest two prickly bushes with both hands, that I recovered my wits and dashed across to help them.

Anyway, we reached the top of that sub-mountain, which seemed like Everest to us after what we had been through. Ilyusha was pale and quiet now, only occasionally spitting on the palms of his hands, but I was strangely excited, and Asror, as usual, didn't say anything.

Have you ever been on the top of any kind of mountain? If you have, then you must know that feeling of sudden detachment from the world, from the humdrum and ordinary life: and the wind, rushing at you with the same strength from all sides, and the sun, as if it has suddenly moved down closer, together with the dense blue sky, and the earth, down there in the distance, looking hazy and dreamy now.... And so we sat there on the top of that red mountain, with its slopes running down and away from us on both sides, and we completely forgot about the purpose of our trip and finished off all the food that was left in our rucksacks.

I don't know how long we sat there, but it was long enough for our hands to turn dark from the "ultraviolet rays" – another phrase from real life spoken by Ilyusha, who was getting lively again now, and then his keen eyes spotted a suspension bridge between our mountain and the next one, which wasn't made of red sand, it was real, with granite shoulders and what he called "alpine meadows". But no matter how hard we gazed in the direction that Ilya pointed, neither I nor Asror could make out a thing. "That's where the rhubarb grows!" our Porthos exclaimed, and we set off after him, plodding cautiously along the ridge of our crumbly mountain. In any case, there was no point at all in going back after what had happened on the climb up.

After a while we also saw the slim thread hanging between the two mountains, and we could hear a river roaring on the bottom of the gorge between them, no doubt on its way out into our valley. But when we reached what Ilyusha had decided was a suspension bridge, it turned out to be a trough for water and at our side it ended in a rusty pipe. It was made of three sets of planks nailed together into a channel that ran across about fifty metres of cables wrapped round it to make a kind of net. Ilyusha had to demonstrate his leadership ability, and so he set off first, walking on his knees along the channel, which swayed from side to side. It creaked and swayed about under his feet. A third of the way across, when Ilyusha was already suspended above the precipice, he turned his head back towards us with a dead sort of movement, because it was impossible to turn his body and whispered quite clearly: "You too..."

Now I remember the entire story with horror, but even at the time, for all our childishness, I knew this was the end: if we didn't go and give him some extra weight in the channel, the swaying would make Ilyusha fall, and if we did go – not to save him, but simply to be with him, we would all end up hurtling down together with the channel and be smashed to smithereens. While these thoughts were spinning round in my childish brain, Asror had already crept out on to the channel, somehow intuitively pacing each slow step to match its swaying. There was nothing else I could do but wait until Asror had covered half the distance between Ilya and

myself, then I moved on to the channel as well. I must admit quite honestly that I didn't stay on my knees: once I was half way on to the channel, I simply lay face down on it and crawled, looking at the plank underneath me. The channel creaked unmercifully, but it was obviously used to bearing weight. I remember it as clearly as if it was happening now. At the time there was a strange sort of predestination about that crossing for me: I didn't want to move forward, I was afraid, but I couldn't turn back, it was impossible physically, because the channel was so narrow, and morally, because of my friends. And then, how would I get back home from the peak of this cursed mountain as red as blood?

That channel across the precipice went on forever: at every creak or beat of my heart, I just wanted to force myself down against those three planks of wood and merge into them, like a chip of timber, or a nail, or the dried silt, anything at all, simply in order not to have to move. But suddenly the channel swayed especially hard, as if it had decided to be done with all this fear and tip us out like splashes of water – and that was followed by a howl from Ilyusha of "I'm here" – as if he was rushing to save us – and I instinctively curled up as tight as I could and squeezed my eyes tight shut, and then suddenly, after death failed to come, I realised that Ilya had jumped out of the channel on to the other side!

Again I can remember those jumbled-up childish feelings shifting in time to that swaying: the channel hasn't broken! Ilyusha's safe! But what about us! It was only when my lowered head touched someone's hand that I realised Asror had either waited for me or simply crept backwards, and in that contact of two bodies I felt that safety was close at hand...

We clambered out of that channel and after that I don't remember the rest: I'm sure we didn't find any wild thubarb in those alpine meadows of Ilyusha's, we must have gone down to the river and walked along it out into the valley, but as I live and breathe, I don't remember any of that.

So that's the story.

Chapter Forty-Seven

Goodbye girl, farewell girl,
free your eyes from the sea,
now your road is from the tracks of the wind,
now there is no halt like me.

The thread was broken, the ferry disappeared,
our clocks went in different directions.
There were two words left unsaid by me:
I remember just one: "end".

Hamid Ismailov

Clashes, wordless looks,
the mysterious nothing between us
now starts a new emptiness,
if the sea will roll up sleeves,

if the sea will run, and rushing
fill my eyes again,
is this death or another death
the reason of this death?

-Belgi

A story from Andrei Rainik, a classmate of Belgi Abutov:

In our class everyone was in love with a girl called Natasha. She was either a Karachai or she came from somewhere in the North Caucasus, but we didn't understand that then, we simply thought she was a miracle of nature. She had braids that were as black as tar, eyes that were like black olives, slim black eyebrows and delicate features traced out on flawless white skin. Belgi was in love with her too, but he never admitted it.

I realised it one day, though. Children are a lot cleverer and more cunning than people who are grown up usually think. One day Natasha was the class monitor, and she stayed behind to tidy up after the Saturday classes: wash the blackboard, wipe the floor. We were playing football on the school pitch. In the middle of the game I remembered that I'd left my briefcase in the classroom and I went back. Natasha was already finishing her cleaning, and I asked her to hand me my briefcase, so that I wouldn't leave tracks on the freshly washed floor. She gave it to me, but when I went back to the other lads, who were already sitting in the shade under a tree, something strange came over me, and I started acting just like Ilyusha Pentakidi, telling them that I went into the classroom and Natasha was washing the floor on all fours.... I went up to her from behind and....

I still remember the way Belgi flushed as all the other lads laughed obscenely, how he walked away, supposedly to get the ball, and didn't come back again that day. But as I already mentioned, all of us said that we "fancied' Natasha, only Belgi never admitted it to anyone. Although later, in seventh class, after his mother died and he went away to a different town to live with his grandmother, the girls told us that Natasha started writing to him, and she had his photograph.

You know the way it usually happens. The most beautiful girls, the ones everyone fancies, end up without anyone, and Natasha was left on her own up until tenth class – everybody took their simple, approachable Lenka, Aichirek or Nuriya, and Belgi's best friend, Yakub Alimjanov, tried to tag on to her, and so did another one – Vityok Guzev, but I don't know if anything came of it.

After tenth class she moved away to Samara, which was still Kuibyshev then. I think Vityok Guzev went there too. I don't know if Natasha was writing to Belgi at that time. But one day, when she was on her way home from a dance, she was hit by a truck and killed – she was only eighteen. I know Yakub told Belgi about it, and he was really shaken.... But as for him becoming a poet, I don't know anything about that....

Chapter Forty-Eight

If Yosir had been called a "war correspondent" he would certainly have been insulted. Apart from the very beginning of the first year, he fought alongside all the others – went out on night sorties, withdrew under helicopter fire, fired and returned fire. Although, when the fighting was over and their multinational team, which, apart from the Uzbeks, included Kyrgyz and Uigurs, Chechens and Arabs, starting boasting in their common language of Russian, defying the fear of death they had felt by counting up how many men they had killed, Yosir usually moved away, and everyone assumed it was to make a report to the Centre. And since no one could accuse him of cowardice or of being defeatist, with a certain degree of irritation they allowed this correspondent to detach himself from the heated conversation around the campfire.

Of course, Yosir had read books by "war correspondents" from the Second World War. He had always felt embarrassed for these "professional" writers, he could tell from every line they wrote that they themselves felt awkward about hanging around at the staff headquarters in the rear, the commanders' dugouts or the field hospitals, and then describing the heroism of the front line. No, the life and the war that Yosir had here were different, he would like to have thought they were genuine, but there was still a strange game-like quality about it all, and even in mid- battle, with bullets flying over his head, Yosir felt as if he were in the middle of the Chirchik firing range for the summer training exercises, at which the enemy was called "the potential adversary". It was the same here. Against whom and for what end were he and his brothers-in- arms really fighting? Against Karimov and his corrupt regime? They were far away in Tashkent, no doubt panting and sweating over a plate of pilaf and a bottle of cognac... For the holy cause of Tahir Yuldash? He was probably sitting down to his pilaf in Kabul with the Arab sheikhs, and panting and sweating, of course.... Another "Comrade Islam"'....

But these thoughts would be knocked out of his head when a mine exploded ten metres away, throwing him behind the rocks, and the shower of shrapnel and pieces of a human body was followed by a hail of bullets intended to take his life....

Hamid Ismailov

He never took these seditious thoughts back with him to Shiver, beyond Hodja-Achkan, when they went back to base and spent a long time washing themselves clean in the mountain stream, getting back into the drowsy routine until the next sortie.

Chapter Forty-Nine

To sea, tired as sky,
to sea, broken as sky,
to sea twilit as sky
when my solitariness worships.

The ladder of the railway is long,
the ladder of the railway is without end,
the ladder of the railway lies down to sleep,
the real name for the clouds is snow.

The wild grass in the dense bushes abounds,
the wild grass in the dense bushes is intertwined,
the wild grass in the dense bushes is like hair,
but instead of lice, dead fish make it their home.

These words don't refer to me, t
hese words were born before me,
these words, these words are instead of a mudbrick wall:
the grass that embraces the dust is waiting for you.

-Belgi

The original of this material, from the IMU file "Autumn 2000", is covered with markings in red pencil and various notes. It is a speech by President Karimov concerning the events of that autumn.

Uzbek leader exhorts "repentant" guerrillas to return home. An extract from a report by Uzbek Television on September 7 (The video shows the ceremony as Islam Karimov is seen off at Tashkent airport). Today the President of Uzbekistan, Islam Karimov, left for New York to take part in the Millenium Meeting at the highest level of the United Nations. The Uzbek president gave an interview to journalists before his departure. President Karimov called for reforms in the United Nations to allow immediate action on the issue of the Aral Sea. Question: Islam Abduganievich, what were your feelings and your thoughts yesterday

when you signed the decree granting exemption from liability to those who had joined terrorist groups in error? (The video shows Islam Karimov, surrounded by journalists.) "I think there are some things that people simply can't understand, whether they happen to be the president or an ordinary worker. It is incomprehensible when men raise their hands to strike against their own people, when men who grew up on this land and, as the Uzbeks say, ate the salt of this land and drank its water, under the influence of certain negative elements in various terrorist and extremist centres, take up arms against their native land. I have to say this, because this is also their land, and they were born here. They are coming back to this land to kill, plunder, burn and bring grief to the mothers who live here. I think this is unnatural. There is no justification for this. That is the first thing.

"And this is the second thing. There are people who are easily influenced, especially when they are young, people who do not have their own convictions, their own ideology, who do not have any firm position in life. They are deceived, they seduced by dollars. I would like to repeat, they are seduced by dollars. Their youthful, pure and healthy aspiration – to do something for themselves, for their families, their Homeland – is turned into its exact opposite. That is, attempts are made to pollute them with ideas that are absolutely and fundamentally false. These are the ideologies of extremism, Wahhabism, Hizb-Tahrir and similar tendencies. Their teaching radically contradicts our sacred religion, Islam. From this point of view, what is happening in this area is being done by those people who are our genuine enemies. These people are dreaming once again of creating a parasitic Uzbekistan. They dream of establishing a theocratic system here, a kind of Islamic state or Caliphate, as they call it. They want to take our country back to the middle ages, to obscurantism, as if we were not living in the twentieth century. That is, they wish to take us back to the eighth and ninth centuries. It is hard to digest this, there is so much rubbish in it for a normal person. But at the same time, this rubbish, this plague and disease, are capable of infecting the minds of young people. Our bitter experience has convinced us of this.

"My idea, my desire, if you like, my earnest desire, is to give those people who have got stuck abroad, above all in Afghanistan and Tajikistan, to give one more chance to those who have repented to return to their homeland. They do not have to beat their chests and weep bitter tears in order to prove that they are repentant. It must be in their hearts. Let them return to their homeland. Let them return to the open arms of their parents, their relatives and families and live like all people who live in Uzbekistan at the present time, our multinational people, which desires only one thing: a better life, peace and stability in our country. They wish to feel certain of the future of our young people and be certain that our old people will depart from our land in peace."

And this is the statement made by the Amir of the Islamic Movement of Uzbekistan, Tahir Yuldash, in one of the interviews he gave to foreign radio services.

"In the name of God the Gracious and the Merciful.

"What is happening in the south of Uzbekistan, in the Uzun and Saryasia districts of the Sukhandarin region is a response to the incorrect policy of the Karimov regime. For eight years we have been warning this regime, and now our warning has been put into effect. In continuation of the holy jihad that we declared against this regime last year, for more than three days now the mujahedin who make up the Islamic Movement of Uzbekistan have been pursuing their jihad there.

Question: Many people note that this region is far away from your centres. What is the purpose of the jihad being carried out there, what goals are you pursuing with it?

TY: We, the Islamic Movement of Uzbekistan, consist of representatives of all the districts and regions of Uzbekistan, and this movement is capable of carrying out a jihad in any of the districts of Uzbekistan and pursuing its high goals.

Question: The Uzbek Minister of Foreign Affairs has just claimed that the armed men infiltrated the area from Tajikistan, and accused the Tajik authorities, and in particular the opposition, of facilitating them. How well-founded are these accusations?

TY: This is an absolutely groundless assertion. We have completely withdrawn from Tajikistan, and a long time has passed since we left Tajikistan. It is our Muslim brothers within Uzbekistan who have begun these actions, after making their preparations. As for this claim – it is a new slander against us by the authorities.

Question: On the first day of these events we phoned the Saryasia hospital and they told us that six wounded soldiers from the government forces were being treated there. Today the Minister of Foreign Affairs stated that three soldiers had been killed in the fighting. Is this fighting still going on, and what losses are there on your side?

TY: These clashes are continuing in the mountain uplands of Saryasia and the authorities' losses are much greater than they state. Several dozen men have been killed and a few men have been taken prisoner. On our side, Allah be praised, there have not been any losses. Our mujahedin are fighting selflessly for their high ideals and the fighting is continuing at this very moment.

Question: On the first day of these events, it became known that shepherds in the mountains had been taken hostage. What has happened to them?

TY: These words are without any basis, we do not have anything against our Muslim people, we are fighting against the regime and the butchers of the Tashkent regime. Everthing else is a slander against us.

Question: You say that soldiers of the government forces have been taken prisoner. What will happen to them?

TY: Time will tell. The regime is holding hundreds of thousands of our supporters prisoner, under arrest. As far as these men are concerned, God willing, we shall decide this matter in the future. The regime is once again spreading slander about us, saying that there are Arabs, Pashtu and Turkmen in our ranks. This is a groundless assertion. Those who are fighting there now are all Uzbeks, devoted mujahedin. The Islamic Movement of Uzbekistan categorically rejects this slander. And in particular the assertion that there are Turkmenis there is an attempt to involve neutral Turkmenistan in these events.

Question: The number of your guerrillas in the area of military action is being given as from seventy to a hundred men. How accurate is this figure?

TY: Our movement has not tens, or even hundreds, but thousands of members. And the movement involves not ten, or seventy, as they claim, but a much greater number of men. And so we cannot tell you how many there are, since it is a military secret, but we can say that we have sufficient forces to oppose the regime.

Chapter Fifty

I have said several times that there are events in Yosir's life that only I know about. I thought for a long time about whether I should tell you what I am about to tell you now, and I can say quite honestly that I am signing off this chapter when everything else in the book has already been written and has even settled into place to some extent. I was worried for a long time by one particular phrase that Zubair let slip as if by accident in one of the letters that were brought to me from Afghanistan. In the middle of a string of flowery phrases, he suddenly mentions, entirely out of the blue, that they all watched the film *Nido* which he and Yosir had made together, "at the Sheikh's place".

In the Islamic Movement of Uzbekistan there was only one man who was called "sheikh" – Osama bin-Laden. Zubair, as a rather mediocre individual, was apparently very fond of emphasising his own position and dropping the names of his contacts. I was told by one western journalist how, after he had been "chasing" an interview with Juma Namangani for a long time, he deliberately played on this side of Zubair's personality, until the press secretary eventually promised to arrange this unprecedented interview, and then one fine day the journalist's telephone rang. It was Zubair, as always over-pretentious and full of his own importance. But this time, according to the journalist, he didn't give the impression of having Tahir Yuldash standing behind him with his hand over the mouthpiece, checking every word. And what he said next was:

"Well now, there is someone here who would like to talk to you" – and he handed the phone to someone.

My friend, of course, guessed who was on the other end of the satellite phone. He was surprised by the thin, sweet voice of the other party, who immediately said: "Assalomu alaikum, this is Jumaboi..." yes it really was Jumaboi Namangani. The time was between the first and second Batken wars, which means some time in spring 2000. They exchanged the standard courtesies, following which my friend said that Juma was impossible to track down for an interview, to which Juma replied: "That's my profession, being elusive". They laughed, and then the journalist asked the commander if he could interview him, since the whole world was already talking about him, and he had never made any public statements. Juma replied: "We're only military men, there are ideologists here who do the talking for us". My friend pressed the point that the world wanted to know about Juma as a personality, and so it would be interesting to record a conversation with him simply about life – who he was, what he was – to which Juma once again replied politely: "When the time comes, we'll sit and have a talk, we definitely will". Then he added: "I'm not a great talker anyway". Like everyone from Namangan, Juma addressed the other man in the third person. They spoke a bit more about this and that, then Juma said: "If you want to know something about us, we have a man here – Yosir – you'll be able to contact him through the people I'm handing the phone to..."

After saying his sweet-voiced farewells, he handed the phone to Zubair and Zubair, even more full of himself now, asked "Well now, do we keep our promises or not?" (By the way, only very recently rumours have begun circulating that Zubair was shot by Juma Namangani for being an agent of the Uzbek Special Services, just before Juma himself was killed, but since Namangani's death itself remains unproven and unconfirmed, it is hard to say anything certain about whether he killed Zubair or find any proof.)

And so, Zubair was always fond of name-dropping or hinting at important connections. But in any case I phoned my friend about that letter in which Zubair mentions the "Sheikh". My friend is a journalist who knew the entire movement from quite close up, in particular Zubair, who used to call him from time to time about "the latest achievements of the IMU". And he confirmed that this meeting had indeed taken place. A little later he gave me the telephone number of one of the Uzbeks in Afghanistan, who told me a few meagre details of the meeting. But later still, when the IMU's tape recordings were left homeless following the American bombing raids and eventually found their way into my hands, I came across one tape which I think is of this meeting.

They – Zubair, Yosir and Umar – were not taken to the Sheikh in the same way as the rare foreign journalists – mostly Pakistanis or Arabs – were usually taken, blindfolded or even worse, with a sack over their heads. No, they were put in a closed jeep with blinds on the windows and two men with automatic rifles sat beside them, supposedly protecting them against any possible incidents on the road. Naturally, they only understood all this in hindsight, before the meeting Amir Muhammad Tahir Farruk simply phoned Zubair urgently and ordered him to take the film with him and wait for a jeep that would call for him at the Headquarters building.

They drove for a long time, but then every road in Afghanistan is long and wearisome. The jeep rattled over the ruts for five or even six hours. Yosir had come off night duty, so he was dead on his feet. Zubair tried to impress the taciturn Arab guards with his Arabic, appealing constantly to the authority of his fellow-countryman, the Imam Bukhari. Out of respect for the Imam, the Arabs did not tell Zubair to shut up, and so they rode on to the roaring of the motor and the ceaseless flow of the press secretary's Arabic. Yosir, half-asleep, was unable to understand why they were driving for so long, since he had assumed they were being taken to someone like Vakil Ahmad Mutavakkil, with whom Tahir Yuldash was on close terms, in order to hand over the film to some Arab who ran the Badr website, or to someone else....

Eventually Yosir lost all sense of time, and when the jeep stopped once, and then several more times, and each time ferocious Arabs stuck their heads in, and then it finally came to halt, and this time the rear door swung open, it was just as dark outside in the courtyard as it was in the jeep. This was obviously not the residence of Vakil Ahmad Mutavakkil: it was a mountain village that reminded Yosir keenly of his own native Eski-Naukat, and the chilly air nipped at his nose: the stars above his head were bright and full... Then they were searched, and every fold in their clothes was checked. But even now Yosir didn't realise where he had been brought. It was funny to watch Zubair showing off and trying to joke in Arabic, but the men here just got on with their job: they barked at the press secretary and he immediately fell silent....

They were led through some dark courtyards, from one yard to the next. Yosir had once been in the alleyways of the Acha Obod gypsy quarter of Tashkent, where he had been surrounded in exactly the same way, until he had finally been relieved of his last kopeck, and suddenly the mischievous feeling of that frivolous gypsy roguery reawoke in him, and he no longer felt afraid of anything. After all these labyrinths of clay and stone, they were led into an Afghan house, where they were searched once again, then through one room into another, and there they were told to sit and wait. An unspeaking Arab sat facing them, swaying in time to his own prayer, Zubair now maintained a haughty silence and

Yosir immersed himself in his childhood impressions of those mountain village houses where you could sit for hours in total idleness, examining the corners and the niches by the light of a dull twenty-watt electric bulb.

By this time both Zubair and Yosir knew perfectly well where they had been brought. About an hour went by and then a man suddenly came in from behind an Afghan rug on the wall, not where there was a door, but straight through a hole in the wall, and he asked them to follow him. They walked through another room with armed *shahids* and entered a small but very comfortable room that smelled of spices, where there were several men sitting along the wall, including the Amir Tahir Yuldash. Zubair suddenly fell to his knees and started bowing his forehead to the ground – or so it seemed to the startled Yosir. He heard the Amir's embarrassed voice speaking in Arabic: "There is nothing we can do about about the reverence that they feel for you". A softer, guttural voice replied: "Worthy of all praise is Allah..." The Amir directed them with his gaze to the place by the door where they were supposed to sit and Yosir supported the overexcited Zubair as he sat down at the copiously spread low table.

There were six men sitting in the room and the Sheikh, who was at the head of the table, was leaning back against the butt of an automatic rifle hanging on the wall above him. Now here is the promised transcript of the meeting:

Sheikh: Why should our brothers suffer such torment?

Amir: Our mujahedin are prepared not only to suffer the temporary inconvenience of the road, but if necessary to give their lives for you, Most Worthy Sheikh....

Sheikh: Allah be praised! Allah be praised! Islam has need of such warriors as will bring victory to those oppressed and enslaved by the *kafirs*....

Amir: These mujahedin, as I said, are from the ideological department.

Sheikh: Ma sha Allah! Whatever Allah desires, so shall all be! Our brothers must know that we have wounded Satan in his very heart! Now he is writhing in his deathbed agony! The hour is near when what has been done by our brother *shahids* will raise up armies of our supporters, and we shall liberate the world from the power of Satan! The law in the world is this: he who is strongest is victorious.

Alish: (clearing his throat awkwardly) Is it true that you... hmm-hmm... once used to collaborate with America? With its special...

Amir: (hurrying to interrupt): In Islam it is permitted for the sake of victory over a great evil to employ the force of a lesser evil.... The

holy jihad that our most worthy Sheikh once declared against the Soviet Empire destroyed the power of the godless Bolsheviks and allowed us the chance, Allah be praised, to return to our Islamic roots ...

Sheikh: Alhamdu Lillah, Alhamdu Lillah! Allah be praised!

Amir: And now that we have done away with the Empire of Evil, it is the turn of the Empire of Satan.

Alish: I think Ronald Reagan was the first to call the Soviet Union the Empire of Evil, wasn't he? Do you recall?

Sheikh: The traces of Soviet propaganda still remain strong in the minds of the young people of Maverannahr. And yet this is the land that gave Islam Al Bukhari and At-Termezi, Al Marginani and Al Zamahshari....

Amir: We are working tirelessly to turn them on to the straight and radiant path of Allah, and Allah will help us in this.... (he changes the subject of conversation). Our brother has made a film about the painful path of this awakening, about the sufferings of our brothers and sisters. And if the most worthy Sheikh will permit, our brother will show this film and our young interpreter will try to the best of his ability to translate this terrible story.

Sheikh: Ma sha Allah... May it be as Allah wishes!

(everybody is silent for a long time, the film can be heard being shown, but its sounds cannot be clearly distinguished)

Sheikh: Well now, the oppressed Muslims shed many tears. But the time requires these tears to turn to stone, to become a weapon in their hands. A cobblestone to use against the oppressors and enslavers....

Alish: Do you mean the cobblestone of the proletariat? And against our own enslavers – our rulers and those like them?

Amir: Them too, but in the first place the most worthy Sheikh has in mind the hosts of Satan – America and its henchmen, who sow mischief on the earth.

Sheikh: Our brothers razed to the ground two pillars at the very centre of their world...

Belgi: But innocent people died in them. People's husbands, wives, sisters, brothers, brides... You say that the tears must become stone, but can blood be washed away with stone and blood? Do not tears wash away blood?

Amir: It is war. *A la guerre comme a la guerre*, as your French say...

Belgi: But the Koran says, let him who has killed an innocent person know that he has destroyed his own soul

197

Sheikh: Alhamdu lillah! Allah be praised! But the Koran teaches us to oppose mischief on the earth. Mischief is worse than death, says Allah. And the Americans are preparing any day now to invade Afghanistan, a Muslim land. Do you think then that we should wait while they bomb every one of us and mingle us with the earth?

Alish: (speaking out of turn) Pardon me, I am no great specialist on the Koran, although they made us learn it off by heart at the Department of Oriental Studies, but we have an Uzbek saying: "The coward raises his fists first"....

Amir: Our people have many different prejudices....

Sheikh: Do not say so, this is great wisdom. Just look at who raises his fist first, who has occupied the holy lands of Mecca and Medina and tramples them with his infidel boots, who is now sending aircraft carriers and B-51s to Afghanistan, who....

(at this point the *azan*, or call to prayer, sounds)

Sheikh: The people have already assembled for the evening prayer. You, brother, lead the prayer. The people have need of an inspired word, and we shall quickly conclude our debate and join you...

I have seen the film *Nido* or *The Groan*. Alish told me that a long time before he made it, Yosir had devised a scenario for a cartoon film. In actual fact, he hadn't really invented it, the scenario was something that happened to him every night in his flat in Tashkent, when he put his little brother to bed. He sat at his brother's feet in the dark room while the boy went to sleep, and he looked out of the window. There was another block of flats standing opposite theirs, and Belgi would examine the windows of the other building: in one window the people watched television all evening, in another there was a palm tree growing and a glimpse of a doorway in the form of an arch, in which a woman dressed in red occasionally appeared, in a third there was an old woman feeding several cats, in a fourth an alcoholic husband was being beaten with a rolling pin by his shrew of a wife. In short, every window was aglow with its own life. And then one after another the windows went dark. There was only one left, in which a man with dishevelled hair was smoking as he tapped something out on a typewriter: he could have been writing a novel, finishing his dissertation or sending in his latest complaint – there was no way Belgi could guess. But even this window went dark, and then Belgi's own face was reflected in the blank window, and the drops of night rain slid down the glass like his tears...

This was the scenario for that cartoon film. And, either consciously or unconsciously, Yosir had tried to repeat it in the film *Nido*, telling one

life after another, lighting up and then extinguishing the windows of people's stories, which ultimately reflected his own life story and his own face....

While the film was running, Yosir recalled that old sensation of the blank window, the impression of the Tashkent rain and the smell of the spring dust, which these men sitting along the walls almost certainly knew nothing about....

After the film, which concluded with the mute face of an orphan boy gazing into the camera as if it were a window, the first to speak was the Sheikh. He said slowly and quietly: "There is very much grief in this film. But grief gives rise to the search for justice, and the sense of justice leads to jihad. We have to show the young people of Maverannahr devotedly following this path of jihad. And this boy, insh'Allah, will become a mujahed..."

As the evening went on, according to Alish, Yosir said less and less and watched the other men, especially the Sheikh, who reminded him so much of someone that the feeling was like a itch, and then only later on he realised that he had seen that morbidly exquisite face with the black shadows under the eyes in an Indian miniature that was a portrait of the last of the Great Mogul emperors, Aurangzeb, seated in prayer.... Just as he was thinking this, he caught the Sheikh's glance on him: glances like that always mean much more than long conversations, because they remain imprinted on the mind – one man perceives the other without words: and that was how they remained in each other's memory – Sheikh Osama and the unknown Uzbek, Yosir - in the clear realisation, shot through with apprehension, that each had understood the other totally.

Chapter Fifty-One

I can feel that my work is coming to an end, but not reaching a conclusion. For how can one draw conclusions on a man's life when perhaps God has not yet drawn his? I look at the piece of paper on which I sketched out ideas as I was just getting down to work, and I see on it the form of a tree which starts from the word "Belgi" and then branches into three parts: "Previous life", "History of power" and "Life in the IMU". So apparently I was intending to review the poet's biography. I gaze at the section on "Previous life", which is, in turn, provisionally divided into "Symbolic scenes" and "Leading scenes". Below "Symbolic scenes" there are two little boxes – "Development" and "Uzbekness", while "Leading scenes" is followed by "Leading to Islam" and "Islam".

Then these two sets of scenes are united under a circle marked "Events", and below that there is a list: "Grandfather", "Grandmother", "The West", "The Gathering", "Moscow", "Tashkent".

The space under "History of power" is empty, although there is a dotted line leading to the abundant material under the third section "Life in the IMU". This life is divided into two: "Hoit" and "Afghanistan". Under "Hoit" there is only one little square, and written in it is: "Division/Writing", followed by "Main events": "Conception", "Tajikistan", "Independent Movement", "Explosions", "Batken", "Saryasiya", "Hizbut", "Afghanistan", "Final". And, finally, below the upper "Afghanistan" there is a little circle with the words "Restored to faith/action".

And the lines come back together again on "Belgi-Yosir".

This is just like trying to analyse Belgi's poetry. Working out what I had in mind, and what has come of it. If I ponder seriously, I can discern my initial logic. And then the way I followed it as I wrote this biography. But on the question of whether I am any closer to an understanding of the broad canvas of Belgi's life, and especially its final years, it is not so much that I remain uncertain, as that I deliberately allow scope for different interpretations. On the one hand, the initial impulse seems to have dictated the way one chapter follows another, but when I take a closer look, there is a fairly large gap between the destination dictated by the plan and the place to which the pen, following the dictates of life, has led.

I have noticed that when I break off from writing this biography, owing to one circumstance or another, I start having dreams with more or less the same subject. You know, surely, how resistant the settings of dreams are to change – the day before yesterday you could go racing along in the car on this same gravel road, under these same trees, on the way to get the shopping, and now, only a couple of days later, the landscape hasn't changed all that much, but the mood is completely different and, accordingly, so is the action, and the theme. And because of that, you simply don't realise that the setting is still the same...

Well then, I found myself in a mountain village with a road surfaced with crushed stone, and I got out of the bus or, more likely, the truck that had given me a lift and set out towards the shadow of a house where someone was supposed to be a waiting for me, or where I once acted out a different life, and all the while I was observing events from the inside. While I was trying to observe if there was anyone in the yard, a man approached me from behind – he had a big thick beard, and so his spiritual authority was incontestably established. I didn't know him

personally, but I must have heard of him, and been even more familiar with his reputation, since I could sense his importance without even knowing who he was.

Let him be Mullah Abduvali-kori – it's a convenient enough title. People of that kind usually wander around in dervish courtyards, exuding a scent of musk, and there really was a kind of cultivated righteousness about him that defined the contours of the place where I now found myself. And yet, he approached me in the way that soldiers approach the cook – out of some ordinary, everyday need, but for me that was enough.

And then immediately I spotted the mountains in the distance, and I thought that over there, between the two peaks that could just be made out beyond the apricot trees, there ought to be a river, and when you looked down on it from above like a bird in flight, there ought to be a camp in the flood plain of that river. It might be surrounded, as usual, by trees, and beyond that by scattered clay buildings, but from up here the camp appeared all of a piece – marked off from everything else by a clearly visible fence and a dense palisade of poplars on sentry duty.

That flight took me into the camp and, observing the river while in flight, I realised that Batken, which, naturally, I could not pronounce in my dream, was there somewhere, further upstream. It was just the kind of feeling that you might get in Shahimardan – further upstream, where the Jordan is – you look up and down the river and think: and over there is the road to Kashgar...

But quicker than this river rushing towards me, quicker than my guess about Batken, I found that I was armed. There an automatic rifle hanging across my chest and I was walking upstream beside the river, moving up from one rocky shelf to the next as they got steeper and steeper. Since the plan of the camp was still staked out in my mind, the rock ledges unfolded as empty buildings, which I had to break into cautiously and spray with a burst of automatic fire – just to be on the safe side. I cautiously made my way up, steeper and steeper, and at every bend I threw up my LA 7821 and belched fire at the startled shadows in the next half-ruined building or bunkhouse.

Something was still lacking to complete the feeling and the picture. It was like a hint at which way to go, but I didn't hear the word Hoit or Batken that seem quite obvious in the waking state, and amid the resounding pronouncement of those bursts of fire, I strove with all my might to catch hold of this thing on which my life seemed to depend. And at the very last moment a burst of fire seemed to explode in my brains, and I cried out together with it, to exalt my rapture, or to crush my fear: "Allahu Akbar! Allahu Akbar!"

Hamid Ismailov

Chapter Fifty-Two

As Pushkin said: "There is an ecstasy in battle, on the very edge of the precipice..." It's true. All our lives we have wondered why the generation of so-called "war poets" remained stuck in a war that was over long ago, as if there was nothing happening in the life around them any more.

And whenever I asked Afghanistan and Chechnya veterans, or men who fought in Batken, what they felt in battle, their eyes glittered and they looked away.

I can only try to guess what Belgi felt as he held his smoke-blackened gun at the ready somewhere high in the mountains, near the Turo glacier that will never be anything more than a geographical name for us – up among the blinding, almost black, snow, behind one of the rare, sharp rocky outcrops that protected them by night from the piercing wind and by day from the unnaturally loud and clear fire of the special unit of "Scorpions" who had been dropped in their rear.

The radio told them not to make a fuss and wait until darkness came, but it was an entire lifetime until darkness, and here the rocky outcrops crumbled away under persistent bombardment, and the whistling bullets set avalanches of snow sliding down into the abyss.

That time they lost three mojahedin and they had to bury them hastily in the icy snow, in order to come back for their bodies later, only that never happened, since that very night, as they were making their way back through the gorge to the base camp in groups of three or four, following paths that only they knew, the first snow of the new season fell. And so those youths – one from Andijan, one from Ferghana and one from Tashkent – were left there, without their guns, beneath those blackest-dark skies, beneath that leaden-grey snow.

After engagements like that, as they were washing their camouflage uniforms – some of them bloody, some of them torn on the sharp edges of the rocks – for some reason Yosir always used to remember the same moment of his life: it was during the trip to Bamberg, when one day they were taken to the house of the local professor of Iranian studies, Bert Fragner, who had as his guest a celebrated Muslim calligraphic artist whose name Yosir simply could not recall. The names of infidel foreigners all bore the distinctive marking of ownership, while Muslim names, and names even from further East, for instance Chinese names, were as if faceless, they were something common and inconsequential, in these parts even poets disdained their own names and addressed themselves in the estranged third person: Hey, Hafiz; Hey, Fuzuli....

That was the way the world-class Muslim artist had referred to himself and to others, the way the men from Namangan here did – in the

third person: "And where would they themselves be from...", "So, they say that they write poetry, and this servant of theirs happens to write pictures..."

That banquet at Professor Fragner's old estate, on the top of a hill from which the beautiful Bavarian town of Bamberg was visible in all its ancient magnificence, had been a great success: superbly subtle Burgundy and Rhine wines, an astonishing variety of delicious international food prepared by the professor, complemented with an incredibly delicious selection of desserts prepared by his wife, and all of it seasoned with profoundly intellectual conversations about Saadi, or Blanchot, or Nichoti or Bo Vey.

Anyway, it had turned out that the artist had rediscovered the geometrical laws underlying Arabic writing and numerology, and had gone even further than that – in a certain sense he had proved mathematically that the ninety-nine glorious names of the All-High or, in the Prophet Muhammad's phrase, "the hundred minus one names of Allah" represented the reality of an infinitely expanding cube, which is the initial dot of Arabic script. As he explained it, this starting point was also the basic atom in both the Universe of things and the Universe of the soul, the Universe of writing. As he spoke, he quickly dashed off the first letter of the alphabet, Aleph, and it consisted of seven dots, just as a standing man consists of seven parts equal in size to the dot of the head.... "But why precisely seven?" he had asked, and immediately gone on to reveal the nature of this number as a mathematical phenomenon by taking his calculator out of his pocket and dividing all the natural numbers by it, and in every single case the magic of the little machine sent the figures speeding off into eternity, and then he immediately sketched a geometrical figure with seven points and again demonstrated the infinite number of ways it could be laid out, and then immediately expanded it through the colour spectrum, and once again certain laws were manifested, which were hard to follow with the mind, but the heart beat eagerly to their rhythm.... "And then, when a man prostrates himself in prayer, he touches the ground at seven points..." the artist had concluded and moved on to further marvels of proportion and harmony.

The artist's endless stream of mathematical revelations had set Belgi's head spinning as he used first calligraphy, and then geometry, and then his calculator to demonstrate the amazingly harmonious proportions of the world created by the All-Merciful, adducing as he went along *ayats*, or signs, apparently drawn at random from the Koran, to confirm his calculations....

That day a little group of listeners had gathered round the artist, but suddenly there had been a peal of thunder in the darkening twilit sky and a storm had begun out of nowhere, driving the guests out of the

garden to take shelter under the veranda roof. Everyone had laughed at this sudden crush, with one person's hastily grabbed-up plate clattering against someone else's silver cutlery, and then half an hour later it had turned fine again and the air was so fresh that everyone had drifted back into the garden, some with cups of coffee and some with bowls of green tea, and then the artist had led the poet aside and told him: "What I was saying earlier was certainly known to Al-Farabi and Ibn-Sina, but neither of them give any more than hints in their manuscripts. The essence of this world is concealed by a veil – so perhaps what happened in the middle of our conversation was a sign?"

In translation, the word "Belgi" means a sign. Perhaps that was why Yosir so often recalled that particular evening and that particular party at the home of Professor Fragner, who himself had an inventive mind and was fond of signs, and under that veranda roof during that merciless downpour, he had expounded his own theory of the *uluses*, those vast administrative districts devised by Genghiz Khan for his conquered territories, saying that once Genghiz Khan had established his four *uluses*, this mental map had been established forever: how else could you explain the fact that Tamerlaine had fought campaigns against Toktamish – driving him all the way to Moscow – and against Bayazid – conquering Istanbul in the process, but he really never left his own viceregents in these places, he simply rearranged the hierarchy of *uluses*...

And so now, when they were on their way back to their winter quarters in the mountains between Tajikistan and Kyrgyzstan, in order to avoid going completely insane, Yosir ruminated on what mental map they were redrawing with their mountain sorties ...

When anyone in this band of Chechens, Arabs and a couple of Uzbeks and Tajiks argued about anything, it was always about the bombings in Uzbekistan having set the pattern for the West and the USA, and how the West would be given the same gift that Uzbekistan had received after February 16 – a jihad, but a jihad in which not only mujahedin, but also rank-and-file Muslims would rise to their feet and fight the oppressors.

Yosir tried superimposing the Bamberg discussions on the Pamir-Alai arguments and arrived at some strange conclusions. But if he had expressed even a hundredth part of his thoughts, not only would he have been laughed down – at best he would have been arrested, but at worst he could even have been shot on the spot either for anti-constitutional propaganda or for undermining discipline and insubordination, and so Yosir then withdrew ever more deeply into himself.

Chapter Fifty-Three

Yosir's only contact with the outside world was through phone calls from Zubair, to whom he reported on the current situation, but only occasionally in the presence of Juma, who did not really like to get too close to the satellite phone, remembering what had happened to Dudaev in Chechnya, and so more often the report was given in the presence of one of Juma's aides, usually his nephew Ilkhom, who always tried to correct Yosir as he was speaking on the phone. But on the rare occasions when Juma was sitting beside him, after his report Yosir always told Zubair that the commander was there and handed the phone to Juma so that he could he could exchange hasty pleasantries with Zubair in his unnatural, sugary voice.

Even though Zubair was now the head of the *Devan*, or political department, of the IMU – a kind of secretary-general, in fact – in addition to being the movement's press-secretary, he still did not carry any real weight. Yosir realised that Amir Tahir had appointed Zubair to this position in order to consolidate his own sovereign power, but as soon as armed hostilities had begun the previous year, Juma's authority had started to grow, not only among his own men, as a direct result of the military action, which he commanded, but also among the Taliban and the Arabs. They started sometimes going directly to Juma, and the press, which was monitored by Yosir and by Zubair in Kabul virtually made Juma the leader of the IMU. Juma himself could feel this now, and so even when he spoke with Zubair after a report, he never asked after the Amir in order to report to him in person, as he used to do: on the contrary, it seemed as if Zubair were reporting to Juma all the petty details of diplomatic activity and the other superficial commotion of the rear line, which was insignificant in comparison with the military action, where Juma was in charge.

It even seemed to Yosir that the decision to commence military action that year in Saryasiya, a decision that was initially opposed by Juma, who after talking to Zubair on a few occasions had even demanded that the Amir come to the phone and fervently tried to convince him that their forces ought to be concentrated on the crucial task, which was to break out into the valley – that this decision had actually been taken by the Amir to counter Juma's authority, to remove that group from his control and establish himself as commander-in-chief of all operations. After all, for example, neither Zubair nor the Amir had ever said anything at all to Juma about the Yangiabad group that they had heard about here on the radio....

As relations between Juma and the Amir grew tenser, Yosir felt more and more like Juma's hostage, and only the fact Juma always valued

those who fearlessly threw themselves into the fighting allowed Yosir to continue with this routine of constant reports to the Centre about engagements, hostages and losses.

Nonetheless, that summer Amir Tahir suddenly turned up in their high-mountain camp. A Tajik helicopter landed in an alpine meadow, its wheels immediately becoming mired in the soil that was unused to bearing the weight of machinery. The Amir followed his automatic rifle out of the helicopter and immediately gave orders for the wheels to be wedged with rocks, keeping Juma and his entourage and his own bodyguards waiting. Yosir noted to himself that the Amir looked rather incongruous in his white Afghan trousers that resembled long underwear with a camouflage jacket over them and a white *tubeiteka*, or skull-cap, with a criss-cross pattern. Then Yosir strode haughtily towards Juma, but it was his own bodyguards, not Juma's, who started firing into the air and shouting: "Allahu Akbar! Allahu Akbar!"

This was the first time Yosir could remember Juma not making any move towards the Amir, but just standing there, rather stooped, as if he were trying to keep clear of the helicopter's whirling blades, and then Amir Tahir was the first to hold his hand out towards Juma, and only after that was there shooting in the air and shouts of "Allahu Akbar! Allahu Akbar!" from Juma's side too.

Juma led the Amir away to his tent, together with only one of the unfamiliar Arabs or Pashtus who had arrived with Tahir, and what they talked about for all those hours, while they were occasionally served tea, or the high-mountain pilaf that had been cooked up especially for the occasion, no one ever found out.

That evening the Amir flew away again in his helicopter, and in the early darkness he failed to acknowledge Yosir among the men seeing him off. Yosir could not tell if this was a good thing or not: he had so far been considered the Amir's placeman here, so did this indicate an offhand attitude towards him, or was it just the opposite – the Amir had acted like that deliberately, in order not to betray any special relationship with him, so that there wouldn't be any excuses for either envy or revenge....

Be that as it may, two evenings later as Yosir was serving his shift listening to the radio, he picked up a report from the Kyrgyz news agency Kabar about the Amir of the Islamic Movement of Uzbekistan, Tahir Yuldash, having been wounded during action in the mountains of the Batken region. He immediately reported the news to Juma's aide, and a little while later Juma himself appeared in the mouth of the cave, looking sleepy. He asked a lot of questions about the smallest details of the report, and then they tried to make an unscheduled call to Kabul but, naturally, the phone there was switched off.

Juma handed the receiver to his deputy and told him to get through to Hoit, and after a while the phone there was answered, but it was one

of the novices who had been left on guard duty with equipment that was not needed for the night, while the others all went off to sleep. Juma shouted furiously at the poor novice, ordered him on pain of death to call commander Yunus and then dropped the receiver into its cradle, having held on for the precise minimum amount of time required for the phone's position to be triangulated. After allowing five minutes for the sleeping commander to be brought, Juma ordered his aide to dial Hoit again, and commander Yunus was already waiting, panting for breath and badly frightened by Juma's fury, and then Juma had asked in his nervous, trembling voice what had happened to the *kori*, which was the code name for the Amir. "He returned to base yesterday," Yunus replied. "Without a scratch?" Juma asked. "He came back the same as when he left," the phone replied. "And he reached you unharmed?" – "With the help of Allah!" Juma immediately put the phone down in disgust. "More games!" he said, with a furious glance at Yosir, as if he were to blame foreverything. Yosir said nothing.

"You'll go on the mission with the boys in the morning!" Juma commanded. "Prepare your weapon and knapsack!" This command was also for the aide, who had a gun, and without saying a word, the two of them walked out of the tent into the opening of the cave, which was barricaded with rocks.

Chapter Fifty-Four

Do not grieve about this,
death in fact is neither high nor low.
It is not death that is greater,
but the thought of the road to death
that overcomes death itself.

- Belgi

Yuriy Loginov, one of Belgi Abutov's fellow students at the Chirchik tank academy recalls:

"Reporting with all due brevity, there are two incidents from our academy life concerning student Abatov that have stuck in my memory. The first incident was on a twenty-five kilometre forced march, when our platoon slacker Linnik suddenly grabbed hold of his appendix side and stopped running, and in this irregular situation student Abutov, taking the initiative, and I, joining him, were obliged to take student Linnik in tow, in the underarm and across the shoulder position, and drag him all the way

to the end of the plan of march, wasting forty-five minutes of time on the five kilometres of the route remaining ahead.

"Incident number two: the examination on the History of the Communist Party of the Soviet Union. Student Abutov advanced to the board ahead of me. The subject on his exam card was 'The Infantile Disorder of Leftism in Communism'. Krasnyuk gives him the lead: 'I am proceeding along a street, there is a crowd of armed bandits. I act in accordance with Lenin's IDOLIC. Abutov replies: 'Position – in the tank: direct aim – fire, reverse – machinegun fire at the remainder' and 'Position – in the infantry: close combat – bayonet attack, automatic weapon fire without closing in!' And Krasnyuk says: 'Student Abutov, mark – two-oo out of fi-ive!'

"Owing to the consequences of this exam result student Abutov memorised *The Infantile*

Disorder of Leftism in Communism off by heart forever!"

Chapter Fifty-Five

No, it's better to deceive you, better to deceive oneself.
This transitory thing is like the whooping cough of my breathing,
the German measles of my face.
One day sometime the eyes will not water from the wind
and the hands will not freeze from the cold,
having agreed on the naked lie of being with you, or the lonely truth
without you.

-Belgi

I myself once used to know *The Infantile Disorder of Leftism in Communism* almost off by heart. And what's more, when I was just getting started, it seemed to me that in the process of work on this book I would have to refer repeatedly to this brochure by Lenin, the "doblyovka" as it was known at my university, from the initial letters of the words in its Russian title. My first feeling was that I would be able to unearth the roots of IMU "leftism" in Islam and explain it as an "infantile disorder". After all, the Taliban, as younger Islamists, proved even more radical than, for instance, the aging mullahs of Iran, who at one time seemed to represent the ultimate limit of Islamic radicalism, so much so, indeed, that these very mullahs began anathematising the Taliban as an absolute calamity.

In rather similar fashion, the Islamic Movement of Uzbekistan, led by Tahir Yuldash and Juma Namangani and consisting of young Islamists who might be called neophytes of Islam, has slowly but surely moved

to the "left" over the last ten to twelve years, becoming more and more radicalised. However, when I recently reread *The Infantile Disorder of Leftism in Communism*, I suddenly realised that the political processes in which the IMU has been involved should be compared, in the first place, not with "leftist communism", but with the development of Bolshevism itself. And at that point it was suddenly brought home to me why the first thing that struck Hamid Ismailov about the Taliban's Afghanistan was its similarity to Bolshevism.

As an experiment, let us go through the main points of *The Infantile Disorder of Leftism in Communism*, comparing the development of Bolshevism with the development of the Islamic Movement of Uzbekistan.

In the first chapter, "In what sense can we speak of the international significance of the Russian revolution?" - Lenin speaks of a shift of the centre of the revolutionary movement from the developed western countries to Russia and the Slavonic world. We can observe in parallel that, following the invasion of Afghanistan by Soviet forces, the centre of radical Islam shifted more and more in the direction of Central Asia, and the West itself played a significant role in this. Much has been written about how the CIA created Osama bin-Laden – the extreme embodiment of this radicalism. In general, the parallels, even between Lenin's actual words and some of the Islamists' exhortations are quite striking: "But no matter how the present struggle in Russia might end, the blood and the happiness[strange but right] of the martyrs whom it will, unfortunately, produce in more than adequate numbers, will not be wasted in vain. They will fructify the young shoots of social revolution throughout the civilised world, making them grow faster and more luxuriantly..." Change a couple of words – and you have a paragraph ready for translation into Arabic, Pashtu or Uzbek.

Chapter 2. One of the basic conditions for the success of Bolshevism (in our case, the Islamists). Here Lenin speaks of the uncompromising centralisation and harsh discipline that are one of the basic conditions of success. I should say that these are the very conditions that singled out the Islamic Movement of Uzbekistan from among the other secular and religious movements as the main opponent of Karimov's regime in Uzbekistan. It is well known that when they joined the ranks of the IMU, warriors swore on the Koran an oath of allegiance to the movement's leader, Tahir Yuldash, and we hardly need to mention the harsh discipline in the fighting wing of the IMU, Juma Namangani's Islamist forces, where men were simply killed for insubordination. The entire movement was led by a narrow circle of men in the political department of the IMU, but supreme power belonged to Amir of the Faithful Muhammad Tahir Farruk – in other words, to Tahir Yuldash.

To compare the two lines of development again, let me reproduce a paragraph from this chapter with an assertion that will prove strangely accurate: "...Islamic thought in Uzbekistan, under the oppression of an incredibly vicious and reactionary regime, has been zealously seeking a correct theory of radicalism, following with remarkable diligence and thoroughness each and every 'last word' of Islam in this area. Thanks to forced emigration as a result of this regime, by the mid-nineties the Islamic movement in Uzbekistan had acquired a wealth of Islamic contacts and a superlative familiarity with the global forms and theories of Islamic radicalism, surpassing any other country in the world".

The quotation from Lenin fits at every single point.

After this the leader of the international proletariat moves on to the fifteen-year experience of

Bolshevism, and we and our Uzbek Islamists follow him.

Here are some quotations from the third chapter of Lenin's work, followed by a two-paragraph outline of what has happened in Uzbekistan during the last fifteen years.

The first stage: *"Everywhere a great storm can be sensed approaching. There is unrest and preparations are being made in every class [of society]"*. During the final years of perestroika, life really did seem to have shifted out of its customary channel: so-called "informal organisations" began springing up on all sides. This process started rather more quickly in the Soviet Baltic republics, with their National Fronts, including Sayudis in Latvia, and gradually spread throughout the entire Soviet Union, reaching Central Asia. Uzbekistan was by no means at the head of this line, but even here the Birlik national movement was established in late 1988, on the initiative of a group of young writers. At the same time, as part of the general fermentation, all kinds of local organisations, including Islamic ones, were set up in the regions, frequently under the general aegis of Birlik. Let me refer you to the initial section of this book, where mention is made, in rather officious language, of the establishment of Islamist organisations like Islom lashkarlari, Tavba and Adolat in the Namangan region. Let me simply add that initially they were associated with the national movement Birlik.

The second stage: *"All the classes act openly. All views on programmes and tactics are tested against the action of the masses"*. During the late eighties and early nineties Birlik held a series of mass meetings. For the most part these took place in Tashkent and initially they still had a "pro-Soviet" character. For instance, the first meeting began with the laying of a wreath at the foot of a colossal statue of Lenin, but gradually the meetings started raising questions about the status of the Uzbek language, the single-crop agricultural system producing only cotton and Uzbek soldiers who were killed in the Soviet Army, and then they

started spreading to other regional centres. In parallel with this there are meetings held by various sections of Birlik which, as they develop, cease to see themselves as sections of something else. Once again, let me refer you to the first chapters of this book which describe, for instance, the famous meeting at Namangan, when president Islam Karimov himself was taken hostage. As you can see, the Islamists are already putting forward the idea of an Islamic state in Uzbekistan.

The third stage – the years of reaction. *"Tsarism won. All the revolutionary and opposition parties were destroyed"*. By 1994 President Karimov had essentially wiped out all opposition within the country and managed to consolidate his own power. The initial persecution was directed against the secular opposition, primarily against the leadership of Birlik, as well as the Erk party that had separated off from it. The militia and armed forces dragged in not only the activists of these two organisations, but also much broader groups of "informal democrats". Many of them fled from Uzbekistan: those who stayed were arrested.

In breaking the secular opposition, one way or another President Karimov's regime drove all dissidence into hiding, in the first place into the mosques. That was where masses of young people first began gathering under the wing of the radical imams. I should add that by this time, apart from the secular opposition, the Ubek authorities had launched a simultaneous campaign against the nascent Islamic organisations: for instance, in 1991 the congress of the Islamic Renaissance Party, which had been founded as a branch of an "all-USSR" party, was broken up in Tashkent. In 1992 the Islamic groups and organisations in Namangan were effectively beheaded: some of the leaders, like Hakimjan Satimov, were arrested, while Tahir Yuldash and his immediate entourage managed to flee to Tajikistan.

"Defeated armies are quick learners", Lenin writes in this chapter, and once again I continue to quote him, merely replacing the Bolsheviks with the Islamists: *"Of all the crushed opposition parties and revolution parties, the Islamists withdrew in the best order, with the least damage to their 'army', with more of its central core intact, with the least deep and least chronic schisms, with the least demoralisation, with the greatest capacity for getting back to work on the widest scale, in the most correct and vigorous fashion"*. There were several factors at work here: although the Namangan Islamists had promulgated their demands – for example, for an Islamic state – throughout the whole of Uzbekistan, at this time they still remained a local movement, a Namangan movement, with some support along the Ferghana valley, and therefore the forces of law and order mobilised against them were on the local level and, as Tahir Yuldash admitted, they actually warned him and his closest confederates about the arrests being planned. Precisely because this was a local organisation, at its

core it was significantly better organised than national movements and organisations. The organised withdrawal was also facilitated by the elements of military discipline that were incorporated into this organisation. And above all, the central core of this movement withdrew to Tajikistan, where the Tajik Islamic movement had already become colossally strong, embracing almost half the population of the country. There was a supportive environment ready to hand.

This led the Uzbek Islamists' movement to the *"years of upturn"*, which Lenin characterises as initially *"incredibly slow.... and later rather quicker"*. The Islamic opposition of Tajikistan had set up base in Afghanistan, where it was initially helped by the faction of the Tajik Ahmad Shakh Masoud, but later it switched to a new host, the Taliban, after which the Islamists felt quite at home in Afghanistan. With bases and refugee camps in Aghanistan, the Tajik Islamist opposition, with which the Uzbek Islamists merged, was still pursuing military action against government forces within Tajikistan, in particular in the mountainous areas of Tavildara. On one hand, in the political leadership of the Tajik Islamic opposition, Tahir Yuldash soon became Saeed Abdullo Nuri's deputy for international affairs, and on the other, the so-called "Uzbek battalion", under the command of Juma Namangani, began acquiring more and more power on the battlefield. As these two advances to take up leading political and military roles, the Islamic Movement of Uzbekistan emerges as an ever more independent faction.

The Tajik war legitimised the Islamic Movement of Uzbekistan. Rephrasing Lenin slightly, we can say that *"in the extremely reactionary conditions of the Karimov regime, the presence of this movement plays a highly useful role for the Islamists. Islamists within Uzbekistan are sent into penal servitude..."* but they are also recruited into the movement itself. A force appears with which they can identify and on which they can rely in their in opposition to the regime. After the signing of a peace agreement in Tajikistan, the Islamic Movement of Uzbekistan acquires distinct shape and declares itself an independent political organisation.

There is one more stage reviewed in *The Infantile Disorder of Leftism in Communism* that can easily be compared with the historical development of the Islamic Movement of Uzbekistan: *"The incredibly chronic decay and obsolescence of tsarism (in our case of the Karimov regime) created an incredibly destructive force directed against it"*. These qualities of decay and obsolescence can be fleshed out with corruption, close integration with the criminal world, veniality and lack of all moral principle, and against this background, for young people with even a shred of decency, a video image of an Islamist with an automatic rifle carries all the allure of Robin Hood and Che Guevara combined.

This stage correlates with the stage in independent Uzbekistan's development that concluded in the bombings in Tashkent in 1999.

Even if we do not go along with the scenario according to which these explosions were, if not actual staged, then at least directed from the wings by the powers-that-be in Uzbekistan, we can still agree with the many observers who assert that "the incredible force directed against the regime was largely its own creation".

At the end of this chapter Lenin drops in a phrase which, applied to the Tashkent explosions, can serve as a key to parallel events of the present time: "History played a trick and made the opportunists of a backward country surpass the opportunists of a number of advanced countries". Of course, we shall have to replace the word "opportunists" with the word "rulers".

Chapter Fifty-Six

How many people and how many different destinies Yosir had seen in the last two or three years. One day a young man of twenty-five had arrived with a group from Khorezm. He had a delicate face that simply radiated light. Although this wasn't a place where acquaintances were encouraged, Yosir could always get to know someone by saying it was for the film that he and Zubair had been making for so many months.

But this time it happened for a different reason. One day, when they found themselves paired together for training exercises in guerrilla warfare, and were supposed, according to the instructions, to find their way – without exposing a glimpse of any silhouette, or shape, or shadow, or flash – to the rear of the supposed adversary and sit there for a couple of days, gathering information and maintaining contact only by means of signals in the dead of the night, when any militant commanders who suddenly turned up would hardly be able to get to them in the mountains, they had suddenly started talking in whispers without any mutual suspicion.

The young man, who was called Anas, turned out to be a graduate of the Bauman Technological University in Moscow, where he had lived for a long time. He told Yosir quite openly that in Moscow he had been a follower of Aum Shinrikio's movement, and then of yoga and Buddhism, but after he was forced to go back to Khorezm by his parents, who told him: you'll get married and settle down, we'll find you a job here, he naturally hadn't found any real work, and he'd taken a job in the regional hospital, keeping an eye on the antediluvian medical equipment – all those dental drills and intravenous drips.

He had lived like that until a close school friend of his turned up in Urgench, supposedly on some kind of commercial business. He had been

the first one to take Anas to the mosque. How delighted his parents had been at the idea that their son had become an orthodox Muslim believer. Anas had gradually worked his way into Islam, and already begun to argue with his parents about the bottles of vodka in the basement, set by for his wedding. His father used to get annoyed and say: "We're Muslims too, but everybody does it, so we have to do it too."

And then his friend Oibek had told him that up in the mountains in Tajikistan there were *hujrahs*, clay huts, where you could spend six months learning the Koran by heart, that there were genuine sheikhs there who could trace their family tree back to Bahauddin Nakshbandi via Ahmad Sirhindi. These names set Anas's head spinning, and he agreed to make the trip. Especially since in Urgench he had no job to match his qualifications, no present and no future....

They set out via Tashkent, with their trousers turned up to expose their ankles, as all true believers did nowadays. In Tashkent they paid a visit to another man from their region, a modernist artist whom Oibek also tried to inspire to take the straight path, after the first thing this acquaintance did was to offer them a drink. They argued for a long time, and in response to one of their assertions, the artist recited a few lines by a poet called Belgi, which Anas had remembered, and they went like this:

Facing this void –
How many names would I not give to it
In filling it.
The only essence/mystery
Is the gap between predetermination and free will

Anas had whispered these words slightly more loudly than the cautious whisper of his story, and Yosir had been forced to tug on his partner's sleeve, but later, when Yosir recalled that night and that story again, he was not entirely sure that he had jerked towards Anas so frantically because he was afraid of being discovered by the inspectors who had been planted all over the place, oh no, it was really because that was *his poetry!* – poetry that he himself had long ago forgotten... But from the way that Anas broke off and lowered his voice back to an inaudible whisper to continue his story about the journey from Tashkent to Dushanbe, and from there to Hoit, Yosir realised that it had not been a provocation, not even an intuition... And neither that night, nor at any time afterwards did he ever admit to Anas or anyone else that he had written these or any other lines of poetry.

And as for Anas, the young intellectual with the glowing face was sent to Chechnya on some assignment, but on the way he was intercepted by the Tajik special services and they handed him over to their Uzbek

colleagues and then, so they say, he was sentenced to a long prison term. But after Alisher had run away from the camp that spring, Yosir had learned not to let his heart attach itself to anyone.

Chapter Fifty-Seven

Was Belgi aware of how famous he was as a poet? Yes and no. On the one hand, he did see the publication of his first book *Yo'l* (*The Path*), which was introduced to its readers by two friends of his, Hamid Ismailov and Kuvanbek Kenja, and I shall include their foreword and afterword to the book shortly. To have won recognition from these two – and especially from the latter – was a great achievement: in his book *A Ground- Drift of Poetry* Kenja had demolished the very foundations of Uzbek Soviet and post-Soviet poetry, but he had quoted abundantly from Belgi as a contrast to everything else. Apart from that, as I said at the very beginning of this book, by that time Belgi had already begun travelling widely and reading his poems in Germany, France and Italy. I therefore assume he realised how much recognition he had won.

But at the same time I am absolutely certain that external recognition was not the yardstick of his own attitude to himself. Every poet must be an alloy of doubt and wilful assertion, but even when Yosir heard his own poetry recited by Anas, up there in the mountains, on that training exercise, as soon he realised it was not deliberate provocation, he certainly regarded it as a simple coincidence – one of those coincidences that a man's life is full of, especially the life of a poet. The rhyme of life – that's the simplest explanation for it. But one of the men who came back from Pakistan in the autumn of 2002 and was not put in an Uzbek jail told me that the last time he had seen his fellow-believer by the name of Yosir, on the night before an American bombing raid in the village of Zulmat, they had been unable to get to sleep for a long time after the evening prayer, and there in the village mosque my informant had switched on his small transistor radio even though, strictly speaking, it was not allowed, and one of the items in one of the foreign broadcasts in Uzbek was about a poetry evening in the Raspaille Theatre in Paris, where they had read the work of an Uzbek poet called Belgi, whom nobody in the mosque had heard of, and Yosir had been the only one to make his way through the tangles of bodies to the radio and put his ear to it from the other side, and suddenly he had starting crying, but since it was dark in the mosque, no one had seen his tears, and so no one had kicked up any righteous rumpus or reported the incident through the appropriate channels.... Or perhaps no one gave a damn any longer anyway....

Hamid Ismailov

At the time my narrator had put it down to homesickness for the homeland and fear of imminent, meaningless death from some random bomb or piece of shrapnel, because he had these feelings inside himself too, but I didn't explain to him the reason for those tears.

This is what Hamid Ismailov and Kubanbek Kenja wrote about Belgi's first book of poetry:

In place of a foreword

This is the third time I have presented the poetry of Belgi to readers. The first time was when I sent a selection of poems – which, by the way, still remain unpublished to this day – to the weekly *Literature and Art of Uzbekistan*: I wrote: "In the late eighties, while I was sitting in a small room in the Union of Writers in Moscow and arguing, in the way that one does, about literature with the occupier of the room, the representative of Uzbek literature, Sabit Madaliev, the door out of the wintry darkness of Moscow opened for a moment and a rather young-looking man appeared in the doorway and asked: "Is this the Uzbek poetry representative office?" I don't remember exactly what happened next, but I think Sabit Madaliev was called out by one of the secretaries and the two us of were left alone together in the small room, sharing a long silence. Snow, yellow in the light of the streetlamps, was falling through the blue twilight of the Moscow window, and the young man handed me a pile of papers with a rather clumsy gesture, saying: "Here, I brought my poems, you can pass them on…" and then, explaining that he had to go and meet someone else, he spoke a rather awkward, hasty farewell and left…

The second time my attention was focused on Belgi's poetry was when I was writing my review of the critic Kuvanbek Kenji's celebrated book *A Ground-Drift of Poetry*:

"This poet's name is Belgi. I have only met him once, in Moscow, in the studio of the artist Shavkat Abdusalamov. Our meeting was, as the Russians say, a bit untidy, and the only trace it left behind was a pile of Belgi's poems that Shavkat Abdusalamov handed to me. Kuvanbek is clearly closely acquainted with Belgi. In any case, in his book he not only cites the poet's verse, he also adduces abundant information from Belgi's life, allowing the reader to build up an everyday image of the poet as well as a poetic one.

Belgi is a poet who transcends distances, the author writes. His poems, whether they are written in Osh or Koktebel, Moscow or Khakasia, Fontainebleau or Bamberg, are the reflections of an Uzbek mind and soul that are open to a journey. This journey is not measured in kilometres of distance, it is, rather, a mystical path, a path of realisation. But Kuvanbek tells us that for this poet, reaching the end of the path is less important than 'wandering in time, or more precisely, the attempt to ford the stream of time on foot, to ford the stream of language.'

Unfortunately, this was never published either. And so now, as I present Belgi's poetry to the reader for the third time, I naturally have the superstitious thought somewhere at the back of my mind: "What if it

doesn't work out this time either?" But a different part of my mind comforts me with a thought that is more characteristic of our poetry: "As the parting is bitter and long, so is the meeting loving and sweet".

I shall not write about Belgi's poetry. He lives in his own poems. And, in addition, this book carries an afterword by Kuvanbek Kenji. My task is merely to raise the curtain, as it were, on the phenomenon of this book, *The Path*. Allow me to introduce you – Belgi.

Hamid Ismailov

And here is my best attempt at a translation of Kuvanbek Kenji's afterword to the same book:

In place of an afterword

What we today call "Uzbek poetry" has blossomed or set fruit as a result of a new encounter or a certain stirring in the air or of coming face to face with the sun. In the first period of the Arabo-Persian world, as if wielding two flinty stones, Navoi struck the sparks of a new poetry out of the Turkic consciousness. If we can speak of a second explosion, then that is certainly Chulpon, when Uzbek *jadid* poetry was grafted on to Russian culture of the late 19th and early 20th century, and in that interval a new Uzbek poetry put out shoots.

Belgi is a poet who has connected our poetry to the modern poetry of the world.

Poetry is the bundle of straw that Hoja Nasreddin held out on a stick in front of his donkey. Belgi already occupies the space to which the national consciousness will find its way tomorrow. The name of that space is not any of those that the poet lists in an apparent attempt to confuse us – Tashkent, Paris or London: it is the human personality. The poet is not actually travelling along a road, he is a spirit wafting in the air.

Belgi has achieved this freedom of soul as a footloose Uzbek in a free world. In this freedom there is no coercion, it has a simplicity of nature. It is not a matter of subjects drawn from daily life, in fact you could not describe a continuous narrative based on his poems, it is a matter of a complete absence of spiritual posturing, the point here is for trial and experience, hope and regret, to be exactly equal to themselves.

Measuring Belgi by one standard or another – comparing him with Navoi, Chuplon or Rauf Parfi – is a pointless exercise. Incidentally, I have written extensively about that in my book *A Ground-Drift of Poetry*. Yes it is easy to find in him this refinement, and this tenderness, and this inward reflection. But he is something else, he is simply Belgi (a sign).

Of what is he a sign, this Belgi?

Kuvanbek Kenja

217

Chapter Fifty-Eight

There are two opposed urges struggling within me: one is to get this story finished as soon as possible and acquire a little clarity, and the other is to write down everything that I know, have heard, analysed and compared, everything that arrives with each new day, with new facts and events from the recent Iraq war, and news of other things yet to come, and then again reach some kind of shoreline. But there is a final gap in what I know about the life of my central character, one that I cannot fill right now: I do not know how his life ended, or if it has ended.

Sometimes I feel like a man who has tied an explosives belt around himself, but someone else is holding the detonator... whose consciousness do I want to blow up, and what I am I trying to prove to anybody apart from myself? But what can I prove to myself, smeared through space in the bloody fragments of this novel?

What are we trying to prove to each other, to our friends or enemies, in this world? What do other people's biographies, other people's lives teach us? The fact that no matter how you might have lived your life, in the end there is no satisfaction in it, no solace, no conclusion? While writing this book, I have become filled with a kind of eternal moan, I want to howl and howl, I want to swear obscenely, brawl, splutter and spit, go insane, I don't want to live. How can all of this have built up inside me, after all, I haven't pushed the emotion to the limit, I have related my narrative cautiously, I haven't even pondered on or hinted at what Yosir might have known as he assembled his concluding manuscript, have I?

Did that film *Nido* ever appear, and what happened to the chronicle itself? Is it all in some American special archive somewhere, waiting for that scarce thing, a translator from the Uzbek into the insensitive English, or was it scattered to the wind by the storm of the Afghan war, lost somewhere in Vaziristan?

But one thing I know for certain: as Heine once said, the crack that runs through the heart of a poet divides the world in two. What I have described in this sketchy experiment in biography as something individual and particular, is actually the condition of the world today, and the story I have told using the example of the last ten to twelve years in Uzbekistan is a model of what is happening today across much larger geographical spaces. Russia is repeating the experience of Karimov, China is repeating it, the West is going the same way. Che Guevara is replaced by Hattab, Hattab is replaced by someone else, and the young men all go rushing to follow them...

But that does not frighten me now. Every minute the world repeats itself, but everyone beats his own forehead against his own wall. And yet, while every heart stores up its own pain, sometimes that pain is reflected in another heart... And so this book is neither *Doctor Faustus* nor *Doctor Zhivago*, and not even *The GULAG Archipelago*. It is even further from being a volume in that notable Russian series "Lives of Outstanding People". It belongs to the category of one heart's response to the pain of another, for there is nothing quite like pain for sharpening our sense of the fleeting happiness of this bitter, mortal, earthly life...

There is a certain delusion in this reality,
the beloved does not pine for the one who is pining.
If you are nostalgic for the earth, there is no homeland
for you and so on... the rest is clear.

But in the bottom of my heart
like the sun on the well water
there is a reflection: either a reflex, or a remarkable sight,
or a stain, or an unending pain
that glimmers. I throw down a bucket
to catch it, and finally
word after word I drag in
the feeling like something slippery and heavy.
O for this pain to end completely. It's as
though the eyewater flows like an irrigation
ditch from my pupil.

It's all clear:
that is a word, and this is pain.
But if this is so, then 'pain' also is a word.

Chapter Fifty-Nine

When I had almost completed this attempt at the biography of a poet and was already seeking a publisher for the work. I started giving public readings of it to gatherings of my friends in Tashkent and, more often, to groups of specialists on Islam in Moscow since, naturally, I realised that I could not publish this book in Tashkent. Then one day I received a strange e-mail message, inviting me to the *chaikhana*, or teahouse, in the Samarkand Darbaze district, including meticulously specific instructions on the time and manner of the meeting. My first

219

thought was that it was from the special services, especially since, following the explosions in Tashkent in March, everyone was expecting renewed persecution of Muslims, and the special services had been put on alert. Apart from that, although I was aware that a biography of a poet who had ended up among the so-called terrorists was not the kind of literature most welcome in contemporary Uzbekistan, I didn't really think I had anything else to be afraid of, and yet I felt a distinct twinge of alarm. But then, having thought it through a bit more carefully, I realised that if it had been the special services, they would hardly have been likely to send me an e-mail, they would simply have turned up at my flat on Kara-Kamysh Street.

So I agreed to the meeting. At the appointed time, when the *chaikhana* happened to be very crowded and no one in it even aroused my idle curiosity, let alone intense suspicion, I took a seat in the booth specified, and ordered, as I was supposed to do, green tea and a bread cake, and shortly thereafter a young man with a clear, direct gaze came in. After the standard exchange of greetings, he told me: "I want to give you this. *It's from the other side...*" and he handed me a bundle, with a nod towards the plastic bag that I had also brought with me by way of ID on his instructions. I hastily thrust the package into the bag – my hands were trembling, but my heart was fluttering even more tremulously, as if any moment it was about to be discovered in some criminal act and punished mercilessly.

I can't remember how I managed to finish my tea. Naturally, I didn't ask that clear-eyed young man any questions, that was quite unthinkable. My heart was pounding away up in my throat instead of my chest, I wanted to run – to run and leave that package, run aimlessly, simply run.... What a dreadful business this was – secrets and conspiratorial meetings! Not for fainthearted cowards like me!

I knew that a caravan of men had arrived from Pakistan some time earlier and just recently one of them had given an interview to Deutsche Welle, in which he said that Tahir Yuldash was now in the region of Vaziristan, at the village of Vanna, and then the Pakistani army started claiming that it had almost arrested him there, saying that he had been wounded, and so had members of his entourage. In all these bulletins and stories I searched for a familiar name – Yosir – but it wasn't mentioned by anyone, although that fugitive from Pakistan told Deutsche Welle that Zubair had died in a bombing raid in Afghanistan, and not been killed by Juma Namangani for being an agent of the special services. But I am digressing. Let me get back to my own adventure.

Some time later, after I had inconspicuously left the package behind a wardrobe at my aunt's place and reached home late at night by a circuitous route, I realised I had acted like a real bonehead in the

way that I'd dealt with the young man and in bringing my aunt in the business. But nobody came to my place or my aunt's during that sleepless night or the following feverish day. After two days I paid another visit to my unsuspecting aunt and, choosing my moment, inconspicuously retrieved the package. Then, with my ears burning bright red, as if I were being scrutinised under some cosmic x-ray, for some reason I came home through the centre of town ... I confess with my hand on my heart that I opened that package in the toilet, after first switching out all the lights. It was a standard school exercise book, its pages filled with fine writing in Uzbek, which was divided up into chapters and occasionally punctuated by Arabic script. That first night I leafed aimlessly through the exercise book, not really understanding what I was doing, or the significance of the thing itself. The next day I realised that the framework for a new book was taking shape before my very eyes – something that had supposedly happened with many of the books I had read in my life, but that I had never experienced. But now *it* was happening to *me*. After several feverish days and nights, I finally realised what it was I had and went dashing to the nearest Internet café to send a reply to the message that had invited me to the *chaikhana* in the Samarkand Darbaze district. Unfortunately, an hour later I received a reply from the service provider, telling me that there was no such subscriber. I sent the message again and received the same answer a second time.

Even after I managed – with the help of a dictionary and my trusty friends – to work out what the writing in the exercise book was about, I wondered for a long time whether I ought to take it into account here, in this book, whether I even ought to mention this one-and-only secret and mysterious incident in my life – perhaps I had got so caught up in the "spymania" that I have written about in this biography that now I was hopelessly entangled, but then, after I told my friends about the contents of the exercise book, we came to the joint conclusion that it ought to appear here at least in part.

And although I didn't find that clear-eyed young man again in the Samarkand Darbaze *chaikhana*, despite revisiting it time after time, like the scene of my crime, and although he never contacted me again by e-mail, I realised that the youth who had delivered the exercise book to me was from *the other side*: he had evidently returned from Kashmir since, in addition to the Arabic script I have already mentioned, at the next inspection I also discovered inscriptions in that decorative Indian writing that links together the tops of all the letters, and an indologist friend of mine read one of the words for me as "Srinagar".

I do not know who wrote that manuscript, especially since I have the impression that it was written with the left hand. I am no graphologist,

and I have not compared the style of the writing with manuscripts by Belgi – I don't happen to have any – and so no, I cannot claim *that Belgi wrote it,* but I would really like to hope that it was him. And for that reason I would like to conclude this incomplete investigation of his life precisely with this mysterious manuscript.

A Second Part

Petals of Sufi Blood

Cast of Main Characters and a Simple Time Line

Shah Jahan – the fifth Mogul ruler after Babur, Humayun, Akbar, and Jahangir. Ruled the Indian Subcontinent from 1628 until 1658. Famous for building the Taj Mahal.

Dara Shukuh – his eldest son, who should have inherited the Empire. A poet and a Sufi, who wanted to bring all religions together, was opposed and killed by his brother Aurangzeb, who called him 'an apostate'.

Aurangzeb – Shah Jahan's youngest son, who took over the Empire. A strict Muslim, who arrested his own father and his own children and killed his own brother.

Zebunissa – Aurangzeb's daughter, a famous poet, who was imprisoned by her father.

Suleiman Shukuh – Dara Shukuh's son, who fell in love with Zebunissa. He was also killed by Aurangzeb.

Jahanara – sister of Dara Shukuh and Aurangzeb, who tried to bring them together;

Raushanara – another sister, who took Aurangzeb's side

1615 – Dara Shukuh is born

1618 – Aurangzeb is born

1628-1658 – Shah Jahan's reign

1631 – He starts building the Taj Mahal

1638 – Zebunissa is born

1657 – Shah Jahan falls ill and the struggle for the succession starts

1658 – Aurangzeb defeats Dara Shukuh and takes over the Empire, arresting his father

1659 – Dara Shukuh is publicly executed by Aurangzeb

1702 – Zebunissa dies

1707 – Aurangzeb dies as the last Great Mogul Emperor

Hamid Ismailov

Shah Jahan, emperor of the mighty India of the Great Moguls, named Sahib Kiran Soni, or Second Ruler of the Universe, gazed through the openwork alabaster window screens of his place of confinement at the finest of his creations – the distant Taj Mahal, where his beloved wife, Mumtaz Mahal, lay at rest. The sunset-red forms of the dome and the airy minarets that were like her ethereal walk were distorted by reflection in the waters of the Indus, or perhaps it was the cloudy tears in the Padishah's eyes that conferred imperfection on those perfect forms which had been imprinted on the lonely old man's heart since so very long ago.

He had been imprisoned in the Agra Fort by his son Aurangzeb, who was now named Alamgir, or Conqueror of the World. A true match for his father: for after all, in his own time had not Shah Jahan rebelled against his own father, the emperor Jahangir, and eliminated all the other heirs to the throne one by one? Why then did the heart of the old man imprisoned in the fort ache so badly? Why this kinship between his bleeding heart and the blood-red sunset?

Shah Jahan listened to the voices of the children in the street below his alabaster window screens: "Nime – derun, nime – berun! Half on the inside, half on the outside!" the children were shouting. Something sharp, like the hook protruding from the palace wall, on which the children usually hung their ropes to play their games, suddenly pierced the old man's heart, and he cried out through the window: "Who's there?" – only to frighten them, really, he didn't want an answer. And for a moment the children's shouts did fall silent, but suddenly the clear voice of his granddaughter via Aurangzeb, the dusky beauty Zebunissa, rang out mischievously in reply:

> At the might of Shah Jahan, Ruler of the World, Both
> the earth and sky did shake and tremble,
> Now see the finger of amazement, bitten in his mouth,
> Half on the inside, half on the outside....

And then there was a fluttering peal of childish laughter....

* * *

Zebunissa, princess of the Great House of the Moguls, daughter of the Emperor Aurangzeb, named Conqueror of the World, gazed through the openwork alabaster window screens of her place of confinement at the bloody sunset in the sky and remembered her fleeting life. How very recently it seemed that she had teased her grandfather, the once mighty Shah Jahan, who had been imprisoned in the Fort of Agra by her father Aurangzeb, and now the book of life in the pages of which she had written, was about to slam shut with a final cold puff of wind.

I searched the library of the world, turning page
after page, I saw your letter and said, my wish is here.

She stood there, thoughtful, in the sunset, dressed all in red, or perhaps it was the sunset that had bloodied her silk dress, and suddenly she heard a voice from somewhere below:

You are dressed in red, my gaze has crept to the lip of the roof.

Who was it? Some idle passer-by, one of the hundreds who were hopelessly in love with her? Or had her betrothed, Suleiman Shukuh, whom her own father had killed, once again crept into her heart uninvited? And then she answered in a low whisper:

Not by strength, nor prayer, nor gold can he creep close.

The only reply she heard was a sigh….

* * *

"When did all this begin?" Shah Jahan wondered in his solitude. Was it after the victorious Mevar war when he, still calling himself Prince Hurram, had returned to the imperial palace of his father Jahangir, and a month later his beloved wife Mumtaz Mahal had given him a first-born, a son, to whom the august Jahangir had given the name of Muhammad Dara Shukuh and the title of "First Rose in the Shah's Flower Garden". Everyone had loved the little boy, his grandfather had destined him for the throne, his father had promised him future prowess in arms. And even when Mumtaz Mahal had borne another three sons after him, neither the plain-mannered Shuja, nor the swarthy and surreptitious Aurangzeb, nor the youngest son, Murad, had ever been showered so generously with honours as was the first-born, Dar Shukuh.

When the Emperor Jahangir later sent his son Prince Hurram to the Dekkan province as vice- regent, he had not kept the first-born beside him for upbringing – the deprivation would have caused the prince and princess too much suffering – he had taken the prince Shuja as his ward,

although in the prince's family this tutelage was understood rather as the taking of a hostage.

Dekkan had flourished under Hurram, making his father Jahangir delighted beyond words with his heir, and only Hurram's stepmother, the domineering empress Nur Jahan, had been overwhelmed by malice and envy. She was the one who had schemed and intrigued to sow discord between father and son and forced Prince Hurram to rebel against the Emperor Jahangir. It was her wrath and fury that driven the prince and his family into foreign exile, and if not for Hurram's faithful Mumtaz Mahal, who shared with him all the hardships of the fugitive's life, what would have become of him then....

It was Mumtaz Mahal who had given him the wise idea of seeking a truce with his father, and as a sign of reconciliation she had entreated her husband to send to the imperial court their most precious possessions – their two sons, Dara and Aurangzeb.

It was wintertime, when the two, aged nine and six, set off on their journey. Following the local custom of that foreign place, their mother scattered rose petals in their path, and who knew then that the end of that snow-white early road on which they were set by the silently weeping Mumtaz Mahal would be as bloody red as rose petals on the snow.

* * *

"When did all this begin?" Zebunissa, the princess imprisoned by her own father in the fort of Salimgarh, wondered in her solitude. Long ago in her distant childhood her teacher Saeed Ashraf Isfahan had told her the story of what happened between her father Aurangzeb – who was then a youth of fourteen years – and her uncle, the deceased Dara Shukuh, whom the mullah had been educating at that time in the subtleties of the literary arts.

It was the fifth year of Emperor Shah Jahan's reign. Just before the beginning of the Lahore summer the Ruler of the Universe had decided to amuse himself with an elephant fight. Two elephants named Sudhakar and Suratsundar were led out into the arena in front of the Shah's balcony. The three young princes – Dara, Aurangzeb and Shuja – decided to observe the fight from close quarters, mounted on horses. The battle did not last long: long-tusked Sudhakar quickly put the tuskless Suratundar to flight and went hurtling after him, to the wild hooting of the spectators. But, suddenly spotting Aurangzeb on his steed, the elephant stopped and went dashing after the horse. The brave youth did not lose his head, but thrust his spear right into the elephant's very forehead. The elephant roared and the crowd howled together, the din of smoke flares mingled with the shrieks of servants. But not even this frightened the enraged elephant, on the contrary, with a shrill screech,

he thrust his tusks into the bulging flank of the horse, but Aurangzeb had leapt from the saddle an instant before the animal began neighing appallingly as it was hoisted into the air. God only knows how all this would have ended if the elephant Suratsundar had not halted his flight and taken advantage of the confusion to attack Sudhakar again...

The agitated emperor ran down from the balcony, the servants and viziers went dashing towards Aurangzeb, and one of them exclaimed to the pale youth who was strolling slowly towards them: "Shahinshah is horrified that you are moving so slowly!" to which the prince muttered through clenched teeth: "I would make haste, if the elephant were here. Now that the danger is past, why should I hurry?" His father rushed up to his son and embraced him, thanking Allah that everything had turned out well. He immediately ordered the valiant youth to be rewarded with five thousand gold pieces, all the time muttering to himself: "Thanks be to Allah, everything could have turned out differently! Such dishonour!" Pale Aurangzeb replied: "If it had gone differently, I would not have been dishonoured! The dishonour lies in the way that my brothers took to their heels!" – and he cast a barbed glance at Dara Shukuh, who was standing some distance away.

* * *

Shah Jahan gazed through the ogeed loopholes of the Fort of Agra at the twilight that was advancing from the east, refusing to accept that the evening breeze was not responsible for the dampness of his eyes. He knew that the warlike Turkish blood of his seven fathers had been diluted for several generations with the blood of wives and concubines from this place, and he blamed his sentimentality on them – as warm and dusky as this same twilight. Had any of his stern ancestors from the steppes ever fallen in love, as was the custom now in his royal clan? He recalled how he himself had lost his head and his reason when he saw a girl at the bazaar, in the row of stalls selling jewellery: her name was Arjumand-Bonu, the daughter of one of his father's viziers. And he, still a young prince, was in that row of stalls to buy adornments for his bride – the Shah of Persia's daughter, whom he had never seen.

He could not eat or drink, he was pining so badly that the marriage with the princess had to be postponed for several days. But he had had to wait much longer – more than five whole years – to marry his beloved Arjumand, who took the name Mumtaz-Mahal and became his second and dearly beloved wife.

She had borne him fourteen children and died in giving birth to the fourteenth. For seven days and seven nights the Emperor Shah Jahan had not shown his face. When he emerged, grey-haired and stooped,

from his chambers, his first-born, Dara Shukuh, had walked up to his father and recited a verse with a numerical value that gave the year of his mother's death. The old warrior could not respond with a verse of equal skill, but in his heart there was born a feeling that was akin to this poem, and he decided to pour this feeling into a building which would have no equal on earth...

In the year that his wife beyond price died, Shah Jahan started building the Taj Mahal – a shrine for the empress...

Now he tried to feel for the familiar forms of the Taj in the darkness with his eyes, but the first stars – those unruly brigands, stole his glance and carried it up into the heavens. And then Shah Jahan's thoughts returned once again to his beloved son, Dara Shukuh. For it was he who had inherited his mother's dreaminess and love of beauty. Beside him, even his sister, Jahanara seemed more practical and determined, not to mention the third son, Aurangzeb.

And then when Dara Shukuh fell in love with his future wife, Nadira-begim, he was dying with impatience for the wedding. Brisk Jahanara had persuaded her father to advance the preparations for the wedding, even though mourning for Mumtaz-Mahal was still continuing, and on the very day of his favourite son's nuptials, the emperor had appeared in public for the first time in the magnificent Divann-Hos, his private audience chamber. Hundreds of musicians played on hundreds of instruments of every possible kind and the echo of merriment returned to the palace. The hands of the prince were painted with henna, as were the fingers of especially honoured guests, whom the servant girls enveloped in shawls of golden thread.

The following day the procession moved in all its splendour through the streets of the city and its tumultuous bazaars, and into the immense reception hall of the palace, accompanied by the three young princes: Shuja, Aurangzeb and Murad. When Dara Shukuh approached the famous peacock throne and bowed bow before the emperor, his father rose from the throne and bound round his neck a gold thread beaded with pearls and a azure diamond, as bright-blue as the sky overhead. And then he placed a crown on his head. Gold and silver rained down on the newlyweds and children, both poor and rich, squealed as they gathered up the coins. These festivities continued for several days, until finally Dara Shukuh invited his father and brothers to his newly built house on the riverbank.

* * *

Zebunissa peered through the ogeed loopholes of the Salimgarh Fort into the twilight advancing from the east, and to her the first stars to appear in the sky seemed to be her own tears. The daughter of seven

Turkish fathers and their sensuous Indian wives, her mind was as clear as the open steppe, but her heart was moist and passionate. Already in those far-off years when her father Aurangzeb ruled the province of Dekkan, while she was growing up at the court of her grandfather, Shah Jahan, the little girl had fallen in love with her cousin Suleiman Shukuh, the son of her oldest uncle, Dara Shukuh, but from the very beginning there had lain between the two brother princes, Dara and Aurangzeb, an enmity that not even their father, the Emperor Shah Jahan had been able to bridge, let alone Zebunissa and Suleiman Shukuh....

Her father, the righteous ascetic Aurangzeb, referred to his brother Dara Shukuh as a "mulhik" – an apostate – for his equal love of both Muslims and Hindus, and from childhood he had harboured an acute sense of rivalry with Shah Jahan's favourite son, and judged his own entire life in comparison with this philosopher and poet. One might think that a man who, for the sake of the throne, had incarcerated his own father and older sister, killed all his brothers and exiled his children, must have a heart of stone, and yet Zebunissa's mother, Dilras-bonu Begim, had told her how once, when Aurangzeb was still a young prince, he had found himself in the town of Zainabad, where his aunt lived, and decided to visit her. Custom requires a Muslim to knock before entering a house, but since the prince was not visiting strangers, he entered the gate without knocking. The first sight that met his eye was a girl of divine beauty gathering ripe fruit and singing in a low and languorous voice as she did so. Unable to control himself at the sight of this sinful beauty, the pious prince fell down in a swoon. Shrieking and wailing filled the air around him, and his aunt, who came running at the noise, began tearing her hair. But the prince was alive.

When evening came he had regained consciousness, and by midnight he had recovered the power of speech. And then he said: "If I tell you what ails me, then swear to me on Allah that you promise to bring the means of my healing!" His aunt flung her arms up and: "Not only healing, I am prepared to give my life!" Then Aurangzeb told her what had happened in her garden. His aunt was greatly frightened, since this girl, Hira-bai, was her husband Saif-han's concubine. "He will kill me first, and then her!" she whispered in fight. "You are right," exclaimed Aurangzeb. "I will think of something myself."

The next day he summoned his servant Kuli-han, who, having listened to the prince's story, then offered to kill Saif-han, thereby opening the way for the prince to take Hira-bai into his harem. "No!" replied Aurangzeb. "I do not wish to make my aunt a widow, and in any case it is against Sharia law! It would be better for you to go and talk to him, perhaps Allah will set him on the right path..."

Kuli-han went to Saif-han and told him of what had befallen Prince Aurangzeb. Saif-han pondered for a moment and said: "I will send a

231

reply a little later with his aunt". That evening the aunt was despatched to the prince with a message saying that Saif-han was willing to exchange Hira-bai for Aurangzeb's concubine, the beautiful Chattar-bai. When he heard the offer, Aurangzeb was so excited that he exclaimed: "For her I would give not only Chattar-bai, but my entire harem!"

And that was not all that the pious prince was prepared to give for Hira-bai for, as Zebunissa was told by her mother, Dilras-bonu, one day in the garden which, as usual was full of music and singing, in exchange for a kiss the beautiful Hira-bai asked Aurangzeb to partake of the sinful wine, and all who heard this were paralysed with fear, but not the prince, who seized a cup and for the first time in his life raised it to his hot lips, which had never known this infernal taste. And only at the very last moment did Hira-bai seize the cup from his hand, whispering: "I wished to test the strength of your love for me: set aside the cup, there is something more intoxicating than this wine..."

And this incident soon became known at court, and Dara Shukuh was quick to comment to the Emperor Shah Jahan:

"Behold the specious righteousness and asceticism of this hypocrite! He behaves like a fox who has broken into his aunt's henhouse!"

But Prince Aurangzeb's sinful happiness did not last for long, for Hira-bai died suddenly in the first spring of their love. On the day she died Aurangzeb was beside himself with grief. Eventually he jumped on to his battle steed and galloped off in a desperate frenzy to the hunt – to give vent to all his fury with this barbarous and faithless world...

Later, when the prince's devoted servant Kuli-han asked him: "What is the hidden meaning of the hunt in such a hopeless condition?" – the prince replied with tears frozen in his eyes:

Weeping at home will not purge the pain or fury of the heart
The heart's torment must be purged in solitude, out in the field....

"And since then music has never sounded in your father's presence..." Dilras-bonu had told her daughter Zebunissa. And she added: "It is strange, but your father says that you are as like Hira-bai as two drops of water..."

* * *

Day after day and night after night, withdrawing into the farthest corner of the Fort of Agra, Shah Jahan recalled his life, grain by grain. This thing that was tormenting him now had not begun in his time or with him, it had always been thus, from the very foundation of this empire by the great Babur Shah, and even before him brother had risen up against brother to inherit their father's throne and power. Had not the

children of the forefather Adam begun this fratricidal struggle, had not Hobul killed Bobul... had not he himself raised his hand against his own brothers before he ascended the throne? Why, then, was he now haunted and tormented by the fate that had overtaken his sons?

In the year when he began building the Taj Mahal, his favourite Dara Shukuh, to whom he had prophesied his Peacock Throne, had built a magnificent house for his wedding on the banks of the Ind. Immediately after the wedding the prince had invited his father and three brothers to the house for wedding festivities. Since the torrid summer was at its height in Agra, Dara had decided to show them his underground room that led to a huge mirror terrace over the river – the terrace had been brought from Aleppo in faraway Syria. Everyone went down into the room and only Prince Aurangzeb had remained sitting on the doorstep. Noticing this, Dara winked to their father and said: "Look where he is sitting..." – at which His Majesty exclaimed: "My son, I know that you have been raised since childhood as an ascetic and a recluse, but you are of royal birth and must know your place. For they say that he who does not know his rank is a heathen! What kind of whim is this, for a prince to sit on a doorstep on which all and sundry may walk?" Aurangzeb replied: "I shall tell you later why I have decided to sit here..."

Some time later he stood up and on the excuse of the midday prayer left the gathering without His Majesty's permission. When he heard of this, Shah Jahan flew into a fury and forbade his third son to show his face in the palace. And this punishment lasted for almost seven months. But after all the father's heart proved softer than the son's, and in the eighth month Shah Jahan sent his eldest daughter, Jahanara, to Aurangzeb to learn the reason for the prince's defiant behaviour.

Immediately his sister asked the prince about this, Aurangzeb gave her this reply: "When Dara invited us into his underground chamber, and then on various pretexts kept walking into and out of the room, I thought that he might close the door, and then we would all suffocate. If he was doing this out of carelessness, then I took it on myself to guard the only door, so that he himself would not suffocate in the vault. But out of a high sense of nobility His Majesty forbade me to sit on guard, and there was nothing else I could do but go and redeem my sins in prayer to the Almighty..."

And then Shah Jahan not only forgave Aurangzeb, but rewarded him. But now the words the prince had spoken at that time gave rise to quite different thoughts in the Shah's mind, or could it be that life had forced him to read those words quite differently now?

* * *

Day after day and night after night, withdrawing into the farthest corner of the Fort of Delhi, Zebunissa recalled her life, grain by grain. This thing that was tormenting her now had not begun with her, but long, long ago – in the very first days of the empire, and perhaps even earlier: the life not only of an emperor's wife, but also of his aunts, sisters and daughters was a tale of wandering through their husbands' feuds; it was their fate, a life filled with emotional torment, when brother rose up against brother, when son rose up against father or a father persecuted his offspring. Who should she recall: Babur Shah's sister, Honzoda-begim, or the sister of her own father, Jahanara? And perhaps she should think of herself, incarcerated here only because she loved her own brother, Prince Akbar, who had rebelled against the order established by their father, in which the Hindus had been deprived of all rights, their shrines and schools had been destroyed, and mosques had been built on the sites of their temples. Aurangzeb had accused his son of treason, and Akbar had been forced to flee from his father's wrath to Persia. Zebunissa had been incautious enough to write a single letter to him there. The letter had been intercepted, and the enraged father had incarcerated his beloved daughter in the Fort of Salimgarh. But her father had not even spared his own sister, the mighty Princess Jahanara, who had interceded several times for him with Emperor Shah Jahan. Aurangzeb had imprisoned her together with the old man in the Fort of Agra, only because she was not only his sister, but also the sister of his abhorred brother Dara Shukuh, whom the new emperor had condemned to death for apostasy.

Aunt Jahanara had told her that when Zebunissa was six years old her aunt had been very badly burned. At that time twenty-six-year-old Aurangzeb was the ruler of the province of Dekkan. The Shah's couriers had been promptly despatched with this terrible news, but the news had reached the prince's ears even earlier through his own courtiers. The Emperor Shah Jahan had guessed that Ali Marhandan and Saeed Mirin and Sadulla-Khan, all of whom Dara Shukuh hated for their duplicity, were spying at court for Aurangzeb, who addressed them in his letters as "faithful friends and teachers of faithful pupils". They were Shah Jahan's finest officers, and so he decided first of all to give his son a warning. He wrote: "My child! Those of royal blood must possess elevation of spirit and inscrutability of intellect. I have heard that you are inexcusably humble towards certain of my officers. If you are acting so improperly with an eye to the future, then know that all has been preordained, and nothing can be changed by this servility of spirit!"

Aurangzeb had written in reply: "Your Majesty, You are right: all is in the hands of Him Who exalts whom He will and humbles whom He wishes. I am acting in accordance with the *hadith* transmitted by Ibn Anas from the lips of the Prophet Himself (may Allah preserve his line):

'Allah exalts him who humbles himself'. In saying this I am by no means contradicting Your

Majesty, but I am certain that Your most worthy letter was written in accordance with the verse:

'Temptation is from the Devil, who engenders doubt in the hearts of men and djins'..."

Aunt Jahanara had told her how furious the emperor had been when he read this letter, he was prepared to curse his defiant son, but before Aurangzeb visited the palace in connection with his sister's accidental burns, he sent the emperor his sword on a belt of gold-woven cloth, as a sign that he was going into voluntary retirement. He did not enter his father's sight, but withdrew into another period of reclusion, and if not for Jahanara, who once again pleaded for his forgiveness, Prince Aurangzeb would have been cursed by his father and possibly exiled or imprisoned. But how could Zebunissa's aunt possibly have thought that this kind-heartedness would end in her own imprisonment and the imprisonment of their father, the ailing Shah Jahan?

> If the blanket of a man's fate has been woven of black,
> The heavenly springs of Zamzam and Kavsar will never wash it white

* * *

Prince Dara Shukuh had inherited from his ancestors, and above all from Shah Babur, the founder of the empire of the Great Moguls, an elegance of spirit, a love of speculative thought and a passion for writing. Since he was a small child he had rummaged though books as if all the wisdom of the world were concentrated in them. By the age of twelve he had learned the mother of all books, the Holy Koran, off by heart: by the age of fifteen he was equally strong in both the exoteric and the esoteric sciences; by the age of eighteen he was capable of commenting on Sufi doctrines, citing ancient Sanskrit texts. Books had developed an arrogance of spirit in him: naturally, none of the courtiers around him could match the stature of those with whom his mind conversed, and therefore Dara Shukuh's feeling of chilly isolation in the midst of these courtiers grew ever stronger. The only companion of his spirit was his sister Jahanara – "the Blessing of Light" – but she became more and more involved in guileful matters of court... Later he was a passionate follower of the Sufi school of Hodja Muinuddin Chishti, since a vision had imparted to Dara Shukuh that the most direct path to God was the path of the Sufi order of Kadyri, founded centuries before by Abdulkadyr Gilani – may the Lord preserve his mystery!

And the prince was initiated into this order by his father Shah Jahan's spiritual master, the saintly sage Miyan Mir from Lahore, in the year when Dara's first daughter died as soon as she was born. Miyan Mir

had succoured the prince's grieving heart with a renowned formula of words from his own teacher Abu Saeed Horasani: "There are countless numbers of roads to God, but the Journey is no more than a single step: take but one step away from your own self and you can reach Him".

When the saintly old man died soon after, the prince's thirsting soul become attached to Miyan Mir's pupil, Maulyan Shah, to whom Dara Shukuh dedicated his first Sufi treatises. He wrote that in the school of the spirit to which he belonged, there is no pain and labour, no asceticism: everything in it is as easy and pleasurable as a gift. Here there is everything – love and goodwill, joy and ecstasy. God is not the Tormentor, but the Benefactor of His creatures and He surely raises His chosen ones up to His dominions as guests, and does not persecute them like criminals.

The emperor really had loved his first-born like a dear guest. He had elevated him in rank above the other brothers and always kept him at his side, while he appointed the others governors and despatched them to the provinces, where Prince Shuja, so it was reported, had abandoned himself to lust, Murad Bahsh drank wine both day and night, and Aurangzeb made war on his neighbours, entirely without permission from the imperial court.

Shah Jahan did everything to make Dara Shukuh consummately accomplished, not only in spiritual matters, but also in affairs of state. In cases when his younger sons had suffered defeat, the emperor fitted out a mighty army under the leadership of his favourite and assigned the finest generals to him. So it was, for example, at the siege of Kandagar, which belonged to the king of Persia. Aurangzeb failed to take it with an army of sixty thousand men, and then Shah Jahan gave Dara Shukuh a mighty army of seventy thousand men for the campaign. But the enlightened prince did not place his reliance in the might of his dozens of canon, hundreds of battle elephants and thousands of select troops, he placed his reliance in the power of vision and Providence.

When the army halted in Kabul, two Sufi came to the impressionable prince, and one of them exclaimed in his trance: "I see that the Shah of Iran is dead!" The second added: "I too see this. But I shall not return until the coffin with the Shah's body falls to the ground!" Dara confirmed what they had said with his own vision: "I shall spend no more than seven days at Kandagar, and the city shall be taken".

Astrologers calculated the time when the position of the stars would be favourable as the twenty-third day of the month of Rabiul-avval for the start of the march, and the seventh day of the month of Jumadius-sani for the start of the siege. Dozens of mullahs accompanied the tread of the army's feet with their incessant prayers, and in addition several magicians were hired, whose job it was to conjure up a myriad maggots

that would teem in the storehouses of the besieged, spoiling their food and so breaking their spirit.

The army set out on its march on the right day, but owing to rowdiness on the long journey, the prince arrived too late for the appointed day of the siege. And then Dara decided to delay the siege for another month, until the next favourable position of the stars. Meanwhile, the enemy continually improved his defences and made daring sallies, and Dara's troops ate up their meagre campaign rations. But Dara Shukuh was counting on his magicians.

One of them, Indira Gir, whom the prince had hired in Lahore for a daily ration of royal viands and a cup of young wine every evening, promised to summon his devas to tear down the fortress walls that were too strong to fall to human siege. And he really did walk casually towards the walls, and easily persuaded the Persian sentries to let him into the fortress to see the head of the city. The commandant of the fortress was also glad to treat the magician to his viands and what was left of his wine, but when Indra Gir decided to go back to Dara Shukuh, the commandant suddenly abandoned his benevolent attitude and put the magician in an item of torture equipment – a kind of gigantic vice – where poor Indra confessed to his guileful plan, and under pain of death was forced to use his magic to make Dara Shukuh's army fall back immediately from the fortress walls. However, the devas would not obey the tortured magician, and then the merciless commandant ordered his head to be cut off and thrown, together with his body, from the top of the impregnable fortress walls to their foot, where the enemy of thousands was waiting, anticipating the assistance of the devas.

* * *

On the day when the Sun moved from the constellation of Gemini into the constellation of Cancer, a pilgrim of holy appearance – a Haji – presented himself to Dara Shukuh and promised to keep the enemy's artillery and rifles silent by the power of the spirit for three hours – a long enough period of time for the fortress to be taken. In remuneration he required not only full royal rations, but also two dancing girls, two thieves, two gamblers, one bull-calf, a lamb and five cockerels.

A week later, at the time fixed by the Haji, when the messengers called out that they were ready for battle, the magician lit a lamp, then sprinkled lentils on it and launched into a strange dance, jumping up into the air in time with the sounds of the bursting lentils. At the end of the dance he threw himself on a stray dog and slit its throat in front of everyone, then drained the lamb's blood while slitting the throats of all five cockerels, one after another. Exclaiming to the dancing girls and the gamblers: "You should also be sacrificed, but I buy you freedom with my own blood!" he cut his thigh and covered the blood of the sacrificial

animals with his own. Then he started dancing again and a little while later he grabbed the commander in chief's sword and dipped it in the blood.

The next morning, when the troops were ready for the attack, the Haji was summoned to the commander-in-chief, who demanded that he silence the enemy's canon for the promised three hours. The Haji rubbed his sleepy eyes and said: "There are three djins guarding this fortress, and I fought two of them all night long, but the third managed to escape. The attack will have to be halted for a week. That will give me enough time to deal with him!"

During that week the Persians must have heard about the magician's preparations and so they took magical countermeasures. They dropped a dead dog with its belly slit open and stuffed with mouldy rice at the foot of the wall. Summoned to the prince, the Haji exclaimed with horror in his voice that this act had brought the previous two devas back to life, and therefore the siege would have to be postponed indefinitely....

* * *

Following the long and unsuccessful siege of Kandahar, when each general blamed another for the failure, and all secretly blamed the prince, when the soldiers who were still alive – Hindus, Pashtus, Turks, and Uzbeks – all thanked the One God in their various tongues for the slushy road of return, Dara Shukuh did not know how he could present himself to the imperial eyes of his father, and only the single thought that God had entrusted to him an entirely different mission, revealed in a youthful vision, soothed the pain of his military fiasco. He was eager to get back to his books, eager to reach the place to which his heart and mind were drawn for a higher task than besieging fortress walls – the task of besieging the unruly heights of the spirit.

On the way, in the midst of the snowy Haibar Pass, he recalled what he had written in his treatises, and this thought, returning to its origin from afar, seemed strange and unusual. There are three stages in the comprehension of the Unity of God. The first stage is the denial of one's own self, when "everything is He, and I am nothing". Here there is still no genuine separation, and the verse reads thus:

> *Beloved Lord, I am not, I am not,*
> *But you are: lover, love and beloved*

He repeated these words to himself and one corner of his mind noted in passing that his desire to conceal himself from his father now was in some way akin to this verse ...

But, lashing his steed with his whip, he drove his submissive thought on as well. The second stage, his thought prompted his memory, is called

the intoxication of Unity, and it signifies the highest stage of ascent. Here the awareness of division and separation between "I" and "thou" disappear completely and the seeker dissolves in the divine unity. He understands that "I am I" and, praying to God, he prays to himself.

> If the infidel is bored with ritual Islam,
> Who shall know the true essence of unbelief?
> Within each idol there glimmers a soul,
> And beneath unbelief there smoulders true faith....

The campfire at the very highest point of the pass warmed his soul with these words. However, the third stage of God's unity is the "sobriety of union", when the world of multiplicity cannot conceal His unity from the gaze of the travelling seeker:

> Hey, you who seek God everywhere
> You yourself are God, not outside God,
> And in the midst of a boundless ocean
> Your search is akin to a drop that seeks the ocean.....

Night lay on the boundless valley, which embraced all the space ahead, and in this ocean of unity all distinction was lost between these dusky Hindus and Pashtus, Turks and Uzbeks, soldiers and generals, their faiths and religions, victory and defeat, fear and hope, travelling and standing still, life and death.

* * *

After the prolonged and ultimately unsuccessful siege of Kandahar, when every general blamed another for the failure, and all of them secretly blamed the prince, when the soldiers who were still alive – Hindus, Pashtu, Turks and Uzbeks – all thanked the one God in their various tongues for the slushy road of return, Aurangzeb knew full surely that he was returning on the orders of the emperor, and he felt dissatisfaction at his father's hasty decision.

On the way, in the midst of the snowy Haibar Pass, thinking of the meeting with his father and his brothers, the prince recalled a verse that invoked the unsleeping vigilance that had maintained the indestructibility of the house of Timur for centuries:

Do not disdain caution when the enemy is courteous
A dagger may be hidden under clothes, like water under grass...

He thought about the valour of the Persians, who had defended their fortress for four months, and the Hindus who were under his command: the Persians' planet was the Sun, which was why their minds were quick

and their foresight was four times as keen as the Rajputs', whose planet was Saturn. But the Persians' weakness, he thought under the starry night sky, is that the path of the Sun intersects with the path of Venus, and so they are full of love. Saturn is closer to Jupiter. One had to be constantly vigilant with these cunning Persians, as this verse says:

When water spreads at the foot of a wall, is it not to undermine it....

As Aurangzeb gazed forward at the night-dark valley, these words reminded him of more than just the failed siege behind him....

* * *

On the day when the Sun moved from the constellation of Scorpio into the constellation of Sagittarius, in the twenty-third year of the reign of the Emperor Shah Jahan, Prince Aurangzeb disobeyed his father's express will and met with his brother Prince Shuja at Agra, where they concluded an alliance against their older brother Dara Shukuh, who was fondly cherished by the aging Padishah. In witness of this alliance, Shuja's daughter was betrothed to Aurangzeb's oldest son, Sultan Muhammad. A little later the alliance of the two brothers was joined by a third, Prince Murad Bahsh.

Shah Jahan, who kept a wary eye on every slightest movement in the country that he ruled, sensed something was amiss and wrote several wrathful letters to Aurangzeb, in an attempt to break off the betrothal, but as always, in opposition to his father's pressure Aurangzeb cited the verses of the Holy Koran and the *hadiths* of the Prophet. Then the emperor sent a messenger to the other prince, Shuja, with a complaint against Aurangzeb, saying: "Your younger brother is not coping with the administration of the province of Dekan, which requires a more mature ruler, such as yourself..."

A little later Shah Jahan, having named Prince Dara Shukuh as his successor and awarded him the title of "Shah of High Predestination", persuaded his son, who had written book after book and had begun translating the Bhagavadgita and the Upanishads, to think about strengthening his own position. Everyone at court knew of the passionate love between Dara Shukuh's eldest son, Suleiman Shukuh, and Aurangzeb's daughter, Zebunissa, but now any idea of their betrothal was out of the question. On his father's advice, Dara Shukuh betrothed Suleiman Shukuh, first with the niece of the most influential Rajput general, Rao Singh, and then with the daughter of another military leader, Jafar Khan.

This was at the time when the Emperor Shah Jahan took the province of Multan away from Prince Aurangzeb and gave it to Dara Shukuh to rule. From his tour of inspection Dara promptly wrote to his father that

Aurangzeb's warriors had destroyed the Indian temples, and hastily set about restoring them. Let it be said that the emperor's spies informed him that this was not entirely true: Aurangzeb had left Multan when unruly crowds had themselves started smashing down these temples....

Aurangzeb was on his way to his Dekan when, outside Lahore, which was an integral part of Dara's domain, the governor of the city came out to greet the prince but, strangely enough, galloped past the prince's procession and then disappeared back into his city. This was a public insult to Aurangzeb's royal dignity and, of course, he saw it as the work of Dara Shukuh, who at that time had set out for Kabul with the emperor.

But he was wrong about this: the governor of the city was afraid of vicious tongues who might report to the "Shah of High Predestination" that his placeman was disloyal...

In short, from that time on Dara Shah called Aurangzeb "holier-than-thou" behind his back, and Aurangzeb called his despised brother "the heretic".

* * *

Prince Aurangzeb had inherited from his ancestors, and primarily from Babur-shah, the founder of the empire, an intransigent intellect and an unquiet heart. He had impressed upon his children since they were little that he who wished to rule the House of Timur must, above all, stand midway between meekness of the soul and ferocity of the heart. For if either of these qualities exceeds the other, it becomes the cause of the throne's downfall. Excessive meekness of the soul inspires in subjects a sense of impunity, whereas an excess of heard-heartedness frightens people. "Look, Sultan Ulugbek, for all his remarkable intellectual virtues, was so hard- hearted that he spilled blood with or without due cause. His son, Abdul Latif, was obliged to incarcerate his father in the fortress of Nihovand." Then, after a pause, Aurangzeb would add: "On his way to the fortress Ulugbek asked one of the beggars to whom he usually threw gold coins: 'What do you think, what was the reason for my downfall?' The beggar replied with tears in his eyes: 'Excessive bloodshed that drove others to recoil from you...' And as for our most august ancestor Humayun-shah, it was his meekness of soul with regard to the unruly Sher-khan that cost him the throne. When Hamayun-shah politely requested Sher-khan to call his son to order by writing him a letter, Sher-khan's father replied: 'He has long ago outrun the bounds of admonition by letter, and I can foresee where this devil-may-care attitude will lead!' "

He would pause again, while his children breathed heavily, and then conclude: "And in addition, the successor to the House of Timur must know no peace, for as the verse says:

241

> *A king, like water must not stagnate on the spot*
> *Water blooms, a king is overgrown with the burden of habit.*
> *In campaigns glory, honour, desire for vengeance*
> *And desire for peace part the foot from the stirrup.....*

"And finally, one must keep a wary eye on servants, and appoint them to positions in accordance with their capabilities. A philosopher will never become a warrior, and a little man should never be burdened with great affairs, just as a great man should not be busied with trifles, for ones lacks the guts to do the job, and the other will be tormented eternally by his shame. And so there will be absolute confusion in the state," Aurangzeb would tell his children, and then fall silent, but his eyes still blazed...

* * *

To this day Zebunissa could still feel that gaze on her: passionate and suspicious, loving and wary, cruel and repentant, but never betraying itself with a single wrong word, let alone action. It was in the twenty-ninth year of the rule of her grandfather, the Emperor Shah Jahan, that nineteen-year-old Zebunissa heard from her aunt Jahanara about the betrothal of her beloved cousin Suleiman Shukuh to the daughter of an Indian rajah. For three days she did not eat or drink, weeping bitter tears, until suddenly she decided to leave the imperial court and go to her mother in Aurangabad.

The autumn Sun was gradually moving out of the constellation of Leo, and when their procession had travelled two days' journey, she was overtaken by a messenger who informed her that the emperor had fallen seriously ill. Zebunissa knew that her grandfather had been ailing for a long time, but for a brief moment a triumphant gloating glimmered in her heart, filled with Turkish blood: after all, he was the one who had given uncle Dara Shukuh the idea of betrothing his son to an infidel Rajput girl...

The Sun really is leaving the house of Leo, the princess thought bitterly and, in contravention of every rule of etiquette, she continued her journey to Dekan. When she arrived at her father's court, her father was already preparing for war. Here she was told that the heretic Dara Shukuh had killed the emperor and usurped power. And as for the emperor still glancing out of the window once a month – that was a eunuch dressed up in the king's clothes!

Riding this flood-wave, Aurangzeb and his brothers Shuja and Murad declared a holy jihad for the salvation of the offended faith. And although to start with Princess Zebunissa understood how laughable the invented pretexts were, and that their only justification was the eternal contest for

the throne, in the end the grievance of her young maiden's heart won out and she immersed herself unreservedly in court diplomacy. Her father Aurangzeb wrote to his brother Shuja that the strength of their tripartite alliance rested on the two of them, while also sending secret letters to his younger brother, Prince Murad, in which he complained that Shuja had fallen under the influence of Shiites, and therefore everything depended on the two of them, as faithful followers of the Prophet, and at the same time he promised this dissipated drunkard another three southern provinces abundant in wine and beautiful women... In addition, he had to lull the vigilance of the court, where the ever-alert Jahanara had sensed that something was wrong and was writing letters to all the brothers appealing for them to unite in peace. But the other sister, Ravshanara, fed them the latest rumours from the court and exhorted them to act rapidly and ride the wave of the Ulema' and mullahs' discontent with the excessively liberal, not to say, she wrote, pro-Indian views of Dara Shukuh, who had already been declared successor to the throne.

Early in the winter of that year the war began. Prince Shuja suddenly declared himself emperor and invaded the province of Allahabad. When the old emperor heard of this rebellion against his power, he was beside himself and immediately gave instructions, through Dara Shukuh, for an army led by Suleiman Shukuh to be sent against "this scoundrel whose soul has only ever known the single feeling of lust" and for the rebel's head to be delivered to him "as a sign of punishment". Dara Shukuh gave his son the finest general, Mirza Raja Jai Singh, and the imperial army began its campaign.

In late winter the imperial army unexpectedly attacked Shuja's forces at the holy city of Benares and completely routed it. Shuja himself escaped on a ship by sailing down the river. However, the combined forces of Aurangzeb and Murad, who at this stage had also crowned himself, launched an attack on Darmat at the opposite side of the empire and inflicted a crushing defeat on the other commander-in-chief of the imperial army, Jasvant Singh.

At precisely this time Dara Shukuh's men intercepted a letter from Aurangzeb to Murad, in which the first prince congratulated the second on his coronation and went on to write: "As for this Servant of God, I have no passion for the secular affairs of this delusive world. There is no desire in my heart, save the desire of heaven and therefore of service to the House of the Lord! You are our chosen brother, and everything that motivates you against the arrogance and injustice of the heretic Dara bears the imprint of a just battle. And in this holy jihad you must rely on me as a friend, support and brother. While our poor father is alive, we must join together to direct our steps towards His Majesty in order to serve him and to punish this upstart Dara, intoxicated with pride and vanity, this one who, under the guise of Sufism, has strayed from the

right path into the heresy of Hinduism in both thought and deed. If this heretic seizes the throne and establishes his power, the foundations of the true faith will be undermined and the claims of holy Islam will be betrayed in favour of unbelief and Judaism. May the Koran bear witness to our alliance and may no doubts or suspicions steal into your luminous mind!"

When the old emperor was read this missive by his eldest daughter, Jahanara, he thought with bitterness of Zebunissa, whose tear-stained face seemed to gaze out at him from this coded letter....

* * *

Shah Jahan could still feel that gaze on him to this day: passionate and suspicious, loving and wary, cruel and repentant, but never giving itself away in a single wrong word, let alone action. Now, when only his faithful daughter Jahanara was left to him, he learned from her that in a battle at Samugarh his successor Dara Shukh, whom he had embraced as if for the last time and blessed for battle when seeing him on his way from Agra, had suffered a crushing defeat by the army of Aurangzeb. The old emperor looked at his daughter with his weak-sighted eyes and he thought he saw his granddaughter, who had declared a hunger-strike against her father's actions in a desperate attempt to call a halt to events that had long ago got out of hand. And how greatly Shah Jahan had desired that impossible wedding between his beloved grandson and granddaughter – Suleiman Shukuh and Zebunissa – as if he wished to bequeath to them what he and Mumtaz had failed to achieve in their lives. And what now? Zebunissa was taking revenge on her father Aurangzeb. Suleman Shukuh had been delayed in the mountains of Benares, so he had not been able to rescue his father, Dara Shukuh, and there was only the ever-faithful Jahanara, reading the report of the battle at Samagarh like a requiem for his vain life.

On the sixth day of the holy month of Ramadan, when the summer sun blazed unmercifully in the sky, Dara Shuruh led out his sixteenth-thousand-strong army for open battle in feverish haste, but instead of attacking the enemy positions, his troops stopped in the middle of the field, awaiting an attack from the troops of Aurangzeb and Murad. A scorching wind from all six directions and a lack of water struck down troops heavily laden with armour. Aurangzeb also mounted his battle elephant but, on seeing that the imperial forces had halted in confusion, after the sunset prayer he withdrew his army to its initial positions.

It was not just the aimlessness of that day that split the army of Dara Shukuh, but also the fact that the Muslims – Iranians and Turanians – were observing their fast in impossible conditions, whereas the Rajput

Hindus, Sikhs and Punjabis found relief from the heat in water and food before the very eyes of the Muslims....

Early in the morning of the following day Dara Shukuh drew his forces up into battle formation: at the very front was the artillery, covered by the following infantry. Further back there were five hundred battle camels standing at the ready, followed by several hundred battle elephants. And then, behind this impregnable defensive screen, there were five divisions drawn up in line of battle. The royal cavalry consisted of ten thousand superbly trained horsemen and, at the very centre, the crown prince Dara Shukah himself was mounted on a gigantic elephant, surrounded by five thousand of his most devoted warriors.

The army of Aurangzeb was drawn up in the same way, according to Mogul tactics.

The attack of the royal forces commenced with artillery fire. The booming and the smoke hung over the sandy valley of Samugarh. Aurangzeb's artillery responded with only isolated shots, and then Dara decided that it had been crushed and ordered his infantry to attack the enemy. Thousands of arrows whistled though the air, carrying with them the smoke and boom of canon shots, and this hailstorm was followed by the clash of crossed swords and blades beating on chain mail. Blood, sweat and tears transformed the sand into thick mush.

The advance units of Dara's son, Sipehr Shukuh, and Rustam-khan almost broke Aurangzeb's avant-garde, and they were already sounding victory on the drums, but then Aurangzeb's artillery made a sudden and powerful entry into the battle, and a well-aimed canon ball shattered the elephant under Rustam-khan to pieces.

And then Dara decided that the moment of victory must not be allowed to slip away, and he advanced with his centre through the ranks of elephants and camels to support Sipehr Shukuh, but he ran into the impenetrable defences of Shaikh Mir. Now his dispositions were irreparably unbalanced: the canon had been left behind with the bewildered gunners, who could not fire at their own men, the battle camels and elephants could not advance, for they would trample their own troops....

And then Dara struck in a dash for the centre of Aurangzeb's defences. But yet again Aurangzeb's artillery, held in reserve, discharged a new squall of fire, and the confused and vulnerable Dara Shukuh decided to dismount from his elephant and mount a horse. But the troops all around, seeing the royal elephant without the crown prince, decided that he had been killed, and their spirit was immediately broken....

That evening Dara, his son Sipehr Shukuh and two thousand of their retainers managed to escape in the direction of Agra....

As Jahanara read this message, the emperor, leaning thoughtfully on his staff suddenly seemed to see their ancestor, Zahriddin Muhammad Babur-shah:

> *Do not give yourself over to power and*
> *do not pledge your hands to labour,*
> *God will surely provide, so strive, and yet be generous.*

* * *

Princess Jahanara read Babur-Shah's reminiscences out loud and the tears slowly rolled down her swarthy cheeks on to the family manuscript handed down from generation to generation:

There were twenty or twenty-five pursuers, there were only eight of us left. If, in the midst of the alarm, we had known their number, then we would have offered stout combat. But, thinking there was a large detachment following behind the pursuers, we continued on our way. Even though those in retreat may outnumber those in pursuit, still they say: "It is enough to say 'boo!' to a defeated man".

The horse under me was weak. Khan-kuli offered me his mount and he and the others gradually scattered off to the sides. Only Mirza-kuli was left with me. His mount also began to fail. I said: "How can I leave you, come with me to share life and death equally". But in the end Mirza-kuli exclaimed: "My horse is exhausted, leave me and ride on, God grant you will escape..." I felt in a strange condition. Mirza-kuli also fell back. I was left all alone.

Two of my enemies appeared in the distance. One was called Bobo Sairamiy, and the other Banda Ali. They started gaining on me. My horse was tired, and the mountains were still far off, but the rocks had begun. I thought: "My steed is failing, it is a long way to the mountains, where shall I go?" There were about twenty arrows in my quiver. I thought: "I shall dismount and start firing from among these rocks to my last arrow", but the first thought was interrupted by another. "I shall get to the mountains, stick the arrows behind my belt and scramble upwards" - since I was certain of the strength of my legs.

With this thought in mind I continued on my way. My horse could scarcely plod along. And the others had approached to the distance of an arrow's flight. But I begrudged my arrows and did not fire. And they were wary and did not approach closer. They kept riding like that. The sun set when I reached the mountains. They shouted after me, through hands held like trumpets: "Where are you heading for like this? You know, all your men have already been taken prisoner!" These words threw me into a fury. If we all fell into the hands of the enemy, there could be no greater danger! I did not answer, but continued on my way to the mountains. Having covered another stage of the road, they started shouting again, but this time more politely. And they dismounted as they did so. I did not listen to their words and continued on my way. I went higher and higher along

the ravine, I carried on until the time came for the evening prayer. Finally I reached a rockslide and turned to look back. Rocks showered down and the horse would go no further.

They also dismounted and addressed me with respect and reverence, even more politely than before. They said: "Where are you riding to in the night?" They swore that Sultan Ahmed wished to declare me a sheikh. I said: "My heart does not accept this, I must not go there. If you truly desire to do me a service, then another such opportunity may never come. Lead me to the khans and I will reward you beyond your souls' desire. If you will not, then be on your way. And my horse will carry me on! And that shall be accounted as your service!"

They said: "We should not have set out after you. Now that we are here, how can we go back? Since you do not wish to go back, we are at your service!" I said: "Swear this!" They swore on the Holy Koran. I said: "Lead me to a place where we can hide during the day and obtain horses during the night, and ford the Hodjent river to find ourselves in Hodjent". They said: "There is a certain secluded place here, we can hide there". Vanda Ali, who governed the town of Karnan, said: "I will go to Karnan and return with all that we need".

We set out towards Karnan and halted on its approaches. Banda Ali continued on his way alone.

But the morning came and he had still not returned. The shivering that shook us was powerful! Banda Ali returned with the dawn. He did not bring any horses, he brought three bread cakes. Each of us put a bread cake inside his clothes and, on reaching the ravine, we tethered our horses and then we all sat there, looking in different directions and keeping watch over each other.

* * *

Dar Shukuh galloped away from the field of his defeat, and the number of men around him grew less and less. They either scattered in safe directions or else they intended to surrender themselves to the mercy of Aurangzeb, who was now beating the drums of victory, or else... Only Sipehr Shukuh, his youthful son, kept pace with his desperate father, but even his horse started to fail, Dara Shukuh galloped on for some time completely alone, the sun was setting behind his back, casting a long black shadow that tangled with the hooves of his weary horse, but, resigned to fate, like its rider, the horse kept moving its legs without stopping. Finally it reached a tree, and Dara Shukuh shuddered, halted his steed and dismounted, and then, after washing in a spring under the tree, he threw off his helmet and sat down, lowering his head on to his knees. His son Sipehr Shukuh rode up, and he heard his father's dull groan: "Whatever is fated to be, so be it!"

They had to try long and hard to persuade his father to mount his horse again and gallop into the darkening night in the direction of Agra. By midnight they had reached the capital, but the news of the defeat

had reached the city sooner and emptied the usually crowded streets. Only a few days earlier the prince had led his supposedly invincible army through these streets and the emperor himself, in seeing them on their way had blessed him for victory. Now his disgrace was greater than any other on earth, and the frowning night was his only helpmate. Dara Shukuh did not show himself at court, but took his wives and family, with all the wealth that could be loaded on to elephants and camels, and that very night before dawn he set out in the direction of Delhi.

* * *

Princes Zebinussa read aloud the reminiscences of Babur-Shah and the tears slowly rolled down her cheeks on to the family manuscript handed down from generation to generation:

> Banda Ali said: "On the outskirts of Karnan there are gardens where it is possible to hide, no one will suspect anything, let us move there, and from there we will send men to the governor of Kadyrberda". With this thought in mind we mounted our horses and made our way to the outskirts of Karnan. It was winter, and it was very cold. They brought me an old sheepskin coat and I put it on. They brought a little soup, and I ate. And I felt so much better! I asked Banda Ali: "Did you send a man to Kadyrberda?"
>
> He said: "I did". These unfortunate men, as it turns out, had conspired to send their man to Aksy, to my greatest enemy, Ahmad Tanbal. I went under the canopy, lit a fire and my eyes would not stay open. And to reassure me, these men tried to persuade me to stay there and not move to another garden.
>
> At midnight I mounted my horse and moved to another garden. Bobo Sairamiy sat on the roof and watched in all directions. At the next noontide he climbed down off the roof and said: "Yusuf Daruga is approaching!" A strange agitation came over me. I said: "Go and find out if he is coming because of me". He went out, and spoke with them and came back. He says: "Yusuf says that your beks wish to make you a Padishah!" I said: "After all these clashes, battles and betrayals, how can I go to them, how can I trust them?" At these words Yusuf went down on his knees and started vowing that he really had been sent by Sheikh Bayazid-bek, who had heard of my whereabouts.
>
> When he said that, I was visited by a strange feeling. Clearly there is no feeling on earth stronger than fear for one's life. I said: "Tell the truth, if this is not how everything is, I shall make my ritual ablutions". Yusuf began vowing again, but who could believe him? I felt impatience within me. I got up and walked into the garden. I started talking to myself. I said: "A man may live a hundred years, even a thousand, but even so in the end he has to die!"
>
> *If you live a hundred years, or but a single day*
> *Still must you leave the dwelling of the heart, like a shadow....*

And I set my mind on death. There was water flowing in that park, and when I bowed my head in genuflection, my eyelids closed for a moment. I saw Hodja Yakub, the son of Hodja Yahya and the grandson of Lord Hodja Ubaidullah, and he was riding towards me on a sorrel horse, surrounded by horsemen. He said: "Be not sad, Hodja Ahrar Ubaidullah sent me to you, saying: 'We shall raise you up to be a Padishah!' And wherever difficulties may arise, let him only remember us, and we shall appear before him. Victory and success are now moving to meet us! Arise, lift up your head..."

And I awoke in great good spirits and meanwhile Yusuf-daruga and his henchmen were taking counsel, saying that I should be bound. I heard these words and said: "You speak of this, well now, let me see which of you will dare to approach me!" I said this, and suddenly I heard a heavy beating of horses' hooves behind the clay fence. Yusuf-daruga said: "If we had bound you and delivered you to Ahmad Tanbal, our affairs would have prospered better. But now he has sent more men to seize you". That is, he began hinting that the hoofbeats were from horsemen sent by Tanbal. On hearing this I shuddered, not knowing what to do.

At that moment the horsemen could not find the gate in the clay fence and simply broke down a part of it and entered the garden. I looked, and saw it was Kutlug Muhammad Barlas and Boboi Pargori, my devoted warriors, who had arrived, having gathered fifteen or twenty men! They approached, jumped down off their horses and, bowing already from a distance, fell at my feet. At that moment it seemed to me that God had granted me life anew! I said: "Seize Yusuf-daruga and these faithless serfs". The men scattered and ran, but they were caught on all sides, bound and brought to me.

I asked my men: "Where have you come from and who informed you of my whereabouts?" Kutlug Muhammud Barlas said: "After we parted from you at Aksy, I fled to Andijan. I had a dream of Hodja Ubaidullah, who said: 'Babur-shah is now in a town by the name of Karna, go there and bring him, since he must rule...'.

* * *

Shah Jahan sat alone in his empty chambers and felt the number of people around him constantly dwindling. The hope of his old eyes, Prince Dara Shukuh, had fled the city without so much as casting a shadow across the threshold of the palace. And now Prince Aurangzeb, who had entered the city to the triumphant sounds of war trumpets and drum rolls, would not cast his shadow across the threshold, but send letters through his messengers. And even Jahanara did not come out of her chambers, either distressed by what had happened, or preparing herself for what was about to happen.

Shah Jahan had tried sending Jahanara to Aurangzeb with a *Farman*, a Most High Order, to call for a halt to the fratricide and offering to leave the Punjab to Prince Dara Shukuh, Bengal to Prince Shuja, and declare Aurangzeb crown prince and bestow on him the title of "Shah of High Predestination", but in reply Aurangzeb had only laughed...

Now Shah Jahan realised that it had not been Aurangzeb laughing at that moment, but fate, who had caught up with the old emperor on the threshold of death. Had not he himself rebelled against his own father, the emperor Jahangir, and also risen up against his own brothers? Had not he himself fought for the throne when his old father was still alive? Why was he now complaining to fate, why could he not accept what had happened against his will?

Now he himself wrote a letter, without Princess Jahanara's knowledge, with his own unsteady hand that was accustomed to the sword, but not to the reed pen. He wrote to the ruler of Kabul, Mahabat-khan, appealing to him to gather his forces and intervene on the side of the crown prince Dara Shukuh. But the longer his trembling hand floundered in the ornamental script of the flowery phrases praising the courage and devotion of Mahabat-khan, whom he had formerly despised, the more keenly the emperor felt his own helplessness, he felt like his eldest son, who had spent his entire life with just such a phantom reed pen in his hand. "The sword is mightier than the pen!" the emperor scratched as his final phrase, and then, despite the imploring style of all that had gone before, he concluded: "But if, under these circumstances, the pillar of the state Mahabat-khan disdains this appeal, then tomorrow, on Judgement Day, my hand will grasp him by his deceitful forelock!"

* * *

Dara Shukuh sat alone in his empty chambers, feeling the number of people around him constantly dwindling. His last hope – his eldest son, Suleiman Shukuh – was still making his interminable march through the Himalayas, and it was simply not possible for him to rejoin his father. Or was he, following his father's defeat and his father-in-law Jasvanta Singh's desertion to Aurangzeb's side, harbouring some dark scheme – had he recalled his love for the daughter of that pious hypocrite, Princess Zebunissa?

Dara had written him letter after letter, and the reed pen, which had once felt so familiar in his hand and now felt so strange, kept trying to remind him of something against his will. He had now reached his Punjab – "the land of five rivers" – which Dara Shukuh had formerly called the earthly image of heaven, but even in this eternal heaven he beheld all the hell of the present, as if two oceans that the Almighty himself had held apart and prevented from mingling, had suddenly fused into one.

And had not Dara Shukuh himself appealed to these two oceans to fuse together, had not he himself, throughout his former life, summoned wave upon wave, had not he himself given the title *The Mingling of Two Oceans* to his last work, in which he had tried to demonstrate the submerged unity of the currents of Islam and Hinduism? A single

God, a single soul, call it Ruh or Atman, the same human senses, both the external: hearing – samia or sabda; sight – basira or rupa; smell – shamma or gandha; taste – zaika or rasa; touch – lamisa or sparsa, and the internal: imagination, attention, memory, intuition, thought – also the same, only designated by different names. And the pain now felt by Dara Shukuh – he who had mingled the oceans of the mystical and the earthly, philosophy and war, book and throne, pen and sword – was not that pain the same for all these senses?

Was not the wonder, as it said in the Koran, that the Lord created two oceans – one with salt water, and the other with fresh water – and behold the miracle, that they do not mingle together, as if some invisible barrier between them....

"The sword is mightier than the pen," Dara Shukuh scratched as his final phrase, but immediately crossed these words out and completed his latest letter to his eldest son as follows: "And so, it is clear that Allah is Self-sufficient, beyond all need for worlds..."

* * *

Aurangzeb sat alone in the empty chambers of Dara Shukuh, who had fled, and scraped with his pen: "The sword has proved mightier than the pen!" – deliberately repeating his father's phrase from the letter that had been intercepted. Then he continued: "May it be known to Your most august mind that the actions of Your humble servant are subject only to the will of Divine Providence. I have always lived in the hope that Your Majesty, with the keenness of intellect typical of You, would not go against Providence by raising up obstacles to the actions of Your humble servant and lighting the path for those to whom Providence has denied her support. I have frequently heard it said that these barriers were raised in accordance with Your orders, and that it was in accordance with Your will that my brothers strove to battle against me, in so doing inflicting deprivation and hardship on the people. Nevertheless, I paid no attention to this and did not swerve from the road of exalted devotion. However, reports of Your Majesty's hostility to me arrive constantly, and Your coded letters in particular testify to this. And so, I am convinced that Your Majesty does not love Your humble servant, and You are still attempting to clutch at what has fallen irrevocably from Your grasp. In these circumstances Your humble servant has no alternative but to take the necessary measures, for the sake of maintaining order in the state and restoring Sharia law, and Your humble servant's mind will not rest until all three apostates have received their due punishment. As long as princely heads remain on their shoulders, there will be no peace in the state. When the affairs of my rivals have been settled in accordance with the will of the Almighty, there will be no more need for these measures dictated by caution."

Aurangzeb did not write to his prisoner that a little earlier he had given orders to arrest the weak-minded Prince Murad, who had already declared himself Emperor and begun minting coins with his own name on them...

* * *

Zebunissa sat alone in the empty chambers of her father Aurangzeb, who was now warring with his brother Shuja, scraping a letter with her reed pen. She did not know to whom she should send it: to the Emperor Shah Jahan, incarcerated in the Fort of Agra; to her eldest uncle Dara Shukuh who, pursuing his desperate flight, was now in Kashmir or Gujarat; to her condemned intended, Suleiman Shukuh, who was stuck in his interminable march through the Himalayas; to her father Aurangzeb, who was ruthlessly settling scores with every possible heir to the Peacock Throne, one by one; to her great aunt Jahanara, who had so far held the empire in her firm, invisible hands, but had now lost courage in the tangle of her equally great loyalties; to God up in His blue heaven, or to herself, here on this earth so black with misery?

* * *

Dara Shukuh circled round India, betrayed in Lahore, in Multan, in Gatch, in Gujarat, in Ahmadabad, in Udaipur and in Ajmir, and with the frenzy of an entranced Dervish he kept moving round and round the same circle. It was as if something from the depths or, perhaps, on the contrary, from the heights, were mocking him, who had long ago passed through all the stages by which the soul develops – all those valleys of Trepidation, Hardship and Despair, all those peaks of Penitence, Resignation and Acquiescence... Now his tardy body was walking the same paths, but this time his expectations were ominous. Why did the path of the soul differ so much from the path of the body?

The prince's eyelids closed in weariness, and to the accompaniment of a constant clopping of hooves he thought he saw the holy Indian sage Baba Lal, whom he had met after the unsuccessful siege of Kandagar. "What is the significance of image-worship among the Hindus?" the young and curious Dara had asked, and now in his sleep, he realised that the question had been about the throne. "The essence of this practice is in concentrating the mind. He who possesses knowledge of the Spirit does not concern himself with form. But he who possesses no inner awareness must, as a consequence, be bound to external form. In exactly the same way as unmarried girls play with dolls, but forget about them when they marry. Such is the nature of image worship. Those who do not possess knowledge of the spirit will clearly seek to acquire it by means of external form, but as soon as they acquire inner awareness, they also will disdain external form..."

The prince's steed galloped through the dense Indian night, and Dara carried on questioning the holy sage.

"In the Ramayana it says that when Rama Chandra conquered Ceylon, a huge number of men were killed on both sides. Then he sprinkled them with the water of life, and his own army was reanimated, but Ravana's soldiers remained dead. How is this to be explained?"

Baba Lal said: "This happened because Ravana's forces had acknowledged the supremacy of Rama's forces on the battlefield. The supremacy is obvious. Blessed individuals, who have acquired *mukti*, or salvation, never return to the human form. They were killed on the field of battle, but before that the thought of Rama was present in their consciousness. Ravana's soldiers had acquired salvation, and therefore their souls did not return to their bodies..."

His steed galloped wearily towards the Indus, and already there was a breath of its misty dawn coolness in the air, and for the first time in long months Dara Shukuh's soul lightly and blithely forsook his exhausted body for a brief period of sleep.

* * *

Aurangzeb circled round Inida, acknowledged in Lahore, in Multan, in Gatcha, in Gujarat, in Ahmadabad, in Udaipur and in Ajmir, swooping down with the frenzy of an entranced kite, ever closer to his prey. He ought first to have dealt with Dara Shukuh, but just as he was about to, Prince Shuja advanced his re-assembled forces against Benares, and Aurangzeb was obliged to turn his army toward the east.

It was already the Indian winter, and the anniversary of the beginning of the war was approaching, when Aurangzeb closed in on the town of Hajvah. The first thing he did, as a faithful Muslim, was to visit the grave of the holy sage Saeed Baddiuddin, better known under the name of "Shah Madar", where he prayed and dispensed ten thousand rupees in alms to the attendants at the shrine.

On the seventeenth day of the month of Rabbius-sani, when the armies met near Hajvah, Aurangzeb mounted the imperial elephant and there and then his court poet presented him with a verse encoding the hour of the start of the battle:

> *May the Koranic sura Taborak preserve you evermore,*
> *And may the crown always adorn your brow.*
> *Long have I sought a date to symbolise your victory.*
> *And my heart has prompted: "May victory be kind to you!"*

Aurangzeb gave instructions for the poet to be given five thousand rupees.

On the first day of the battle only the canons fired. When evening came, Aurangzeb returned to his camp and spent the whole night in prayer, imploring the Almighty for speedy victory. But in that hour just before dawn when a white thread cannot be distinguished from a black one, a heart-rending scream rang through the camp.

What had happened was this. Rajah Jasvant Singh, who had crossed over to Aurangzeb's side from the forces of Dara Shukuh, had suddenly betrayed his new master. By arrangement with Prince Shuja, he was supposed to attack Araungzeb's baggage trains and then flee in the direction of Shuja's army. When Aurangzeb's soldiers went dashing in pursuit of Jasvant, they would become easy prey for Shuja's troops, poised for attack.

But Aurangzeb never lost his head on the battlefield. None of the brothers had waged war as often and as eagerly as he had, and therefore, not only did he know all the cunning tricks and ruses of the enemy with his mind, he could smell them. In the midst of this Rajput pogrom, when the camp was filled with wailing and shrieking, Aurangzeb deliberately did not mount his elephant, but ordered a *tahti ravon* – a kind of litter entirely unsuited for combat conditions – to be made ready. And when the troops saw their leader swaying on the shoulders of the bearers as if he were crossing a peaceful square in Agra, calm returned to their ranks and those who had not fled – with the merciless prince's curse pursuing them – were ordered to remain as they were and maintain battle formation.

No one went dashing in pursuit of Singh and the few accursed adventitious military commanders who fled in fright, and in the morning Aurangzeb's army emerged for battle in appointed order, led by its commander in chief on the imperial elephant.

From this battle Zebunissa gleaned the story of three gigantic elephants belonging to descendants of the Prophet Muhammad from Barh who were hostile to Aurangzeb. These elephants had immense chains attached to their trunks and, like three adamantine mountains, they swept away all around them: every stroke of a trunk felled hundreds of men and dozens of horses – Death himself seemed to be using them to reap Aurangzeb's soldiers. And so when these three black elephants broke through the thick defences in the very centre of the army and advanced in the direction of the imperial elephant, it seemed that in only a few moments they would trample the solitary colossus with the emperor perched on his back. And then Aurangzeb ordered the legs of his elephant to be tied with chains so that it would stand fast. A second later he ordered the sniper Jalal-khan to shoot the driver on the central enemy elephant, and he fired immediately, instantly killing the man who was driving his crazed monster into the attack with a rod of iron. Another instant, and one of Aurangzeb's men had clambered on to the enemy elephant and pulled it up short. That stopped the other two elephants dead in their tracks.

And then, lo and behold, facing the other way, the elephants began mowing down Shuja's soldiers with their chains. Aurangzeb merely wiped away the sweat that had sprung to his brow, or perhaps it was his prayer, but however that may be, victory was now his.

* * *

Jahanara sat alone in the empty chambers of her father, the Emperor Shah Jahan, who had been imprisoned by Aurganzeb in the female quarters of the palace, and scraped out the story of recent days with her reed pen. Her cloudy tears rolled down her cheeks, falling by turns on her own manuscript and the manuscripts of her great ancestors, lovingly preserved by the imperial family.

Prince Dara Shukuh had suffered yet another defeat by Auranbgzeb near the city of Ajmir, and now he and his family were in no-man's land beyond the Indus – in the Pashtu zone with Malik Jivan – a half-Turk, half-Indian, whom the princess had always regarded with disdain and contempt. What lay in store for her beloved brother now: the fate of the Emperor Humayun, who fled from his own country to Persia to the protection of the Persian Shah? Or was the proverb right when it said: "A defeated man is never sated with combat"? Would he now start relying on the Pashtus and the governor of Kabul, Mahabat-khan? But would they gamble their own peace for the sake of some dubious adventure? To rise for new victories following defeat you had to possess the spirit and the sword of Babur-shah, and that sword was now in the hands of Aurangzeb...

Jahanara turned away for a moment from the manuscript and read once again the secret letter sent to her by the European doctor who had been with Dara Shukuh, crying continuously as she did so: "I have spent the last three days with Dara, whom I met by chance in a strange way. Being in a depressed state following the death of his beloved wife, Nadira-begim, and unable to bear the hardships of the fugitive's life, he asked me to accompany him and his few remaining family and retainers as their doctor. I must describe the circumstances of that day when the prince received a letter from the local ruler, denying him refuge. The women in his harem wept bitterly. We gazed at each other in horror, not knowing what fate now had in store for us. We observed Dara walking, more dead than alive, from one person to another, stopping and talking, asking even the lowliest soldier for advice. He could sense the alienation in each of them, and the mute awareness that he had been left without a single follower was growing in his eyes..."

It was almost the end of Holy Ramadan, the first one since the beginning of the brothers' war for the throne, and also the first year of Aurangzeb's rule. He had finally crowned himself on the twenty-

first day of this month. The gates of joy and festivity at the imperial palace had stood wide open at his royal command. Music was playing in every corner, the walls of the palace were adorned with carpets and decorations. Coins with the name of Abdul Muzaffar Muhidddin Muhammad Aurangzeb Bahadur Gazi – that was what he was now called – had been put into circulation, and Princess Jahanara herself had received five hundred thousand rupees in these coins. No one else in the kingdom had been accorded such great honour: even Aurangzeb's favourite, Princess Zebunissa, had only been awarded four hundred thousand of rupees.

But to whom could the Padishah-Begim Jahanara tell the feelings that were in her heart?

* * *

To this day Aurangzeb could still feel that gaze on him: passionate and suspicious, loving and wary, cruel and repentant, but never betraying itself with a single wrong word, let alone action. Dara Shukuh's story had come to an end and his star had finally set. The same Malik Jivan whom the prince had once saved from execution by trampling by an elephant had seized the prince and his family on a mountain track as they were on their way to Persia. This guileful Pashtu had written to Aurangzeb to say that in his grief after the loss of his beloved wife Nadira-Begim, Dara Shukuh had not even raised his sword. Only Sipehr Shukuh had fought to the end – but what could the prince do against this gang of bandits, Aurangzeb thought disdainfully.

Dara Shukuh and his son had now been brought to Delhi in chains and given into the charge of Nazar-bek. As God was his witness, Aurangzeb would have preferred his brother to flee to Persia, from where there was no return, but now he would have to find a punishment for Dara Shukuh that would frighten his enemies and inspire his allies. This is what Aurangzeb would do: before gathering the Islamic judges and pronouncing sentence on this heretic and kafir, he would order Dara and Sipehr to be paraded through the whole of Delhi, facing backwards on a dirty elephant. From the Lahore gates through the two largest and most crowded bazaars Chovki Chandni and Saadulla, then past the fort to old Delhi and then finally this route of shame would end at the Hvaspur prison. But parading ahead along this route with his gang of bandits would be that jackal, Malik Jivan, on whom Aurangzeb would confer the title of Bahtiar-khan.

Aurangzeb knew perfectly well what kind of reception the people would give Bahtiar-khan, how the women would pour basins of slops and urine on him from the rooftops and the boys would pelt the gang with rotten eggs and fruit! And he would arrive at the palace for his audience in that state!

But Aurangzeb did not guess how, at the same time, the people in all the quarters of Delhi would sob and weep at the sight of the two princes dressed in rags and chained to the bare back of a she-elephant.

Under the fierce summer sun Dara Shukuh shuddered on the back of that elephant as it ambled through streets in which he had known such incredible honour and glory. In the bitterness of his shame he did not even raise his eyes from his rusty shackles and only once looked round at the cry of a beggar who exclaimed: "Dara, when you were king, you always threw me a gold coin. Alas, today you have no alms to give me!" What could the prince throw to him, except a tearful glance or a heavy sigh? But he tore off a piece of gold-threaded brocade that was left on his sleeve by chance, and tossed it to the beggar.

A howl ran round the market of Delhi...

* * *

Dara Shukuh gazed though the ogeed loopholes of the Hvaspur Fort at the twilight advancing from the east and refused to admit that the dampness of his eyes was not caused by the evening breeze. His son, Sipehr Shukuh was cooking lentil soup in one corner, while his father, who had moved away to the opposite corner, was recalling his life, grain by grain. For some reason Dara Shukuh saw a snowy road on which his mother, Mumtaz Mahal, had scattered blood-red rose petals, and himself at the age of nine, hugging his six-year-old brother, who was trembling from the cold, and trying to warm the little boy's icy hands with his breath.

Then he saw two holy sages: the pillar of the Sufis, Mulla Shah, and the ascetic yogi, Baba Lal, holding out to him at the same time the Most Holy Koran and the Upanishads, which in some strange way were combined into a single book of revelation, and then Dara Shukuh asked the sages:

"When a Muslim dies, he is buried in the earth, when a Hindu dies, he is burned, but what happens when a dervish in an Indian cloak dies?" Bab Lal answered him: "First of all, being buried in the earth or burned is a matter of corporeal existence. The dervish will not be concerned about his body when he has left it in order to immerse himself in the ocean of delight that he has discovered in God. He leaves the sphere of material existence in order to be incarnated in a form that has no materiality, as if it were Nothing. As a snake returns to its burrow without a thought for its cast-off skin, so the dervish has no concern for his body, let people do with it as they will..."

Mulla Shah Badahshani continued: "Let it be known to you that the completion of any work involves pain and suffering. Exert yourself! He who is sincere of heart in this work is truly enamoured, and he who is enamoured is worthy of blessing and revelation. The ideal man is

he who is not censured by anyone, neither ordinary people nor adepts of the mysteries; the ideal man is he who does not disdain any labour ordained by the Shariat and the Tarikat, or Path, and also the Hakikat or Truth. Inwardly every action must be verified by Truth, and outwardly all actions must coincide with the common sense of ordinary people…"

Dara Shukuh's cloudy tears slid down his cheeks on to these holy books in his hands and then the door of his prison opened behind his back and, turning in the direction of life, the prince saw the jailer, hunchbacked Nazarkuli-bek, and Aurangzeb's executioner. Shafi-khan. And they were accompanied by several armed men with naked swords. Holding out towards them his empty hands, Dara cried: "Have you come to kill us?" They replied: "We know nothing about killing, we have only been ordered to take your son to a different fortress!" Sipehr Shukuh went down on his knees beside his father. The hunchback Nazar barked: "Get up!" And then Sipehr fell against his father's knees. Father and son embraced with tears flowing down their cheeks. The hunchback shouted louder than before: "Get up, or we'll drag you out by force!" One of the executioners approached the young prince. Dara Shukuh wiped the tears from his face and said to the hunchback: "Go and tell my brother to leave his innocent nephew here…" The executioner replied: "We are not messengers, we are carrying out the king's orders". And with these words they threw themselves on Sipehr and started tearing him away from his father.

And then Dara Shukuh ripped open his pillow and pulled out a pen knife, which he thrust into the hunchback's body with all the passion of an enraged father. Metal scraped on bone, but the knife would not come out out, so deep was it stuck in that abhorrent body. Dara fought like an elephant whose child is being taken away, but there were too many of those base slaves. Seven of them dragged Sipehr away into the next room, and the last thing that the young prince heard as he lost consciousness was his father's wail: "La ilaha illallah! There is no God but Allah!"

It was Dara Shukuh's severed head calling through bloody foam on the torn pillow, and the down flew threw the air like snow, and like rose petals on snow.

* * *

Aurangzeb gazed through the ogeed loopholes of the imperial palace in Delhi at the twilight advancing from the east, and behind his back he felt the bloody sun sinking below the edge of the world like a severed head. He had summoned the highest Ulema and judges for a private audience in order to resolve one question: should he have Dara executed, or should he keep him prisoner in the state prison of Gavalior, where the other prince, Murad, was already in detention?

The first to enter the discussion was Doonishmand-khan, who had been out of favour with Dara Shukuh for a long time. But strangely enough, he said that there was no need for extreme measures, and imprisonment in Gavalior, with an increased guard, would be quite adequate. And then a shrill female voice spoke up from among Aurangzeb's entourage. It was Princess Raushanara-begim, sobbing as she demanded death for this heretic and apostate for the sake of calm in the state and the consolidation of the faith. Aurangzeb knew that she was fighting her own war with Princess Jahanara for female primacy in the House of Timur. He merely smiled into his moustache and cast a glance at the others.

In different circumstances Halilullah-khan, Shaista-khan and Takarrib-khan could have supported the first speaker, but to oppose Raushanara, with her womanly vengefulness meant condemning yourself to death sooner or later, and with one voice they chose Dara's death instead. "The foundations of Sharia Law and the Faith were repeatedly shaken during his lifetime. Therefore, in the defence of the Faith and the Holy Law, and also in the interests of the state, the Emperor has decreed that, as a disturber of the public peace, Dara could not lawfully be left alive."

The next day they brought to Aurangzeb his brother's severed head. "Ill-fated man!" Aurangzeb exclaimed. "I did not look into his face while he was alive, I shall not look into it now!"

A day later, as the Sun poured down its scorching heat from the constellation of Leo, Dara Shukuh's head was set on the back of that same dismal she-elephant and once again paraded through all the crooked, narrow streets of Delhi. Women openly threw rose petals at the feet of this procession and wept into their sleeves....

* * *

Princess Zebunissa had inherited from her predecessors, and above all from the founder of the Empire of the Great Moguls, Shah Babur, and his magnificent sister, Honzoda-begim, elegance of spirit, subtlety of taste and ardency of imagination. But even her mind was unable to accommodate what the foreign healer had said – or could she possibly have imagined it in the fever that he was trying to cure with his bitter herbal lozenges? Supposedly Princess Raushanara- begim had persuaded the Emperor Aurangzeb to have the severed head of crown prince Dara Shukuh wrapped in gold-thread brocade, placed in a gift chest bound with beaten gold and sent to the Emperor Shah Jahan, who was incarcerated in the Agra Fortress.

The old man whom everyone seemed to have forgotten was so delighted when he saw the chest that he immediately instructed Jahanara to prepare as a reply the diamonds from the robe of his eldest son Dara, who had never even tried this robe on. And then they had both opened that precious chest, unfolded the brocade and....

Zebunissa's fever raged for seven days and seven nights: she shouted out, imagining that she was the emperor, or tore her hair and tried to bite through her own veins, calling herself 'the miserable Jahanara', or lay there without breathing, like a dead body, and the foreign healer carefully turned her gleaming black braids away from her motionless head.

* * *

Prince Suleiman Shukuh gazed through the ogeed loopholes of the Salimgarh prison into the twilight advancing from the east and shared the heartache of imprisonment with Aurangzeb's eldest son, Muhammad Sultan. The sun seemed to be setting on the House of Timur, and the two princes recalled its history, full of majesty and fury, grain by grain. The black thread and the white thread interwove, and it was impossible to tell them apart, and in this fabric where day mingled with night, the couplet left to them by Babur-shah simply could not be transcended.

> *Kunduz o'lsa tungacha aytaymu bepoyon g'amim*
> *Kecha o'lsa tongga degru holu zorimnimi dey?*

> *If the day lasts till the night, shall I tell of my limitless sorrow?*
> *If the night lasts till the day, shall I tell of my miserable state?*

Suleiman Shukuh asked about his bitter love, Zebunissa, but Muhammad Sultan changed the subject to his uncle Dara Shukuh's latest book. "Is it true that she still refuses to marry anyone?" Suleiman Shukuh persisted, but Muhammad Sultan only gave a hasty nod and hurried to ask his question: "In his latest work *The Greatest Mystery* my uncle cites a verse from the Koran: "Truly this is the most glorious Koran, in the secret book, no one shall touch it, save only the purified. This is the revelation of the Lord of worlds,' – and he says that the Upanishads are that very secret book. Does this mean that he can expound the obscure places in the Koran, and is this in agreement with Sharia law?"

Suleiman Shukuh explained at length what he had heard from his deceaased father, but his thoughts slowly and surely returned to Zebunissa: "Is it true that a heartless young poet by the name of Bedil has appeared at court and that he vies for fame with Zebunissa?"

> *Pur bekasam imro'z, kasero habaram nest....*

> *I am totally empty today, no news from anyone.....*

"But that is precisely the answer that my uncle suggested concerning the two conceptions of Sufism – Ibn Arabi and Sirhhindi. One spoke of 'vahdati vujud' – unity in the flesh – and the other of 'vahdati shuhud' – unity in witnessing…"

Thus was the fabric of their conversation woven, from day to day, from night to night, and they did not know that Suleiman Shukuh would be poisoned by Aurangzeb in the Gavalior prison and Muhammad Sultan would spend ten years in prison with another cousin, Sipehr Shukuh, and then be pardoned together with him and that, in addition, his father Aurangzeb would give his daughter Zubatunnisa-begim in marriage to Sipehr Shukuh.

Also concealed from their eyes in the book of fates was that Princess Zebunissa would inherit from them this cell in the prison of Salimgarh and also their incessant conversation, related to her by the kindly jailor, who had inherited his post from the hunchback Nazarkuli bek, who had failed to recover from the enlightened Prince Dara Shukuh's final thrust of fury, but she would have no one with whom she could share her thoughts in her absolute, empty solitude...

* * *

On the day when the Sun halted in the constellation of Scorpio, marking the beginning of the twenty-first holy month of Ramadan in the reign of Emperor Aurangzeb, Zebunissa received in her prison a precious mirror, as a gift from her father. There was a certain ambiguity in this gift, as there is in all relations between emperor and princess, father and daughter. Since Aurangzeb Alamgir had ascended the throne, during the first days of Ramadan he had forbidden music to be played throughout the empire, or forbidden Hindu religious schools and meeting-houses, or ordered their shrines to be destroyed, or forbidden the celebration of Navruz, but this year he had cancelled the celebrations for the anniversary of his ascent to the throne. Now it was forbidden to offer him gifts, scribes were forbidden to use silver ink, officers were forbidden to greet each other by throwing one hand up in the air. Now the emperor was not supposed to appear at the window before the people or wear his gold-thread finery. But there were another two prohibitions which wrung the lonely princess's heart.

The Emperor had forbidden the growing of roses in gardens, apart from the two imperial flower gardens, Anzabade and Nurbari, and, secondly, it had been forbidden from henceforth to use lapis lazuli in decorating the palace walls.

And suddenly, in the midst of all these prohibitions – this gift, a precious mirror with a handle in the form of a gazelle, decorated with an immense blood-red diamond. A gift as a riddle that the princess had to solve, but surely the princess knew everything, so what, then, ought she to see in this mirror? Her own solitude, her own imprisonment, her own tears, her own life, which she was gathering together from day to day, from night to night, grain by grain?

Come, a beauty with curly hairs and mascara eyes is here,
The beauty who kills with a warm look is here.

Her coquetry is a knife, her eyelashes are daggers, her sight is a diamond,
If you need a martyrdom, the steppe of Kerbala is here.

If paradise smiles to you, don't be deceived,
Don't go outside of the wine-house, because the place is here.

From feet to the head – wherever you look,
The coquetry breaks the heart, the place is here.

I searched the library of the world, turning page
after page, I saw your letter and said, my wish is here.

If you give a charity of beauty to God,
Come here, a begging Zebunissa is here.

How could the princess touch this stone, which she remembered from her childhood, when she and Suleiman Shukuh were running through the imperial palace and uncle Dara Shukuh came out of Shaha Jahan's chambers, looking distracted and happy, and this stone on his Indian gown rivalled the bright blue of the azure sky and the celestial blue of the waters of the sacred Indus. The lapis-lazuli of her long-ago childhood.

They say that when Aurangzeb tore this stone off Dara's robe, which he had taken from the dying Shah Jahan, in her usual manner Raushanara had scattered a handful of rose petals on her brother and the stone had instantly and forever taken on the colour of blood....

"Who reflects whom, who expounds whom, who tells whose story?" the princess thought, gazing into this mirror as if she were looking at the twilight of her life standing in front of her, and suddenly, like the answer to this sinister riddle, for a moment the face she saw in the mirror was not hers, it belonged to Hira-bai – the girl with whom her father had been so fatally in love, and at that moment the gold gazelle made a sudden leap, the mirror darted after it and shattered to pieces with a crash. The gazelle lay there with its bloody insides ripped open on the ground under the high walls of the palace and the shards of the mirror lay like bloody petals, reflecting the road from nowhere to nowhere....

* * *

Aurangzeb, emperor of the mighty India of the Great Moguls, named Alamgir, or Conqueror of the World, gazed through the open-work alabaster screens of his imperial palace at the twilight of his life

advancing towards him, and refused to admit that the dampness in his eyes was caused by belated repentance. He had just written his will with his own hand, a hand that had known the sword, and not the pen, all its life, but evidently the heavens had turned in their cycle so that, at the last, the pen had proved mightier than the sword even in his hands, the hands of a tireless warrior. The heavens had turned in their cycle so that everything he had revered all his life as a just and rightful cause had proved, now that life's river was about to merge with the sea, to be no more than cause for regret; and if it were more than that, it was not for him to judge, but for the One who had sent him on this deceitful ordeal known as life.

"Praised be Allah and a blessing upon those servants who are in agreement with Him, and He in agreement with them." Here is my testament.

"First – in the name of this sinner who is weltering in his misdeeds, cover the holy shrine of Hasan – may peace be with him! – for those who have drowned in the ocean of sins have no other protection save for sanctuary at the Gates of Mercy and Forgiveness.

"Second – Ai Bek has four rupees from the price of caps sewn by me in person. Take this money and spend it on a shroud for this defenceless creature. There are thirty-five rupees from payment for copying the Koran in my own purse. Give them to the beggars on the day of my death.

"Third – those interring me bear responsibility for which rituals are permitted and which are not, for a dead man is not responsible and relies on the assistance of the living.

"Fourth – bury this pilgrim in the Valley of Rejection of the True Path with his head uncovered, for any abased sinner who appears before the Supreme Judge with his head uncovered shall be granted forgiveness.

"Fifth – cover the upper part of my shroud with material of snow-white. Eschew the strewing of any rose petals.

"Sixth – it behoves him who inherits the throne to deal kindly with those helpless slaves who, through the guilt of this shameless sinner are loitering in the wildness of desert places."

The emperor hurried in his effort to recall the sixth point of his will, for all his thoughts had become stuck in the preceding instruction. It had been the same a few moments earlier, when he was writing the will, and then he had resorted to cunning by handing over his thoughts to the eternal warrior inside him, and had soon begun writing a seventh, an eighth, a ninth and a tenth point, comparing the Persians with the Turks, and the Turks with the Hindus and finally with the Saeeds of Barh, none of whom he trusted, and exhorted those to whom he was leaving this

will to do likewise. But that was the entire snag, since he knew that there was no one to whom he could leave this empire, it had culminated in him, and that was the reason why he had lived to such a great age before writing his will.

His errant thoughts turned to his own father, the Emperor Shah Jahan, but ninety-year-old Aurangzeb immediately mastered that thought with an incredible effort of will, and his trembling hand traced out:

"Eleventh – never trust your sons and do not treat them benevolently for as long as you are alive. If the Emperor Shah Jahan had not favoured Dara Shukuh with special devotion, the affairs of this individual would not have ended so lamentably…"

Even here the pen had proved more cunning than he. He read through what he had written in such feverish haste as his final testament and stopped short on the phrase "the affairs of this individual would not have ended so lamentably". Whose affairs? Shah Jahan's, Dara Shukuh's or his own – the sinful creature of God Aurangzeb Alamgir's? Or perhaps the affairs of all of them, all the heirs of the great House of Timur, the heirs of Babur-shah? And why had he only mentioned sons, he wondered, his heart suddenly pricked by the thought of his beloved dusky Zebunissa – who all his life had secretly reminded him of his bitter love Hira-bai, and for that he had buried her alive in prison. And then he began scratching at the paper with his pen again, as if he were venting the fury of all the cats scratching at his heart:

"Twelfth – the main support of the state is to be well informed in every detail of the state. A momentary negligence becomes a torment for many years…

"Twelve is a sacred number. I end with the twelfth of my instructions."

God knows from what depths of his mind there sprang the verse with which he concluded his will and testament:

If you should learn something, then bless you,
But if you go against everything, woe, woe unto you!

And suddenly he saw that there was snow – white, fluffy, swan's-down snow – falling on the black night and the black earth of India, and the childish weakness of a six-year-old boy sent on a journey down a strange road against his own will stirred within him like a sudden emptiness, and someone bigger than he was took hold of his frozen hands and started blowing an enticing, spicy warmth on to them, and the emperor's head was struck by a squall of the bloody petals of death....

Hamid Ismailov

A Poet and Bin-Laden

A reality novel

Glagoslav Publications